Books by Renee Hayes

Rim Walker Novels

The Girl Who Broke the World
The Girl Who Freed the Darkness
The Girl Who Forged the Light

Renee Hayes has crafted a richly detailed post-apocalyptic world with a plot that offers surprise after surprise, and well- developed characters with complex relationships that you absolutely root for, or love to hate. Strong female protagonists remain in the minority of fantasy fiction and, as a parent to girls, having a character like Zemira is really important to me. Like all who are coming of age, Zemira has to learn how to live with her power and what its limitations are. This means she has to be smart and think outside the box in situations where her power is diminished, like when she is exposed to borenium. Overall, Hayes gives us the promise of an exciting new series and I look forward to seeing where we are lead next. **5-star review by Jamie Michele for Readers' Favorite**

So captivating and enchanting! The way the author describes her characters and each Rim Territory is fascinating and magical. The storyline with each chapter makes you want to just keep reading and not put it down! It is wonderful to read something that is exciting, intriguing and original! I can't wait to see what happens next! *Myra Cumming, Verified Amazon Reviewer*

Fantastic Read. Really, really enjoyed this book. Colourful, relatable characters in a beautiful and dangerous, futuristic world that reminiscent of Avatar or Narnia. Looking forward to the next book in the series and will be purchasing a few extra copies for Christmas gifts!
Verified Amazon Reviewer

Top-notch fresh take on a YA Fantasy. *The Girl Who Broke the World* explores the theme of inner demons and the choices we make in our lives in such a clever way that you are left wondering if you would have done the same. I loved every second of this book but that ending had me in a choke hold. I can't wait to see where the story goes in the coming books!
Skye, Verified Australian Reviewer

RENEE HAYES

THE GIRL WHO FORGED THE LIGHT

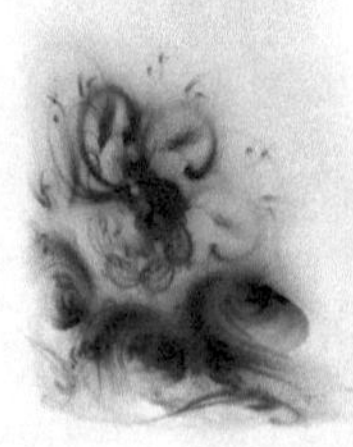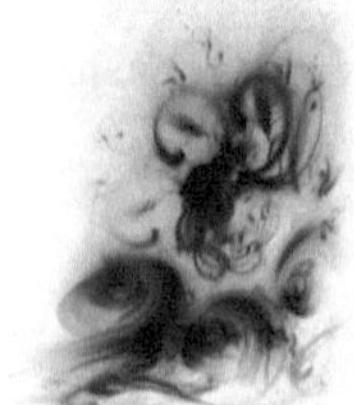

Queensland, Australia

Cover design by Judith San Nicolas
Typeset in Goudy Old Style 9 & 11 pt/Harrington 24 pt
Printed and bound in Australia by IngramSpark
Prepared for publication by The Erudite Pen: theeruditepen.com

A catalogue record for this book is available from the National Library of Australia

The Girl Who Forged the Light ~ 1st ed.
ISBN 9780645587142
eISBN 9780645587159

Dedication

For all the readers of weird and wild things, I wouldn't have made it this far without you. Thank you, this book is for you.

Contents

Map of the Dark Rim

Map of the Rim Territories

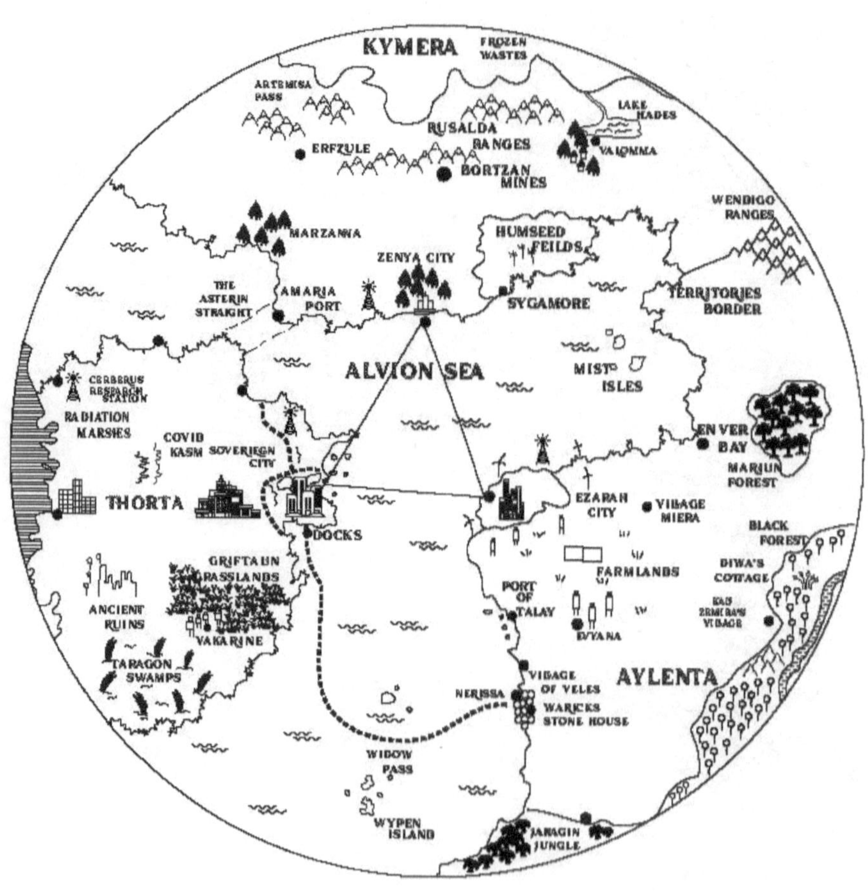

Part I

Prologue

Outskirts of The Dark Rim, 2532

The vision of the metallic black dragon dripping with rain blended into the walls of the damp cave behind it. Through his one blurry eye, Ravaryn Black tried to focus on the image swimming before him. The pain that had blasted his legs and stiff neck was now numb from the frigid temperature all around him. Almost like a blessing, the cold seeped into his aching muscles and bruised bones. The fire that had just burst from the beast's maw now crackled and sizzled to life, igniting the pile of bones to the far side of the dank cave he found himself in.

Where in Mother's earth am I? Ravaryn thought, alarm creeping in. *Mist... flying... shoulder... there had been so much pain in my shoulder. And fire... great plumes of brilliant orange and white fire, setting the forests ablaze, and turning everything to ash.*

In front of him, enormous wings shook away the rain, and his mind focused on the present again. The intimidating creature dropped a carcass on the cave floor before Ravaryn, dripping with rain and blood, which mingled into the dirt. The stain spread out like ink on parchment, mesmerising his clouded mind for a moment.

The dragon moved, and a flickering of each iridescent black scale caught his eye once more. Out of nowhere, black swirling mists encompassed the dragon's shape, transforming it before him. A man now towered over Ravaryn. Shock reverberated through his core, as it was like seeing himself thirty years into the future. The older version of him had the same chiselled face, but his dark hair was sprinkled with a few silver strands, and a short, messy beard surrounded the tight-lipped expression the stranger wore. But that's where the similarities ended. Those eyes... they were Ravaryn's, but also not. Those luminous gold rims surrounding the deep black wells practically illuminated the stare that bore straight into him. His head swam again. A wicked grin lit up the dark features. The man's weathered but still-handsome face dripped with the frigid rain as his eyes crinkled slightly at the corners.

Why is this man smiling at me? Where the hell am I? Mother's earth, my body feels like it's been dropped from the side of the Artesian pass... confusion swirled in Ravaryn's mind like a leaf in the rapids of a downpour.

As the gold-rimmed ebony eyes met with Ravaryn's silver dappled ones, the man spoke. 'Hello, son.'

His voice was deep and velvety, and the rim of gold in his obsidian eyes flickered in the firelight, making his eyes luminous, otherworldly. 'So nice to finally meet you.'

Ravaryn's heart stabbed a painful thump in his chest and raced faster and faster with every passing second. Panic swept over his body, and a cold sweat broke on his forehead. He felt like he was going to vomit, but didn't want to give this man the satisfaction.

'Where am I?' he demanded coolly. 'And by the way, my father is dead.' He untucked his hands from around his chest, but his ribcage felt like it was constricting in on itself. He needed more air. *Just who was this stranger, pretending to be his father? And where was Zee?*

He tried to push his body up further against the wall; the king in him despised being towered over by this deranged shifter. Pain shot like lightning up his back and simultaneously down his legs, despite the numbing cold. A grimace forced out through his clenched teeth as he fought to control his breathing.

'Is that what she told you?' A menacing laugh boomed from the man, his eyes glowing in a way that would make anyone cower before them. 'Oh dear Diwante, tsk tsk tsk. You deceitful little fae.' He replied to his own question like he was speaking about a disobedient pet. Shaking his head, his expression looked almost amused.

Ravaryn's vision was blurring at the edges, stars speckling all around the man. The way he cocked his head to the side gave Ravaryn chills. And with the animalistic grin, he seemed even more malevolent now, like he was partially insane. *Diwante?*

The word echoed around in Ravaryn's mind. *Diwa? Mum?* His head felt light between throbs of pain.

'From your confused expression, it seems your dear mother didn't tell you who your father truly is. Or what she did to me...' Pure venom leaked from his voice, which darkened his entire being even more. 'Well, let me enlighten you.' That velvet voice, so deep and resonant, belied the evil emanating from him.

'I am Salvador.

I am the black dragon.

I am the dark one.

I am your father, and I am going to take back what is mine!'

The words floated towards Ravaryn. His grasp on his mind slipped, and consciousness evaded him as Salvador spoke.

'And you and I, my son, are going to rule over this entire world. Anyone or anything that gets in our way will burn to ash before they even have time to exhale.'

Blackness crept in around his vision, leaving only the rings of gold etched in Ravaryn's mind as he succumbed to the pain, confusion and darkness.

Demons

Salvador's Stronghold, The Deadlands

Thaylon's stride was measured as he patrolled the hall of cells in third level of the ancient building, black mould adorning the crumbling walls of concrete and steel. His large hands clasped behind his back as his eagle eyes roamed over each creature he passed, as if appraising objects of their value.

'That one.' He pointed to one of the cells on his left, his steady voice deep and authoritative. 'He's ready.'

The man following in Thaylon's wake replied, 'Yes, master.' He was human, but his eyes conveyed only emptiness as the hollow sickly-green irises studied the floor. His once-tall muscular frame slumped as he approached the cell's locked metal-bar door.

Thaylon eyed the creature pacing within for a moment longer with hooded eyes, as if cementing his decision. Then he clasped his hands behind him once more as he walked away. Down the row of cells he strode, towards the exit of the galley-like corridor lined with prison cells.

The glow of brilliant blue sky-pine light emitted from the sconces on the walls as the flame bounced around the seed. Taking a sconce in one hand, the human man's other hand started to shake as he handled the lock to the cell that his master had chosen. A chitter escaped the cell, setting off a chain reaction through the prison corridor. The monstrosities within all screeched in a rising crescendo as the man removed the lock from the door.

'It's just like the rest. It's just like the rest...' he whispered desperately to himself as he entered the cell, the sky-pine sconce clutched tightly in his white-knuckled, perspiring grasp.

The chittering died down in an instant, and the silence became even more terrifying than the roaring chorus of the otherworldly creatures. The beast paced before him, its eight thin legs moving in rhythmic timing back and forth, back and forth, with majestic precision. Multiple eyes scattered to and fro in different directions as it moved. It momentarily paused, still as stone, as if only now sensing that the man now stood in the cell before it.

'It's just like the rest, It's just like the rest...' The man's whispers fell fast from his lips as the creature, which may have once been human, sniffed at the air.

Slitted nostrils flared in the centre of its distorted face. Although the torso that connected to the spiderlike lower body may have once been human, its skin was as black as tar, and its eyes were ghostly voids of grey that clouded over the pupils. Head tilting to the side, it skittered to pinpoint all those monstrous eyes on the man. The movement was so quick it caused him to drop his sky-pine light in fright. The creature opened its jagged maw, and long, sharp teeth glowed from the eerie blue coming from the torch on the cell floor, now surrounded by an assortment of bones and filth on the damp ancient concrete.

A click, click, click emitted from the creature's throat. The man's eyes grew wide, the white surrounding his entire iris. Then it lunged. Huge fangs burst forth from within its double-rowed mouth. It grabbed the now-screaming man with mantis-like arms, and the fangs sank deep into his eye sockets, its jaw dislocating to fit its prey inside. The sickening screams echoed throughout the concrete dungeon. The other creatures heard the commotion and clicked wildly in chorus, their own sharp-tipped arms clanging on the bars of their cells and stretching out towards the smell of fresh blood. The muffled screams died down as the man was devoured by the monster.

The crunch and squelch of flesh and bone was the music now soothing the others' hysteria. The kill was over. They resumed their pacing, eyes darting all around once again like soldiers awaiting their next command.

As for the eight-legged monstrosity that had just devoured the man, there seemed no human left inside of the creature that had been created in this soulless place. Just an insatiable hunger that had been satisfied for the moment. It had enjoyed its first kill.

The sky-pine's light flickered from the cell's floor and caught in the golden webs of smaller golden orb spiders that littered the walls and ceiling of the imprisoning cell. With relish, they had watched their newest, somewhat distant, distorted cousin consume its meal.

Boots sounded at the end of the hall as Thaylon re-entered the third level. 'Cole! What's the hold up?' he bellowed, anger lacing the sharp words. He marched to the cell where the man was no longer and stood almost eye to eye with the beast, its maw dripping fresh crimson and its eyes focusing their foggy sheen on him.

'Oh, for fuck's sake!' His brow furrowed together as he exhaled, displeasure creasing his smooth features.

Thaylon entered the cell and edged around the beast, herding it forward. 'Out! Out with you!'

The creature's legs skittered, and it snapped its jaws towards Thaylon in annoyance. He dodged its rows of jagged teeth and pair of fangs and blasted a ball of bright red flames at its multiple legs. The creature screeched and teetered forward rapidly out of the cell, colliding with the iron bars on the way out.

'The lord wants you all ready by the week's end,' Thaylon boomed, addressing the cells full of monsters. 'If any of you Arakanai want to play the same game as this one here just did, you'll be ash before you can blink all your fucking grotesque eyes at me. Hear my words!'

Thaylon's voice shook the walls. Crumbling pieces of stone and dust trickled down from the decaying structure as he stormed out of the third level behind the large Arakanai that had just eaten his top herder. His large right fist clenched powerfully at his side. *Now I have to find another filthy little human with the balls enough to be a herder for me. These fucking creatures are getting on my nerves.* Thaylon's large boots clipped up the wet stairs as he stalked after the freshly created Arakanai, frustration seeping from his pores.

The Queens Who Walked Worlds

Maya Village, Lamiria

Diwa Mumasumi, or so she called herself, sat on the bed in the birds-nest shaped room of Maya Village. She hugged Zemira Creedence as the tears freed themselves from her familiar starry silver eyes. Yet they slid down a much more youthful face, smoother and with a glow that hadn't been there before. Diwa's sweeter but still-comforting voice whispered into Zee's ear as she embraced the young woman. 'We will get him back. We will get him back, I promise.'

Zee withdrew from the embrace with a sadness of her own staining her guilt-wracked face. 'Did you know this would happen, Diwa? Did you know about that *thing*, that *monster* inside the Dark Rim, with the prisoners? Did you know about the prisoners this entire time?' Her voice shook. *'Did you know that I would break the wall and release it?'* As much as she tried, Zee couldn't keep the accusation from seeping out and snaking through her words.

Diwa raked her hands through her loose hair. 'I didn't know that you would dissolve the wall with your magic, Zee, I swear.' Diwa's voice was almost pleading.

'But you did know about the monster within the Dark Rim? The black dragon?' Zee said the words carefully, waiting for Diwa to confirm that she really had seen an enormous fire-breathing dragon that had snatched Ravaryn from her grip.

A deep breath rattled from Diwa, and her body sank forward. Her shoulders slumped and took up a position that was more familiar with the Diwa Zee had known and loved since her childhood.

'And what has happened to you, Diwa? Are you even still you? You look decades younger, and you...you don't look like you.' Zee's eyes stung, as a hollowness opened up within her. The hurt, the loneliness and the lies filled the hollow with a darkness. A darkness that grew stronger with every deceptive twist and turn revealed to her along the way... and with every second that she didn't know whether Ravaryn was alive or dead.

'Zemira, I know I have a lot of explaining to do.' Diwa was sombre, squeezing Zee's hands with her own. 'I owe you the truth, the *whole* truth. I want you to know everything as I'm too old to keep secrets anymore. They are wearing away at my soul, and I'm ready to release them.'

Zee felt relief wash over her. Not once in her entire life had she gotten a straight answer or a promise of the truth from this woman, so the feeling of relief was foreign, and she almost didn't trust that this was really Diwa.

Hearing the wooden platform behind her shift with weight, Zemira turned to see who was approaching the first-level room that was suspended in the rainforest's floating village. Orion's emerald gaze locked with her own. It took but a second for her to take him in. She was his daughter, his little wolf. Even though a grown woman now, she would always be his little wolf, in her heart.

Her father lunged forward at the same time Zee stood from the bed, and the pair embraced in a fierce hug. Orion squeezed the pain and worry away from her last few weeks with every second he held her in his strong grasp.

'I'm so sorry, Zee. I'm so sorry I wasn't there for you, that I didn't see what was happening to you. Are you hurt?' Orion pulled her out at arm's length and surveyed her to see what she had been through, physically.

He spied the blackened vines trailing down her arm, twisting and connecting to the now-onyx fingernails on her left hand. Grasping it in his own large tattooed hands, he inspected the patterns adorning her where Kyeitha, the former forest queen and Zee's own grandmother, had left her curse. But instead of it spreading and consuming her, Zee had ended Kyeitha by using her own power against her.

As if reading the story the vines portrayed, a proud smile lit up Orion's face. 'You did it,' he whispered, his eyes glassy. The lines at the corners of his eyes made him look all the more handsome in the relief shown there.

'I—I had help.' Zee nervously pulled her arm away from Orion's grasp.

The look of relief fell from his features. 'So I heard.' His voice had returned to its usual stoic sound. He said nothing further as he gazed past Zee, his eyes finally recognising the other person in the room who was still perched on the bed.

'Dee?' Confusion furrowed his brow. 'Is that you?'

She laughed, but only a slight resemblance laced the sound, unlike the cackle she had once produced. It still sounded like Diwa though, and it was more befitting the woman who resembled his old friend, but whose appearance was drastically different.

'Sure as a raven is black.' She winked.

It was Diwa all right, and Orion bent to embrace her in a less-desperate hug.

He eyed both Zemira and Diwa. 'The pair of you have some explaining to do, and I want to hear everything.' His deep voice was again laced with relief.

'Diwa first,' Zee said, wanting answers immediately. 'I've been waiting a lifetime to get straight answers from her, and I've finally been offered them.'

'Well, you know what makes a story even more enjoyable.' Diwa's Cheshire cat grin finally resurfaced, making her more-youthful self look positively radiant.

'What?' Zee said, deadpan. She thought Diwa was up to her old tricks and about to defer the entire situation, leaving her in the dark once again.

'Tea, tea and more tea!'

Zee laughed. She actually laughed after all the horrible things that had coated her soul in misery over that past year, and the laugh fractured her sadness just a smidgeon.

Orion held out his hands to her. 'Sounds good to me, and I know just the place. I just came from there, actually, and this woman makes a mean brew. Nothing on your tea of course, Dee, but it has a certain kick to it.'

The three wove through the suspended bridges of Maya Village as the people still mingled and rejoiced below. Orion led them to the centre of the village and its largest tree with the enormous hollowed-out meeting place, and the healer's den within it. It felt like a lifetime ago that Zee had been here, in front of an entire village of people. They'd watched on as she'd struggled in another realm, using their energy to weave herself a healed arm from their collective hope, love and life-force. And Ravaryn, Ravaryn had been there, supporting her the entire way. Her chest constricted along with the blood blooms adorning her right arm. The tattooed vines moved slightly and curled the buds tightly shut.

Gods, please be alive, Ravaryn. How she ached for him, body and soul.

A dull pain snaked through her hand and up her arm as Zee entered the healer's den behind Orion, with Diwa trailing behind her.

'Back so soon, white wolf?'

A sharp-toothed grin glowed in the yellow light emitted from the hanging blossoms that illuminated the dark space. The room was cluttered with everything under the sun. The clutter filled the tightly packed shelves, the floors, the nooks in the walls, and even hung from the ceiling of the carved-out dwelling.

Sahara's dark skin glowed golden in the light, and her eyes shone with an otherworldly light at the trio.

'We're in need of some of tea, and I was wondering if you'd be so kind as to oblige.'

Sahara eyed Orion as he spoke, then Zee stepped out from behind him.

'Rim Walker! You live. Well done! And who do we have trailing behind you?' Sahara's jaw dropped as she squeezed past Orion and Zemira, without even spying Diwa first. Her bracelet-laced arms made her chime and jingle, and she moved like a ruffled brustlehen.

'Diwante! You look like shit. What happened to you?'

Diwa's laugh echoed through the space, while Zee and Orion looked at the women in confusion.

'Good to see you as always, Sahara. It's been... an age,' Diwa replied.

'Hmmf,' Sahara huffed, taking in Diwa's refreshed appearance.

'Tea?' Diwa suggested.

A smile crept over Sahara's face, those glistening, pointy teeth appearing again. She tilted her hair to the side, her high bun of dreadlocked white hair flicking with her movement. 'Fabulous idea. I have just the brew.' Her eyes squinted with her genuine smile.

Zee though she looked like a crocodile about to attack. She said nothing of the sort though, just watched the two strangest woman she'd ever met in her entire existence, realising they were old acquaintances – friends even. *Of course they bloody were. Why would the nutcases not know each other?*

Once the three were settled deep in the tree's core of the den, Sahara returned with a metal teapot and three cups. She chinked her hands together, rattling the bracelets, then scurried off into some other unknown section of her eerie maze. The tea was dark, like a clear deep-mahogany stream, almost as if it were trying to match the same shade of the ancient forest giant that they were now deep within.

Diwa poured them all a cup, after inspecting the porcelain, and handed one to Orion, then Zee. Zee sniffed at the brew. It didn't have the usual colour that Diwa's teas always possessed, but it did have a sweet, thick caramel-like quality to it. And a fresh, sharp lemony buzz that materialised in the after-taste. It was soothing and warming at the same time and actually calmed Zee's fried nerves ever so slightly. She sighed with relief as the tea worked its wonders.

'Alright, you two both deserve some answers. Some, Orion, you've already been privy too.' A deep sigh left Diwa, 'I just want you to know,' she eyed Zee, her silver-speckled gaze pleading. 'I have done things that I regret. We all have, but I fear mine are heavier than most. All I ask is that you please try to understand. I did not make any decision lightly, and not all of them were things that I could foresee. I think it's better to show you rather than to tell you...' she trailed off, placing her dainty cup back in the centre of the mat they all sat cross legged around.

Surrounded by the healer Sahara's strange collection of junk, bones, feathers and ancient artefacts, Diwa's silver eyes shone then clouded over as her hands waved in the air before her. Zee placed her tea cup back down just as Orion did. Her eyes widened as she realised this was not just a cloud-like vision that Diwa had shown them before. No... the spinning colourful mist that was forming before her grew larger and larger, engulfing the whole room, until images started to appear within it. This just wasn't a vision; this was as if Zee and Orion were in another actual world. Then she realised they were *inside* one of Diwa's *memories*.

Two young women were foraging in the woods, baskets in hand. One basket was full with fresh red raspberries and the other an assortment of wild mushrooms. The first young woman had silver eyes and a wide, vibrant smile. The other dark-haired woman had full mulberry lips and stunning spring skies in her eyes. They contrasted incredibly with her pale moon-like skin. The pair laughed and strolled through the unusual-looking woods. Plants and ferns of the strangest colours surrounded them, like nothing Zee had ever seen in the old Rim world, or even in Lamiria.

A giant rumble, like a crack of thunder, shook the earth beneath them. The sound was deafening, and Zee felt like she was inside a vicious storm. A prickle of fear rippled over her skin as the women started to fall. They fell fast through a deep, dark gash in the earth, leaving their world on the other side, and the images spun and transformed around Zee and Orion. The women now found themselves in a different world, where they came to be in front of a shimmering lake. Little millowisps tended to the blooms on the lily pads growing on the water's surface. Gaia appeared, as though out of nowhere, and spoke with them. She crowned the silver-eyed woman queen, presenting her with a crown of twisted vines laced with small blooms and crystal-like gems that glittered between the fine vines.

The images shifted again. The young women were now in Tangaroa, the city in the Valley of Rivers. Zee recognised the glowing valley with the sun reflecting on the water, making it look like a stream of golden silk. Sahara had taken Zee there when she was in another realm searching for answers to heal her cursed self and lost limb. Another image then replaced the one in Tangaroa. The silver-eyed queen's smile was wide again, and she was with a man – a young, attractive man who looked strangely familiar. His chiselled face was striking, and he had a luminescent quality about him. His eyes were as dark as night, but had a gold rim just visible around their border.

The other raven-haired woman appeared in a similar memory. She was staring into a man's eyes, his huge frame making her appear miniscule in his arms as he kissed her. His hooded dark-ocean eyes looked into hers with both admiration and ownership.

The next vision was of the silver-eyed woman handing the crown of vines over to the delicate porcelain-skinned woman before the entire city of Tangaroa. The two men stood off to the side, hands neatly tucked behind their backs and bowing their heads as the crowd cheered and the former queen cradled a pregnant belly.

Time sped forward as Orion and Zee silently took in the images. Zee's mouth opened slightly in awe at what she was witnessing. But the next scene was a fight, where the handsome dark-featured man was arguing with the woman with silver eyes. He lost his temper, smashing objects around. Then he transformed into a monstrous beast... a black dragon. He pinned the tiny woman to the earth in the forest, her huge stomach protruding from her delicate frame. The image shifted again and showed her holding a small black-haired baby. She was all alone in the woods. Casting a spell, she hid the infant in an orb of protection. It slept soundly in a small cave filled with life, where creatures glowed all around and a crystal-clear turquoise spring sparkled in the distance. Zee had seen this place before in the tunnels that ran under Lamiria. Ravaryn had taken her through these to the temple.

Another memory appeared. It was of the woman – the young Diwa. She cast her magic out into a blackened world, and the more magic she expended the older she grew, leached of youth. Her wrinkles grew deep, and her back curved forward while her hands became knobbly and aged with spots. Tears cascaded down her face as her teeth grit together in a grimace of pain but still she expended her magic outwards, casting a tall wall of protection over a black sea, a dark space before her at the edge of the world.

When she was done, she collapsed to the ground. The image trans-formed into a dark mist. The dragon had found her, alone in the forest, and he was angry, *furious*, at the sight of the withered old woman that was once his. His rage multiplied when he realised that she was no longer pregnant. Shifting into his man-form, he threatened her again, his large hand engulfing her delicate neck as he lifted her against the trunk of a tree. Her small feet dangled in the air as her colour reddened. Her pan-icked face moved back and forth frantically as she clutched at the hand starving her of oxygen, trying to pry it from her throat.

She was dropped to the ground.

Another memory took its place.

The old woman stood at the edge of the darkened vista of the black sea and pointed forth into the iridescent wall of magic she had created. The man's rage-filled face poured pure venom into the look of hate that he gave her, and his hand struck her face violently, causing blood to spray from her delicate old mouth. He transformed into the black dragon and flew into the landscape beyond. The woman watched, her expression changing the further the dragon flew from her, and into the invisible bar-rier that Diwa had created. Straight through and into the prison that was now the Dark Rim. Her face came to rest in the most familiar smile in Zee's young life. Diwa's look of satisfaction was shining in her eyes, and the Cheshire cat grin that lit up her weathered face up seeped victory.

Diwa turned from the Dark Rim and never looked back. She retrieved her baby from the sleeping safety of the cave, where he was still inside the protective orb she had left him in, and woke him with her remaining magic. Tears of joy streamed down her face as she knelt, hugging the baby to her chest. She rocked back and forth, happiness and triumph shining from her face in the glow of the grotto's bioluminescent light.

The mist stilled and disappeared from all around Orion and Zee as the healer's den materialised back around them. Coming into view before them was a more youthful Diwa than they were used to, and her sparkling silver eyes had just a touch of a shine to them now. But there was a small, sad smile on her face.

'I did what I had to do,' she said. 'I-It was the only thing I could think of to keep my son safe. To keep him from that monster's clutches. Salvador is so powerful, and he tricked me into thinking he was good and kind in the beginning... that he was like me, stuck in a new world without a way back. But the world he had come from was very different to mine. We came from a world full of ancient magic, where the fae ruled their kingdoms through the royal lineages. We knew of the demon realms in our old world, as our world had a long history with them. It was forever being invaded through tears in the fabric between the fae lands and the demon worlds created by old magic, which we struggled to heal. But that fateful day when your earth world changed, *our* world was rocked by a blast so powerful it tore multiple fissures in the already thin fabric between our realm and Lamiria. Kyeitha and I found ourselves falling through a tear, which instantly disappeared, and we were trapped here this new realm called Earth. Later on, we found the only other beings whom we thought had suffered the same displacement: Thaylon and Salvador had fallen through a rip in their world to this one, too. But their world... it was dark and ruthless. Yet Salvador is Ravaryn's father.' Diwa's voice was strained. 'He is a demon... and I was a fool.'

Diwa's eyes found the floor, and Zee's widened as all the information fell into place. Ravaryn, the kind, protective man she now loved, the strange dark soul that had entwined himself around her very core somehow, was born of a demon.

Blaze and Astrid

The sweat on Paxton Raker's hands turned icy the moment he reached the roof of Zenya castle. Blowing in sharply from the south, the wind brought with it the scents of Zenya city laid out below. His knuckles cracked as he flexed them together in the sudden cold. Today was the day. He was going to find Zee. He was going to find his best friend, and hopefully she was healed from whatever magical uncertainty had been poisoning her, sickening her, since she discovered who and what she truly was.

Was it really only a year ago that she had ended the forest queen's reign over both worlds? It seemed like a lifetime ago that Zee had destroyed the Rim wall, the shimmering barrier that had protected the last of the humans for more than five hundred years. Pax had always known that Zee was different, special, but he'd never guessed in his wildest imaginings that she had magic. That she could conjure the elements, manipulating them and the world around her to her will.

Pax had also never imagined that she would use that power against him... or that she would leave him behind. He should have guessed it when he found out she was more, that she wasn't really human. She had never really fit in, or belonged. Well, how could she now? She had left him here with the humans in the old Rim world. Where he should stay. Where *he* belonged. Where he knew he should be safe from the otherworldly creatures and forces he was definitely not equipped to deal with like she was.

But none of that mattered. Nowhere felt safe; nowhere felt like home without her. Or at least without the knowledge of her being okay. He had to find her, and he had to see that she was still her, that she was still Zee, no matter where she was or who she was with.

His teeth clenched forcefully inside his jaw as he came to the far edge of the castle's roof. He looked down to his right on the village below. The townspeople were scattered like ants, moving in and out of the carved-out tree bases of the gargantuan sky pines and going about their day. They were none the wiser of the new world that lingered behind the edge of where the old Rim wall had stood.

A few snowflakes settled on the shoulders of his deep earthen-coloured Moscow jacket, sparkling in the sun's rays that forced through the thickly clouded sky. Catching his eye, a glittering ray bounced from the glass roofs of the newer buildings to his left, between the village and the dark Alvion Sea. The new buildings' tunnel-like structures had glass-domed roofs and stretched out in long lines, their blurry contents a shimmery evergreen within. Heat wavered from the snowflakes that melted against the heated glass, disappearing in a mist upon contact with the warmth.

A gust of icy wind tore his attention away from the new glasshouses and interrupted his wandering mind. The gust was followed by a magnificent snow-white creature, it's perfectly lined thick-feathered wings slowing its graceful descent onto the roof as it powerfully blasted up freshly fallen snow. Paxton held his ground, his fists now tight inside his pockets for warmth, as he watched in awe just like the first time he had seen the creature – the duellerat.

Mazda glided the snow beast to land beside him. She had a huge smile as she sat comfortably perched upon Blaze's furry back, his multiple eyes flicking to and fro, some taking in his surroundings, others monitoring

Paxton. Mazda leapt from Blaze's back with the energy to match a freshly born fittle deer, her vibrant auburn curls following her in stark contrast to her deep-blue coat and black-gloved hands.

'I've found one!' she proclaimed, play-punching Pax in the arm. Her wide smile was almost wicked, that's if anything could ever be described as wicked about Mazda. The only thing that would come close was the way she smiled at Paxton. It had only been a few weeks since he had arrived at the castle demanding to see Zemira. He had been prepared for the worst – seeing Ravaryn, the King of Kymera again, who was 'supposedly helping her heal'. But instead he had found neither of them, just the new captain of the guard, Barrack, and a fiery young woman who tended to the king's duellerat, Chester, as well as her own – Blaze.

'She's a little sketchy, but she'll do just fine.' As if she were talking about a reliable old piece of machinery – not a giant untamed flying creature that could gut him, if it did so choose, in one swipe with its taloned feet, most likely without a second thought.

'You say that like it's a good thing.' Paxton's heart raced as he met Mazda's shimmering blue gaze. Her perfect wide smile spread as her cheeks bloomed pink from the icy wind of her morning ride.

'You'll be fine! You've practised plenty with Blaze over the last few weeks, but it's just that he can't carry us both. And there is definitely something wrong as Ravaryn and Zee haven't returned yet. You'll do fine, and she'll be here any minute.'

Mazda moved to his side to look out at the same space of sky he was surveying, now wringing his hands. The sky she had just emerged from with Blaze.

'She?' Paxton questioned, turning a raised brow to Mazda.

She didn't meet his eye, just watched the grey skies and swirls of snow before her. 'Yes, *she*. Her name is Astrid, and she's incredible! Just wait until you see her. I won't even tell you what I had to bargain for her. You owe me big time.'

'And what do you possibly think I could give you in return?' Pax questioned her, perturbed. 'What could you possibly think I possess that you would want. I'm an orphan from Aylenta with nothing and no one to my name,' he said self-consciously.

He lowered his eyes to his booted feet, now stamping in the snow underneath them. A delicate finger raised his chin towards a bright magnetic gaze. 'Oh, I don't know about that, Paxton from Aylenta. I'm sure there's plenty of things I could think of that you could give me.'

Paxton's face heated instantly at her words, just as a gust of wings and a shrill cry saved him further squirming under her direct attention.

The majestic duellerat landed with a jarring thud on the roof before them. Paxton's eyes grew as wide as sunflowers in the morning sun. The snow creature's feathers were sleek and mottled a beautiful shade of grey and white. Astrid towered higher than Blaze, and her vermillion eyes searched the pair of them rapidly, assessing her humans with pinpointed accuracy.

'Ah... she's *incredibly* bigger than Blaze.' Paxton's voice threatened to betray him as it shook.

'I know, right!' Mazda nearly squeaked with excitement for the adventure they were about to undertake.

She shoved his still form forward, her two small hands pushing him before Astrid's terrifying gaze. She towered over Paxton; he had grown used to Blaze's height over the last week or so, whose large eagle-like head and smooth fox ears came just above Paxton's.

Astrid stamped a clawed foot in the snow before him and huffed her hot breath unnervingly close to his face, which ruffled his chestnut hair.

'Well... say hello!' Mazda nudged with her elbow as if the gigantic thing before him were a cute little kitten or something.

Pax cleared his throat and thought of Zee. Zee, who had needed help but hadn't been able to ask, who had been there for him when no one else was. Zee who had rescued him from the mines where he thought he was going to die. Zee who needed him now.

Now, Paxton, he commanded himself. 'Hello, Astrid!' He tried to sound regal, authoritative and sure of himself. But he just sounded like an idiot yelling at a creature that could split him in two if she were to decide she felt like it.

Mazda nodded at his side encouragingly, and Blaze padded over to see how the introductions were going, coming to stand at Paxton's other side. Blaze trilled an odd sound out to Astrid as if conversing, and she lowered her head down to meet Paxton's eyes with her own multiple ones all locked on him, so very close.

His breath caught in his throat, and Mazda actually moved so as to grip his arm or pull him back, the light hesitation on his part making him all the more terrified. Within a second, he had come to regret his actions, *ridiculously* regret them. But he held his ground; he didn't move an inch to back away from Astrid's soul-penetrating gaze or to show the fear swimming rapidly through his veins.

Astrid screeched an ear-piercing caw right in Pax's startled face. His eyes forced shut at the sight of the blue inside of her sharp-toothed beak. Blaze trilled in reply, trotting over to Mazda, and Astrid moved back, shimmying her feathered wings and neck like a parrot that'd just had a bath. Paxton's face drained of colour, and Mazda burst into a breath-sucking laugh beside him.

When she gained enough composure to speak again, she offered, 'Wow, that went so much better than I was expecting! Astrid said she's never *not* eaten an offered rider before! Well done, Pax! I knew she'd love you.'

Paxton almost fainted. 'You had better be kidding me.' His tone was far from impressed.

'Oh, come on, it was a 50–50 shot. Now we get to see you two ride!'

Blaze clucked his tongue and spun his eagle head to the side, ears tucked down to blend into the thick, soft fur behind his feathered head.

'I swear to the Mother, you delight in scaring the life from me.'

Mazda laughed. 'Well, yes! It's hilarious, and besides, this place has always been so dull. I've never had anyone to mess with other than Rav, and he never takes it as well as you.'

At the mention of Ravaryn, Pax's mouth soured. The moment of adrenaline-filled teasing vanished like ash on the wind. Mazda watched his expression change and felt her own fun seep away. She knew she shouldn't have mentioned the king. Paxton had a hatred for him that went deep, Mazda had discovered, after some prodding and prying. She just wished people could see Ravaryn the way she did. But she knew deep down that no one probably ever would. He had done unforgivable things in his blinded, vengeful state before his curse was ended. Yes, most would never see the good that the King of Kymera had done. Only the bad.

'Come on,' she prodded a little more gently. 'Let's go find Zee. Astrid seems to like you... enough.' She snickered. 'I promise you'll be fine. It's not every day I get to ride with someone else. We're the only two in all of Zenya with duellerats, so please don't take my fun from me just yet!' Her eyes were laced with mischief, and pleading.

Paxton couldn't resist and returned a stiff smile of his own. 'Alright, alright. Let's see if I can stay on Astrid any better than I could Blaze.' His face lit again with nervousness, but with a tiny bit of exhilaration seeping through.

He couldn't help from catching Mazda's infectious excitement. Her bright smile shone as she flung herself onto Blaze's back with one smooth jump, sliding into position with such grace she seemed like she were born to it.

'Astrid.' Paxton tried to use his most polite tone once again.

She clucked but once, without eyeing him this time. A short, sharp command as if to say, 'Come on, human. Let's see what you've got.' Turning slightly to the side, Astrid tucked her wings in half way, ready for Paxton to mount, her silvery grey feathers ferruling down her body in a ruffled wave – with possible apprehension.

Paxton took a deep breath and rubbed a hand over the back of his neck before marching over to the duellerat that was most definitely twice his size. He proceeded to mount the terrifying creature with a lot less grace than Mazda had. Once securely on Astrid's back, she stepped side to side as if adjusting to Paxton's weight upon her, or just in eagerness to try their first flight.

'Ready?' Mazda called out, her sweet voice sliding towards him through the frigid wind.

Astrid cawed in answer, and Pax yelled back as his fists tightened around handfuls of thick grey feathers and fur. 'Ready as I'll ever be.'

Astrid pounded her powerful legs forward and spread her wings wide as she leapt from the castle's roof and plummeted with such speed it was as if Paxton's stomach had been ripped from within him and left behind. He blinked furiously as the pair spiralled through the air towards the glittering lights of the village below, his body braced like a dam wall about to burst, teeth grinding as he forced them together. His knuckles, balled tightly into Astrid, were now as white as his surroundings. It was all Pax could do to hold tight and keep the scream from tearing from his mouth.

Poison and Power

Salvador's Stronghold, The Deadlands

Ravaryn's head swam with visions of flickering black scales as the urge to vomit racked his body. As he became more conscious, he realised he was sitting up against a damp, dripping wall. With one eye still swollen and tightly shut, he strained to take in his surroundings. Ravaryn was no longer in the cave, and from what he could tell, he was alone. The drip, drip, drip of water seeping through the mouldy walls echoed eerily out from the dark cell he found himself in.

He tried to stand but pain blasted through his legs. His muscles quivered with the effort as he clenched his teeth. He was going to die. He was going to die *here*. It suddenly dawned on him. A cold sweat was creeping over his skin. *Infection.* Blood poisoning. Then death. A pretty wretched way to go - a wretched way for a once wretched king. And Zemira, his Zemira, would never know what had happened to him. The pain of that realisation hurt him more than the pain tearing through his body.

'Is anyone there!' The growl took more effort than he had. 'Why the fuck am I here? Are you going to let me die down here? Is that it, you bastard?'

A few moments passed with no reply, and the dripping water reeked with a stagnant tinge. Rotten wafts of the ancients' rancid poisoned water dripped from the old stone ceiling. Not stone. Concrete. He was in a concrete building, a concrete cell. He must be in the dead lands. But why would he bring him here? Ravaryn's head clenched with painful, sharp throbs, and stars were circling before his vision. *The black dragon, my father... Salvador, he had called himself.* It was all coming back to Ravaryn in shards.

The Dark Rim prison. The survivors. Zee's patterned dark vines entwined in his own grip. A kiss. A scream – and a creature ripping him away. Flames, fire, destruction, pain, a cave and a monster.

Footsteps sounded from far away, the boots striding through layers of puddles on the prison's hallway floor as they approached. Ravaryn tried to focus, but he now felt cold all over. Then his pulse quickened. Before his cell door, a man's form stood, shrouded in shadow. Not just a man, a giant. Ravaryn could just make out a huge frame, muscled torso and hooded eyes. They gleamed in the dim light, and a smile crept over the stranger's mouth, a sight that made the nausea in the pit of Ravaryn's stomach intensify tenfold.

'Well, well, well.' The man's rich, deep voice was steady and almost held a pleasant tone as he fit a key into the rusted old lock of the cell door. He carried a bag over his shoulder, which he placed on the floor as he entered and came to stand before Ravaryn, appraising him like a weapon that he would very much like to wield. How could anyone look down on him like that in his state? He felt near death; he *was* near death.

'Nice to meet you, Ravaryn Black, King of Kymera, the *black dragon* of the old Rim world.'

Ravaryn was struggling to stay conscious, but he managed another low growl. 'What do you want with me? Who the hell are you?' Ravaryn laced the words with as much hatred and venom he could muster.

Thaylon's laugh boomed, echoing around the walls of the dank cell and ricocheting pain through Ravaryn's skull.

'We want to help you, Ravaryn Black.'

The man's eyes glowed with something that made Ravaryn want to turn away from his powerful stare, but he held his gaze. Crouching down on his haunches before Ravaryn, closer than he would have liked anyone to get in his defenceless state, the stranger reached for the bag he'd deposited on the floor when he had entered. He spoke softly as he withdrew something from within it. Metallic notes filled Ravaryn's nostrils, mixing with the acrid scent of the poisoned water all around them.

'I am Thaylon. We journeyed here long ago, your father and I. You could call us comrades, friends even.' His sinister smile surfaced again, and with that look he seemed familiar. Ravaryn couldn't place his features, but it was like he had met this man before. Recognition hovered just out of his gasp.

'We're a team, your father and I. I'm the poison, and he the power. And you, Ravaryn Black, will help us. You want to rule, don't you? After all, you are a king, yes?' Thaylon lifted the contents of the bag out onto the cell floor – an old dented metal plate.

'We've waited a long time to be reunited with you. Your father is finally free, and to have found you right there... as one of the ones who freed him. Well, it's like fate. You found your way to us after all.'

Thaylon's hand reached back into the dirty sack, and he withdrew something wrapped within a cloth. A cloth seeping red from whatever was within it. The metallic sour tang intensified in the thick air of the cell.

Ravaryn tried to focus, but his vision was blurring, and he could feel himself inching away from consciousness again. 'I did not free him,' he snarled.

'Oh, I know. And I also know who did.' Thaylon's smile was wider, prouder. 'You are Salvador's heir. But it seems I have an heir all of my very own.' His voice was even, assured.

Ravaryn felt panic sweep through him. Some unknown fact was hiding from him in plain sight, and his mind was trying to piece together whatever dark puzzle he was now involved in.

'You will rule beside us. And you will eat, or you will die.' Thaylon unwrapped the cloth in his hands and dropped a large chunk of raw meat onto the dirt-encrusted metal plate next to Ravaryn, and lifted it to his face. Thaylon closed his deep midnight-blue eyes and sniffed the meat like a delicacy.

'I am not a dragon. I am something... different. A fire demon and a blood mage. I create. I transform. I live and gain my strength from lower life forms. Their flesh, their energy gives me power. It can heal you too, as you have dragon's blood, *demon's* blood, in your veins, Ravaryn Black. You've just never been shown the way...' His blue eyes glowed as he dumped the plate onto Ravaryn's lap.

'I don't know what you think I am, and I don't know who the fuck you are. But I'm not eating whatever poisoned shit you're offering.' Ravaryn scowled at the lump of red meat in front of him. 'Whatever this sick game is that you and that monster think you're playing at, I want no part in it. Let me go now because I want nothing to do with either of you. I'm no dragon, and I'm no demon. And I'm of no help to whatever you think you're planning. You've got the wrong man.'

Thaylon laughed, the cells around them echoing the menacing sound. He seemed deranged, a little insane. 'Oh, I don't think I have, son of Diwa.'

The mention of his mother's name ripped fire through him, and a sense of rage and clarity helped him focus just a little from the edge of oblivion. 'How do you know that name?' Ravaryn demanded.

Thaylon stood, leaving the meat before Ravaryn, and he began to pace the cell with his hands behind his back, huge fists clasped together. As he spoke, his eyes roamed the dirty walls of painted mould. 'Oh, I know many names. I have been here since the very beginning, since the humans' demise, just like your father. Who do you think taught dear Kyeitha about blood magic? Who do you think taught her how to create her pathetic creatures of the damned? But she was such a disappointment! Kyeitha had so much promise and could have ruled alongside us. She could have conquered this world, yet instead she chose to betray me... to banish me. And she stole my true heir from me, stole my magic from his very veins before he was even born, leaving him untouched, ordinary, useless. But my magic poisoned her, didn't it, Ravaryn Black? She couldn't fight the darkness any longer. But I've still got my heir. She just skipped a generation, that's all. She must be bloodthirsty, powerful, just like me...' His smile was horrific now. '...to have killed her own grandmother. Her power must be incredible.' Thaylon's eyes gleamed with pride as he spoke, his pupils widening into dark wells, his voice like that of a leader reciting a powerful speech to his soldiers.

Ravaryn's body begin to shake as realisation dawned in his mind.

'You will eat, or you will die.' Thaylon stopped pacing and stared down at Ravaryn, his face now set like stone. 'And Salvador will not be pleased if you die. But still... if you do, we have another heir out there who will take your place. But once a demon eats mortal flesh, he will hunger for it always. Eat, and it will fill you with so much power your wounds will heal, and you will be whole again. Afterwards, you will hunger for nothing else.' His words were quieter now, like he was reciting something holy.

Ravaryn's onyx eyes widened with horror as they tore away from Thaylon's deep blue wells to the hunk of raw meat in his lap. He flung he metal plate away from himself in absolute disgust with the only bit of energy he could muster. It clanged with a jarring sound against the concrete floor, and he twisted his broken body to the side and retched, his stomach howling as he emptied his its contents beside him.

Revulsion coursed through him at Thaylon's words, at what he expected Ravaryn to do. Then came the realisation that he knew what Zee was, and his need to find her shook him to his very core.

'You're a monster.' He spat blood and bile on the floor next to him. It was all Ravaryn could growl before the darkness edged around his vision.

Thaylon smiled down at him as if it were a compliment, pleased as he went to leave the cell. 'You will eat, or you will die.'

A Forest Aflame

Maya Village, Lamiria

Zemira was reeling from what she had just witnessed, the *memory* she had just lived through, the one Diwa had shared with them using her regained powers. The essence of those memories and the aura around Diwa were incredible. For the first time they showed just how deep her secrets ran, like roots reaching far into soil below the top layer, unseen but always there, binding her to this very world.

'Is Ravaryn unharmed? Can we see him?' Zee couldn't hide the fear coating her voice. Without even having to see Orion's expression, she sensed his anger permeating the perfumed air around them. Zee ignored it, ignored her father. When suddenly, deep within the ancient tree, screams filled the clutter-laden den. Screams from the village outside, which a moment ago had seemed like a world away, tore the three sharply back to reality, cutting short the answers Zee desperately sought.

'Something's wrong.' Orion's deep voice almost sounded relieved for the abrupt distraction.

Orion and Zee leapt up simultaneously, with Diwa not far behind as the commotion grew louder, more desperate. They didn't encounter Sahara on their way back from her den, so Zee swept the colourful beaded curtain away from the entrance. The light struck her eyes for a moment, and it was too bright... too hot. Hot white and orange flames engulfed the tree's limbs, flames licking rapidly towards them. Orion raced to the balcony through the heat to see the village below in chaos. People ran in all directions. Some were consumed by the flames and were screaming in agony. Others were screaming for their families in the midst of the blaze.

Orion's face paled at the devastation that had occurred so rapidly. Diwa caught up with the pair, Zee now frozen next to Orion as they took in the scene below. It was like a war had broken out before her in this peaceful place, without a second's warning.

What in the Mother's name was happening? Zee's heart burst forth in her chest. Diwa took them both by their arms, pushing her slender but strong frame between them, her voice panicked. 'Salvador... he's here. Hurry! We must help the villagers!'

They didn't need any more urging. Sour panic coated Zee's mouth as a look of pure fear misted over Diwa's silver eyes. They sprinted down the flaming stairs of the mammoth tree, now burning swiftly to its demise. Zee slipped on a crumbling step, her hand catching the scorching rail. Pain burst forth on contact through her left hand, but it quickly disappeared into the flesh, the blackened tattoo of blood blooms and vines somehow absorbing the pain for her in an instant.

The three leapt from the last few steps just as the wooden staircase collapsed into a blackened pile of food for the fire. Zee's hair swept in front of her as a huge gust of wind burst from behind her, and an ear-piercing screech ripped the air in two. She spun around, and coming straight towards her was the menacing black dragon that had taken Ravaryn from her in the Dark Rim.

Silvery fangs glistened in two perfect rows as its scaly obsidian maw opened into a sneer. Its wings slowed its gigantic body as a crackling sound of static buzzed the hot air around them. With a moment of foresight, Zee grabbed hold of a momentarily frozen Diwa and a stunned Orion, and screamed, '*Move!*' just as a stream of flames poured out from the dragon's mouth, blasting the earth where they had stood a second ago.

The three scrambled for purchase in the chaos, only then noticing the mutilated and charred bodies strewn over the village floor. They ducked within the tree trunks on the edge of the main clearing in the village's centre for refuge. Zee's rapid breaths were stinging her throat as she tried to fathom the scene before her. Anger ignited in her veins as Orion tried to comfort a clearly frightened Diwa. The pair had never, ever seen her afraid, and her fear was like a noxious weed trying to rapidly invade their systems. But Zemira's veins pulsed with energy, anger and power. *How dare this creature steal her people and destroy this village.* Her pupils flared with a deep glowing green, and before Orion or Diwa could protest, Zee ran from the thickness and protection of the trees and into the clearing where the black dragon had just attacked them.

Her palms erupted into flames, licking higher as they trailed up her arms to her elbows. Energy sizzled from her core, sparking like lighting around her. To the left, on the far edges of the clearing, Maya village's warriors were attempting to fight off the dragon's attack. Now earthbound, with his wings tucked into his shimmering black body, he moved like oil through water. *He was too fast.* It was as if the warriors and the dragon weren't even on the same plane. Even though the warriors were highly trained and fought in perfect unison, they were barely inflicting a scratch upon him. Sharp talons knocked them down like a scythe to wheat.

Zee spotted Aytac, Kyeitha's former black wolf shifter guard, and his twin sister Sayde at the forefront of the attack. The dragon's claws contacted with Aytac's shield and body, flinging him with a crunch into a nearby tree trunk. Sayde's fury was a living thing as she dodged and weaved the attack, managing to come up under the dragon's breast. In an act of pure hatred, she thrust her spear into the dragon's sternum with all her might, a scream tearing from her.

A roar of flames burst in anger from the dragon's maw as it felt the attack that had slipped by him. Sayde slid under the dragon's belly and out of reach of the razor-sharp talons that now sought her. Zee took the distraction, the moment, as a sign. And she ran. Her feet flaring with flames and speed, a yell tore from her as she blasted pure energy from within her. Her flames engulfed the dragon's face as she expelled everything within her, not holding back.

He turned towards his attacker, Sayde forgotten. Now blistering heat burst forth towards Zee as more of the villagers fled, while Sayde ran to where Aytac's crumpled body lay and dragged him into the forest. Zee held the dragon's flames as long as she could, sweat dripping from her face and down the centre of her spine. Her teeth clenched with the effort as they were forced together within her jaw. The flames of the black dragon stopped, and Zee's own flames blasted into his face, catching the right side of his monstrous head just as he turned. With an almighty sweep of his wings, he took flight. As his wings expanded, his powerful tail pounded Zee mercilessly into the earth, like a giant crushing a fly.

Zemira's green flames retreated as she tried to move the earth around beneath her, her mind working faster than it ever had, anger and adrenaline fuelling her bravado. She managed to combat some of the force of the blow by moving the earth underneath her as she was hit with the solid blow of the tail, her hands digging into the soil as she moulded it around her. But stars permeated her vision, and she nearly lost consciousness as the power of the dragon's tail and sharp metallic scales crushed her into the earth as it leapt from the village floor, retreating from its attack. Large obsidian wings carried it into the sky above Zee, as it flew further and further into the distance, leaving Maya Village burning and broken all around her. The screams had died down but not disappeared completely.

Strong hands wrapped around Zee's shoulders, the pain crushing her insides. *Gods, her ribs must be broken.*

Orion said wildly, 'Zee! What were you thinking? Get up, we have to go. The village is collapsing all around us.'

Zee's head swam as she let Orion lift her from the small pit of dirt she lay in, her eyes searching the charred bodies strewn everywhere, horror filling her stomach like acid. She saw movement to the left as a small body hunched over a blackened form. Zee pulled weakly against Orion's grip. 'Over there.' She twisted her head to motion towards the person as Orion dragged her away from the clearing now littered with death.

Orion almost kept moving her to the forest. 'Dad...' Her eyes finished the rest of the sentence for her. Orion took a second to read her plea, and a growl left him as he rapidly steered them towards the injured villager.

Smoke cleared as flames rose when they reached the small figure. Weeping filled their ears as a blonde head rested forth on a blackened form. Orion cursed, and Zee's heart fractured. Mirabel wept, covered in blood and slightly blackened by flames herself, over her grand-folks' bodies. Her small hands were squeezing Flinder's motionless ones like she was holding onto the last flicker of him within her palms.

As Orion gently put her down, Zee stumbled forward. 'Mirabel! We have to go!'

A tree creaked and snapped as it crashed down just metres from them in a shower of coal and fire, but Mirabel wailed unmoving before her fallen family. 'Dad, grab her. I'll manage on my own.'

Orion's deep eyes assessed Zee for a moment, then he acknowledged her with a stern nod. He scooped Mirabel up into his arms, and the three dodged and weaved their way through the wildfire blazing around them now.

Zee had never felt heat such as this. Her skin burned all over, and her eyes were misty and stung like a raspor's bite. Her ribs begged for her to curl up into herself and just lie down in the forest to sleep. Her throat rasped as she tried not to inhale the noxious smoke into her lungs.

Orion reached a large hand back to her, and she clasped it with her remaining strength as he pulled her along through the flaming forest around them. After what seemed like a lifetime of running, the flames were barely behind them, and there was no sight of anyone else running from the village. Zee had no idea where they were. She felt the magic within her totally exhausted as she tried to call on the air, earth and water's power around her. Yet she came up dry like she had swallowed a mouthful of sand on a hot beach. Flames encroached in front of them. They had somehow been caught in the wildfire's snare.

'Dad! You have to shift to carry Mirabel out to safety', Zee said desperately.

'I can't carry you both as Wolf, Zee.'

'I know. But you have to shift.' Tears stung Zee's bloodshot eyes as the smoke became thicker, the heat making her dizzy.

'You know I can't do that. I can't leave you.' His deep voice was laced with anger... and fear.

Zee flailed her fists against his chest with the sliver of energy she had left. 'You have to save her!' Then she crumbled, her head dropping as she leaned into him in defeat. 'Dad, ...'

Orion squeezed her tightly against him and Mirabel's crumpled, weeping body in his arms. Just as the flames licked at their feet, Zee felt the earth fall out from beneath them. Darkness replaced the blinding glare of the wildfire as all three fell into a cold, murky body of stagnant water below. Orion thrashed as he let Mirabel go, but she seemed to have come back to reality as the cold water hit her shocked body. Orion reached out for Zee, and they made their way into the darkness, away from the flames above.

Gaia is Gone

Zee was walking through the cauldron-mushroom glen, but the small flying lizards that zipped between the blooms before her were all sapped of their colour. Some squeaked as smoke trailed after them, and their scales fell from their tiny charred bodies.

'Gaia!' Zee called out for the Earth Mother, and it felt like she had been searching for her for hours. From the lake and the neon forests to the mushroom glens and the ancient rainforests, finally she reached the outcrop that looked out to the deadlands.

'I need you! I need to speak with you! Gaia, please, we need your help,' Zee begged, desperation lacing her words and making her voice high. It scratched at her throat, while her bones begged her to lie down in the dead earth beneath her and rest. But she wandered on, past blackened trees and cracked earth until before her stood a crumbling structure in the desolate desert of the ancient ones' biggest failure: the deadlands.

The blood blooms on Zee's left arm flared a bright blue within the black petals, opening and stretching towards the massive concrete and rusted metal structure that stood up from the poisoned earth like a temple of decay. Zee looked at her arm as she turned it over and wriggled her onyx fingers before her... her arm spoke of danger, but it also beckoned for something within the structure too. All the blooms were striving forward, towards the place as though it were the sun and they had been surviving only in the dark.

Ravaryn... Zee's heart sang to her. Ravaryn must be in there. She stepped forward, determination injecting strength into her as she marched on towards the ancients' building, just as the ground began to rumble beneath her. The earth churned, and her weary legs shook until Zee fell on her arse, hard. The earth began to mound high above her, and a huge face filled with rows teeth gaped forth. A mud muncher screeched its ugly greeting at her and lunged down to swallow her whole, just as Zee's hands flew before her face and she screamed.

'Zee! Zemira, wake up!'

The scream ripped from her throat as she woke, and her eyes begged to stay glued together as she was roused from the fitful sleep. Decaying plant life and a damp tang filled her nostrils along with the lingering scent of smoke. It was Orion, and they were lying in a damp, dark but most thankfully cool place, where no engulfing flames of any kind lingered.

Weeping echoed around them, and Zee remembered Mirabel, the attack, the fire... and the fall.

'You passed out as soon as we reached the edge of the water,' Orion confirmed.

'Where on earth are we?' Zee questioned as she sat up, her head blasting pain as if daggers had been forced into her skull through her eye sockets.

'I don't know, but from what I can guess, we fell through the roof of an old ancients' structure that the forest had grown over. The walls are stone-like and so is the floor. But how are you feeling, Zee? Are you strong enough to summon a light?'

Zee scooted herself upright, ignoring the sharp pain digging into her middle. 'I'm okay. I... I was looking for Gaia.'

Her eyes looked haunted in the faint light; Orion could just see her outline with his shifter wolf eyes glowing through his human form. His heart constricted at seeing his daughter's fear seep forth from her.

'I couldn't find her. I couldn't find her anywhere... I came to this this building... and then Ravaryn, and...'

'Shh, you've been through a lot.' Orion's large hand cupped her shoulder. 'You've expelled too much energy, and you nearly drained yourself in the attack. Zee, you have to be more careful.' His voice softened. 'We can talk about this later, but for now we have to figure out where we are, and find what's left of Lamiria. My best bet is that the lake of life and the temple will be where everyone would head. Ancient magic protects its land and walls. We'll get out of here and head for the lake, alright?'

Zee nodded, then concentrated through the pounding in her brain to conjure a flame of light from her palm. As soon as she did, it illuminated their surroundings and the weeping mess that was Mirabel.

The walls were mould-stained stone, the ancients' stone – concrete – like some of the buildings that still remained in Thorta city. The walls curved to a round ceiling, like they were inside a giant tube that sloped downwards into the pit of water they had fallen in.

'You have to get Mirabel out of here.' Zemira made her way to the weeping girl, the light flickering the ominous surroundings, making Zee feel as though she were in a dungeon.

She reached for Mirabel with her free hand and squeezed the young girl's shaking body tightly against hers. 'Mirabel, we're going to get out of here. We're going to get somewhere safe.' Zee's emerald eyes shone as they locked on Orion's. 'Orion's going to get you out of here, but you have to do something for me, okay?'

Mirabel had quietened down, her head pressing into Zee as though hiding away from the truth of what had just transpired in her village, to her home and to her family. 'You have to be strong, just for a little while longer. Can you do that for me?' Mirabel sniffled and nodded her head into Zee's protective embrace.

'The wildfire will have passed by us by now, so Orion will fly you out in his eagle shifter form to find the others. He'll take you somewhere safe. But you'll have to hang onto him, Mirabel. He can't fly and carry you, do you understand?' Zee released her grip and waited for Mirabel to acknowledge what she had just been told. No words left the girl's mouth. Zee was afraid if she tried that more sobs would burst forth. And she could see the girl was barely holding herself together. Mirabel just nodded very slowly, and her dark eyes connected with Zee's, hopeless and full of horrors. Zee emitted a weak smile for her, but that was all she could muster.

Orion lit up the pit with a blue streak of light as he shifted into his huge eagle form. Zemira knew he didn't want to leave her exhausted and alone in the ancients' strange underground structure, but he also didn't really have a choice. He wouldn't want to fight with her, and there was no reasonable excuse that he had to disagree. He knew she was right: Mirabel was a quaking mess ready to break. Before Orion shifted and swept Mirabel upwards into the blackened forest above, he told her with a rumble to stay put.

'Like I'm going to go shopping at the market or something, right?' Zee quipped back and rolled her eyes. 'I'll be fine. Take your time. I'll enjoy the serenity while you're gone.' She was exhausted and needed rest.

Orion had grumbled back. 'I'll be back soon.'

Zee's head still throbbed violently, and she had no plans on exploring just yet. She did, however, desperately need to find Gaia. She needed answers. Zee remembered the deadlands she had seen, with the ancient structure towering up before her out of the poisoned land... and Ravaryn... her heart felt a pang as she remembered her arm being pulled like a magnet towards the crumbling fortress in her mind.

He's alive.

Lowering herself down against the curved wall of the cylindrical structure, Zee sat with her back against the wet mould-painted wall. There was enough light emitted from the hole in the roof that the three had fallen though to see the outlines of the space she was in for the moment. So she let the light in her right palm dim. Why was she always so spent after using her magic? What was she doing wrong? Sure, she had given nearly everything to fight the black dragon off, Salvador, but all she had done was deter its attack. How in the Mother's name were they going to stop such a force? How were they going to protect themselves? And why had Diwa been so paralysed by fear when he appeared? The Diwa she knew had never been afraid of anything. A shiver ran through Zee, goose pimples appearing after it on her skin, but then she felt a flutter of heat sweep through her. Hot and cold at the same time. That was never good. Maybe she was growing a fever?

Zee felt empty and hollow, a feeling that was all too familiar. She rested her head back against the hard wall, and even if she'd wanted to cry, no tears would come. She had passed the point where releasing sorrows would give her any sort of relief. Her left arm felt like sweat was pouring through the pores of her skin. She looked down in the dim light and saw one of the blood blooms wilt and twist into itself, disappearing from her arm altogether. Zee blinked, clearing her vision. Was she hallucinating? She sparked a flame for light and swept it close to her vined arm. All the blooms twisted in on themselves like the first one had. And a deep pang of pain crept through the vines. Thorns elongated on her skin, and a whisper of a name slid through her mind. '*Zemirahhh...*' Ravaryn's usually deep silken voice sounded weak, pained and barely audible.

She bolted upright. '*Ravaryn?*' Zee's panicked mind answered back. How was this possible? What was going on? Had she spent her energy so much that she was merely hearing his voice as her mind's way of trying to comfort her? Zee waited, then again, there was a pang in her arm and a whisper in her mind.

'*Zemira... I'm sorry. I'm sorry ... I can't, I ... just ... can't ...*'

'*Ravaryn!*' her voice was desperate in her mind. '*Ravaryn, hold on!*' she screamed back at the wisp of his essence. '*Hold on! We're coming. I'm coming for you!*' Zee had forced her eyes shut with concentration, not wanting to lose track of the weak connection, whatever it was within her. It faded, and when she opened her eyes, another blood bloom twisted in on itself and died.

He's alive.

Hope didn't bloom as brightly within her as it should have. Zee had never heard his voice sound so defeated, not even the day in the forest when he'd spoken to her about Liara and his babe. It was truly Ravaryn, but fear crawled over her skin as she feared what was left of him... what his father had done to him.

'*Hold on...*' Zee breathed into the clammy air around her. '*... I'm coming.*' She let exhaustion overtake her as she again rested her head back against the wall and shut her eyes, letting sleep come so she could search. Search for Gaia, search for answers she desperately needed, and search for the man who had somehow wound himself around her very core, who was a part of her, who needed her and made her feel like she wasn't the only one of her kind on the planet.

Zee fell into a fitful sleep, drifting into the realm of the Mother. She once again started her search, leaving her body behind her in the gloomy underground structure.

Creatures

Zenya, Kymera

Orion felt weakened not just by the flight and effort it took to carry Mirabel, but by the weeping she couldn't keep inside the whole flight over the blackened forests of Lamiria. He spotted a group travelling close to where the fires had died away, and where the protected lands around the temple must have begun. There were only a handful of villagers that had fled Maya Village and the attack that morning by the black dragon. What had Salvador's reason been? To instil fear in the forest folk? To destroy their home? Just to kill? Or the answer that Orion feared, the one that made his brow furrow with dread: the possibility that he might just have been looking for Zemira.

Orion thought the idea irrational, a father's fears, but what if by chance he knew? He knew of Zemira, her powers, her heritage? He had somehow clearly known who Ravaryn was the first moment he had laid eyes on his grown son. Maybe he could sense the blood flowing within him? For as soon as he was freed from the prison Diwa had locked him within for decades, Salvador had found Ravaryn instantly. Orion shook the thoughts of paranoia away as he slowly descended to the group of survivors.

He spotted a slightly hunched-over Aytac nursing his right side. A ferocious-looking Sayde ran forward to meet him, spear firmly gripped in her hand as he landed. He shifted after gently coaxing a rattled Mirabel from his back.

'Is everyone alright here? Anyone badly injured?' Orion asked the question that could be just as easily answered with his own eyes scanning the group. But he didn't know what else could be said.

'We gathered all that were still with us before we fled,' Sayde replied, then her eyes pinned on her brother. Aytac buckled and wobbled. 'Sit, you stubborn man!' Sayde scolded him instantly as if it weren't the first time she had said the words that day.

'And to think how much I missed you, sister. Your sweet concern for me is heart-warming.' Aytac had fewer barbs to his voice than usual, the hint of a weak smile trying to lift his stiff upper lip as he dropped to sit on a nearby stump.

'And who do we have here?' Sayde questioned, looking to the crumpled Mirabel, her knees tucked into her chest as she sat still and now silent, her tearstained face hidden from the world, and from the reality she did not want to face anytime soon.

'Mirabel.' Orion led Sayde away as he explained. 'We found her in the midst of the attack. Her grand-folk, Belladon and Flinder... they did not make it, and we don't know if the rest of her family made it out.'

A pained look crossed Sayde's face as her eyes became dark and hollow, a sheen glassing over them. She sucked in a deep breath and replied, forcing her eyes shut to absorb the trickle of emotion there for just a quick moment. 'We'll look after her. We're headed to the temple, and there's no safer place in Lamiria that we can go. With Kyeitha gone, maybe we can finally return to the Valley of Rivers.'

Orion nodded, his eyes approving the decision. Sayde gave a sharp dip of her own head and proceeded over to Mirabel. She sang smooth, calming words to her, trying to coax the girl from the shock and sorrow she was living through, her hand gently resting on her shoulder. Mirabel finally looked up and seemed to reign in her emotions; for now, she seemed she would manage. Hopefully she could keep her anguish at bay until they reached their destination and the group were safe.

Orion walked over to where Aytac sat, rolling his shoulders that now ached a little from the flight. 'I'll be back,' he said. Aytac's large yellow eyes were still focused on Sayde and Mirabel. 'But I have to go and get Zemira. She was severely weakened by the attack. We fell through the forest floor, straight into an ancients' old building, as the fire was upon us. We were lucky...' Orion paused. 'Do you know if many others have made it out?'

Aytac's eyes found the leaf litter at his feet, and he ground his boots in just a tad more. 'Just who is with this group. I'm sure there are others, though. We'll know more when we reach the temple.' His gaze finally met Orion's, his yellow irises contracting as he zeroed in on him. 'We'll need her, Orion. We'll all need her to open the doors to Tangaroa...'

Orion nodded, his heart aching a little as he absorbed the words he didn't want to hear. 'I'll be back with her as soon as I can. Get to the temple safely. We'll see you there.'

And with that, he shifted and flew up into the thick smoke-fogged sky to trail back the way he had just come to retrieve Zemira. He used his inner sense, his heart's desire instead of a sense of direction from the unrecognisable smouldering landscape, to guide him back through the mottled skies, back to the young woman that was once his little wolf.

*

The air slowly but surely warmed just a little as the crisp white landscape below started to morph into actual colours, not just varying shades of grey and white. Paxton could feel he almost had a nose again. He couldn't tell whether it was from the rise in temperature as he and Mazda, astride the duellerats, neared the border of the old Rim wall. The radiant smile Mazda wore on her adrenaline-filled face, freckled cheeks glowing in the wind as she glided beside him through the crisp air, made him warm in his very core. She and Blaze were majestic to watch, a duo seamlessly blending into each other. Mazda looked like she belonged on the back of the graceful flying beast, like she were born to it, her fiery tangle of curls streaming out behind her like a river of autumn leaves in the wind. Pax could tell she loved the duellerat, and Blaze seemed to exude the same happiness Mazda did.

Paxton, on the other hand, still feared losing a hand or a finger upon landing, given how tightly he gripped onto Astrid's neck feathers with his frozen hands, but his heart had finally slowed to a slightly more respectable pace. Pax did feel he was getting the hang of riding the creature. It was simple – just don't fall off, and don't rip out any of Astrid's feathers or fur.

Mazda slowed, falling behind him, and when he turned to look her way she motioned with her hands that she was going to descend for a break. Pax still wasn't sure about how to really communicate with his chosen duellerat, Astrid. But as he spoke loudly over the wind, the creature instantly spotted Blaze and followed suit. They both gently glided down where the stark shining snow had faded, and where new forest growth bordered a larger, much older, forest. The old trees looked like they had been standing since the dawn of time, and the mist mingled in the dips of the canopy as they descended.

Paxton could hardly catch his breath; he had reached the lands outside of the old Rim world. The *only* world humans had known for more than 500 years since their very-near extinction, and he was now outside of the Rim's safety. He descended closely behind Mazda and Blaze, coming to an abrupt but not nearly as graceful stop beside them. Astrid skidded upon the hard earth meeting her feet, adjusting for Paxton's added weight and digging in with her taloned claws.

'Are you doing okay back there, Astrid?' Mazda called out. 'Paxton hasn't made you bald yet I hope!' The exhilaration from the flight and the rush of the adventure further illuminated the beautiful pitch that was Mazda's sweet yet powerful voice.

'Ha... ha!' Paxton drawled, drawing out the two syllables sarcastically like Zee would have. Gods, he missed her. But still riding an adrenaline rush of his own made it easy to push away the worry. For now.

'I'm fine. Thank you for asking.' Mazda laughed back at his flat tone.

Astrid was clearly not impressed with his steel grasp even though they had landed. In an instant, she reared back and bucked him from her with a sharp caw. Pax landed square on his arse. A fit of laughter burst from Mazda, and a strange noise erupted from Blaze. Paxton guessed it was the duellerat laughing at his expense. A clucking noise came from Astrid as well. The laughter was contagious, it seemed, as she joined in at his expense.

His cheeks turned beetroot red, but he couldn't be too embarrassed – he was sincerely impressed he had survived his first flight and had stepped foot into the lands beyond the old Rim world. The lands Zee had said they called Lamiria. After a few moments of clearing his head and willing his legs to not feel like jelly beneath him, Pax looked around. The sun shone through a densely clouded sky behind them from the west, from Kymera, and ahead scarce dappled light shimmered through the weaves of the rainforest's canopy. Intricately patterned leaves of all colours shone within the forest before them, an eerie vibe seeping forth.

Pax was captivated, and like a moth to the flame, he headed forward straight into the forest to investigate further. 'Have you even seen anything like this?' his awestruck voice questioned a just-as-stunned Mazda who now followed after him.

Tiny luminous creatures flitted in and out of the undergrowth, and a furry echidna-like rabbit darted away before them from one patch of ferns to another. It was a floxel, unbeknownst to the pair. A few leaves sparkled with a luminescent glow upon being brushed by. The only noise around them was the quiet hum of wind gently stirring a few leaves from the forest's floor. Intoxicated by the magic of the eerie forest engulfing their senses, they didn't see the oncoming threat that crept towards them through the dense vines on long, thin legs, perfectly blending in with the fungi-coated trunks of iridescent yellows and oranges.

Click, click, click.

The unfamiliar noise broke the stupor Paxton and Mazda had both been in, as if the forest had held them in a trance. As Pax turned to Mazda, the sheen coating her eyes faded, and they grew wide as they met Paxton's. Indeed, her bright blue eyes like blooming cornflowers shone with worry at him. She'd heard it too... a rattle, like the wind through humseed stalks, followed the eerie click, click, click, and the pair spun around to where the noise was coming from behind them.

Two rows of sharp, jagged teeth appeared before them in a jaw that seemed to hinge far too widely open. Sharp spidery legs vibrated in front of the creature's body as they rubbed together, emitting the vibrating sound towards them. The creature reared up and towered high over the pair.

'*Run!*' Mazda screamed.

At the same moment she legged it, the creature lunged forward at a stunned Paxton. It wasn't the shock of seeing the vile-looking thing that stunned him, as Paxton could still remember the close encounter he and Zemira had had with the Vipen when crossing the Alvion Sea from Thorta to Aylenta. It was that its contorted face somehow seemed... *human.*

Paxton dodged its snapping maw as a screech shot forth from it. He tripped over backwards and fell on a rotting tree limb, but rolled and leapt to his feet, following as fast as he could after Mazda and back towards the edge of the forest where they had left Blaze and Astrid. Horror seeped through his veins like ice as he heard sharp spider-like legs pound into the ground right behind him, inching closer with each step.

Just as he felt it was nearly upon him, Pax ducked and rolled to his side and into a thicket of tangled plants behind a wide tree trunk. The creature pounded after him, spindly legs carrying the half-human torso forward with furious speed. But suddenly its pursuit ended, and it was gone. Pax heard a scream that seemed to render the forest still. *Mazda!* His heart exploded in his chest. What on earth had they been thinking, coming into this place unarmed, the pair of them. He should have known better. He should have *been* better. This was entirely his fault. He found his feet and flew to the spot where they had landed; Mazda was on the ground underneath the creature's barbed front legs, which pinned her down in place.

Large fangs were protruding from within its maw. Closer and closer they reached for her face, purple saliva dripping onto her from its disjointed maw. In a flash, Paxton remembered Zee's knife. He had kept it from the day Kyeitha had taken her over in the Black Forest – when she had tried to kill him. He snatched the knife from his waist and ran like his legs were on fire, sliding under the creature to come up next to Mazda. With all his might, a yell of fear-coated determination left him as he thrust the knife upwards into the roof of the creature's gaping mouth. It rapidly snapped its large fangs back within its jaw, and sharp-rowed teeth scraped a layer of skin from Pax's arm as he pulled the blade back, moving as fast as he had plunged it in.

The creature's legs shifted from pinning Mazda as it momentarily jumped back from the attack, and a sharp-as-metal point of a front leg pierced straight through Paxton's inner thigh. He grunted in agony but forced himself upwards, dragging Mazda along with him. His breath came in gasps as blood seeped from his skinned arm. It stung like wildfire, and his wounded leg pulsed as blood pumped from the deep wound.

Blaze and Astrid pounded towards them. 'Let's get the hell outta here!' The words flew from Paxton's pale face.

'Pax, look out!'

The creature had recovered and was stabbing its front two legs out in the air like spears towards him, trying to pin him down like it had done to Mazda moments before. Astrid reared up as she defended her rider, and her two powerful front claws tore shreds into it as Pax tried to stumble away from its attack. It screeched, reared back and click, click, clicked its throat as if assessing whether or not the fight with the duellerat was worth the prize it sought. Then miraculously, it backed away and fled into the forest from whence it had first appeared.

'You saved me...' Pax's shocked voice carried over to Astrid. She nudged his side with her head as if to say, *Don't worry about it, human! Let's get the hell out of here before that thing comes back.*

'Maz! Are you okay?' He began searching frantically for her, just as she reached him, Astrid and Blaze standing guard behind her. Her trembling hands reached forward and skimmed Paxton's face, searching his eyes.

'Thank you,' she breathed, then slid her hands around his neck and forced him into a vice-like hug, his own hands having nothing to do but awkwardly embrace her thin waist.

'It was nothing... you're welcome. I mean, you would have done the same for me, right?'

She pulled back, a weak smile on her pale face as she nodded and let him go. Pax wobbled a little before her, and she instinctively looked down, her voice rising an octave. 'Your leg!'

'Oh, shit.' Paxton had been distracted by Mazda's embrace, which gave him the slightest reprieve of the pain from his flesh-stripped arm and injured leg. But the pain returned as soon as he sighted it, even more blood seeping forth.

Mazda didn't hesitate. She bent down and roughly ripped at her long skirts layered over her fitted flying pants and knee-high boots. She tore a long strip and began to wrap the beautiful fabric over Paxton's seeping wounds. He sucked air in through his teeth as she tightened the fabric with a knot. Kneeling before him, she quickly wrapped his thigh, her red hair shining like a goddess before him.

Get yourself together, Pax.

He focused on watching her small, nimble fingers work the fabric and gently tie the last knot, but a screech from Blaze tore their attention from the task. The duellerat was away from the pair and still eyeing the edge of the forest, while Astrid stayed guard and stood close to the two. Movement caught Pax's eye, and there from the edge of the forest, two more of the spider-like creatures now attacked Blaze in unison, working together to violently pin him down.

Mazda screamed and turned to run towards her duellerat, her dearest friend, but Pax's strong hand grabbed her roughly, fisting into her dark coat and pulling her back.

'No, Maz! We have nothing! No weapons. We can't fight them off! We nearly just died… we will die.'

'*No!*' Mazda roared in anger, realising Pax was right all too soon as one on the monsters started to spin a golden web around Blaze, constricting his thrashing wings and claws. Astrid started screeching, but stood guarding the two humans in her care.

'We'll get help. We'll come back, Maz. Please, we *have* to get out of here.' A scream of anger and desperation tore from her in a violent burst, and she spun around to grab Paxton just as forcefully as he had gripped her.

'I know.' Her eyes met his, defeat within them. 'You're right.'

She raced towards Astrid and helped Paxton get up on her back. Mazda flung herself behind Pax just as a third spider creature emerged from the forest and headed straight for them. Its loud click, click, click echoed around the trees and melded in amongst Blaze's cries in a sickening song. It tilted its ugly head to the side as it took in the three and ran towards them, its legs skittering it forward at such speed.

'Astrid, go! NOW!' Pax roared, but she didn't need the command. She pounded forth powerfully and lifted the pair into the air just as the creature leapt, trying to pin her with its front barbed arms, maw gaping open.

Mazda's hands gripped Paxton tightly around the waist and she turned her head to see the pair of creatures drag Blaze away. He thrashed and roared wildly in a tight spool of golden thread. Angry tears emerged from Mazda, but they mingled into the wind as Astrid flew higher and farther into the cloudy skies above the ancient forest.

Fever

Zemira awoke with sweat coating her entire body. Her legs ached, and her lower back stung with sharp pangs. A tingle ran down her backside, numb from falling asleep while sitting upright against the hard concrete wall. Her vision wavered before her eyes; once again while sleeping she had searched the realm where she should have found Gaia, but nothing. There was not a sight of the Mother of the earth.

Zee tried to stand, her head swimming, and she stumbled forth in the dark stagnant space. She had to get out of here. How long had she been sleeping? How far away would Orion be? She would rather wait in a blackened forest than in this dank hole any longer. It reminded her of a cave, and she hated dim claustrophobic spaces.

Traps.

Her mind seethed as it supplied the word. With a deep breath in, she steadied herself at the edge of the molasses-like water that had broken their earlier fall. Far above her, faint light filtered in through the ceiling of the space. Zee spread her hands wide and out to her sides as she absorbed the energy of this place all around her. The water was strong and thick, and it contained stories as old as time. She felt the animals that had perished within it, their energy contained, but also the plants that it had given life to, and the creatures that had lived within it.

She breathed deeply and absorbed the energy of the concrete that held strong and true, keeping the secrets of this place for all this time. The concrete had been home to the ancients, who had optimised its strength by mixing particular types together. Then she absorbed the energy of the stone that had been forged by Mother Nature's hands, volcanic and longstanding in its natural state.

Gaia. Worry flickered like cicada wings in Zee's gut. *Where on earth are you?*

She willed the hard stone beneath her feet upwards, shaking with the effort of using her powers. The floor underneath her rumbled and cracked as a huge chunk lifted her aloft. It was steady beneath her, but the sweat increased on her brow, making her feel smothered and sickly. All she had to do for now was get out of here, and then she would wait for Orion. She couldn't be in this place any longer, as for some strange reason it felt as though she were trapped in a prison cell. Her father's voice rumbled in her mind. *Stay put.* Oh well, it wasn't just him she didn't listen to. It wasn't like she listened to anyone else, either.

The stone was level as Zemira crouched down on it, willing it forward with all her might across the water's surface. Once she was just under the hole of sunlight, she channelled the molasses-thick water to lift her upwards. A smooth sweeping sensation slid through her veins, and she swept her hands in circular motions upwards to her freedom, her muscles protesting against the movements. She had no idea whether or not she could make her actions work, but she had to try. She had to try *more*, Zee realised. She needed to actually see what she was capable of, to practise her skills instead of just hoping she could pull off whatever she wanted when the time called for it.

Maybe if she could fight better, wield her powers *better*, Mirabel's grand-folk would still be alive. Maybe the village would still be standing. Her anger simmered within at herself, and she felt the water swirling and churning beneath the slab of stone as she stood up out of the crouch, nearly there. Her teeth clamped together, and slowly but surely, Zee lifted herself towards the light.

Her panting breaths started to rattle her, and her head was cloudy. *Shit.* She was sure she was ready to pass out. Just as she reached the top, she let the water and stone drop, her hold on the elements ceasing as they were too heavy to hold onto. But she didn't need them anymore. Zee jumped and landed with her torso on the edge of the opening. Her slender hands scrambled for purchase on the charred forest floor, and she gripped a vine that tumbled down. It was still attached to a seemingly solid core, so she wrapped it round and round her wrist, then pulled herself forward.

All around her in the burned remains of the forest were creeping dark shapes... some were small, some the size of her palm, and some were larger... like dinner plates. Spiders... golden orb spiders were scuttling haphazardly across the ground all in the same direction, like a creeping wave before her. Zee blinked, and just like that, they were gone.

Gods, was she hallucinating?

Once her legs were free of the hole, she rolled onto her back and stared up at the forest's emptier canopy. It resembled thin, creeping blackened fingers stretching towards one another. It was getting late, with the light fading in the still-settling smoke of the dark sky. Zee was definitely ill, she knew it. She'd never felt anything like this before. It was different than when Kyeitha's spirit had possessed her body, slowly poisoning her. But she knew she was in trouble.

Soon the stars would be winking at her, and the orcles would awaken to see the destruction the fire – no – the black dragon had reaped on their beautiful lands.

Would they mourn? Would they be able to regrow if no seeds had survived?

Zee felt her eyes close, sadness cradling her soul.

How were they going to stop such a force? How was she ever going to get to Ravaryn? What if she never saw his stupidly handsome face again?

How she longed to hear his silky voice tease out her name, his lips soft yet firm against hers. Zee regretted not having more time with him, not forgiving him sooner. There was so much unsaid between them, so many emotions she had yet to truly acknowledge. How could she feel this way about someone she barely knew?

Then there was the other half of the coin, in that sometimes she felt she had known him her whole life. The things he said, the faces he made, she understood them all like she'd known him a lifetime. But he was such a strange soul, and she was afraid of getting closer to him. Not because of who he was, or even what she now *knew* he was. It was because she was worried about what other people would think. Pax, her father, *Gods...* her mother. How pathetic. When had she ever truly cared about what others thought of her? Why was she holding back now?

Zee felt a sharp pang in her left arm and lifted it to see her marks. Her arm felt like it were wrapped in lead, and as she inspected the tattooed blood blooms she saw another bloom twist, wilt and disappear before her eyes.

Ravaryn, where are you? she whispered to herself, her heart now feeling just as heavy as her arm.

*

Orion found Zee asleep on her back and lying under the emerging stars, her left arm cradled against her chest within her right hand.

'I thought I told you to stay put,' he rumbled, his deep tone not as harsh as usual, as he approached his sleeping daughter. But she didn't stir. His large hand gripped her shoulder gently to rouse her from sleep. They had to get back; they had to get everyone safe inside the magical walls of Tangaroa, the Valley of Rivers. He felt her shoulder, damp and yet not cool with the night's incoming air, and his hand swept to her forehead. She was burning up. Gods, she was *burning*.

'Zee.' He shook her again.

A mumble left her lips, and her eyebrows scrunched. Orion scooped her up into his arms, but flying was out of the question. She felt light and clammy against his broad chest. His throat felt tight, looking down at her. He had never had to suffer through her getting ill when she was little as the forest folk didn't get sicknesses like humans did. And even though

Zee was half human, she had rarely been affected by sickness at all. He hoped it was just a reaction to using so much power while fighting Salvador, and that it wasn't something more sinister.

Her sweat was seeping through into Orion's dark shirt, causing his legs to move faster. He was already exhausted but there was no way he would let anything happen to his daughter while he was still breathing, so he trudged on through the remains of the blackened forest. The twisted bare limbs looked like demons in the night, some still smouldering, and red coals flickered within them like eyes. He forged ahead, trying not to let the despair that breathed out of the destroyed ecosystem enter into him, towards the temple with his little wolf in his arms. His heart ached for Verena, Zee's mother, and he prayed to the Mother like never before that she was safe for the time being from Salvador's reach.

Blood Bond

Exhausted bodies littered the temple floor, its expansive sandstone veranda full for the first time in decades. Every muscle in Orion's body screamed as he made his way towards the lake of life in the moonlight, avoiding the villagers sleeping away the pain, fear and heartache they had recently endured. Millowisps glided through the air to meet him, trailing vibrant colours from their little bodies of light and circling him and Zee in a chirpy greeting.

The water was cool and sweet as it enclosed Orion's ankles then his burning calf muscles as he entered the healing waters with his daughter in his arms. The millowisps from nearby Lilypad blooms all fluttered closer to inspect the pair. Light twirled and flickered about as Orion submerged Zemira into the cool waist-high water. He knew that the magic had not been able to heal her from Kyeitha's curse, but he had hope that this was different.

Just under the surface of the water, Orion held his breath as he fixed his eyes on her face to watch for a trace of movement. A few tiny air bubbles tricked out of Zee's nose, and then her eyes flew open under the clear moonlit water. Orion lifted her body out of the water as Zee awakened, coughing and spluttering. He carried her back to the shore and sat her down beside him.

'You scared me,' he admitted, his large hand encasing her shoulder for support, the other raking over his ragged face.

Zee's eyes were unfocused as she spied the lake, then Orion. She took a few slow blinks to try and clear the water away then tilted her head up to the night's sky and took a deep breath in.

'I still don't feel right,' she said, her voice weak.

'You just need to rest. I'll find Diwa, and before you know it, you'll be crushed in one of her hugs. And she'll sort you right out with her healing as well.'

Zee spluttered, a chuckle leaving her chest with a cough, brightening her face just a little. 'That, and some tea, and I'll be as right as a sun raven.'

Lying back on the sandy shore, she let her eyes rest. Before long, she fell into another fitful sleep, searching in her mind's realm for Gaia.

*

Zee awakened to warm sun reflecting off the lake's tranquil waters. No, not warm, but hot... too hot. She sat up, her head pounding, and swept a hand across her forehead. She was covered in sweat again as heat licked up her body, the fever back. Feeling woozy, Zee struggled to creep away from the direct sunlight warming the small shore. People were milling about, sitting or still sleeping under the vined roof of the temple's open pergolas.

Zee took in the large monsteras and ivy vines weaving around the pillars as she searched for a familiar face. Dirty, soot-stained and sunken faces met her all around, and she felt dizzy once again. She turned away from a stunned villager blocking her path and spun into another. The brunette with deep earthen eyes grabbed Zee as she teetered on her feet.

'Zemira. You okay? You look like you're about to pass out.'

'Sayde?' Zee recognised Aytac's twin sister.

'Here, come with me. You need to sit.' Sayde led Zee to a seat in the middle of the temple. No, it wasn't just a seat – Kyeitha's throne blurred in her vision, and memories of her melting Kyeitha into oblivion flashed into her mind. But flashing even more violently were the memories that the former forest queen and guardian had planted of Zee's loved ones turning against her, as she'd tried to weaken her to kill her.

'No, not there!' But Zee was too weak, and Sayde had grabbed her around the waist and sat her down on the forest queen's throne before she could protest a second longer.

'You need to sit, Zee, or you're going to faint, I swear.'

The tiny mushrooms and miniscule flowers that grew all over the grand throne opened towards Zemira's presence. They glowed with bright silver light and began to encase her body with tiny thread-like vines that rapidly started spinning out from the stone.

Sayde stepped back in alarm, her wide doe eyes growing larger, her mouth now hanging ajar. Everyone in the space turned to see where the bright veil of light was coming from and witnessed the vines engulfing Zemira's body, then twirling away once again. The light dulled and faded, and Zee now sat straight-backed and still as a statue. She had been transformed anew. She wore a gown of midnight and emerald, perfectly matching the soul within her – half-forest, half-darkness. Her hair was braided in intricate swirls of braids against her scalp. Dark kohl rimmed her eyes, and the worn leather necklace holding Ravaryn's ring was now replaced by an actual necklace of woven silver-metal vines. It encased what seemed like the same stone, but larger. She now had a quail egg-sized obsidian opal at her throat.

Zee still didn't move as the flowers and fungi gently vibrated a sweet tune that hummed an ethereal sound, filling the pergolas. The plants twirled and changed around the villagers, bursting forth in bright blooms of moonflowers and jasmine, and jade vines crept along the roof. Their luminescent flowers hung heavily, lacing the ceiling with crystals the same colour of Kymera's sky-pines.

Orion had located Diwa, and together they raced through the immobile throng of people towards the throne and Zemira. Diwa's hand stopped Orion from reaching out and touching his daughter, as the transformation that was underway was not yet complete. Diwa stood there, and a proud smile crept over her knowing face, mixed with just a touch of nostalgia.

After time had slowed around them all, shifting the very winds and magic of the temple, the throne stilled. Then the stones crumbled away beneath Zemira and abundant vines rapidly replaced them, transforming the throne into a new seat that suited Zemira well. The dress she now wore was fit for a queen, the *new* queen of the forest. Sheer deep-green sleeves swept down from her shoulders, patterned with two glowing Luna moths on each shoulder. Delicate silver vines spiralled up from her waist, contrasting against the black velvet at the centre of the gown.

As Zee stood from the newly transformed throne, vines of jasmine and tiny chamomile flowers sprouted in her wake. An emerald flame flickered deeply within her eyes, and her new demeanour was like a spirit being led towards its destination, beckoning her forward. Some of the people knelt before her as she passed by, while others gasped and a few slowly backed away.

A zephyr of coloured leaves floated elegantly through the open space, and millowisps danced around her as she glided through the crowd. Zemira came to stand at the far back wall of the temple's grounds. She stopped at the place she had once travelled to with Sahara, and her blood bloom-tattooed hand ending in onyx fingernails swept over the story carved into the stone wall. Her fingers found their way to the half-crescent moon that protruded from the wall, to the intricate stone handle that Zee knew was the key to the entrance of the protected city beyond. It glowed brightly under her touch, and the temple wall rumbled under her power. The wall cracked then split into a wide opening, the glow dissipating as Zemira's hand fell, right before she collapsed on the floor. The air instantly stilled around her crumpled form, and the song of the vines and fungi ceased as the millowisps fled from her presence, retreating to the safety of the lake. As Diwa and Orion rushed to Zee moments later, a loud screech sounded. A duellerat carrying two humans skidded roughly to the lake's edge, splashing up water. As one human slid from the creature's back, the other was thrown unceremoniously into the cool water of the deep lake.

*

'This isn't a normal fever, Orion. I can't just heal her from this.' Diwa's voice was strained. 'Look at her arm. That mark is a blood bond. When Ravaryn healed her arm after removing Kyeitha's curse, he gave a part of himself to do it. He is suffering, and therefore so is Zee. I'm sorry, but there's nothing I can do. Even her becoming the forest queen isn't powerful enough to break their blood bond. What affects one will affect the other.'

'So she's just going to lie here and die!' Orion's bloodshot eyes glared at Diwa.

'If Ravaryn is dying...' Diwa's voice shook, '... then, yes, so is she.' Her voice hitched as she stood over the motionless Zemira.

'Well, that settles it.' Orion paced, and dust that had been lying dormant for so long marked his trail across the floor. He rubbed a hand roughly over his exhausted face. 'I'll find the bastard and bring him back. You can heal him, whatever is wrong with him, and Zee will recover. Am I right?'

He pinned Diwa with his steely gaze, willing a straight answer to come from her for once in her life. The words uttered by Sahara, the Maya Village healer, just before he had been reunited with Zee reverberated in his mind.

The choice is yours.

Sahara had known... she had known the pair were connected and implied it would be Orion's choice to let old wounds die and make amends with Ravaryn for Zee's sake. But he hadn't thought she'd meant for the sake of her life! And how would he explain this to Verena? Anger rippled from him, his usual cool and calm demeanour officially fractured.

'Watch over her, Dee. I will fix this.' And with that he took one last look at Zee in the gown the forest had crafted her after making her it's new queen. He bent down to kiss his daughter's fevered brow and strode from the room.

*

A healed Paxton waited impatiently outside the carved wooden doors to the room Diwa and Orion had taken Zee. Astrid must have known that the lake would heal his wounds; either that, or she had become accustomed to throwing him from her back upon landing, and he was luckier than he would have liked to admit. Mazda was at his side, sitting in one of the seated alcoves, twisting the silver ring on her thumb around and around.

'I can't take it anymore,' Pax complained, hand rubbing the back of his neck. Just as he went to pound on the door, it opened before him, and he came face to face with Orion, his gaze leaking anger. The man looked like he hadn't slept or eaten for days, because he *hadn't* slept or eaten for days.

'You two shouldn't be here.' His words were harsh, short, and not like the Orion that Pax knew at all. Even though Zee's father, especially as Wolf, had been protective of Zee – as a man, he had been a bit friendlier towards Pax.

'Orion, I have every right to be here. The last time I saw Zee she was possessed! Now let me through.' Paxton was shocked at his own words, and Orion raised his brows at the fire coming from the young lad.

Orion stopped him with his large hand just as Pax went to push past him into the room to see her. 'She's healed from Kyeitha, from the curse. But it seems we have a bigger problem now. I'm sure Diwa will explain everything to you. Just know that I'm going to fix this. I'll be seeing you, Pax. Look after them. Apologies for my shortness.' He broke eye contact and let him pass, his deep eyes conveying more to Pax then his words.

Pax digested what he had just said as Orion nodded a greeting to Mazda, who had just witnessed their conversation. She stood abruptly and nodded back politely at Orion, her worried eyes like turbulent winds growing before a storm. With that, Orion left them to reunite with a feverish unconscious Zemira.

Paxton looked around the room for the eccentric old woman he remembered from the Black Forest of Aylenta, but could not see her anywhere. He did note a slender young woman tending to Zee, and was about to stride over to her when she turned around to face him. His mouth dropped open in shock as her silver-speckled eyes locked on his. It was Diwa, her was sure of it, but... not Diwa.

'Diwa?' Pax gasped. 'What happened to you? You're so young! I don't understand.' He shook his head, wondering if he was hallucinating.

The younger Diwa smiled at him...

Paxton's shoulders twinged with a sharp pain as he ran his hand over the tight muscles in his neck, tilting his head to the side. He eyed the new version of Diwa that stood before him, trying to focus. So many strange things had happened in the last year. Was this really any different? But there had to be a reason for this massive change. Diwa wasn't vain, in any sense of the word. It wasn't like she would have gone out and found a way to do this to herself. No. Something had happened to change her like this. 'What happened to you, Diwa? How are you... like this?' His hands swept over her in up and down motions.

'Do you know where he is? How hurt is he if Zemira is unconscious!' Mazda's voice rose, ignoring Paxton's concerns for her own.

'I don't know, love, but Orion is going to get him back, I'm sure of it.' Diwa looked worn. Even in her younger self's body, she appeared tired with age.

'Ravaryn helped her just to curse her himself! He's a beast.' Paxton's anger was like daggers to Mazda's and Diwa's hearts. He cursed Ravaryn as he ran his hands through his long tawny hair.

'It's not his fault, Paxton,' Diwa corrected. 'If you want to blame someone then you can blame me. I have something to tell you that I think you should know. The both of you. Come sit,' she ordered.

Paxton huffed loudly and followed the pair to the sitting area, ready to absorb the explanation and hopefully gain some understanding of what was going on. His head started to ache and his chest felt too tight.

As Diwa revealed her truths, it was like peeling off layers, peeling off the years of the costume she had worn to keep them all safe. Keep them in the dark. She told them of Salvador, of Ravaryn and of the Dark Rim. When she had finished, Paxton and Mazda sat before her, mouths gaping.

'That's a lot to keep to yourself for so many years...' Paxton admitted. The fact that Salvador was now released upon their world, and sounded a thousand times worse than Ravaryn, did nothing to help the pain that was constricting Paxton's chest. Then Diwa told Mazda that she must take her rightful place as Ravaryn's appointed heir and ruler of Kymera.

'You must take charge, Mazda. It's time for you to step up as queen. We need the territory armies to know the threat they must prepare for.'

'Wait, what? Mazda can't be queen! She's just a stable hand at the castle!' Paxton was reeling from the avalanche of information he had just been forced to digest, and now this!

Diwa's silver eyes flitted to Mazda; she raised one brow and offered a comforting close-lipped smile.

Mazda's eyes slowly left the ground. 'It's true, Pax. I am Ravaryn's protégé, and I am to be Queen of Kymera.' She tore her eyes away from Paxton's shocked face. His mouth hung open as he stared back at her.

'There's something else, Diwa.' Mazda ignored his shock for now. 'We encountered these... *creatures*... at the edge of Lamiria. They took Blaze...' her voice shook as she explained. 'They were like... they looked half human, half spider, like two species had been morphed together... just like Kyeitha's creatures. It was like they had been *made*.'

Diwa could not hide the brief flicker of fear in her eyes. She chewed her lower lip then bit down on it as her eyes narrowed. 'Salvador has already started to change our world for the worse it seems...' Then she straightened in her chair, her chin lifting as she spoke, her voice becoming firm. 'And it will take all of us to stop him. Whatever his plans may be, they will not come to light as long as I am still breathing.'

Soul Flame

Ravaryn wafted in and out of consciousness... a memory consuming him, as though his mind had forgotten it and was now telling him again of its occurrence... but there was a shadow in front of his bleary eyes. Something was in the cell with him, and he was speaking truths to this shadow within his fractured mind, as fever and blood poisoning ravaged his body.

'I never thought I'd see her again,' he spoke to the shadows, a blood-curdling scream echoing inside his skull, calling his inner demons out to play that he usually kept reigned in. His weakened mind swirled them into formation as they surfaced again and again.

His skin broke into a cold sweat as soon as he laid eyes on her in his mind... Zemira Creedence, the Rim Walker who was to break Kyeitha's curse and free him so he could finally exact his long-awaited revenge on the forest queen. Zemira's resemblance to Liara made his breath catch in his throat as if his very soul had stopped breathing. He had just stared into those eyes, so familiar, but a deeper shade of green, hatred reflecting back from them.

Now those eyes were an emerald field he knew he could easily lose himself in; lose his wits in. But back then, as they'd bored pure hatred back into his own sinister gaze, all he could do was force himself to wield the mask he had perfected, slamming it back over his features. He had tried but failed to break their powerful connection.

'I am a vengeful king.

I am a murderer.

I am a monster.

I will kill the queen of the forest.'

He had repeated the words to himself like he had for decades. All for it to be undone with just one look from Zemira...

His heart had fractured piece by piece at the look of hatred the young woman had pierced him with when they'd first met. His onyx eyes had met Zee's emerald ones as though magnets were drawing them together. The very fibres of Ravaryn's being had felt like they were reaching out to her. Time had slowed to a stop, as if the universe was trying to weave her into his very soul. It had taken much more focus and strength than he'd ever experienced to drag himself away from her and back to his task. His task of freeing himself from his curse and taking his revenge on the former forest queen.

Ravaryn's mind forced the memory away, only to have it surface again and again. His eyes flickered in and out of reality. 'Don't you see? I failed her. I failed her, and now I'm doing it all over again.'

His voice was barely a whisper, and his chest was heavy, making it hard to suck in the next breath of putrid air lingering within the cell. He was talking to the shadow, and he knew his time was near. His eyes were glassy with emotion as flies buzzed around the rotting piece of human meat that sat on the cell floor with him. Stomach swirling again at the thought, he tore his mind away from it.

'I just can't...' he admitted to the shadow, now somewhat more opaque.

A voice filled his mind and the cell all at once. It was like the first light of a new day breaking over a meadow at dawn. 'I know, Ravaryn, I know. I'm so proud of all that you are, and you don't have to.'

Ravaryn thought that he had surely passed from the world in one last pathetic, stubborn act of defiance against what he thought was wrong. The shadow shifted and moved closer, until a tall, ethereal woman stood before him, with eyes like that of a newborn doe. They fluttered with long lashes that curved to the side, and her ears poked out from the finely woven vine-like hair that twitched this way and that.

She knelt down before him in the muck that lay over the floor, looking ridiculously too beautiful and delicate to be in an environment so harsh, filthy and desolate of joy. Her head tilted to the side, and small antlers protruded through her braids of vined hair, tiny buds creeping up their edges. One antler seemed to be broken away in half, and a smile fluttered gently on her pale sage face.

'She is a soul flame, Ravaryn. A reflection so true to your very being that no other soul could ever be a match within millennia. That is why you pine for her so, and that is why you couldn't bring yourself to eat the flesh.'

Ravaryn's sucked in breaths as his head spun. 'Zemira?' he questioned.

'Yes, Zemira,' she answered.

Ravaryn couldn't fathom the energy to even ask what the woman before him spoke of.

'I'm dying, aren't I?' he asked, fear rattling his bones. Not fear of death, fear of leaving Zee all alone in a world that would never fully understand her, what she was or who she was.

'Yes, my child. I'm so sorry I took so long... I was far away.' Her eyes strayed from him like she felt guilty at the explanation. 'Needed elsewhere, I was. But you didn't break, you stayed true to who you are.'

Ravaryn had no idea what was going on, but he knew that he was closer to death than he thought. He was hallucinating, and this vision was to ease his pain.

'Will you look after her? Will you keep her safe for me?' The words stung, and a small tear broke free from the corner of his eye.

The woman took a long, elegant hand and swept the tear from Ravaryn's pale cheek before it could slide away and mingle with the filth that he was imprisoned in. 'No,' she replied, her voice monotone.

His heart shattered as the pain tore him in two. Zee would be all alone in this world. He had failed her. Ravaryn crushed his eyes shut as the ache of sadness rippled over him.

'Because you will.' The woman smiled again, the tiny buds opening to yellow blooms along her undamaged antler. 'I didn't reincarnate your soul flame for nothing, my dear Ravaryn.'

As her words weaved into Ravaryn his eyes opened to see the woman's skin shining like the stars that resided within her.

'My soul flame?'

'Yes, Zemira. You were devastated by the loss of your Liara, but you were destined for an even greater love: Your one true soul flame, yet another incarnation of Liara's soul.' The woman turned to look towards the crusted-over rotting lump of meat on the cell floor, and Ravaryn followed her gaze, 'There will be much more suffering, Ravaryn, much more. But I can help. I will do what I can.'

She turned back and came so very close to Ravaryn's face. He saw eternity in the woman's eyes. Within these darkened depths was a galaxy spinning, a rainbow and a cacophony of colours that then shone out through her ethereal face. She lifted an elongated finger coated in a fine layer of moss between them, and his tear hung like a small dewdrop from her fingertip. Then the woman opened her sensuous lips and breathed life.

The tear left her finger and swirled into Ravaryn's open mouth. He tasted the sun on a crisp, frosted morning on Zenya city's summit. She opened her own mouth and tiny iridescent white moths flew out from within her. They swarmed in a thin vortex and filled his throat, his chest, his stomach. He felt the wind cascade over his wings and his skin as though he was feeling it for the very first time.

Ravaryn tasted spices and fruit so fresh it matched the taste of Zemira's first kiss that he had stolen in the underground oasis. He felt the warm earth of Aylenta between his toes in Diwa's gardens, and the scent of cinnamon and rosemary filled him with warmth like one of his mother's hugs. Into his mouth Gaia breathed life back into Ravaryn's broken vessel of a body, and into his soul that had held on to the very end of his life, never betraying him. The temptation of healing through the death of another human's flesh was not even a second thought to him. Ravaryn breathed in clean, cool air that tasted of meadows and life. A finger lifted his chin just a little, till his eyes met with hers, and an otherworldly expression illuminated her face.

'Who are you?' Ravaryn asked, with eyes that matched a full moon, exhilaration and life bursting within him.

'Why I am the Mother of the Earth. I am Gaia, and I will need your help.'

Hidden Library

The Valley of Rivers, Tangaroa

Sayde walked the overgrown trails of the valley road that hugged one of the main rivers. The entire city weaved in and out of beautifully crafted waterways that brought fresh, clean water and life throughout the valley. Although overgrown from being abandoned by its people for years, the valley's beauty still shone through. This place, the home she had grown up in, was a tribute to the people who had once lived here before Kyeitha's destructive reign.

Her thoughts wandered to Aytac as the scents of wild mint she crushed under her boots wafted into the cool air. It grew everywhere along the river's edge and through the city, along with watercress and creeping daisy, and its fragrance had coated her childhood. Sun ravens and ripple finches glided past her in a blur of rainbow colour, calling to each other and joining the groups feasting in large mango trees opposite the river until they were drunk with fermented fruit, happy and full.

Beautiful lotus flowers scattered about the waterways in clumps, blooming life and beauty all around, while squid-like fish shot sporadically through the waterways, darting around the glowing yabberis scavenging along on the sandy river floor. Though the city embraced her return with warmth and life, none of it truly penetrated Sayde's soul. She felt her sadness growing each day like a cancer. The attack on Maya Village had been the last seed on a dying plant that was her composure. She was going to kill Salvador if it was the last thing she would do ever do on this earth – before she was reunited with Noah again in the afterlife.

Sayde needed knowledge; she needed to know everything about the dragon shifter, or demon, or whatever in the Mother's name he was. She reached the luminous waterfall that towered metres about her in the air, spilling like a silver spray of mist, tiny water droplets caressing her face and landing in her hair. The waterfall fell from the cliff above the entrance tunnel – the door to Tangaroa – the door to the city of the Valley of Rivers. The very same door that Zemira Creedence had opened days before, and before the eyes of the entire village.

The saviour.

The queen killer.

The Rim Walker.

The new forest queen.

Sayde still didn't know exactly what Zemira was, but she knew that she was indeed different. Sayde pondered the strange woman. She was young, yet she seemed like she had walked this earth before. She had immense power yet she wielded it like a tornado in a teacup. Zemira seemed heartless at times, but spilled emotion with her green eyes. Sayde had felt awe slide through her upon watching the throne of the forest claim her, *transform* her. She wouldn't have believed Lamiria had a new queen if she hadn't witnessed it with her very eyes.

Zemira, Ravaryn, Salvador, Diwa, Kyeitha, Aytac, queens, dragons, prisoners and the Rim Walker. She needed to formulate a plan. Taking a big gulp of air, Sayde dove into the cold waters pounding at the feet of the waterfall that fed the valley. She glided her arms through the water and swam deeper under the waterfall's shield to what they camouflaged, what they *hid* from the world. Gulping for air, she emerged on the other side. Water misted everywhere, and sunlight was blocked out by half from the water's shielded veil. Sayde reached the slick rocks and climbed up and out, and without hesitation followed the carved opening in the wet rockface through a small tunnel that led to the library. The library of realms of information, tucked deep within the mountainside.

Sayde fidgeted in her pocket for the tiny seeds of poppies and sunflowers mixed in the inner wrapping of stratalite leaf – a waterproof plant – which had kept the contents mostly dry. She withdrew the seeds from the tight bundle and sprinkled them out before her as though she were in a cottage yard feeding chickens their grain. She emptied her bag, returned it to her pocket and waited in the misty space with the roar of the waterfall behind her.

After a minute or so, she wondered if it were for naught, if she should have just brought a flame stone with her, but just as she was about to turn and retrace her steps, she heard them. A pitter patter of thousands of tiny legs sounded on the smooth tiled floor of the ancients' library, and lights began to glow before her. Many lights. Tiny glow millipedes had consumed their bribe from the floor, each lighting up as they ate the seeds. Some had a bright green glow, like a fresh lime on a summer's day. Others exuded a gentle violet light, like the night sky just upon twilight, but most shone brilliant white with a tinge of blue.

Dozens and dozens of them crawled with too many legs to even count, over and under each other, creating a mass of moving light that resembled a ball of wriggling yarn. Once they had sufficed that every single seed was gone, they departed all in separate directions, their light growing as they retreated. Each millipede returned to its home and curled into a ball within it, looking like glass orbs on the ceiling and sides of towering book shelves. The dusty library was now lit up, and even though it had been years since Sayde had set foot in it, a smile still tugged at her sunken face.

She had always loved the wonder and the secrets that the hidden library held. The lies and the wars, the wonders of the ancients' technology, the mythical facts about the creatures of Lamiria, and the knowledge and the lore of the forest folk. The tales and fiction from places of indeterminate origin had always been her favourite. Books that had no tell as to where they had been created or from where they had come. Sayde breathed in the musty smell of book dust, a hint of vanilla skirting her nose from the pages as she flipped through a book from the closest shelf. She would find a way to kill Salvador, and his demise would be worthy of every single soul that he had taken from this world. Even hers.

*

Zee's fingers tingled as she tried to move them, but her eyes refused to listen to her command of opening. She had searched for what felt like weeks in the realm of dreams for Gaia, panic filtering through her frazzled nerves at not finding her. Gaia was gone, and Zee didn't know where, but worst of all, she hadn't been able to find anyone. And now she could barely force her traitor of a body to wake.

Straining, Zee thought she could hear voices, and it sounded like Paxton's voice was echoing around her. It couldn't be though. She had left him, safe and alone in Kali, after Kyeitha's' possession had made her attack him. And she had run. Guilt made her efforts to move even harder, and she felt herself grow even heavier within. There was another voice though, a sweet one that sounded torn, and one so familiar that Zee didn't even have to think twice. She just *felt* that Diwa was there.

But why couldn't she wake up? Frustration zinged around within her as she willed her body to listen to the sounds. She felt her eyes flutter and her hands twitch. But that was all. Exhaustion of the greatest level defeated her from the pathetic effort of miniscule movement. Zee couldn't fight the sleep that claimed her back within seconds.

*

Aytac, took a deep breath and dived into the water's cooling abyss under the falls approximately fifteen minutes after his sister. His side still ached and welcomed the cooling effect the waters that enveloped him gave in-

78

stantly. He knew Sayde was still grieving deeply for the man she had lost inside the Dark Rim prison. He should be giving her time, space. But after standing there alone just staring after her, he had to check on her. She had been short, dismissive and not at all herself with him. At least she wasn't the self he remembered before she was banished to the Dark Rim. It had changed her, sculpted her in such a way that he didn't recognise her anymore. And he worried about her. They had never been more distant, not even when they had been separated by their previous circumstances, when he was forced to be the queen's right hand, and she was imprisoned a world away. Aytac surfaced behind the falls and saw a faint glow coming from the tunnel entrance into the hidden library.

Dragging himself from the water, glowing millipedes lit the walls in a colourful illumination of light reminiscent of his childhood. The shelves and high ceilings of the first chamber of the library sang to him as Aytac entered. He followed the wet splotches left on the floor in search of Sayde and found her at a large table in the second chamber. A violet millipede lit the books she had open. She flicked through pages, clearly in search of something in particular, as Aytac approached her.

'You know, I would always find you in here when we were kids. Every time you and him had a fight, I knew this is right where you'd be.'

Sayde's mahogany eyes looked up from the text she was scanning. 'He was a piece of shit, and anyone who knew him wanted to be as far away as they could from the man.'

Aytac continued, 'Remember the day you finally shifted?' He pulled out a cobweb-coated timber chair opposite her.

A small smile tugged at Sayde's top lip. 'He regretted ever laying a hand on me that day, didn't he? I wonder if he saw it coming. I mean truly saw it? Or do you think he thought I would be a weak little child forever? Our father was a fool, a coward, and he tasted like shit.' A sardonic laugh came from Sayde as she shut her eyes a moment.

'He deserved what he got. I just wish that I had done it.' Aytac paused. 'I wish that I had protected you. That I had been there for you.' He placed his clasped hands before him on the table and studied them.

'Aytac, we were children.' Sayde's reply was matter of fact.

'Still, I'm sorry I didn't protect you like I should have. I'm sorry I wasn't there for you then, and I'm sorry I wasn't there when you lost Noah. I never even got to thank the first man that treated you right, Sayde.' Aytac's eyes pleaded with her to share her grief, to share *something*.

Sayde blinked for a few long moments, willing the tears that threatened to spill to leave her eyes. 'It wasn't your fault. You can't always protect me, big brother. I thought you would have realised that by now.'

'I know. But, Sayde, let me in. I've been in agony for years knowing you were trapped, yet not knowing whether you were alive or dead because of me. And thinking that you would never forgive me if you were.'

Anger flared in Sayde's eyes, shooting daggers into Aytac's pleading yellow ones. 'Forgive you? You're my brother, so there's nothing to forgive. It wasn't your fault, it was mine! I chose to betray Kyeitha. I *chose* to try and assassinate her, not you. I should be apologising to you! You don't always have to be so gentle with me! I'm not going to fucking break!'

Books flew from the table as Sayde hands flung them out of her way. She leaned forward over the table towards her brother, her eyes constricting into irises like that of a cat in the purple light. 'You can't always protect me. I want you to stop trying, to stop giving me your pity.'

Aytac withdrew his hands from the table, his eyes laced with pain. 'I don't pity you, sister. I worry about you. That day... when you did what you did to father... it changed you. I don't blame you, and I don't even care that he got what he deserved. I just fear that a little bit of you died along with him.'

'Maybe it did. Now if you're done dragging up our skeletons from the past, can you go? I have things to do here.' Her eyes found another book as she sat back down.

Aytac eyed the books, his heart heavy as he accepted his dismissal. He took one last look at the stranger before him and turned to leave. As his gaze landed on the books strewn over the floor, a page had been left flung open on dragon mythology. The text was littered with drawings of dragons of all shapes and kinds. Aytac absorbed the information until it sat like a stone in his stomach. He went to say something but thought better of it, so he bit the inside of his cheek and left the hidden library, fists clenched at his sides. Without looking back, he strode away from the woman he barely recognised as his twin.

Tea Party in Bed

The Valley of Rivers, Tangaroa

Orion had slept only a few hours but it had been enough. He pulled tightly on the leather strap across his broad chest, having found the armoury in the palace that clung to the side of the mountain overlooking the valley below. The city that he had grown up in weaved through the river. As he slid the dagger into its sheath on the strap, he felt the sufficient weight of the rest of the armoury that he now carried. He had not only been a watcher. Once upon a time, he had been trained as a warrior, a soldier, a killer. He grabbed the bag of supplies he had gathered, but he just needed one more thing before he set off on his way to save a man he loathed with every fibre of his being. A man whose very presence made his blood boil. A man he would never be able to escape now that Ravaryn was blood bound to his daughter.

Orion's teeth cracked as they ground together, his fists flexing at his side. *Fucking Ravaryn Black,* his mind seethed. He left the dusty armoury and set off to find the last thing he needed: his shifter opposite, the black wolf to his white. They had been on different sides before, but Orion knew deep in his core that Aytac was a loyal, genuine man of honour. And he needed him to help retrieve the rotten King of Kymera, to save him so that he could in turn save Zee.

*

Zee's eyes fluttered like butterfly wings emerging from within a cocoon. Mazda slept soundly on the large lounge in the centre of the open-aired room, while Pax sat vigil at Zee's bedside. His head was slumped to the side, resting on his elbow, as he fought sleep of his own. His anger about the blood bond still simmered in his gut, but the longer Zee slept, the more it turned to fear that she would never wake. A gentle breeze flowed in through the opening facing the outer hallway from the valley below, and bougainvillea trailed the edges, their vibrant flowers framing the picturesque scene.

The breeze swept over Pax's cheek and nearly caressed him into sleep. He took one last look at Zee's still form, adorned in the gown that made her look like a goddess, and saw a flutter of her lashes. He shot up in his seat and retrieved her hand in his own; it was no longer clammy with sweat. In fact, her brow was dry and her face looked a normal shade of her radiant bronzed skin.

'Zee.' He squeezed her palm in his own, inspecting the new art adorning it that spiralled up her arm. It was better than the blackened seeping patch of darkness that Kyeitha had marked her with, but knowing that the art was what joined her to the king made Paxton hate it all the more. The flowery patterns on her skin wavered before his eyes, then they *moved.* Untwisting from tight buds and opening to bloom with a velvety shine on each petal, every flower unfurled on her arm simultaneously. A gap where there seemed to be two missing grew tiny buds that remained shut.

Paxton felt his breath catch. Zee was truly amazing, just like she always had been to him. *Magic.* That's how he had always seen her, from the very first day they had met in the school yard years ago. He filled his lungs with air and his anger dissipated, his heart remembering why he was so worried in the first place. She was his best friend, his only family.

'Zee, I'm sorry I took so long to find you, but if you wake up and forgive me, I'll do anything you want.' His eyes glassed over, and through his blurry vision he saw her lashes flicker again. This was followed by the slightest opening of her eyes, and her hand squeezed his back.

'Zee.' His voice cracked. 'You scared me.'

She stared at him for a long moment, eyes adjusting, and his heart skipped a beat. *Was this the same Zee?* She looked so different. So much had happened, and a worrying thought crossed his mind in a flash. What if somehow Kyeitha were still in there, especially now that the forest had chosen her to be its new queen? *Was this really his Zee?*

'I scared you? I scared myself...' she croaked out.

Paxton felt relief wash over him.

'How are you here? Actually, where is here?' She sat up and looked around, then down at herself. 'And what the hell am I wearing?'

Pax let out a laugh. 'I never thought I'd see you in a dress, let alone a gown,' he teased.

'Ugh,' Zee scoffed loudly, rolling her eyes and scrunching her nose. 'I remember now... I remember sitting on that throne... then. *Shit.*' Realisation hit her and she covered her face with her hands.

'Should I be calling you your majesty or just Queen Zee?'

'You ever call me either one of those things again and I'll throw you from the raspor cliffs!'

The pair laughed together, and Zee slid forward and squeezed Pax into a tight hug. 'I'm so glad you're okay. I'm so sorry. I'm so sorry I ran...' she whispered into his ear while still holding him tight.

Pax squeezed her a tad more, and breathed in her jasmine scent, his face in her midnight braids. 'I'm just glad you're alive. That you're still you.'

After a long moment, Zee let Pax go, and the world seemed almost right again.

'With more badass art it seems...' His eyes fell down to her right arm, as his question lingered in the words.

His hands embraced her right one as he inspected the tattoos while she decided on her words. 'Pax, I – I'm sorry, but it was the only way to end her curse. I didn't know it would connect us like this. Connect me to him.'

Pax's deep gaze searched Zee's emerald eyes. 'It's okay, Zee. I knew that one day someone would take you away from me. You were always above me, in another league. *Mother's earth*, you were in another realm above me, Zee, even before I knew you had powers. I just never guessed it would be someone like *him*.'

Zee tried to hide the hurt on her face. 'It's not like that, Pax, and he's not really like the king you remember. That was just an act, a mask he wore.'

Paxton's jaw clenched, and he bit his tongue. 'I don't want to fight with you about him, Zee.' His eyes found hers again. 'Besides, I never win anyway,' he added with a gentle tone, letting lie the subject of Ravaryn- for now.

Zee eyed the large, dusty room they were in, evading his face. She couldn't bear to see the disappointment or hurt or whatever may lie there for the moment. A spot of vibrant red curls caught her eye on the elegant lounge in the centre of the room.

'Is that...? Is that Mazda!' Her face lit up, but she kept her volume under control not wanting to wake the sleeping beauty. Even from all the way across the room, Zee noted the dark rings lingering under Mazda's eyes as she slumbered.

'Sure is.' Pax followed Zee's gaze.

'How on earth did you met Mazda? And why is she here?' Zee wanted to know.

'I met her when I went looking for you,' he explained, tone slightly annoyed.

'You went back to the castle?' Zee's voice registered her surprise.

'Diwa told me who you went with, and I had to know you were okay. I don't trust him as far as I can spit, Zee. You shouldn't either.'

Zee exhaled, not wanting to be lectured about her choices, but knowing full well what Ravaryn had done, the lies he had spun and the damage he had wrought on the old Rim world.

'So what do you think of Kymera's future queen?'

Zee ignored his previous comment about Ravaryn and raised a brow.

'To think,' Pax explained, 'that only hours ago I was under the impression she was a stable hand for the king's duellerats, and that she'd played me for a fool.'

'Pfft, never. Mazda doesn't have a dishonest bone in her body. Did you actually ever ask her whether or not she was in fact just a stable hand? Or did you do what you always do, assume and then judge people by your first impression?'

'Are we talking about Mazda here... or someone else?' Pax countered.

'Don't fret, Mazda probably loved that you didn't know who she really was. Don't take it too personally. She's got a lot on her shoulders, Pax. She probably doesn't need your judgement on top of that weight.'

'Her and you both, it seems.'

Zee rolled her eyes. 'I seriously don't know what the forest was thinking.' She threw her hands in the air, and they landed in her lap dramatically. 'Back to Maz though. How fun is she, am I right?'

Zee's face lit up, and Pax could clearly see the love there she had for Mazda. 'Yeah, she's pretty wild. I've never met anyone with more guts, except for maybe you.' He laughed. 'Would you believe she taught me how to fly? That's how we got here. I have my own duellerat,' Pax boasted.

'What?' Zee was truly shocked now. 'You! The boy who cringes at woverbine slime, who nearly became a raspor's kebab, actually bonded with a duellerat?'

'I'll have you know, Astrid and I are like two peas in a pod.'

Zee flew into a fit of laughter that couldn't be restrained. Mazda stirred on the couch as the pair swapped insults and filled each other in on the last weeks. Once awake and aware of her surroundings, Maz climbed sleepily over to Zee and Pax in the generous bed and slid Zee into a groggy hug.

'I'm so relieved you're still in one piece, Zee. Paxton would have had a pink fit if we hadn't had found you any sooner.' She smirked.

'I'm glad you found him, Maz. I don't think he would survive without one of us holding his hand.'

Pax's mouth fell open. 'Oh, I see what's happening here. Sure, gang up on me, it's not like I don't deserve it. Who else would be crazy enough to consider having two wild women like you for best friends.'

Mazda's ocean eyes sparkled as her top lip curved into a stunning smile. 'We're your best friends?'

Paxton locked his amber eyes with hers, the golden flecks within them catching in the sunlight. 'Yes, your majesty, you're stuck with me now.'

Mazda flushed, her face showing relief that he was using the word as a joke, as it meant he must no longer be mad at her for not telling him who she really was.

'Well then, now that's settled.' Mazda straightened up on the bed, appearing fully awake now. 'There is something definitely big going down. Those spider creatures that have been made—'

Zee cut in. 'Spider creatures? On top of the black dragon trying to burn Lamiria to the ground?'

Mazda and Pax both paled a little. 'It looks like we need to make a plan. Something's brewing, and the last thing we want is to be unprepared,' Pax surmised.

The door to the far wall between two large bookcases creaked and an elegant Diwa entered, a tray in her hands. 'Oh good! You're all awake.' She smiled widely. 'A plan, you say. That's exactly what we need! But first cake and tea! Mint or pear, lavender or salamander hair?' she sing-songed her familiar tune.

'Tea and cake? How on earth did you possibly whip that up?' Zee was amazed and shocked at the same moment, but her stomach growled loudly at her and she found she didn't really care.

A cackling laugh followed, one with not as much age and bite as before, cleaner and crisper, but rest assured her beaming face was the same Diwa as she had always been. She just had more of a spring in her step, and more honey coating her voice.

'Oh, I have my ways. Don't forget I used to live here. Now, maybe the leaves will give us some direction.' She gave an all-knowing wink as she settled the tray between them and handed them each a unique cup.

'Do you want us to move to the lounge area, Diwa?' Mazda inquired, not used to this woman she had heard so much about, whom she idolised, really. Diwa was a living legend in her mind.

'Of course not, love. Haven't you ever had a tea party in bed? What has that son of mine been teaching you all this time?' She feinted actual shock.

Mazda laughed. 'Just boring, ruler-y mumbo jumbo, nothing quite as serious as when and where one should consume tea.'

The pair eyed each other with a deep knowing look, smiles wide.

'Ahh... there's still much for you to learn, child.'

And all of them laughed at that, then settled in planning and strategizing while having tea and cake in bed.

The Glasshouses

Zenya City, Kymera

Tyson Bramble stood tall as the icy western winds of Kymera swept his shoulder-length fiery red hair about. He strained his neck in wonder as he took in the beauty that lay before him. The curved dome structures that rose up around the ice and snow like translucent tunnel worms gleamed like beacons in a storm, shining even in the dim cloudy sky of a typical day. His eyes grew wide as he got closer, and the vibrant green blur behind the frosted glass came clearer into view, making his pulse quicken.

He had thought long and hard about the king's offer, yet the hurt, the hate and the fear that plagued him from the Borztan mines still crept below his skin like a Sparalinx through the walls of the city buildings. But his mother had changed his mind and his heart. Kyra Bramble was a testament to the true power of healing and the right mix of medicinal herbs.

Tyson had always felt a pull to the art of healing and caring for others, but it wasn't until he witnessed the miracle that was his mother healing from and surviving snow lung that his faith was truly cemented into his heart. He now knew with every fibre of his being that this was what he was meant to do with his life, that this was his purpose, that this is what the Mother had put him here on this earth for.

Moving his feet through the thick layers of freshly fallen snow, Tye trudged up to the intricately ornate glass doors of the closest glasshouse. He felt silly knocking as there were no translucent shapes of people within that he could see. He reached for the baroque metal handle of Kymera's symbol, a snowflake tipped with spears, and twisted it open. Warm air poured from within. Scents of Aylenta ticked his nose, and he quickly entered out of the cold.

Growing tables stretched along the sides of the cylinder glasshouse, with one in the centre stretching down the length. Plants of all colours, sizes and origins hung from the centre of the domed roof where it reached its highest point. The centre tables were lined with groups of potted plants that changed in species every metre or so. Tye reached out a finger to feel the leaf of a plant that was dusted in a light layer of purple fur. Then another that resembled rosemary, but its tips ended in strange translucent orbs as if raindrops had attached and suspended themselves there. Tye curiously popped one of the small spheres, and a powerful scent of lime and eucalyptus vapoured into the air. He lifted his fingers to his face, fingers now sticky and turning a shade of deep mahogany, which smelled like summer in a bushland forest. He lifted his fingers to his mouth.

'I wouldn't if I were you.' A clear drawl voice sounded to his right.

Thick muscled arms were crossed over a broad chest. Blond sandy hair, trimmed short, hung over the man's forehead, and his neat eyebrows framed the brightest icy blue eyes Tye had ever seen.

'Your tongue won't stop burning for a week, and everything will taste like ash, trust me. It's definitely not worth a taste.' He raised a brow as if daring Tye to defy his knowledge.

Tye quickly dropped his hand and wiped it on his trouser leg, then produced it to shake the stranger's hand. He tried to hide his embarrassment as he gave his name. The sandy haired man was shorter and broader than Tye, and solid like a rock. His eyes scanned him up and down before finally breaking into a stunning smile, all straight even-sized teeth making his eyes light up even brighter if that were possible.

'I know who you are. It's nice to finally meet you, Bramble. I wasn't sure whether we were ever going to see you or not. But it seems you accepted the king's offer after all. I'm Hamish. Welcome to the glasshouses.'

Tye shook the strong hand that crushed his own just a little and smiled stupidly back. 'I took my time, I guess. But my curiosity got the better of me.' His heart fluttered as Hamish still held his hand firmly in his own. The two stared into each other's eyes, transfixed, for a long moment.

Hamish broke the moment just before Tye was about to. 'So, I hear you're the famous Kymerian who's bought a cure for snow lung back from Aylenta.'

Tye's cheeks warmed, and not just from the humid caress of the greenhouse's temperature. He removed his moscow coat and scarf that Juniper had made him, with scraps of horrendously colour-dyed Moscow wool. 'I didn't realise that anyone knew?' His words hung in the air as a question.

Hamish tilted his head just a smidge to the side, blond hair sweeping across his brow in the same direction. 'King Ravaryn informed me about you, and said you'd have the cure upon your return to Aylenta for snow lung. He said he'd offered you a position, but he didn't know if you'd ever show or not. You had some kind of run-in with him that he thoroughly regrets.'

Tye swallowed, his anxiety making his heart race as he tried and failed not to think of the mines. 'Yes, well, I'd love a tour,' he deflected, eyeing the plants to his left and running a hand roughly through his long deep-red, almost burgundy, hair. He smiled, trying to seem polite. He didn't want to be rude, but the last thing he wanted to talk about was his 'run-in' with the king.

'Yes, of course. Get ready for an information dump. If there's one thing I love more than a hot cinnamon stout on a cold day, it's talking about plants.' Hamish's eyes lit up and crinkled at the edges as he led Tye deeper into the tunnel that was bursting with life.

Tye followed behind, getting a good look at Hamish as he walked and talked passionately, his hands sweeping in the air before him, pointing this way and that. He caressed some of the leaves of various species of plants Tye had never seen, all while leading him through the green maze. His smile stayed put, and he could feel the flush growing on his freckled cheeks as he realised more and more with each passing second that he had indeed made the right choice to come here today – if not for the plants, then *definitely* for the company.

*

Sayde's eyes felt heavy in the fading light. The glowing millipedes had burned through their bribe of seeds and were staring to dim. Soon she would be engulfed in almost darkness. *Time to go.* She would gather more supplies and return again later. Nothing would stop her from finding something, anything, that would help her seek her revenge. She added the book she had just finished searching through, again having come up with nothing useful, to the pile to her left that was stacked high with wasted time. A deep numbness swept over her, and she dropped her head into her hands, pressing her palms against her eyes for a moment.

Standing on hollow legs to leave, her eyes fell to the books she had swept unceremoniously to the floor when she had lost her temper at her brother. *No*, when he had pushed her, once again making her snap at him. She knelt down to pick up the scattered books, some of their pages now crinkled and bent, and she felt just a tad guilty for the precious piec- es of history. The last book she reached for was lying open with sketches of dark talon-tipped wings, scales and jagged-tooth maws, scribbled with information and *warnings...*

Sayde lifted the book and shut it to see the cover. There was no title, and the book was bound in thick burgundy leather, with scales running downwards in a diagonal direction. It felt smooth under her fingertips as she ran a hand over the strange tome. And there in the centre was a shut eye... or an eyelid that had been roughly *sewn* shut. Tiny spikes evenly laced the edge of the lid.

A shiver shot through Sayde's lower back. The light dimmed all around her now, the millipedes truly falling back into a dormant slumber. She left the second chamber of the hidden library with the book firmly in her grasp, reaching the faint light that filtered through the rushing falls at the entrance to the underground building of secrets and knowledge. Sitting down, she crossed her legs and opened the book in her lap. The more she read, the more she consumed the book. Her tired eyes strained for focus, and then finally... *something* she could use.

This book somehow indeed hid information and facts about dragons and demons, whether they be mythical scribblings or actual facts, she didn't know. But for the first time since Noah was taken away from her, she felt a tiny spark of an ember inside of her, a precious flicker of hope. A small whimper left her as tears pricked at the edges of her eyes; she held a hand to her mouth as she read and re-read the words that lay before her. They were salvation like sunlight after the darkest of nights. It wasn't a weapon... no, if it were true, it was something *far* more valuable to her than that.

For the top of the page in the centre of the book read: *How to retrieve a soul that has been lost to a dragon...*

Materials to Forge

Tangaroa, Valley of Rivers

Diwa and Zee sat in the kitchen after leaving Mazda and Pax in the great room. Zee inspected the teacups one by one as Diwa filled a sink to rinse them out. She perched on the bench in the large kitchen that once must have held so much energy and life.

'Ah, mine kind of looks like a cat's eye. Very good!' Diwa chirped. 'And Paxton's?'

Zee placed down her teacup adorned with cherry blossoms and small finches, and replaced it with the cup Paxton had drunk from that had a flurry of bees and daisies on it, all yellow sunshine and crisp white.

'I don't know, maybe a crown.' She turned the cup and tilted her head, her nose scrunching with frustration. 'No, a snake. Gods, how do you tell anything from these?'

Diwa laughed as Zee placed Paxton's cup down and traded it for Mazda's. 'Oh, this is easy, a cockroach.'

'That's a wild guess, Zemira Creedence! You try again.' Diwa scolded, all smiles.

Zee spun the teacup around and saw a tiny movement before her eyes. Just the tiniest fraction of a change, and there before her, instead of a splatter of dark leaves... 'A spider?'

'Very good,' Diwa praised.

'But what on earth does any of that mean?' Zee raised her brows, exasperated.

'Oh, that's the hard part. The *real* art,' Diwa teased in her song-like tone.

'Well, what about yours then?' Zee swiped up Diwa's cup. Within it was a perfect round blob in the middle, an orb. 'Yours is easy, a big blob.'

Diwa waved her hands in the air. 'Pish posh.' She neither confirmed nor denied that it was or wasn't said blob.

'Come now, Zemira. We have some things to discuss that may or may not relate to that blob.'

Zee, utterly confused as always when with Diwa, just nodded, but the feeling was strangely familiar and comforting. She slid from the high bench as Diwa finished rinsing the cups and followed her through the maze-like corridors of the inner castle. They stopped at a seating area that looked out at the vertical mountain cliff to the back of the majestic sandstone castle. The cliff was growing with all sorts of alocasias and peperomias, ferns and creeping plants. They were clinging to the cliff face, all fighting for purchase between each other. They made up the long vertical garden on display, with a small cascade of water right through the middle of the foliage.

The deep rust and sapphire-coloured velvet lounges Diwa led them over to were opulent, although they had seen better days, with a layer of dust dulling them. But they were still so elegant to Zee. The pair sat in the stunning room, lined on all walls with books and artefacts, rocks, fossils and large chucks of crystals. For some reason, the room reminded her of her mother, and Zee felt a sharp pang in her heart. Her mother. How she missed her. Verena must be out of her mind with worry, and Zee prayed that Salvador had not found her yet.

Diwa withdrew her backpack from underneath the stone coffee table that sat in the centre of the room. She withdrew a timber box from within, one that tickled the edge of Zee's memory, one that somehow looked as familiar as Diwa herself.

'I have had this for longer than I care to remember.' She handed the box over to Zee, silver eyes serious.

Zee held the ordinary-looking box in her hands, and a memory flashed back to her. She had seen this box in Diwa's cottage a few times throughout her childhood, always in the same spot on the old wooden table.

'Open it.' Diwa's voice was soft and it shook a little, causing Zee to bite down on her inside cheek.

Diwa's hands fiddled with each other in her lap as she watched Zee open the timber box. Within it, nursed in deep crimson velvet lay an object, a round almost-translucent crystal, a shining orb. Zee reached to take it out from the box, and the orb was surprisingly light, deceivingly so. It swirled and shifted as though it were full of glimmering pearl-like liquid. A strange pulsing energy thrummed from it into Zee's hand as if it was vibrating without movement.

'Okay, I'm curious. What is this thing?'

'I call that "the light". That, my dear, is our failsafe, and it may be the only thing we end up having that can stop Salvador... for good.' There was no song to her voice now; it was flat, and she was dead serious.

Zee tried to not be completely confused. 'How is this going to help us stop Salvador?'

'Because you are going to capture the energy of three deadly things within it. You will morph them together inside the orb, and when the time is right, infect the black dragon with its poison.'

Zee swallowed, her throat instantly dry.

'There's only one problem. The three things you need to collect aren't in Lamiria, dear. There is a place that Gaia couldn't protect from the radiation blasts just outside of the Rim and Lamiria. But the inhabitants, they didn't perish like the rest of the world. Whether they were exposed to less-potent radiation, or for some other reason, Gaia and I don't know. But they have been habituating the ancients' city for more than 500 years... they aren't alive but they're not quite dead. Gaia and I refer to it as the city of the undead ones.'

Zemira's hair stood on end as Diwa continued.

'Gaia can't end their lives, or stop their suffering. She was created to bring life to this world, not death. So she has contained the city and let them be within it.

Zee's eyes bulged. 'You're completely serious, aren't you?'

'Yes, unfortunately, I am. But that's not all. You cannot, under any circumstances, let any of them bite you. Their state is contagious.'

'Are you mad? Why me!' Zee practically whined.

'Your fire, dear. You're the only one who can do it. I'm so sorry. But they will run from your flames like mice from a viper.'

Zee's shoulders slumped. 'So this weapon... you're sure it will defeat him? Will it bring Ravaryn back to us?'

'I'm sure. It's the most powerful vision I've had, and I've had it over and over for years.' Diwa's eyes darted from Zee's. 'I have seen it many times, and it's always the same. It will kill him and banish his presence from this world.'

'Diwa?' Zee felt a spike of worry at Diwa's guilt when she spoke about Salvador. Zee knew none of this were her fault. Her sudden melancholy shook Zee, and she wasn't quite sure but she sensed sadness within the other woman.

'This is what I was made for, right?' Zee's tone changed, as she brought her joking tone back.

'That and so, *so* much more, my dear.' Diwa met her eyes and took her hands in her own, squeezing them tightly, her silvery eyes shimmering. 'So much more.' Her smile was gentle, and knowing.

*

Zee hugged a defeated-looking Mazda goodbye. 'I'm so sorry about Blaze.' She spoke gently as Mazda hadn't even been able to admit out loud to Zee that Blaze was gone. Paxton had been the one to fill her in on what had happened when they'd both landed in Lamiria, beyond the old Rim world.

Withdrawing from the hug, Zee promised, 'I'll be seeing you before you know it, and I'll bring that former king with me.' She winked, all fake bravado, as she felt the same way on the inside that Mazda portrayed on the outside. But she had to be strong, as people were watching. An entire city now relied on her, and watched her, whether she wanted them to or not.

Paxton stood steady as the two future queens said their goodbyes, his heart heavy on the quiet mention of Blaze. Mazda turned to him to say a goodbye, but Pax suddenly stopped her.

'Wait.' He searched Mazda's eyes, the deep pools of blue now gentle lakes, not the wild ocean waves he was used to seeing in her. 'I'm coming with you.'

He then eyed Zee, watching for her reaction. He had fought her tooth and nail only hours ago demanding to stay with her and help with her part of the plan. But the hurt, anger or annoyance he thought he would see on her face at his immediate backtrack wasn't there. Instead, a small, gracious smile took its place; she raised one eyebrow and crossed her arms over her chest in front of her.

'I think that's a great idea. It seems similar to the one a certain someone had only hours ago.' Zee's emerald eyes glowed at him, and then they did a slight eye roll as Paxton's huge smile couldn't be kept from his face.

'Well, I can't leave Mazda and Astrid alone to do all the work without me, you know,' Pax jested.

Mazda beamed and squeezed him in a tight hug. 'So true! Who knows what kind of mischief I could get away with without a sounding board such as you, oh noble Paxton Raker.'

He hugged her back, his chin brushing her flaming wild curls. 'Can't let you have all the fun.'

Zee watched the three leave through the tunnel to the temple, Astrid's giant form trailing after the two small humans. The sight made her chest swell, until they disappeared into the dark trail that led from the top of the waterfall. A deep breath left her. At least in the old Rim world they would be safer. This is what she had wanted. Paxton had fought with her, as usual. Finally, something had gone her way though. But now she would be all alone for *her* mission.

Come on, Zee, what's the worst that can happen?

She didn't care about that right now though, as the sight of Pax and Mazda made her happy in a way she didn't even know she could be. She had always known his feelings for her had grown, changed and shifted over the last few years. But Zee had never wanted to go there. If it hadn't worked, she wouldn't have just lost her best friend, she would have lost the *only* friend she'd had since childhood. He was a staple in her life that she was never willing to give up: a brother, a comrade – *family*. Knowing that the pair of them would look after each other made her worry ease, and that in itself was priceless to her.

Zee turned from the tunnel entrance and made her way over the flat expanse of land at the peak of the mountain to the rushing falls that poured life into the valley below. Her feet suddenly felt too soft, too comfortable in the black velvet flats that accompanied her new look. So much for Zee the warrior.

The sun lit up the winding reservoirs of water that gently snaked in and around the stone buildings, glowing almost golden in the bright light. The water sparkled back at her like tiny stars, carrying its magic in and around the homes of the people who had returned. Zee closed her eyes and took a moment to herself, letting it fill her with peace like a rainbow appearing after a vicious storm. She knew now that Orion and Aytac had already left to find Ravaryn. Yet she cringed at the imagined scenario in her head playing out that was her father finding Ravaryn. What would they say to each other? Would Orion even get him out of wherever he was alive? If it were true what Diwa had said about a blood bond, her father didn't have a choice but to not harm him.

Gods, this was a twisted, awkward mess. Hopefully Ravaryn was now healing, wherever he was. He must be, as Zee's fever had passed; therefore, she believed that so too had Ravaryn's. Her body healing was a clear sign that he too must be okay, for the moment. How she missed him, body and soul.

The fresh scent of the falls filled her lungs with life. She felt the plants that grew strong and vibrant all around her. The small dragonflies flittered in and out of the lotus blooms below, the power in their tiny wings tenfold compared to the proportioned size of their bodies. Colourful birds flew in abundant flocks, their wings moving them elegantly through the air as they weaved in and out of the hills laced with ripe fruit of all kinds.

Wings... her mind wandered then. Two large black wings and a starry night filled her mind, and the chill of crisp, icy air brushed her face despite the warmth and humidity of the valley she stood in. *Wings... where are you?*

A flash of obsidian eyes, sprinkled with silver, bored into her mind. 'Zemirahh,' the deep, silken voice slid through her mind, then caressed her skin. Her arm lit up in gooseflesh, hair standing on ends at the phantom touch. The velvet of the blooms on her arm felt warm and smooth as if Ravaryn were right there, embracing it within his own large hands.

'I thought I might find you here.' A different voice ripped Zee away from the connection, a sharp but sweet feminine tone.

Zee was instantly grounded, and she turned to find two wide mahogany doe eyes taking her in.

'You don't disappoint, and you sure as hell wear it better than the psychotic bitch did.' Venom coated the words referring to Kyeitha.

'I guess it won't be hard to do a better job than she did. Just don't go insane, kill and imprison a bunch of people, and I'll be good, right?' Zee smirked.

Sayde almost laughed, her deep eyes sparkling back a little. It was the first time Zee had ever seen a lick of emotion from them other than numbness since they had met.

'I think I like you, Rim Walker.'

Zee laughed a little at that.

'I think we have a lot in common already, so we're off to a great start.' Sayde eyed the ground, then stared out at the vista before them. 'Speaking of things in common, I hear that you're off soon to retrieve something that might help us win a fight against the black dragon.'

Zee paused a moment. 'That's true,' she answered cautiously. *Diwa*. If she'd told Sayde, it meant that she trusted her with the information. It meant as always that Diwa knew something that no one else did, and she was weaving the future she'd seen in accordance with the future she wanted. How hard it must be to walk in her shoes.

'I want to come with you. There's nothing for me here. If I stay, I'll go mad. The only thing I want is revenge on that sick son of a bitch who took my balance away from me.' Sayde's voice spat hatred at the mention of Salvador, and Zee's heart ached for her.

Without a second thought Zee answered back. 'You know what? I was just thinking how bored I would be without someone else coming along.'

Sayde's lip curled just a little, her hands crossing before her chest now. 'Sweet, it's settled. But first things first, we have to get you out of that... *frock*.' Sayde waved a hand up and down at Zee, a little teasing in her tone.

'I'll have you know this is the first *frock* I've ever been caught in, and I didn't really have much of a choice. I distinctly recall a certain someone leading me right to that throne and making me sit down... so really this is all your fault.' Zee's smile was playful.

'Alright, you got me there,' Sayde admitted. 'But I can fix this.' She waved her hands again at Zee's gorgeous albeit ridiculous gown for a mission.

'What did you have in mind?' Zee looked down, running her hands over the impossibly intricate weaving of silvery green vines in the midnight fabric and light, transparent sleeves of deep green.

Sayde actually almost smiled, and Zee thought it made her glow. She was striking to say the least, with her rich pine-bark hair, petite mouth and earthen eyes that glowed with a golden sheen against her honey skin, but that smile lit her from within. The young woman was stunning when she smiled.

'Oh, you're gonna like this. Come with me, queeny.' Sayde reached for Zee's arm and hooked it in her own, leading her from the top of the falls back through bougainvillea blooms, creeping fig and variegated monsteras, and towards the castle clinging to the mountainside.

*

A gasp left Zee's mouth, an actual girly gasp. 'There's so many! And they are all so *gorgeous!*'

Zee had never been one to fawn over clothes, except for maybe Mazda's creations. But the outfits that hung before her in the large armoury glittered like glow beetles in a dusk forest to her. They were the clothes of the watchers, the warriors of Lamiria, and consisted of all manner of plated tops, equipped with straps for weapons. The garments hung in rows of shielded areas in the abandoned, dusty room.

'I told you I could fix it,' Sayde smirked. She nudged Zee's shoulder now standing beside her at the entrance to the armoury's stores and motioned her in.

Weapons adorned the walls: knives, cutlasses, axes and swords. Zee let her fingers trail over a black jacket that had intricate woven leather on the shoulders, almost like feathers. Another jacket was adorned with belts patterned with golden mandalas where the shoulder blades spanned out on the back.

'This is awesome!' Zee grabbed a handful of outfits and dropped the large pile behind a beautifully carved timber screen set up at the far side of the room. She guessed this was for fittings as there was a floor-to-height mirror against the wall behind it.

She started to strip off the delicate attire of the queen of the forest, and flung it gently over the screen. As delicate and light as the gown was, Zee felt as though a massive weight had lifted from her shoulders once it was off. A weight she wanted to deal with later, *much* later.

Sayde sifted through the racks of outfits searching for something that would suffice. She landed on a deep midnight-blue top, tight-fitting black pants that stretched comfortably as she moved and a black vest that buttoned securely at her front, full of handy pockets. After strapping a large machete-like knife over her shoulder, brown boots finished the ensemble off.

Zee finally emerged, and Sayde's mahogany eyes widened ever so slightly. 'Nice.' She nodded as she appraised Zee's choice. 'Definitely suits you more than the gown.'

'And Mother, it feels so much more comfortable! You clean up alright too.' Zee turned to look at herself in the mirror, still foggy with dust and dirt. She swept a partially gloved hand over the surface, cleaning it away to get a better look at herself. She had picked an outfit that suited her to a tee. The deep moss-green cotton top fitted her form snugly underneath the black jacket filled with pockets, silver metal buttons and clips. The same black pants as Sayde wore were just as comfortable as the ones Mazda had once made for Zee, so she'd chosen them as well. Her waist was adorned with a thick black leather belt, a small pouch on the side, the leather stamped with swirls and leaves.

'I'm ready if you are.' Zee turned to Sayde, happy she wouldn't be alone, and glad that Diwa must have somehow sent Sayde her way.

'One last thing.' Sayde walked over to the weapons wall and gazed at the various pieces hanging there. She picked a nearly arm-length dagger ornamented with a deep-purple gem on the handle that had been artfully crafted into the claws of some beast. She ran a finger along the blade up to the sharp tip, inspecting the curve thoughtfully.

'This one.' She spun the blade in her hand and offered the handle to Zee.

Zee eyed the beautiful dagger then took if from Sayde. She felt a small warmth within her grow, like it were a gift. 'This is perfect.' Adding a leather holder to the belt at her side, she slid the dagger into it. It hung securely from her waist, its weight comforting against her leg. 'What about you? Just the machete then?'

'Oh this?' Sayde tilted her head to where the machete rested against her back. 'This is just for clearing brush. I don't need any weapons when I shift... *trust* me.' Her eyes were devious.

With that, the pair retrieved the packs prepared for them full of supplies. They set off in search of the materials they sought to forge a weapon that might give them a chance against Salvador. Zee took Sayde in. She already looked like a weapon in that outfit, and with the powerful way she walked, Zee didn't doubt her words for a minute.

Mother's earth, what was her shifter form?

Orcle Songs

Forest of Orcles, Northern Lamirian Border to the Deadlands

After having said her goodbyes to Diwa and Mirabel, Zee and Sayde had left the safety of Tangaroa on the hunt for the three materials Zee needed to forge to defeat Salvador. Mirabel was now a shell of the girl she had been when Zee had first met her. Not only had she lost her grandparents, her oldest sister had also been taken in the attack. Mirabel hadn't spoken much at all, so Zee had gathered the information from her mother when she arrived at the stone building they were now calling home. After she had been directed to their new dwelling by Diwa, Zee had wandered through the valley city, taking it all in. It was beginning to come back to life all around her as people worked to clear the waterways and paths.

The valley was beautiful and perched right along one of the main waterways, although it did nothing to ease the pain the villagers had already suffered. Zee was glad they were all safe within Tangaroa's protected valley. But her cheek still hurt where she had bit down with such force, trying to hide her pain at Mirabel's hollowed-out appearance. Salvador had to be stopped. He had already done too much damage. Already within a few short weeks of being free, he had taken far too much.

'Here's as good a spot as any.' Sayde dropped her heavy pack on the hard dirt between five tallow pines as dusk wound its way through the forest, stirring the change from day into night. Rhinoceros beetles the size of Zee's palm, a deep iridescent-blue with stripes of white, hissed as they extended their wings and flew from the small clearing, vacating it for the oncoming night.

The pair had made it to the edge, where Lamiria looked out to the north over the deadlands. A tiny spiral of fear coated Zee's mind at the memory of the dream she'd had about the mud muncher – the larkaden attacking her. *How many of them were out there?* Zee shook the grotesque image away.

'This spot is great. It just needs a few more things...'

Sayde eyed Zee curiously from her spot on the ground as she sipped from her water skin. 'Like what?'

'You'll see.' Zee's smile was cocky. She dropped her own pack and wiped the back of her arm against the sweat on her brow, now cool with the oncoming change at dusk.

Squatting, she looked around the small clearing once more then planted her palms on the earth, closed her eyes and concentrated. Her palms emitted a gentle green glow into the earth beneath them, and all around the pair at the edges of the clearing, tiny swirls of spiky plants burst upwards. They grew and weaved into each other metres above their heads, creating a fence, like the two were now birds inside a cage without a roof.

Two patches of miniature leaves emerged from the ground at opposite sides of the space in long rectangular forms; sweet mint filled the air, the patches becoming thicker and spongy. Zee's eyes crinkled as she concentrated further, Sayde just watching with an impressed look on her face. A bright white-green flame grew in the centre of the space, and at the heads of the mint beds, thick pillows of soft moss crept densely over the ground. Zee's hands stopped glowing, and she opened her eyes to witness her small creations.

'That's a bit better!'

Sayde eyed Zee's changes to the space around them as she did a quick inspection. 'Nice work,' she appraised, 'but walls of thorns?'

Zee shrugged her shoulders. 'Don't forget, I grew up inside the Rim... I have no clue what creatures are out here, and the ones I have encountered so far scare the shit out of me when they try to make me their dinner.'

Sayde chuckled. 'Fair enough, at least you're honest. But someone with your skills shouldn't be afraid of anything in this forest, especially now that you're queen.'

Zee felt uneasy at the words. 'I'm afraid more power still doesn't mean I know what the hell I'm doing with it all, or how to wield it, or how to help anyone.'

'You'll get there,' Sayde said gently. 'After all, you have a lifetime to learn. You're lucky you grew up inside the Rim, not knowing what you were.'

'Why do you say that?' Zee asked, as her brows knit together.

'No one knew what you should or shouldn't be capable of. No one pushed you or forced you to wield your power, to become the best, to make your entire existence about your gifts. It sounds like you just got to gently exist, for a little while at least.' Sayde offered a stiff smile.

'I never thought of it that way.' Zee's voice was quiet, her eyes focusing on the flames she had created easily now in the centre of the small clearing the two women shared. 'I guess you're right, but I always felt stuck, bored, trapped. My mother was... *strict*. And I didn't realise till just recently that my father was actually there for me all along, just stuck and cursed in his shifter form by his mother. Kyeitha. My grandmother.' A shudder passed over her.

Sayde's eyes grew dark, like venom was pooling within them at the mention of the former queen of the forest. 'I guess we all don't realise what we truly have until it's taken away from us. Only looking back can we really see how lucky we were.' Sayde's eyes misted over, her hands clasped taught in front of her knees as she stared into Zee's flames.

Zee guessed she was talking about something else entirely. 'I'm sorry I didn't come sooner...' she said, her voice trembling a little.

'You couldn't have known. Aytac told me that the very moment you were healed of your curse and knew about our whereabouts, you left that very morning. I thought that being inside that hell, that prison, forged on the end of the world was the greatest misery any of us could have endured. Starved, fearful every day one of us would be taken, struggling to survive for crimes we should never have been punished for – until I met him.'

Zee's eyes moved from the flames to Sayde's face as she spoke. Her voice changed and her whole demeanour softened as she stared transfixed at Zee's magic fire, like she was truly faraway as she spoke.

'He lit up the days with light, he *made* it. He made me smile, he made me melt around him, and he made the worst nightmare of my entire life my happiest memories.' Tears escaped Sayde's eyes, just a few, and a throaty laugh slid from her delicate throat, as she shook her head a little.

Zee could barely see the sheen of the tears, but they were there, visible in the encroaching dark all around them.

'He was my balance, my light, my *soul flame*. I just know it.'

Zee didn't know what words to say to comfort her. Sayde's pain a real living thing permeating the air around them, making Zee's own heart constrict inside her chest and her own throat ache. 'Soul flame?' the words from Zee were gentle and curious.

'You've never heard of a soul flame?' The question pulled Sayde a little from her trance.

'Rim kid, remember?' Zee reminded her.

Sayde almost chuckled. She wiped a hand over her face and swept away the emotion along with the tears, her eyes focusing back on reality.

'A soul flame is a love, but not just any love, not just a balance you find in someone that complements you in every way, filling your faults, smoothing your weaknesses. It's more – it's a love that you feel you've felt before. Like in another lifetime, like somehow before you even meet the person you already know them. It's a twin flame to your own, a fated soul for this life and the next. It's a rare thing and not everyone finds it in their lifetimes. But I *know* that Noah was my soul flame. And when I die, I will walk straight from this life into the next and into his waiting arms.'

Tears stung Zee's eyes at the beautiful words, making her heart ache more for Sayde and Noah, and with the worry and fear she felt for Ravaryn. Her left arm felt tight as the vined tattoos constricted around her there, along with her chest.

'And before I leave this realm, I'm going to kill the fucking monster that took him from me. I'm going to rip him to pieces if it's the last thing I ever do. The last breath I ever take on this planet will be the scent of his blood on my tongue.' Claws elongated into crescent moons with shining pearlescent tips from Sayde's clasped fingers, and her huge doe eyes constricted just slightly, the irises within them flickering into thin vertical lines. They flickered like the flames before her, shining out into the dark – one second animalistic and wild, then gone the next second, and back to large round orbs of shining mahogany.

A high-pitched sound echoed through the forest towards them from the east, followed by others. More and more of the eerie wails sang through the cool night air. Similar to howls of wolves, but higher, sweeter and sadder.

Zee turned around in the directions of the unsettling sounds and checked the forest through her walls of thorned vines. The sound correlated simultaneously with Sayde's slight change in appearance, and her dark words had Zee involuntarily jumping a little in her skin. Not from fear, but from the sliding cool sensation as water began to glide within her, like she could feel the orcles filling themselves with the cool liquid they needed for their night's work. It was incredible; she could enter her consciousness into theirs and feel their emotions gliding through her as if they were her own. It was a brand-new connection to the inhabitants of the forest instead of just the plants and elements. This new power felt surreal, and Zee knew it must have been gifted along with the role of the forest queen.

'It's the orcles,' Sayde supplied. 'They have awakened and are mourning the parts of the burned forests. They will every night until they start to transform the damage, calling to each other for help to regrow and to mend the destruction of their home that *he* raped without remorse. We won't need the thorn fence, but if it makes you feel safer, keep it up. But you'll have to come to terms with your new position. You may have been the Rim Walker child, but now you'll have to learn how to be the forest's new queen.'

Sayde moved to the soft bed of mint that Zee had created for her, tired and weary, her thin and nimble body portraying how she must feel on the inside. 'But this is a nice start.' She added the compliment as she lay back and rested her hands behind her head on the mossy cloud-like pillow and looked up at the stars that were now bursting into the inky sky. More and more blinked a hello each second that the night grew. 'A girl could get used to a friend who has gifts with such perks.'

'Anytime you need a fence and a pillow, I've got your back,' Zee replied sarcastically. 'Hopefully I'll figure out how to do more useful things being queen than just make a comfy camp.' Zee huffed out a long breath and joined Sayde on her mint mattress. Lying opposite each other around the fire's dim glow, the stars winked at her, and the songs of weeping orcles continued in the distance.

But all Zee's mind could do was think of deep onyx eyes, glittering with silver specks, a cocky smile, a velvet voice and black wings that could take her away, anywhere she longed to go if she wished it. *Ravaryn.* Her heart squeezed like she had known that name an entire lifetime, maybe two. It warmed her inwardly, like a spark was glowing within her the more she thought of him. His smile, his voice, his earthy bark-and-pine scent. The flicker of heat turned into a soft dancing flame within her. *Ravaryn...* her heart ached for him. Burned for him, as though *her* soul were singing to *her* soul flame.

Smoke and Ash

Salvador's Stronghold, The Deadlands

Ravaryn's eyes adjusted to the dim space before him, thick lashes fluttering, his breath steady and deep. Warmth spread through his now-calm body, sweeping away the agonising pain from within him. His mind raced to the obvious answer of the instant relief, and he felt like weeping at the reprieve of pain. It had gone on for so long... how had Zee survived it for so long? Kyeitha's curse? Maybe he actually hadn't... *Gods, maybe he was dead?* He had finally let his iron grip on life go – worn, empty and completely depleted, he had given up.

His head slowly turned to the left. He was still in the cell though, the drip, drip, drip of putrid water steady. The smell of damp and rot still covered his senses. And to his left on the floor, there was nothing there... the cell was entirely empty except for himself. Only a darker patch of liquid sat in the thin puddle, but the rancid meat was gone.

No, No, NO. I didn't... I couldn't have.

Panic swept over him, his chest filling with a thousand tiny wings, then tiny claws scratching at his throat. He forced his eyes shut to escape the empty cell. *I didn't.* His memory finally burst forth from its slumber, and images, flashes of the woman, the vision, filled his mind. The Mother, who had kneeled before him in the filth, her elegant touch still lingering on his skin. He lifted a hand to his face to run it over the skin there, and his arm felt normal. No lead in his bones weighed down the movement.

Ravaryn remembered the woman, the vision, no *the* actual Mother. Gaia. She had come to him, somehow the Mother of the earth had saved his soul from crossing over to the underworld. He pushed himself upwards and braced for the nauseating spin of his head that he expected, the throbbing headache that should be present, but there was nothing. He was ... fine. Actually, he was better than fine. He was *healed.* It had been real, and she must have disposed of the human meat.

Ravaryn's heart beat faster and faster as his mind got clearer and clearer. Anger flared to life at the thought of Thaylon, and at his father, Salvador. Black smoke seeped from his alabaster skin as he repeatedly clenched then opened his fists before him, conjuring heat within them. Within him, he now wielded a dark, smouldering power. Not flames, but a darkness that could char, melt and incinerate upon his command. He watched as the smoke around him obeyed his command. It was like snakes sliding over his flesh, pouring from him. His power returned tenfold from his previous depleted state. But he couldn't just escape, he couldn't just leave this place, as much as he wanted to flee and find Zee. To hold her, breathe in her comforting jasmine scent. To hear her voice, a sarcastic retort to know that she was okay. He had to find out where and what this place was, what they wanted, and what Thaylon and Salvador planned to do now, that after all this time, they were free.

They would presume he had eaten the flesh, succumbed to the temptation of the repulsive way to heal himself and to gain power. Blood magic, dark magic, one could *never* come back from. They wouldn't suspect that he had chosen otherwise, another path, and that his loyalties lay elsewhere. Ravaryn's mind ticked over. He would have to be patient; he would have to be careful and play it safe, for just a little while. Because if they were capable of maiming and capturing him, Salvador's own son, then what chance did the rest of Lamiria have? Even Zee?

He wouldn't risk their safety; he wouldn't risk Zee's safety. If they found her... a shiver of anger and revulsion physically shook him. Oh yes, he could play along for a little while longer. He could wear yet another mask to see what his father and Thaylon had in mind for this realm. And what the hell they wanted with him. They wanted to control him, that much was obvious, by the lack of choices he had been given: consume blood magic or die. *You will eat, or you will die.* Thaylon's flat words slithered through his mind.

So they either they wanted him on their side, or on no side at all. Ravaryn opened his fists and ash crumbled to the floor. He walked over to the cell bars and gripped them tightly, his obsidian smoke swirling around the rusty filth-encrusted metal. He heated them with his power and fury within, and the metal wavered and disintegrated into powder at his touch. The metal was gone, dissolved in one touch as his eyes glowed with the same darkness he wielded all around him. Ravaryn stepped from the dank cell and strode to the entrance at the far end of the long hall. He ascended the stairs slowly, to find out where in the realm he was, and to seek out Salvador. To find out why the black dragon either feared him, or needed him controlled. To find out what he really sought and *why*.

Ravaryn's eyes smarted at the bright light; it was harsh and in stark contrast from the last few days, or possibly longer. Who knew? He had seemed to lose track of time as he ebbed in and out of consciousness with fever. Squinting to adjust his eyes, he made his way from the dungeon below. The walls were protruding with sharp pieces of rusty metal here and there that poked out from the mouldy structure of the ancient ones' building. The entire floor was empty around him. Large openings that must have once all been glass windows opened out to the grey and lifeless deadlands as far as the eye could see. Cracked, poisoned earth surrounded the formidable building he stood within, like a dormant sea. A few areas of the earth mounded up in lumps and piles. Larkaden tunnels,

Ravaryn guessed. They came close to breaching the surface of the dead soil, and were no doubt the only life it held and sustained.

Ravaryn proceeded to investigate the large expanse of the compound further. He made his way through several stairways, until finally a noise broke the silence around him and lured him towards a doorway to his right. He followed it deeper into the heart of the colossal structure. It amazed him that this building still stood after so long; the ancients were long gone, but their knowledge and skill must have been vast to create such a feat. Too bad their skills at keeping the peace with each other hadn't been as advanced or he might not by standing where he was right now. He might have *never* stood in this world.

The floor changed to a thick rug underfoot, and the hints of mildew and stagnant air faded. He smelled freshly burned wood smoke, leather and something else, not sweet but almost like liquor, brush his keen senses. This part of the building at least looked inhabited by something other than a prisoner.

The light inside dimmed, and his eyes adjusted again. And there, at the back of the long room, was Salvador. His eyes were cast down upon a large wooden desk. It was littered with maps and paper, and a quill in his hand was scribbling away, a glass of amber liquid sitting to the far right of his work. Ravaryn was momentarily taken aback once again at the resemblance he had to this man.

Salvador had shaven his face and donned clean and sharply cut new clothes since the first and last times Ravaryn had seen him... when his father had dragged him unceremoniously away from the Dark Rim to rest in a dank cave... and finally to this hole, legs broken and nearer to death than he had ever been.

'I see you made the right choice.' Salvador's voice had a stern, malevolent tone. He looked up from his work, eyes emotionless as they came to rest on Ravaryn's diminished state.

Ravaryn schooled his features with all his years of practice, not sure what to answer. He should reply, but a tiny trickle of something made him feel on edge. Fear? Loathing? Shock at what was happening around him? 'It wasn't much of a choice.' His voice was flat, unconcerned, as if they weren't discussing the fact that Salvador had nearly cost him his life, and that they were discussing the weather.

'I couldn't have you just wandering off after finally finding you now, could I, son? Besides, wouldn't you like to see what we've been cultivating while you've been no doubt anguishing in that cell over whatever morals you thought you had? Before you abandoned them all and finally decided that blood magic and life was the answer? Hmm?' Salvador's reply was mocking.

Ravaryn's eyes glowed with fury, but he kept it contained the best he could. 'Should I not be concerned about stealing another life's source to sustain my own?'

Salvador raised his shoulders just a tad. 'Their lives don't matter, son. They're merely cockroaches to the likes of us. Flies for our webs. Our power is unmatched by any other beings in this fragile realm. It's our right to take what we want. They have run rampant for far too long while I was *contained.*' The last word came out like a threat, causing Ravaryn to note the particular crack in Salvador's even expression.

'Come.' He stood, then strode from behind the desk into the centre of the darkened room to stand in front of his son. Salvador was tall, but Ravaryn matched his height – the two were equals in that one sense. Ravaryn unconsciously straightened his posture as Salvador's eyes scrutinised him closely. 'I'll show you what world we will create, and get you cleaned up. After all, you've been through a lot in the last few weeks. The least I can do is make sure you are comfortable... *son.*'

A pang of revolt shot down Ravaryn's spine. He knew exactly what Salvador had put him through; he'd nearly killed him, leaving him sick, injured and dying in a foul cell beneath the deadened earth of this place without a second thought. Without a choice... but his father didn't know about the Mother's visit. He couldn't have. Ravaryn matched Salvador's gaze, fury in check – for now – onyx flecked with silver staring into gold-rimmed pools of midnight.

'Good then.' Salvador smiled after a beat, his canines slightly longer than the rest of his teeth in that perfect, broad smile. A smile that did not, however, reach his eyes. 'I will show you exactly what's in store for this primitive little realm and its human pets. I'm sure you'll be impressed by what we've already accomplished.'

Ravaryn felt bile swirl in the pit of his stomach. If this was the way he had been treated, Salvador's own flesh and blood, his own son, what horrors could he possibly be eager to show off to him now? Ravaryn followed after the monster of a man. He had to find out what they were planning whether he liked it or not, as he had to know to defend himself and his people. Salvador clearly had his sights set on the entire realm's inhabitants by the sounds of it, including conquering Lamiria and imprisoning the humans of the old Rim world.

He didn't know why, and he didn't care. Ravaryn just cared about stopping his father before he got his claws too far into this earth, before the damage was too great to undo. Dragon shifter or not, he wasn't unstoppable. Everyone had a weakness, and Ravaryn would do whatever it took to find out exactly what it was.

Salvador led him through more open-aired desolate walkways and rooms filled with the ancient ones' technological junk, and furniture covered in dust, rubble and other debris. A few human bones could be seen in and around the mess of the past. And sprinkled throughout the entire building were webs... webs containing hundreds of spiders ranging from the size of a thumbnail to a dinner plate, their silky golden webs shimmering all around him as they passed. Golden orb spiders littered the stronghold. They finally reached an old metal door, orange and brown with rust, but still very solid as it held out the light that leaked around its edges from the other side.

Outside, Ravaryn guessed. And that was when he heard it – a faint ticking. No, a *clicking*.

'The humans in here,' Salvador's words overlapped the faint sound Ravaryn was trying hard to decipher from the other side of the rusted doorway, 'are weak and ill-fitted for survival.'

He turned from the door so he half-faced Ravaryn, his hand still on the handle as he spoke. 'Unlike us, as we are strong, survivors, winners, *rulers*. So even though it has taken some time to prepare, I needed to *create* an army for our cause rather than just *recruit* one from the meagre pickings this place had to offer. You've already met my right hand, Thaylon. He possesses certain skills that are remarkable to wield and morph. Thaylon is a flame demon, but also a blood mage. It comes in quite handy, I must say.'

The clicks grew louder, and the sound of hard footfalls connecting with stone or earth echoed in the distance also. 'I believe you were a king in the humans' lands and commanded your own army.' Salvador raised a questioning brow, his eyes focused, a sinister glint shining within them.

'I was a king, of sorts,' Ravaryn replied carefully, not quite sure what Salvador was getting at.

'Oh, don't be so modest. I've heard about the battle you won against Kyeitha's pathetic "damned ones".'

Pathetic they were definitely not. Ravaryn refrained from rubbing a hand over his shoulder that still held slightly purple scars from one of the monstrous creatures he had battled. That creature had nearly torn him in two, and they had barely survived the battle. His army would assuredly not have won if it hadn't been for Zemira ending Kyeitha's control over her creatures. That battle had taken Caden and countless others from this world.

Ravaryn's body went rigid as he wondered what in the Mother's name was on the other side of that door. And how on earth would they stop it if it made the creatures of the damned *'pathetic'*? He felt bile tickle the back of his throat as the clicks turned into shrill screeches.

Salvador produced that sickening grin again, one Ravaryn was coming to associate with vile things, as he turned the door knob in his hand. Standing back, he let Ravaryn get a good look out of the door as it creaked forth on old hinges out into a dusty field and into a yard of creatures scattering about. Long, spindly, barbed legs held up monstrous-looking torsos that resembled once being human. Sharp-toothed jaws and eyes flickered about in all directions. They scattered around the open pen as Thaylon wielded a whip to an actual human man, who looked as though fear had cemented his feet to the ground. Ground stained with what Ravaryn could only assume was blood or faeces as Thaylon instructed him this way and that, pointing and commanding him to try and control the herd of insect-like creatures.

'Behold the first batch of my army. *Our* army.' Salvador corrected himself as he slapped a hard, cold hand on Ravaryn's shoulder and pushed him out the door into the yard of wild screeching, clicking mutated abominations. Ravaryn could not, even with all his mastery, hide the revulsion from his face. His eyes followed creature after creature, noting the areas of their build that were human forged with arachnid.

'We call them Arakanai,' Salvador continued explaining, as though Ravaryn cared, his deep tone filtering out as Ravaryn could barely hear his words. Beyond them, out into the open expanse of the deserted land, were pen after pen full of the things. They were skittering about within, and just as he thought he couldn't hide his horror any longer, that he could school it in, Ravaryn heard... 'I want you to command them.'

The words sounded far away, and instead of letting himself drown in the horror, he tried to take the creatures in, tried to learn. How else would they be able to beat these things? The more he could learn about them, the better.

To the far left, a set of feathery wings fluttered above the quarry just above the Arakanai. This caught his eye, as it couldn't take off. It couldn't make it but a few measly feet into the air. Chains were holding the large struggling creature down on the dead ground as he snapped and tried fend off the circling Arakanai at the edges of his smaller pen.

Ravaryn recoiled as the chains held Blaze in place in the centre of the pen, surrounded by the horror that was Salvador's Arakanai army.

Part II

Gaia

The forest of Orcles, Northern Lamiria

Sleep found Zemira after a long while of lying there breathing in the soothing smells of the forest and her mint bed. The orcles' sad songs turned to a lulling tune instead of a distressing one as she finally fell into sleep. Sayde was right, she shouldn't fear anything in this forest; she should learn how to command it. But once again, Zee was left with a position and powers that she hadn't chosen and had absolutely no clue how to use properly.

In her dream state, she was walking through the forest, the moon bright in a cloudless sky. It filtered down through the trees in bright strips as glow beetles gently buzzed around her, their bright lights guiding her through the ancient forest. Her arm was warm despite the cool air that gently blew around her, the breeze not strong enough to stir the glowing leaves of the plants as she passed, but just enough to caress her skin with a cool, calming sweep.

She wandered like she had every night in search of Gaia. Was she alright? Had something happened to her? Had Salvador hurt her by burning so much of her ancient forests, the last she truly had left on the poisoned earth? Zee felt worry prickle in her gut, and she started to run, becoming frantic. The wails of the orcles grew louder, and she felt the forest reach out to her, its new queen, as she sped through it on determined legs.

Vines and large leaves all reached towards her, but to Zee it felt suffocating, not like the embrace she guessed it should be to the new forest queen. Her breath quickened as the cool breeze disappeared, replaced by the smell of charred wood and smoke. She was panting heavily now as she hurdled over decaying logs, tangles of vines and large tree stumps. The sounds were growing clearer, sadder and stronger. The moonlight grew brighter as there was more space for it to creep in through as the forest started to thin out.

Zee tripped at the last second, just as she reached the opening of light. Then there was darkness as she fell face first into the blackened earth coated with a layer of ash. It covered her face and stung her eyes, and as she panted, she sucked up a good layer into her nose and her mouth. It coated her tongue, and she spat wildly. Sitting up, she rubbed at her eyes with the hem of her singlet as she tried to stop the sting.

A deep sadness tore through her as the ash settled within her. It was a pain like no other, and her heart felt as though it were struggling to beat, as though made of glass. Zee gripped her chest as tears sprung to her eyes, clearing them. But the pain that forced its way out from behind them was the greatest sorrow she had ever felt. She felt like she was dying, her ribs constricting as if she couldn't get in enough air, she couldn't breathe.

As she opened her eyes, spread out before her was land burned to nothing but ash and painfully broken trees, the largest protruding were but a quarter of their original size, diminished... dead. Also before her were large slow-moving blobs of translucent blue and white gliding through the debris, wailing their song of sadness and mourning the forest that once was as they dispersed their seeds and water in the clear, now still, crisp night. Zee wailed and screamed and poured out all the pain and emotion that gripped her so savagely, joining in mourning with the orcles until she felt hollow and bare. Covered in soot and ash while sitting at the edge of the destruction, she now felt pathetic and empty. But after a long while, anger filled her. It wasn't just *a* forest Salvador had destroyed – it was *her* forest.

My forest...

The thought brought power whizzing into her veins as her energy returned, and somehow the anger calmed her. She got up from where she had fallen and went back into the forest a short way, searching on the floor between the leaf litter for something precious. After a while, Zee had pockets and handfuls of the gems of life: seeds. She walked out into the damaged black vista and began to move along the orcles, bending every few feet as she moved along, planting and healing, renewing her land with them.

Zee's seed bank was now depleted, but she wasn't tired as she knew her body was sleeping where she'd left it safely camped with Sayde. So she turned back to gather more seeds; she would plant all night with the orcles, with *her* orcles. The thought settled deep in her bones, and it felt right. Along with the wails of their song, Zee distinguished a different type of anguish, one she hadn't heard before. The sound was even more distressing than the ominous wail of the creatures milling about around her, like these cries of pain were pure agony.

Zee rushed towards it, and the closer she edged to the lush, unburned forest, the louder it grew. And there in the bright moonlight was a bent-over form cradling the powered ash and earth in her elegant hands and rocking back and forth like a small child would. Her mouth was hanging ajar, eyes forced shut, and a song of pure anguish tore out of her at the destruction.

Gaia.

She wailed like nothing Zee had ever witnessed before. The sound was pure anguish, the pain of the forest impacting her like she had been struck through with an arrow to her own heart. Zee felt it too, still fresh and raw in her own heart, and came to sit with Gaia. A gentle arm wrapped around the Mother's stooped shoulders, and she looked up to see that it was Zemira. Gaia rested her head on Zee's shoulder, her antler shorter on that side, broken it seemed, and it pressed against Zee's throat there. Gaia cried tears that landed on Zee's skin like drops of ice; they emitted a numbness wherever they contacted with her skin. The two mourned together, and not a word was needed between them as they both felt the same sadness in their souls.

After a long while, Gaia sat up from where Zee embraced her, and the two women now sat cross-legged in the soot. She wiped a slender, elongated mossy hand across her face, the tears gone, but tiny sparkles on her cheeks still present as Zee took her in.

'Where have you been, Gaia? I've looked for you everywhere, for weeks. So much has happened. Are you alright? Were you hurt?' Zee asked her gently, finding her voice cracked and broken from the pain she'd suffered.

Gaia sniffled a little more and took in a deep breath to calm herself. As soon as she let it go, the scent of rain laced with wildflowers hit the earth, overtaking the pungent scent of ash. 'I had to help someone very far away...' she tried to explain, her sweet voice still a little shaky. 'I was gone, for just a little while... then when I returned...' She waved her hands out before her, motioning to the forest that had been decimated for kilometres before them.

'And Ravaryn, he— I...'

Zee's heart jumped. 'What about Ravaryn? What has that monster done to him?'

Gaia turned, a tiny, sad smile creeping onto her face, her eyes becoming gentle and relaxed again, their sadness drowned out by something else. 'I made it to him just in time.' She grasped Zee's left arm as if only now just noticing the patterned vines there. 'You too, were ill. One and the same you are now, one needing the other just as much. United, joined, now one.'

Her words seemed far away and cryptic as always, but deep down there was stirring in her core at the thought, and Zee knew what she meant. 'Thank you, Gaia. Thank you for saving us. We'll make it up to you, I promise. We will stop him. We'll stop Salvador and save you and the forests from any more pain. I promise.'

Gaia truly smiled now. 'It should be me protecting you, not you protecting me, my child.' Pain crossed her delicate features.

'No,' Zee countered. 'It should always be us protecting you. You give us everything, you are everything. You are life. And we'll all fight for you, every last one of us. He will not win.' Zee's words were strong as they left her lips. The time for mourning over, she was filled with an energy of steel and strength. It seeped up from below the earth and into her, grounding her, settling her into her course.

'Diwa has told me of the undead city. She told me there were things there I can forge together to stop him.'

Gaia was saddened again, and looked out to the orcles still pacing far out from the edge of the forest, diminished to half their original size from when the night had started. 'I am the Mother, and I cannot bring myself to needlessly take their lives, so I protected the world from them,' she explained. 'Only flames can end them, and they cannot escape the city. They cannot harm anyone, but Zee, you must be careful. Whatever it is Diwa wants you to find and retrieve must be a powerful weapon if she has asked you to go to that place for it.'

Zee felt unease curl its claws around her heart. 'I'll be fine,' she reassured Gaia, her voice sounding steadier that she expected. 'I've also got Sayde with me. We'll be in and out, we won't linger. Diwa's explained what the items are, what they look like and what they should feel like when I seek them out. Sayde will have my back, and we'll be back in Tangaroa before you know it.'

Gaia's misty eyes returned to Zemira's forest ones.

'Are you okay?' Zee asked once more.

Gaia nodded. 'I've been through worse. I'll heal.' She smiled. 'After all, I have my children to help me.' She bumped a flower-coated shoulder against Zee's shoulder with a small smile.

The act as though they were just two normal friends messing around was so strange to Zee that she laughed. A ridiculous, contagious laugh burst out of her.

'What?' Gaia asked confused. 'What is it, child?'

'Nothing,' Zee wheezed, in between her laughter. 'It's just that this is nothing like I could have ever imagined my life to be when I used to wish for adventure, when I thought the world was simple and straightforward inside the Rim. Boring even.'

Gaia laughed now, joining in with her. Warmth and sunlight shone from within her, the sound like water crashing over rocks, birds singing in the trees. 'I would never have let you lead a boring life, Zemira Creedence,' Gaia revealed. 'You were made for so much more.' She stopped laughing and rested her head against Zee's should again, her child, her friend. Her queen of the forest. 'I'm glad the forests chose you.'

Gaia's words were as sweet as honey to Zee's ears, making her feel like for the first time since she had sat in the throne in front of the lake of life, that maybe... just maybe, so was she.

Salvador's Stronghold

Salvador's Stronghold, The Deadlands

Orion had located a brooding Aytac in Tangaroa, who didn't need much convincing to accompany him to retrieve Ravaryn. Something was eating away at the watcher, but Orion didn't have the time or attention to ask him what it was. All he could think about was his daughter – saving her, healing her, and what that would entail.

The pair had reached the edges of the charred forest that had surrounded the northern part of Maya Village, between it and the deadlands. Salvador's wildfire had caused so much damage here, and seeing it destroyed was like drowning just centimetres away from the air. Knowing the pain and destruction had happened but to not have been able to stop it was torture. They would retrieve the former king and prepare their defensives. This couldn't be allowed to happen again. When they returned to Tangaroa, they would be safe because the forest had chosen Zee; they would have a stronghold to rebuild within and organise their forces. But first they had to find Ravaryn and heal him.

Orion's teeth ached from being clenched, and his jaw was complaining. Zemira and Ravaryn were bonded, tied into each other's lives forever. There would be nothing Orion could ever do to that man that wouldn't in turn hurt his daughter. He guessed Sahara meant that the choice would *never* be his. It would just be a choice on how he would deal with this situation, not whether or not he agreed with it. Verena was going to go ballistic when she found out.

Aytac followed silently behind Orion through the crunchy charcoal and ash-coated forest floor. Orion tore himself away from his own ruminating, realising he had barely managed a few sentences to the other watcher.

'Thank you for agreeing to help on such short notice. I know it doesn't seem like it, but I'm grateful to you. I don't know what we'll encounter in Salvador's stronghold, but Diwa said to be wary as he has amassed forces of some kind. It won't be easy to sneak in and find the king.'

Aytac grunted, 'We'll manage.'

Orion turned to eye Aytac as they reached the edge of the deadlands. The other watcher's face was its usual stoic grimace, the scar cutting a stark line down through the right side, barely missing the bright yellow of his iris. But there was something within them that swirled with unease. Resentment? Anger? Pain?

'What is it, Aytac? What ails you? You look as though you've eaten poison grubs and they're eating away at you from the insides. And you've barely said a word, which isn't unusual for you, but it's definitely less than normal. So out with it.' Orion crossed his muscled arms over his chest, tattooed markings stretching over his bronzed skin, his emerald eyes not leaving Aytac for a second so he couldn't escape the inquiry. Orion didn't need him to be distracted on this mission. *Nothing* could go wrong; nothing could happen to Ravaryn that already had. They couldn't risk it. They couldn't risk Zee. Not just his only child, his little wolf, but now the queen of the forest.

Aytac rubbed a calloused hand roughly across his brow, thumb catching on the scar there. 'It's Sayde.' The words were clipped and quiet. 'I'm just worried about her. Ever since we got them back from the Dark Rim, it's just—,' he exhaled. 'She's different, she's not the sister I lost.'

Orion listened, his gaze pained. 'We've all gone through hell because of Kyeitha, but you and Sayde suffered more than most. None of us are who we once were. Give her time, Aytac.'

Aytac's eyes were distant for a moment then met with Orion's, and a curt nod was exchanged. 'How far away is the stronghold?' he asked, his concerns for his sister put aside. Orion was right. There was nothing to be done, and only time would be capable of healing such wounds.

'It's another hour or so north. I can feel it... a large congregation of anguished energy.' Orion's brows furrowed, and loose strands of his long silver hair whipped across his serious expression. 'Once we reach the stronghold, we wait for nightfall and search for the king by scent. We get him out of there without any more damage than what he has already sustained.'

Aytac nodded. 'Stealth mission, I get it.' He clapped a hand on Orion's shoulder. 'We've got this. We'll have that conniving little bastard with us before the day's done.'

Orion growled deep from within. 'I can't wait.'

His sarcasm caused a stiff smile from Aytac, the irony of the situation not lost on him. 'Who knows, he might even be happy to see your face.'

'Don't push your luck,' Orion grunted, then he shifted before the other watcher. Brilliant white fur now shone stark against the charred ground, emerald eyes bright. Aytac followed suit and stood beside his shifter brother, his dark coat contrasting against Orion's, night and day, shadow and light. Aytac's luminous yellow eyes were focused and ready. Large paws pounded deep in the earth as they set off into the desert-like deadlands for Zemira's blood-bonded other, imprisoned within Salvador's stronghold.

*

Ravaryn was struggling to lock down the mask over his features. He had to get the hell out of here, had to get back to Zee, to the people, and warn them what Salvador was planning. But he couldn't leave Blaze behind. Not here surrounded but these ghastly mutated beasts snapping at him in the chained pen. It was only a matter of time before they got to him and devoured him while the mighty duellerat was pinned down and defenceless. He couldn't leave him to that fate. And if they had captured Mazda's duellerat, where was she? Ravaryn felt sick to his stomach. He had trained her to take over from him as the Queen of Kymera, but she was still a young woman. Had she been captured as well? Was she even alive? What would become of his people? Ravaryn had to get out of here fast.

Salvador droned on about power and ruling and what they would craft this realm into as they walked through the pens of half-human, half-spider creatures. Ravaryn tried to keep his disgust in check as he had to learn as much as he could before getting far away from this sickening mess; otherwise, they wouldn't stand a chance against his father in dragon form, plus this growing army of soldiers. Thaylon's sinister grin and hooded eyes followed Ravaryn as he passed by with Salvador, but the heinous creatures did not come anywhere near their master.

'How do they know not to attack us?' Ravaryn tried to sound like someone who was genuinely curious about commanding this army. As if he was assessing the Arakanais' capabilities, and not trying to figure out how much intelligence or skills these creatures truly had. He needed to find the best way to fight against them when the time came, and the more he knew, the easier it would be.

'They were created with blood magic,' Salvador explained, his tone flat, his deep voice loud over the noise of the clicking, scuttling herd. 'My blood runs through them, so think of them like a hive mind. I am their master, their leader, and now that you have consumed the flesh riddled with magic-tainted blood, so too can you command them, if you wish.'

Ravaryn swallowed, his throat tight. 'Why spiders? Why did you choose such a creature to meld with the humans?'

'They are impressive are they not?' Salvador's lip hitched as he eyed the closest Arakanai. 'The first group of humans Thaylon herded here for me actually gave me the idea. I dove into the minds of them all with the aid of his blood magic. What terrified them the most, collectively, was close and abundant here. The golden spiders that hung from the walls around their cells elicited such an instilled fear. I couldn't help myself. They were perfect. So many legs for balance, strength and attack, along with a few tweaks to the maw and other areas, they were just the right mix I was looking for. Their simple minds can be controlled in large numbers. The rest of the human population will all easily accept my rule once I reach the human lands. The image of their kin mixed with the creatures most of them fear will be very persuasive indeed. Should you choose to reign with me, son, they will be at your command.' Salvador's black eyes bored into Ravaryn's, taking in his expression at the offer he had presented.

'What do you plan to do with the humans and the forest folk once you've conquered Lamiria and the human lands? Scare them into submission with these creatures?' Ravaryn's words were again flat and inquiring, as though he was considering the offer.

'Any who won't submit to our rule will be turned into Arakanai. Any who fight against me will die a slow, painful death. Flames are my preferred method, as you may already have guessed.' His thick brow rose. 'Do you also possess the dragon form? Or did your mother's blood foul your gifts too much?'

Ravaryn's jaw clenched, and his bones ached for him to shift and rip Salvador's throat from his neck where he stood. No one had seen his true shifter form but Diwa, for he had had to hide the monster he became upon shifting. His mother had feared that he would be ostracised from Lamiria if anyone saw his dragon form, so he had fought himself and practised powerfully to only half shift – to only produce wings and talons when needed, and not his entire true form. She had always known what the future held, whether she would share what she knew about his fate or not while growing up, Ravaryn was too smart not to heed his mother's words when it came to such things. She saw and knew things like no one else ever could, with her powers as a seer both a gift and a burden.

'My shifter form was not sullied by her magic, if that what you are wondering.' His words were like acid.

Salvador just chuckled like a smug son of a bitch at his son's barely contained fury. 'We'll see about that soon enough. I hear that Thaylon also has a successor. He caught wind of the information on his way through the lands before arriving here. Not his son, surprisingly, but a granddaughter who ended Kyeitha herself. An extremely powerful elemental who also wields fire, his *demon* fire. The first of her kind in this world, I presume.'

Ravaryn stilled at the words, his mind working overtime. His fists clenched so powerfully at his sides that cracks emitted from his bones.

'We will have to find this Zemira, and see if she also wants in on the change that will be coming to the realm. She will be a powerful ally.'

Ravaryn's heart caught in his chest, his teeth biting his cheek to keep from roaring out at Salvador. Rage filled his eyes, their shards of silver glinting brightly as he held his mask in place by the tiniest of threads.

'Come, I'll show you to your chambers, and you can get yourself cleaned up a bit.' Salvador's eyes roamed up and down Ravaryn's fouled state as if only just noticing he had been left injured and dying in his own blood and filth for the better part of a fortnight. While he, Salvador, ignored his very existence.

'Lead the way.' Ravaryn's false smile matched Salvador's perfectly, like a dark mirror had been put before him. He could fight against this kind of man as he had once pretended to be this kind of man.

'I think I know this Zemira you speak of,' he offered, his voice slipping into a cool calm after swallowing his instant fury moments ago. 'If I'm to be a part of this new birth, this new reign over the humans and forest folk realms, let me be the one to find her. To prove to you my loyalty and gratitude for the blood magic gift you have given me.'

Ravaryn almost gagged at the thought of the control and power Salvador would have had over him if he had been weaker, if he had eaten the flesh and succumbed to the dark magic to heal him. If Gaia hadn't appeared... he slowly took in a deep breath, waiting for Salvador's response. Salvador already thought he had won. Already thought he had control over his son, so to speak. Ravaryn fought to calm the hatred and anger growing like a virus within. His wings and talons struggled to burst from within him without his permission. Is this what the demons from the realm Salvador had come from all did? Was this just the beginning of what he had in stall for earth, should he somehow reign?

Ravaryn would fight and he would win, because unlike Salvador, he had something, *someone* to fight for. And he would burn this world to the ground before Salvador got the chance to if it meant keeping Zemira from his grasp. If it meant keeping her safe.

Salvador's jaw worked as his eyes narrowed just a fraction. Ravaryn could sense the turbulent energy within him as he rolled the idea around, coming to decisions. Searching for all the possible hidden betrayals that might lay within the offer. Why Ravaryn would offer this.

'I shall grant you this first task. To prove your worth to me and the cause. You have one moon cycle. If you don't return with her, I will descend upon the realms myself, as we are nearly ready to begin our conquest. But I'll give you this time. Do not fail, *son...*'

Fury and Flames

'*Fuck, Fuck, FUCK!*' Ravaryn's fist punched into the cracked concrete walls of the room, shattering rubble and dust from the blow. Blood seeped out of the torn skin there. His heart raced. He had to get out of here. He had to warn Zee, and he had to protect her from his father, and from her *grandfather*. Ravaryn was part demon, he knew it now, and so was she. An icy numbness seeped into him. *Fear.* He needed to see her; he needed to know she was safe. He needed *her.*

Despite the rest of the dilapidated building, this room, like Salvador's office, was respectable. Not grand in any way but there was a fire lit to warm the tub's water that appeared clean enough, and new clothes were supplied with boots and a black coat that looked as though it had come from Kymera. Food was also supplied in metal containers that sat sealed beside the clothes on the neatly made bed. The crisp, cool air of Kymera suddenly permeated Ravaryn's mind, and Mazda's bright and wild image clenched tightly around his chest. If Blaze was here...

No... don't think like that.

Ravaryn swallowed, not sure of the last time he had been so afraid, so afraid for people he had finally allowed in since he had lost his family all those years ago. He sat on the edge of the single metal-framed bed in the centre of the room and stared at the tub. The realisation hit him... he actually had people he cared about in his life, all this time after losing his heart, his soul. He had found happiness again, and it was all under threat.

There was no way in the seven hells of the underworld that he was going to let a monster like his father take that away... not again. Ravaryn breathed deeply, stood up and forced the food into his hollow gut. He tore the ragged clothes from his body and scrubbed his skin raw in the large metal tub that sat within the rooms he had been given. He dressed his muscular, scarred body in the clothes from his territory, which he now knew was under threat from a far greater evil than the former forest queen had ever been.

And then he sat and waited for night to fall. He would free Blaze, and with his powers ask his old friend what had happened, and if Mazda was hurt, if she needed him. Why was Blaze here? What would have possessed Mazda to leave the safety of the ice castle in Kymera? Did she leave, or just Blaze? To find him? Unless she didn't leave by choice... unless she had been taken...?

Ravaryn's fist clenched around the dark swirls of shadowy smoke that slid out from his being and grew thicker. It wrapped around him as his mind worked, and he watched as the sky over the deadlands through the large windows of the room begin to fade. And he waited until darkness was his ally.

*

Orion and Aytac made it to Salvador's stronghold in the deadlands as the sun's light through the clouded sky started to fade into dusk. Aytac's yellow eyes roamed over Wolf's stark white coat, and without words, he knew what Aytac's gaze said. Orion started to dig in the dead earth between his powerful paws, and he ripped the earth to dust in a large patch.

He then rolled his huge Wolf's form in the loose powder. It stained his coat like soot, not quite a black but a muddied grey that blended him into the terrain like a ghost. Then they crouched low from their vantage point and waited for the cover of night to camouflage their mission.

The night wasn't pitch black, but the moon couldn't break entirely through the clouds' thick cover. It was time. Eight powerful paws soundlessly padded their way towards the dilapidated building that towered high over them, the relic that still stood from the ancient ones' reign. Noises flicked their powerful ears this way and that as they approached. Clicking sounds grew louder, along with footfalls that sounded like thousands of legs connecting with earth all at once. But it was a faint chorus of noise, as though whatever things were emitting the sound for now were at least calm.

A shattered window led into the building, and both wolves sniffed and stalked their way through the ancient debris. They smelled the poison on the bones of the many human skeletons that lay in the scattered mess, and the dust. There were so many webs – thousands of golden webs littered the walls and ceilings of some of the rooms and long corridors they searched. The golden orb spiders were spinning their webs and crawling through the spaces as though they had lived here longer than any other beings.

Wolf shivered through his now deep-grey coat at the thought of so many spiders, but he had Ravaryn's scent. His heart pounded, hoping that what he found was still breathing, still living, for the sake of his daughter. He silently followed the trail with Aytac on his heels, through the rubble and discord of the building until he reached a shut door. Wolf shifted, and within a moment so did Aytac. The pair exchanged a nod, and Orion turned the handle as quietly as he could while he held his breath. As he entered the room, the king's scent still lingered, and it was strong; he had been here. Just been here. Shit. Orion took in the sullied water in the tub and the rags on the ground covered in filth. He bent to pick them up and horror filled his face as the scents of torture, poison, infection and filth filled his nose and his heart with desperation.

Aytac's voice cut sharply through the quiet terror filling Orion's mind. 'He was just here. Orion,' he nudged him, 'that means he's still alive. Let's go.'

Orion dropped the rags and tried to keep the panic growing like a storm within him at bay. This time, he followed after Aytac as they sought out the scent that had changed slightly after Ravaryn had discarded the scent of filth and pain. To the lower level they stalked, to a rusted door where the strange clicking got louder. It was swung open to yards of creatures, all of the same species, gently swaying and clicking in groups.

Orion and Aytac crept with the stealth of shadows as they passed the seemingly entranced creatures, making their way to the edge of the pens to scout from the edges.

*

Ravaryn had made his way down into the pens as soon as he deemed it dark enough, and before he thought Salvador might come seeking him for something, having given him plenty of time to clean himself up. Smoke seeped from his pale skin, shadowing him in the night, and he whispered a gentle rasp out to Blaze.

'Blaze, my friend.'

The duellerat's head lolled to the side as he rested, blood pooling from where the chains bit into his skin below the fur and feathers. The metallic smell stung Ravaryn's nose. Anger flickered within him, and as soon as Blaze's eyes all opened, they adjusted to see that it was him. He crept swiftly towards him and started to melt away the metal with his hand, pouring the furious energy out and melting the metal within moments. Ravaryn spoke as he moved onto the two front-leg chains, ignoring the growing clicks from the surrounding Arakanai, sleeping or stunned he didn't know, but he didn't want to linger to find out.

'Blaze, why are you here? Is Mazda okay? Was she with you? Please tell me you did not come looking for me.' Ravaryn's words were rushed whispers into Blaze's soft fox-like ears as he stroked his friend's face.

Blaze cooed a soft caw that Ravaryn understood. 'Mazda and the Aylentean boy Paxton were worried for the Rim Walker. Astrid, the boy's new duellerat, and I flew them to the forest, but these creatures—' Blaze's six eyes scattered as he eyed the things that surrounded the edges of his pen. 'They attacked us. Mazda is safe, Astrid got them out. I was attacked and captured, and these things took me here.'

A shudder rattled through Ravaryn. 'You did well, old friend. I'm eternally grateful.'

'Mazda is safe,' Blaze replied with his soft caw.

'Blaze, you did well, and I thank you. Are you able to stand? To fly? To get yourself as far away from here as possible?'

Blaze slowly lifted himself upwards and stood on shaky legs, ruffling his wings as quietly as he could and stretching out the aching muscles that had been restrained for far too long. 'Yes, friend.'

Ravaryn nodded and grasped Blaze's large head, gently bending it to rest against his own. Thanking him, honouring him. 'Fly well, and tell that queen to stay put in Kymera where she belongs, or the next time I see her it'll be her neck I'm after.'

Blaze clucked at the threat, knowing full well they would both protect the fiery young one with their last breaths.

Blaze blinked and then looked at Ravaryn one last time as he started to pound his wings, trying them out after being confined for so long. The clicks surrounding them grew, and all the creatures in the pens encircling them turned and faced their way. Their multiple eyes opened and glowed with a golden luminous ring, all at once coming to rest directly on Blaze and Ravaryn with pinpoint precision.

'Fuck, GO!' Ravaryn urged, and Blaze took off as the screeches tore from the Arakanai all around them. He barely made it into the air just over the first yard of them, jumping and tearing at the air to get at him with their barbed insectile-front legs, open jaws snapping sharp teeth.

Ravaryn tore out of the pen in the opposite direction, and the Arakanai all around him violently grabbed out towards him. He spewed black smoke, incinerating any that came close to his skin. They turned to ash upon contact, and Ravaryn made it rapidly to the outer edge of the yards. He slid under the last rung of the metal fence, straight into two sets of luminous lupine eyes and sharp, exposed teeth.

A growl rippled from Orion's throat as he bared his teeth over the top of Ravaryn. The former king's eyes widened as realisation set in. 'Fuck me,' he breathed.

Orion's gaze was torn from Ravaryn as a bone-rattling roar sounded from the top of the crumbling building. Bright orange and stark white-yellow flames blasted light all around the chaos and into the sky where Blaze feverishly flew away from the compound. The black dragon leapt from the concrete perch, his powerful back legs pushing off and sending large chunks of rubble falling. Orion shifted into his man form and grabbed Ravaryn up from the ground.

'Let's go!' His words were like finely sharpened steel. The trio fled from the yards back around the building and towards the open deadlands and the charred forests beyond.

Ravaryn's pulse hammered in his brain and wings sprouted from his back. Just as he pounded them to become airborne to help Blaze, hands from either side clasped him powerfully to the ground.

'What are you doing?' Ravaryn seethed. 'I have to help him.'

'There's no time,' Orion growled. 'We have to get you out of here.'

There in the sky his wild eyes found Blaze's form, and a shriek of pain seared onto Ravaryn's ears like daggers and the dark sky was illuminated with fire and fury. The black dragon had caught up with the injured duel-lerat, and it blasted powerful fire directly at Blaze's struggling form, engulfing him in a bright wave of deadly flames, incinerating him in a plume of death. Ravaryn's face contorted in shock, his eyes misting over, the size of full moons, as he watched his friend disappear from the world. His entire body went numb, and an icy fury filled him. Orion and Aytac tore him away from the horrific scene and dragged him along through the darkness, far away from the black dragon's fury.

The Undead City

Northern Lamirian Forest, Edge of The Deadlands

A warm ray of light warmed Zee's cheek as her eyes fluttered open in the early morning of the forest around her. Sayde was already up, chewing on some dried meat from her pack, and she spoke in between chews.

'Geez, finally. You sleep like the dead. Up and at 'em, Zee. Prune your fence and let's get going before the morning's gone.'

Zee felt as though she had just left Gaia, but within a blink she waking in the lush forest, untouched by the flames, that they camped in. Zee moaned a reply and rubbed at her sleepy eyes, remembering the sting of the ash as though it was still in there, scraping against her corneas.

'Ugh, you're a morning person...' she groaned at Sayde with mock malice.

'Ha, precious queeny needs her beauty sleep, huh?' Sayde teased. She was in such a good mood, maybe having something to do, or maybe just being away from Tangaroa was a good enough distraction for her. 'Come on, let's get going. I want to see what this city of dead things is all about. You and the old woman have me intrigued.'

Sayde swung her pack over her shoulder giving Zee no more time to wake herself up. Sitting up, Zee placed her palm on the ground, and the barbed vines crept away in a doorway-sized patch to her right – in the direction that Zee felt within her that they would find the city of the dead.

The pair traipsed through the forest until they reached the desolation of the deadlands. Zee felt a heavy, putrid zap of anguish before them. *The city.* 'It's straight ahead. I can feel something... *strong.*' She had no other word for it and didn't want to elaborate on the sickening tug that pulled at her bones.

'So are you going to explain to me what we're actually looking for in there, other than our own demise?' Sayde questioned, her voice indifferent. As her boots kicked at a small rock on the dead soil, it skittered out before her bouncing and rolling into the nothingness that engulfed the two now. A desert free of life, or so it seemed.

'Sayde!' Zee smouldered. 'Aren't you afraid of the larkaden? Of attracting their attention or something?'

'Pfft, nah. They only really come out at night, so don't stress, Rim kid.'

Sayde's relaxed words did not in fact reduce Zee's anxiety. She reached out with her powers and investigated the foul earth below. Most of it closer to the edge of the forest had felt cleaner, less-heavy with pollutants, but the farther they ventured into the deadlands, the thicker and more pungent the energy became. It felt like a sickness surging through her.

Zee shook it off, along with the anxiety clawing at her throat. 'The first thing we need will be relatively easy... I think. Diwa said that the city is protected from any of its inhabitants ever getting out by an organic-type barrier that grows rapidly and is poisonous to the touch.'

Sayde let out a huff. 'And that's the easy thing?'

'Yeah... hopefully. Once I figure out how to get the essence of it inside the orb, I should be able to easily trap the other two things inside of it. But I've never done anything like this before...'

Sayde opened her eyes wide, letting her curiosity filter out towards the rolling tundra of black and grey. 'I'm sure that once we try the first thing, when we get inside the city we'll be fine. What are the other two poisons you have to add into the orb thing?'

'Something called a virus, and another thing that the ancients created called plastic.'

'This is all so strange.' Sayde kicked at another rock. 'But if anyone can pull it off, I'm sure it's you.'

Sayde's words filled Zee with the tiniest seed of confidence, but her palms felt clammy as they walked through the eerie open lands of nothing. 'A few more hours and I think we'll be getting close,' Zee stated.

The two trudged on in silence, captors of their own thoughts, as they neared the city of undead things. A city that had lived untouched and unknown alongside them all this time, and they didn't know who or more precisely *what* they would encounter inside it.

Walls of bright red-orange towered high above Zee and Sayde as they drew closer to the fenced cage-like structure that withheld the ancient ones' destroyed, but partially still-standing, city. Zee had never seen coral, or a reef, other than in old school texts and picture books, but that was just what this fence or barrier reminded her of.

'Whoa, what is this place?' Sayde's voice actually had a hint of awe at seeing the towering barrier of crusted coral-like spires. Her hand reached out before her as though she were in a trance to touch the deep red of a solid chuck before her. Tiny tendrils curled in the air towards her fingers, willing to greet her skin.

Zee turned from the area she was scanning and a yell ripped from her mouth. 'Sayde, *no!*' But she was too far away, she wouldn't reach her in time. Zee swept a hand up in panic and a gust of wind blasted Sayde back from the strange organism that was the barrier to the city.

A gruff of pain left Sayde as she flew metres back and landed heavily on her back, her pack hopefully taking some of the blow. She sucked in painful breaths, slightly winded, and rolled with another grunt to her side, eyes like daggers meeting with Zee's.

'Are you okay?' Zee's voice was high.

'What the fuck, Zee?' Sayde pushed herself upright and turned back to stare at the wall where she had just been. The small anemone-looking tendrils shrank back into the thick columns of the structure, empty of their prize.

'It's poisonous! It's... it's like a living, breathing fungi or something. If we touch it, and we're infected... we die. I can feel its energy... It's alive, and it's old, *really* old.' Zee's eyes were saucers, the emerald flickering within bright in contrast to the dull landscape and bright sunset shades of the eerie wall beyond.

Sayde swallowed hard. 'Well then, thanks, I guess.' She grunted and pushed herself up off the ground. 'Okay, I've got it. Don't touch the coral – the reef fence of death. Anything else I should know?' She brushed herself off and looked up with a new perspective, one less filled with awe at the structure.

'Just don't touch anything in this world. If anything happens to you, and I have to explain it to Aytac, I think I'd rather let the undead eat me.'

Sayde scoffed. 'The undead are going to try *eat* us? Yuck.' She cringed. 'Well, this mission just got way creepier in the last two minutes.'

Zee chuckled. 'I know, right.'

'So no climbing the hungry wall. Then how do we get in?'

'I've got an idea, but first I have to try and forge a piece of this "thing" into the orb. Once I figure that out, it'll be safer to enter into the city and search for the virus and the plastic.' Zee rummaged through her pack and pulled from it the lightweight orb that seemed the shift and move within on its own accord.

Sayde crossed her arms and stood back with a slightly raised brow, lips pursed a little like she wanted to see how this was going to work.

Zee sat cross legged on the hard, dead earth to face the intricate columns of coral-like fungus that connected into a strong, protective fence. It ran so high, metres and metres into the gloomy clouded sky above them. She took one look back at Sayde before she began, her pulse racing a little through her now.

'I'm going to close my eyes so I can concentrate. If that stuff gets anywhere near me, please for the love of the Mother get me away from it as fast as you can.' Zee waited to see Sayde give her a reassuring nod. Zee then inhaled deeply, the air smelling of char and something like mushrooms in bloom. With intense focus, she tried to will a bit of the structure before her, to coax its volatile and deadly form to bond within the orb, or 'the light' as Diwa had called it.

A Cure

Lamiria

Ravaryn's core was frozen over with the pain cracking into fissures throughout his body, like a thousand shards of ice were slicing through him from the inside. Blaze was gone; it had only taken seconds for Salvador to snuff out his friend's life from this world. Orion and Aytac didn't let go of their steel-like grip on Ravaryn until they were far away from the deadlands' stronghold, until the buzz of the forest and its glowing light safely hid them within its chaos of plants, vines and thick trees. Hours had passed by in a blur, and Ravaryn blinked slowly as if he was in a daze, the forest caressing his skin as the three passed through without a word.

Gradually, the two watchers loosened their grip on him, but eyed him warily. Ravaryn looked back with nothing in his eyes, his core still numb. No flickers of silver glinted in his gaze; no mask covered the defeat on his face. Orion and Aytac didn't utter a word about what they had witnessed in the dark night sky, when it had lit with orange and white plumes of death, understanding the loss seeping within the distraught king.

'We must get back to Tangaroa.' Aytac's deep voice broke the silence.

Ravaryn's onyx eyes met with Aytac's yellow ones, and he nodded once. An agreement and also an explanation that he would follow. He no longer needed to be dragged like a prisoner. There was nothing he could do. There was nothing left behind him, other than death and the promise of revenge.

'Yes, there's a lot that has happened... I'll explain along the way,' Aytac offered.

Orion just growled and pushed past them to lead the way back through the profuse forest.

Tangaroa's glittering lights that filled the city once more brought a flicker of life back into Ravaryn's dark gaze. He stood in the city once again after so long. The city sparkled with life once more; it was open, it was free and it was beautiful. Glowing light littered its expanse and gave the illusion that it were somehow floating, as if the vines, blooms and bougainvillea tendrils held it in place against the cliffside alone. Warm, sweet air drifted over his head, but none of it penetrated the cold he felt within.

Ravaryn stood at the edge of the flat cliff clearing near the rushing falls and looked down into the city that had been empty and abandoned for so long because of Kyeitha's twisted reign.

Orion growled a greeting as he approached, the scent of hate thick in the air as Ravaryn turned to acknowledge him. 'If it weren't for the blood bond, I'd have ripped your throat out and let you die before you ever got to see her again.' His eyes glowed with fury.

'I know,' was all Ravaryn could conjure. No clever barb, no hateful retort. He felt empty and lost without her, and understood Orion's hatred more than he could know. He didn't ever bother to shield his face with a mask of arrogance, or hide the guilt there. 'I did it to save her from your mother's curse. You have to believe me that I didn't know about the blood bond.'

Orion's eyes flared with the sarcastic blow he had expected from Ravaryn, but as he looked at the man's defeated face, his anger was doused.

'I am sorry, you know, for all the "games". But you have to agree you didn't look back when you took Verena. You took what you wanted because you thought it was right, and you didn't look back.'

Orion stilled, realisation sweeping over him, as a fresh breeze reached them from the falls. They were two men fighting for what they loved; it just so happened that somehow they had ended up on the same side.

'Do you truly care for her?' The words forced their way out, Orion nearly biting his own tongue, like a lump of coal was within the words burning his mouth.

'I do. More than I do for my own life.'

'That may well be, but as Aytac explained, if anything happens to you... it happens to Zee. So I expect you to better take care, King, because if anything, *anything* happens to her, I will hunt you down in the underworld and make you pay from beyond the veil.'

Ravaryn could feel Orion's fear leak through his furious façade, the fear that lingered in the deep emerald of his glowing lupine eyes, and guilt rattled him. The words tore from him without his permission as Orion glared at him, trying to see if there was a smattering of goodness anywhere within his wretched soul.

'She's my soul flame...' Ravaryn's voice was quiet, strangled.

Orion's eyes went wide, and his jaw muscles flexed. He turned to leave but Ravaryn grabbed his muscled arm, halting him. Orion turned to meet his gaze again.

'I would live a thousand lives of pain to keep her from danger, Orion. Please, you have to take my word. I mean it.'

Orion growled once more and tore the icy grip from his arm, the twisting black smoke along with it that leached from the deplorable creature that stood before him. The creature that held his daughter's heart and soul in his hands. He got as far away from Ravaryn as he could before he could no longer reason with his own mind. Before he tore him to shreds and let his blood spill down the falls into the waterways of the Valley of Rivers.

*

Tracking back, as Ravaryn reached the large veranda to the palace, he stilled, noticing a lithe silver-haired figure awaiting him. Diwa was wrapped in a burgundy and violet shawl, as if she had been rooted in that spot all night. She walked quickly towards him and outstretched her arms to embrace him, her more-youthful face creased with worry lines. But Ravaryn barely seemed to notice her more youthful appearance, the shock of what had happened to Blaze still shredding his heart into sharp pieces.

Diwa led Ravaryn into the entrance room of the palace and sat with him on the lounge. A pot of tea with a few warm wisps of steam trickling intermittently from the spout sat on the wooden table before them.

'Son, I'm so sorry.' Diwa's voice was a high as she spoke the quiet words.

Ravaryn's eyes were pools of swimming ebony as he stared at the teacup before his clasped hands. His posture straightened as he leaned back, adding inches to his large, masculine form. 'You lied.' His voice was low, but steady, the accusation slicing the air as it slid out towards his mother. 'You said he was dead. I never questioned you... I trusted you, with everything, my entire life, I just believed every word...'

'Rav, please, I can expla—'

'Maybe if I had known, he would still be alive!' Ravaryn boomed, his voice wild and laced with gravel, a deep growl echoing behind the words.

Diwa closed her eyes for a few seconds, holding in the emotion and stilling herself against the outburst.

'He's dead. Blaze is dead. It took that fucking monster seconds, SECONDS to end him. If I had known maybe just how vile, how dangerous he was, I could have done something different, could have saved him...'

Ravaryn sank back into the couch, keeping his dark gaze directly before him, not trusting himself to meet his mother's eyes in case the fury there could somehow hurt her. His arms snaked with smoky shadows.

154

Diwa's lips thinned as she chewed on her lip. 'I did it to keep you safe, especially when you were a child. I lied about that one thing, yes, because I didn't want you to grow up thinking you were destined to become something that you're not. I wanted nothing negative to sway or affect the man you would become. I wanted you to have a choice.' Diwa's voice steadied as she spoke, the words she had held in for so long growing power within her as they were released.

'I did what I thought was right. You have become such a powerful, thoughtful, strong yet gentle man. I am proud of everything you are despite what has happened to you along the path in this life, in this world. Yes, I lied. But there is nothing in this world, no knowledge that would have helped or prepared you for what your father truly is. There is nothing that will change his nature, and the fact that he is a demon. And there is no light within him. I'm so sorry for Blaze, dear. I truly am. There are so many things that I wish I could change. So many. Please forgive me. My love for you is more than anything in this entire world. More than my magic, my youth, my own life. There was nothing I wouldn't have done to keep you safe, until you were old enough to protect yourself. But tell me what happened, what he did to you. Are you still hurt?' Diwa's eyes searched his as if she could somehow see any injuries that may be present before he had a chance to explain.

'No. I'm fine. Now.' Ravaryn paused for a brief moment to gather his thoughts. 'We reached Kyeitha's prisoners, inside the Dark Rim. But he was there, and the moment I sensed him, he was upon me. I was dragged across Lamiria. Injured severely then left to die in a putrid cell with broken bones, open wounds, fever. All I was offered was dark magic as my only way to heal - from Thaylon, Zemira's grandfather. He's a vile creature in his own right.'

Diwa gripped Ravaryn's hand as she spoke, squeezing it within hers.

'But somehow I was saved. The Mother - Gaia appeared in the holding cells before me. I didn't take the dark magic into me, I didn't eat the poisoned flesh. I couldn't. I'd rather die than live that way. I thought she was a hallucination... but she was real. She must have been.' Ravaryn's face scrunched in anger, disgust. He growled at the memory, then his head snapped up. 'How did you get away from him all those years ago? How did he end up trapped in the Dark Rim?'

Diwa let a slow breath out, 'I made the Dark Rim, and I trapped him in it. I expelled every grain of magic I could to create it, to keep you safe. When he found me after you were born, he was furious, insisting that I give him his newborn heir. I told him that I had hidden you on an island far from the coast, and that it had caused my magic to seep my youth away. He struck me, leapt from the ledge and never looked back. He flew straight past the invisible barrier of the Dark Rim wall I'd created and trapped himself within. I did everything I could to keep all of us safe. It not only drained my magic reservoirs but also my body, and my youth. But it was all I could do to keep him at bay. Now that he is free there's no telling how far he will go to seek revenge and control over Lamiria and the old Rim world.'

'Gods, how did you keep it to yourself for all these years?' Ravaryn squeezed her hand back now, awe and pride shifting inside him at the realisation of what she had done, what she had given up to protect them from Salvador. 'There is no mercy within him. If he sat by while I waited on death's door, his own blood, there's no telling what horrors he will create should he gain power over us. And he's already started. They are amassing an army. Creatures like that of Kyeitha's but worse, far worse. And he burned Blaze from existence without a second thought... fucking monster.'

'None of this is your fault, nor should you feel guilt for the part of you that came from him. You are good, you are strong, and you are nothing like him. And you never will be.'

Ravaryn stayed still for a moment, his gaze softening. 'I'm sorry. I know. I know. Gods, but how will I ever tell Mazda? Blaze was her everything.' His heart swelled as he thought of his own castle-bound duellerat, Chester. His sweet demeanour, his carefree abandon and fierce loyalty. He probably had Ilga wrapped around his little talon the second Ravaryn had left Zenya. She doted on him like he were a pup, not a full-grown snow creature living in the castle. Capable and smart despite his deformity.

Ravaryn's gaze refocused as he turned to take in his mother. He studied her now, and her face, similar but different from his childhood, smiled back at him gently. 'How was I lucky enough to have you for a mother?' He forced a small half-hitched smile, trying to eradicate the worry that edged around Diwa's eyes.

'Only Gaia knows,' Diwa quipped, a small smile replacing the tight frown for a moment. 'Now, let's have some of this tea, and I'll see what the leaves tell us. And, yes, there's definitely a touch of whiskey in there.'

'Only you would drink whiskey from a teacup.' Ravaryn shook his head, accepting that the younger version of his mother next to him was indeed the same woman he had known all his life.

'Well, I knew you were returning... I just didn't know quite what state you would return in.' Diwa raised one brow.

'Orion and Aytac were not my first pick of chaperones, by the way. I can't believe there was no one else.'

Diwa laughed. 'I'm sorry, but your first pick is elsewhere. She's gathering important poisons for me, things I know in my heart that can stop Salvador.'

'So I heard.' Ravaryn's eyes dropped again to his tea.

'Don't worry, she'll be here before you can sufficiently brood her absence, I'm sure.' Diwa said. 'She is well. She is with the shifter Sayde, Aytac's twin, and stronger than ever now that the forest has chosen her to be its new queen.'

Ravaryn wandered through the halls of the palace that clung to the hillside overlooking the valley. After meeting with his mother, his mind was still processing the younger, more vibrant version of Diwa. He took in the empty rooms that had started to be cleaned and filled with life again since the forest folk had returned. Since Zee, their *queen*, had opened the doors to Tangaroa.

Ravaryn's brow knitted. *Queen...* would she be the same? Or would the power consume her like it did Kyeitha? He swallowed, his throat as dry as ash, even after drinking the soothing tea since being reunited with his mother. Which had eased his aching heart ever so slightly. He looked around at the room he now stood in. It had been cleaned upon his mother anticipating his safe return, and she must have known he would make it somehow. Did she know that he had met the earth Mother? Had he even met the earth Mother, or had his mind made him believe so? *No. He had.* There was no other explanation for his body healing without touching the dark blood magic in that foul meat.

He shook a shiver of revulsion away, then shifted slightly so his large wings were present. They centred him, balanced him in a way that made him feel like his true self more than his human form had ever. It had been torture not being able to shift, to have his magic bound while he had been cursed by Kyeitha and banished to the human territories; she'd known that it had been the worst punishment for him.

A trickle of fear seeped into him again thinking of Kyeitha, not of her, but because of what may happen to Zemira now that she was the reigning forest queen. He gazed out into the dark city below, glow beetle lanterns flickering, which lit the now-occupied houses with a calm, warm light. Ravaryn had to do something; he couldn't just wait around here like some injured pup until his love returned. His mind drifted to the cell he had been imprisoned in, so badly injured he couldn't call on his magic, couldn't even call on his body to move. But the being, the Mother, she had truly appeared. Her words slid towards him, *'I am the Mother of the earth, and I will need your help...'*

Help? Help with what? What could he do that the most powerful being who created life itself could not do? But just the thought alone was enough to distract him from his brooding and clear the swirling of unwanted emotions, so Ravaryn gripped it like a predator would prey. *I can help in some way.* Now, he just had to find a way to see Gaia again. He'd been near death when he had seen her, but re-enacting that state would definitely not be an option. Diwa would know. His wings gracefully followed his movement as he prepared to seek Diwa out, but there watching him in the shadows was a tall, flowing figure with large eyes and a curious sheen glazing over them.

Gaia stood in the dark room before Ravaryn as if the very thought of her name had conjured her here.

'I– I was just thinking of a way to see you,' Ravaryn explained, looking like a startled deer.

Gaia laughed at his wide eyes. 'I know. I could feel your pull, for we are connected, you and I.'

Ravaryn couldn't comprehend what she'd just said, as his mind was like thick honey, his thoughts trapped within, by the sheer awe of her presence. *She was real.*

'You look much better than the last time I saw you, Ravaryn Black.' Gaia's smile was sweet, and the air filled with the scent of humseeds in the sun and the crisp air before a storm.

As she walked towards him, his wings tucked tightly away then vanished, as though hiding what he truly was from her, not wanting this being of absolute goodness and life to see the real him.

'You don't have to hide them, my dear. I think they're one of the most beautiful things about you.'

Ravaryn's heart melted at the compliment, like a small child being told they had done a good job at something they thought they had failed horribly at.

'Do not hide them, Ravaryn. People should see the real you.'

Ravaryn took a deep breath, like he was submerged in deep water, the air thick as he pulled it down his throat. Then without thinking, he shook his huge dark wings into existence again behind his back, eyeing Gaia warily.

'There he is, my dark knight.' Her hands swept towards the elegant deep-sapphire lounge that faced the city below. 'I have something I need to tell you, something that I cannot change, nor can I stop the pain and suffering that is happening.'

Ravaryn followed her lead and sat beside the elegant woman, tiny insects and vines moving slowly over her skin like gentle snakes through the forest floor. 'The Arakanai, the creatures Salvador has created... She sucked in a deep breath of her own, her skin growing a dark shade of forest green, blooms along the surface snapping shut as if hiding away from the words. 'They are suffering... they are still in there... the *humans.*'

Gaia's elongated fingers reached for Ravaryn's large hand to hold it in hers, her eyes swirling storms of sadness and pleading within. The moss on her hands was so soft, like a small floxel's fur. 'The human souls that Salvador has turned into monsters are still inside the Arakanai, in pain, locked inside a prisoner they cannot escape. I need you to find a way to free them, find a cure for the blood magic, before it's too late. Before they lose their minds and are trapped within those creatures forever.'

Ravaryn swallowed, his eyes like far-away galaxies in the moonlight that was fading into morning before them. 'We have a plan. We are going to war, and we will end Salvador,' he assured her. 'Salvador said that they are like a hive mind, possibly the same way Kyeitha's creatures were all under her command.'

'Yes, that may be, but once he is gone, they will run wild and rampant. The cure must be ready, as if they remain that way for too long afterwards, it will be too late.' Her hand squeezed his powerfully. 'Unfortunately, there is nothing I can do. The wildfires have weakened me, and if there's much more suffering and destruction, I'm not sure that I will be able to recover this time...'

A tear welled from Gaia's eye and dropped onto the fabric of the lounge between them. Blood blooms sprouted from the point of contact, blood blooms like on Zee's arm. If she was off retrieving a weapon to fight for them, to fight for Gaia, he could do this. He would help while he waited for her to return, before they prepared for war against Salvador.

'I will, I promise. You saved my life, and you saved Zee's life. I'll get a cure for those trapped souls, I promise. Hang in there; we all need you, as there's no life without you.'

Gaia nodded her head in gratitude, and her grip slipped from Ravaryn's hand. 'Would you like to see her?' she said, her body transforming into a plume of Ulysses butterflies as the wind swept them out of the open verandas and over the breaking dawn. One lingered... it doubled back from the departing swarm and hovered above Ravaryn's head. Circling gently in the air it dissolved into glittered dust that drifted down upon him. Drifting over his bewildered face his eyes grew heavy, and he slumped back onto the lounge into sleep.

The forest hummed around Ravaryn as his chest vibrated with an urgent pull towards something. Someone. *Zemira.* He could feel her. She felt close to him, and this sensation was stronger than the whole time they had been separated. Since he had been taken by Salvador from the Dark Rim. His pulse quickened and his stomach clenched. He had to see her.

Black wings materialised behind him as he raced through the dark forest, the vegetation humming with just enough glowing light for him to sense that dawn was nearing. At almost a run, he couldn't bear the pull that had now become a growing ache. An ache for his other half, his light, his warmth, his *flame.*

His onyx wings spread wide and pounded the cool air as Ravaryn leapt into the sky, the forest canopy flashing past and the clear, crisp night opening up all around him. The moon emitted a half smile, as if it were mocking him. The deadline Salvador had given him pulsed in the back of his mind but was easily pushed away when he focused on the pull in his chest. Zemira was close, she was all he wanted, all he could fathom in that moment. He just wanted to see her, to hold her. To breathe in her soft jasmine scent and feel her tight in his arms.

He turned around to survey the forest below, and a gentle glow tugged him forward. A soft green glow filtered out through the thickness below, and in the darkness Ravaryn spotted his light. He instantly descended towards the aura like a moth to a flame. His soul flame beckoned to him.

Landing hard, Ravaryn searched for Zemira and the glow that had called to him.

'Wings ... is that you?' Zee's voice was all warmth laced with disbelief.

Ravaryn's eyes travelled over her lithe form, and he raced forth, sweeping her up into a crushing hug.

'Is this real?' his heart raced as the words came out gruffly, his voice tight with emotion. He pulled back and cupped her face in his large hands.

Zee smiled and leaned forward to plant a demanding kiss on his full lips. Ravaryn's hands dropped from her face to hold her against him again, one hand around her waist now holding her firmly to him, the other sliding into her silky dark hair. Zee pulled back for a moment, and her eyes roamed all over him.

'You're okay,' she breathed, and her shoulders relaxed as she bit into her lower lip. 'I think we're in a dream,' she said. 'I've been here before. In this... "dream realm" before, with Gaia. It's real, but I think we're both actually asleep.'

'I'm so sorry.' Ravaryn's gaze darkened, his eyes lowering from hers.

'For what?' Zee asked, her tone high and sharp.

'For the pain you must have suffered, because... because we're, I mean...'

Zee reached for Ravaryn's rough chin, lifting his gaze to meet hers again. Making him see her, making him meet her halfway like he had done to her so many times before.

'I know...' she simply said, 'and don't be sorry for anything. None of this is your fault.' A small smile graced her features. 'I've missed you,' she added, her eyes sparkling mischievously as she pressed herself into his firm embrace just a tad more.

Ravaryn's heart swelled and heat flashed wildly thorough him as he squeezed her even tighter to him, not wanting her an inch away from him. A half-hitched smile reached his face, then he kissed her again. Rough and fast. His hands began roaming her body, caressing her.

Zee let a small, satisfied moan free as he made his way to her neck, the sound stirring a growl from deep within him as if in answer to her.

He steered Zee forward so her back came to rest against the sturdy trunk of a nearby tree, while she slid her hands further into his curly hair. Her grasp became tighter as she forced his head back upwards and to-wards her mouth. He felt her desire escalating, and he was relishing the quick breaths she now took in between the passionate kisses.

All of a sudden, the forest around them became brighter, noticeably so, even with their attention deeply focused on each other. Dawn was upon them all too quickly, although it wasn't enough to stop them. But as if it were a warning, Ravaryn sensed this moment was slipping away fast. This gift Gaia had bestowed upon him was nearly spent, and he pulled away from Zee. It took every last drop of control he possessed, as it was the last thing he wanted to do in that moment.

'I think we've run out of time.' His voice was a deep caress.

Zee groaned back in reply, side eyeing the light peeking through the forest behind him as she pouted theatrically. Her disgust at their time being cut short stirred a hearty laugh from within him, and pure happiness coursed through his veins laced with adrenaline and want at just holding her so close. Knowing she was okay, and having her if only for a moment with him, safe and sound.

He kissed her one more time, slower this time, deepening the kiss and exploring her soft lips and mouth more gently while committing every second to memory. When he opened his eyes this time, he once again saw the valley before him. He was awake and all alone on the lounge in the palace on the hill.

Trapped

Orion's scowl grew larger the closer Ravaryn got towards him, his face recoiling as though Ravaryn were some infected, contagious thing. *I guess I deserve that.* The former king came to stand before Orion and Aytac, and they both stopped talking as soon as he was within ear reach, their eyes burning into him like hot coals.

'I have something I need to discuss,' he said smoothly, some of his former charisma returning. 'With both of you.' Ravaryn held his head high and met their gaze with an air of authority. It wasn't the first time the watchers had shunned him, but he was used to this behaviour. Even before he had been banished from Lamiria, he was treated with hate and suspicion. Like his half-shift was something they could catch, as though he were truly some infectious thing. Little did they know he could fully shift all right, and the creature he became would have buried those snide doubts deep, deep down. But he had listened to his mother, possibly one of the only times he had, and hidden his true form.

'I have seen the Mother. Gaia.' The words were straightforward, and strong. He had no idea what reaction the two stoic men would give him. But he didn't care if they didn't believe. He needed their help. Orion's one brow raised ever so slightly, the hate in his gaze shifting to curiosity ever so slightly.

'Okay, all-seeing one,' Aytac mocked.

Orion shot him a slightly amused look.

'I'm serious. She was there when...' Ravaryn took a second and swept his hand through his thick ebony hair. 'When she healed me in the cells beneath Salvador's stronghold. How else do you think I came back from near death? You said yourself, Orion, that Zee's fever was sapping the life from her. I nearly died, and the Mother saved me. Now she has asked for *my* help.'

*

The mention of Zee's state swept any amusement lingering there from Orion's face. He had expected to see her well and healthy and *here* upon their return, but Diwa had filled him in that she had recovered soon after he had left to retrieve Ravaryn. But she and Sayde had gone on a mission to gather poisons from the undead lands to forge a weapon they could use against Salvador. And Thaylon. Orion's father. He was not impressed, but if Diwa had willed it then he knew that *she* knew they would make it back safely, so he had to let his anxiety wash away. And he needed to let his grip on her loosen, no matter how hard those things were for him to bear. He would also have to get word to Verena in the old Rim world, and soon.

'What does she need from us then?' There was no mocking in Orion's tone. If what Ravaryn said were true, he owed the Mother Zee's life. He had seen and learned so many wild things in his life that this was not that big of a stretch to fathom.

'Those creatures, the Arakanai at the stronghold, they were forged from people... humans from the old Rim territories.'

'We had our suspicions.' Orion's words were gruff, and his face all of a sudden dropped, his eyes focusing far away for a moment as a painful constriction in his chest bloomed at the thought of Verena alone in Kali. He needed to go to her. Bring her to the valley where she could be safe from the Arakanai, especially if they were stealing more and more humans to transform and grow their forces. Who knew how long it would take them to venture from Kymera into Aylentean villages? He shook away his growing anxiety, focusing on the king and what he was divulging.

'Paxton arrived here with your protégée just as I left to find you. Diwa said that they'd had a run-in with those creatures, and that they had captured the duellerat ... the one that Salvador flew after.'

Orion saw the silver leave Ravaryn's eyes, becoming black wells of despair, so he changed the direction of his words. 'The duellerat defended them. Paxton and Mazda got away, but the girl told Diwa that she had seen the humans in them, and had connected the dots as to the villagers going missing of late in Kymera bordering Lamiria.'

Ravaryn stilled, his composure returning. Orion and Aytac saw the pain that had entered into him disappear in a second.

'Is she unharmed?' his words were quiet.

'She seemed well, and the young lad Paxton who is with her, he will look after her.'

Orion saw Ravaryn digest this information, his relief at Mazda's well-being etching away at a small piece of the worry on his face for now.

'Gaia needs us to find a cure for the Arakanai. The humans' minds are trapped in the warped bodies forged with the spiders,' Ravaryn said.

Aytac seemingly coming around, joined in with his thoughts. 'We should capture one of them. Diwa has knowledge of healing, and so does Sahara. They will know where to start.'

'That's a good idea.'

Orion saw the relief slide over Ravaryn's face like water dripping down a smooth leaf. 'And how do you suppose we contain one of these things? And where would we take it? The last thing these people need after all that has happened to them is what future awaits them if Salvador wins.'

'We'll take it to the ice castle,' Ravaryn supplied.

'In Kymera?' Aytac said. 'That's too far.'

'No, it's not, and there are secure cells beneath the castle. There are also glasshouses there that contain every catalogued plant in Aylenta and Lamiria combined. Diwa has seen to it that they were all collected as soon as the Rim wall was broken and the curse on us both shattered. She told me of their importance. This must have been what she was preparing them for.' Ravaryn's lips curled to the side, realisation blooming without his consent onto his face. He chuckled. 'That fox, sometimes I swear she knows all.'

That look, and Ravaryn's reaction, tipped Orion's mind into Ravaryn's favour. He was telling the truth. Orion knew it because he had been there before, when Diwa's words, plans and all-knowing of upcoming events had all fallen neatly into place at the precise right time. The wonder he saw on the king's face had been his own reaction one too many times. *Crafty old fox indeed.*

'We will help you,' Orion relented.

Aytac just nodded, a grunt of agreement leaving his mouth. 'What plans do you have in mind?'

'First of all, thank you,' Ravaryn offered.

Orion snapped back. 'It's not for you. It's for the poor souls that are likely trapped in their own worst nightmares as we speak.'

'Very well...' Ravaryn continued. 'Here's what I think we need to do.' He took a seat next to the watchers on the stumps of round wood that surrounded the small circle where they sat. Aytac continued to sharpen the knife in his hands as he listened. Orion bristled, straightening his back ever so slightly as the king explained his plan to capture and deliver an Arakanai to Kymera.

Orion ignored the burning hate still there for the man. Right now, they had bigger things to deal with. His heart ached at the thought of Verena in danger. But if they were going to capture one of the Arakanai and transport the thing to Kymera, he could go to her in Aylenta as soon as the task was done. It was on the way, and Ravaryn made a good point. There would be no victory if the humans inside the Arakanai were lost, even if they put a stop to Salvador and Thaylon. A word with Diwa and a vision would help ease his fear. She would be able to give him a sense of Verena and whether she would be safe for a few more days in Kali. But he had to get to Aylenta and bring Verena to the safety of Tangaroa.

Forging the Light

The Undead City, Northwest of The Deadlands.

It took surprisingly little time for Zee to grasp the essence of the poison in the living wall's structure that held back and protected the earth from the undead within it. Sayde let a little gasp free as a wisp of red liquid seeped from the fence. It floated in the air before Zee's hand, which was held out before her, clutching the orb. The viscous liquid was a deep blood red, and Sayde imagined if she were to touch it, it would coat her fingers like honey.

She watched as Zee sat cross-legged, back rigid and still as stone. Her eyes were shut as she coaxed the poison into the orb. The liquid within swirled from a light grey to a deep blood red mixed with a hint of purple – like a rich wine. Zee's hand dropped a little in the air as though the weight was now heavier within the orb. The wall creaked and groaned before them, making Sayde step back just a fraction with its warning, but that was it. It was done, so Zee opened her eyes and let loose a huge breath it seemed she had been holding.

Sayde approached her cautiously, 'Are you done? Is that it?' She searched Zee's spacey eyes.

'That's it.' The forest queen blinked a little as though she'd just returned from somewhere far away, and her tone became normal again. Looking into Sayde's deep mahogany eyes, a small smile played on her lips as she said, 'Why? Did I make it look easy?'

Sayde smiled back. 'Yeah, kind of. Show off.' She pushed Zee's shoulder playfully as she had returned the now deep-red orb to her pack, and stood beside her companion.

'You want the good news or the bad news?' Zee offered.

'Come on, out with both,' Sayde countered.

'Well, the good news is I know how we can get in.'

'What's the bad news then?'

Zee's shoulders dropped. 'It's not bad news for you, just for me. We'll have to enter the city under the ground, far beneath the wall. It's too dangerous to try and make our way through it or over it. I could try to manipulate the coral that makes up the wall like I can with other plants and elements, but it's got a strange composition. I don't know what might happen as it may have defences. It's almost like it's got a consciousness, like I had to ask permission to take a piece of it. I think the safest way is to move the earth underneath it and create a tunnel and enter through that way. *Far away* from the wall, its poison and its root systems.'

'Sounds fine to me,' Sayde agreed without argument, and she practically heard Zee's bones groan as she thought about being underground again.

*

The tunnel Zemira had created went deep into the dark earth under the city wall. She started 500 metres or so back to avoid any of the poisoned roots or spores that may reside in the ground there. Zee's chest constricted like wire was bound around her as she and Sayde made their way through the dark passage, just a flicker of a flame in her hands to light the way. As they entered the city from under the ground, her heart only stopped racing once daylight was again upon her face from the clouded skies above.

With her hands, Zee sealed the tunnel's entrance temporarily and left a patch of sunflowers standing high and tall to mark the spot for when they were ready to leave this desolate place. That in itself could only be all too soon for her. She looked around at the ruins of the city that once held greatness and had buzzed with life, and a heaviness like lead sank in her stomach.

'How did they fall so far...?' her words were echoes in the streets splayed out before her.

In the shadows, towering, crumbling buildings were everywhere. No plants clung to their sides unlike some of the old relics in Thorta Zee had seen during her escape with Paxton from Greymouth's lab. No animals were present, not even the flutter of a bird's wings in the air, nor the hum of a cricket or the call of anything else.

'Let's get this done,' Sayde said, tone harsh. 'This place is like a giant monument to death himself.'

'Agreed.' Zee's skin felt tight and she resisted the urge to scratch it. 'We need to find the virus, and the plastic. Diwa explained that there is a building with a symbol of two red lines crossed over each other, one vertical one horizontal. Like a hospital or a lab.' She shook the shiver away from her mind at the memory of Dr Greymouth's facility and its energy in Thorta: the crisp sterile walls, the shine of the luminescent lights reflecting from the floor of the shiny hallways and the disinfectant tang that clung to the walls. The tubes of poisons that they had pumped into her body with fine needles, and the weeks she had spent there, Greymouth's beady eyes boring into her mind and making her temples ache.

'Once we find the building, there should be vials and things inside containing the viruses. As for the plastic, Diwa said it would be literally everywhere, but I have no idea what it looks like or should feel like.'

'Seeing as you're the one who can sense it, I'll follow your lead and watch your back. This place doesn't feel right... and I'm not sure why we haven't seen any of the undead that are supposed to be here yet.'

Zee tried to ignore the pain pulsing at her temple as the pair walked through the silent city filled with debris. Old transport vehicles and human skeletons that had perished here long ago flashed before' Zee's mind, like flickers of the past.

'There.' Sayde pointed, causing Zee's eyes to track to a wide building larger than those around them, topped with a red cross, similar to the one Diwa had explained. A hospital.

'Right, so far so good then.' Relief flooded her words as the tension eased just a tad from Zee's tight chest.

They entered the hospital through shattered doors that were once made of glass. Dirt and mildew coated the walls, and relics were strewn all over the first floor of the building that they scoured. Dark patches emitted a metallic scent in the air that pricked at Zee's overly stimulated senses. *Blood.* Rooms with beds and flat boxes hung on the walls. She recognised them as old vision screens. Chairs sat empty along with stands that held tubes and sacks of liquids on hooks, crusted with grime.

After two stairwells, they reached a third level, where rooms with giant machines, built like the arms of large monsters, hung from the ceilings with round mirror-like panels and handles along their edges. Zee sensed the energy, and it had but one difference from Thorta: There was something here that Zee had felt nowhere else but in one place before. The relic she had found in Sahara's den appeared in her mind's eye. The small, flat black rectangle that she had held in her hand, the one that had a fruit depicted in elegant silver on the back of it.

Sahara had had a fit when she had seen it in Zee's hands, and explained that it had poisoned the ancients' minds. Yes, that energy coming from the strange mix of materials within it – there lay the plastic. Now she had made the connection, Zee felt the strange sizzle of the material all around her, and it did in fact lie *everywhere.* She touched the ancients' machines and swept the layers of grime from the object that hung from the ceiling over a bed centred in the room. Like a cocoon, the plastic wrapped itself around something metal within it. Zee felt the outer layer, the plastic, and saw that almost everything in this room contained some of the strange, strong material Diwa had explained to her.

'It's here,' Zee whispered to Sayde, who stood on edge behind her.

'What's here? You've found the virus?'

'No, the plastic,' Zee corrected. 'It's in everything,' she said, before closing her eyes.

Flashes of the old world flickered to life in her mind's eye. Ingenious containers made from the substance, thin translucent film for their food, water skins made of the stuff, toys for children, little bells for babies to suck on, vessels for their plants to grow in. Everything about their lives contained the plastic, then Zee saw it sparkle like diamonds on a microscopic level. She concentrated harder on the image, the new power of the forest queen filling her with awe as it sought the information from the past.

Zee realised that the sparkles were in fact the indestructible plastic. Its tiny shards had cut their way through the humans' bodies, via their stomachs, through food that had picked it up from the soil. It was also in their blood cells, careening through their veins and lodging into the sides of the cell walls there. Into their hearts it forced its way, digging into the lining of their bowels, causing sickness, pain and death from within, just like a virus would, she realised. It had poisoned them; they had overindulged in the greatness of their creation, yet it had in fact started to poison them from within. That's why it was second on the list of poisons Diwa had instructed her to gather.

Zee pulled away from the images in her mind. Opening her eyes, she whipped her hand just as fast from the machine coated in plastic before her, *poison...* and didn't relay what she had just seen to Sayde, keeping the horror to herself. Instead, as quickly as she could, she withdrew the orb from her pack, wasting no time. She wanted to be out of this place as fast as she could.

'I'm going to scour the rest of this floor while you do—,' Sayde eyed Zee up and down and motioned her hand before her '—whatever it is you do. I'll be back in a few minutes.'

Zee nodded her reply and concentrated on the material, forging it into the orb as quickly as she could, careful for none of the tiny melted droplets to come anywhere near her. The orb accepted the mist of plastic, the contents getting heavier again just slightly this time and the swirls thicker and slower, changing to a sluggish green colour – the kind you'd find in the algae of a thick stagnant waterway devoid of life.

*

Sayde strode among the items strewn along the filthy floor of the creepy building, not needing a weapon to wield as there was nothing here: no sound, no sign of life, no trace of the undead creatures she and Zemira had been warned about. She felt almost annoyed at the lack of action that they encountered. Her mind craved distraction, lest her sadness creep back in with its claws sufficiently sharpened once again.

There were just relics of the old ones – junk, ruins and creepy poisons that had destroyed their once-great civilisation – but that wasn't enough to keep her demons at bay. It was then that Sayde heard it, a rustling to the far end of the corridor. She left the room she was in and, feet light as feathers, she crept to investigate the sound. Ears alert, her eyes constricted into slit irises, fingernails protruding into claws as Sayde peered around the doorframe of the room the sound came from. A hiss burst from her lips as the creature she'd startled leapt at her. A whimper and high-pitched scream like that of a hurt child filled the air as the skeletal thing leapt not at her, but past her and into the hall like a flash of lighting.

Sayde raced after the thing, barely keeping up as it headed along the stretch of hallway in the building towards where Sayde had left Zee. *Shit.*

*

Crouching on the floor, Zee spun around after placing the orb back inside her pack, just before a mass of spindly long legs, a tail and a fine long-boned snout careened into her. Another sharp shriek emitted from the creature, but it now curled into a ball, somehow bending its long legs into her lap, shaking bones and scraps of flesh trying to hide there. Two large smoky-white eyes looked up at her with sadness and fear, the edges of them the opposite from hers: black where the whites should be and vice versa.

Sayde slid into the room, catching herself on the doorframe, and calling out for Zee. She froze within a second upon seeing the creature curled up in a wobbling mess in Zee's lap. Zee's hands were held out in the air above the skeletal creature, then instinctively caressed its sleek little head with those large eyes looming up at her in fear.

Zee's heart melted, and instantly she felt a bloom of warmth and emotion flood her. It felt like she had been injected with sunlight as it moved through her, and memories of Wolf cradling her soul with love from her childhood sparked as she patted the hound's head, for intuitively she knew it was a hound, and its terrified shaking ceased a little.

Sayde's mouth fell open. 'What happened to not touching any of the things here!' Sayde protested.

'I can sense it,' Zee reassured. 'It's afraid, but it's not dangerous to us, I promise. It's ...' Zee trailed off as she looked down at the skeletal animal draped with chunks of long-ago rotted flesh-like strips of leathered old skin and fur. Pity and instant love filled her eyes. 'I think it was once a dog.'

'A dog?' Sayde grunted, not convinced.

'It's a creature the ancients sort of created,' Zee struggled to explain. 'I learned about them at school. They descended from wolves. And after centuries of living alongside the humans, the wolves became something different. It must be affected somehow by the radiation from the blast that ended the ancients. Strange magic is intertwined in this place. I can feel its energy, like its life has been preserved for so long. The radiation has somehow kept it alive, in a way... along with Gaia's magic. It must be why the undead are still here after all this time.'

Sayde scoffed now. 'You're saying that wisp of a thing is related to Aytac's shifter form!' Sayde howled. 'Oh, this is too good.'

Zee felt the prickle of humour invade her too at the thought of Orion's huge, powerful shifter form that was Wolf being related to this cowering skinny creature in her lap. 'Aww, it's okay, little pup,' Zee cooed as she patted it. 'You're not a monster, are you? No, you're a little angel, all forgotten about and scared.' She turned to Sayde. 'The poison here mustn't have affected this animal the same as it did the humans, as it seems harmless. I can feel it's got a pure energy within somehow.'

Sayde's eyebrows hit her forehead, and Zee noted her expression. 'I'm keeping it,' she said.

'What! That thing smells like death on a stick! And you can't keep it! It's probably poisonous, like everything else in this hellhole!' Sayde argued, her voice high with exasperation.

'It's not, I can tell. It's somehow not affected, I swear on my life. It's got goodness inside it.'

'It's got nothing inside of it! Zee you can see right through it! It's a walking skeleton!'

Zee looked down again, closer, past the sweet yet eerie light-blue smoky bulbous eyes of the dog in her lap to the patches of rotten fur clinging to the indeed skeletal frame of its more-than-half-missing body.

'I can fix it.'

'And the smell?' Sayde's nose crinkled intensely into the middle of her face, baring her top teeth.

Zee chuckled. 'Okay, and the smell!' She pushed the dog gently from her lap and moved from sitting to a crouch before it, holding its shut jaw before her face. It truly looked terrifying, but if Zee couldn't have felt its energy exuding from its core like the smell of Diwa's heart-warming cinnamon cakes from her cottage in Kali, she never would have seen the sweetness that lay within.

'I'll fix you, you darling little thing,' she cooed again, as if to a baby. 'Don't listen to nasty Sayde, she's just judging your terrifying outside, not your beautiful soul.' Zee felt Sayde roll her eyes from the doorway. The dog stopped shaking, and the long bones of its tail flicked back and forth in the air like a fish gliding through water. Zee didn't know why, but the movement made her smile even more.

She placed her hands on the bones that protruded from where she felt the dog's front legs should have been, and a light-green and yellow light glowed from her palms. The dog didn't balk, it just stood in front of Zee and produced a leathery strip of foul-smelling skin that she guessed must have once been a tongue and licked Zee's face with it. It was dry like sandpaper, or more like jerky.

Sayde gagged loudly, her audible disgust shared by Zee this time. 'Oh gods.' Zee tried not to gag herself. 'I'll fix that too.' And with that, tiny tendrils spread forth from her hands, weaving in out of the bones as they formed bulges where muscles should be. Muscles and tendons knitted together within the skeletal dog's frame, and thicker vines followed. Bit by bit a thin, muscular body was built around the dog's hollow core, then a puff of deep bright moss sprang from the top layer of foliage and sprouted all over the now solid-looking dog like a smooth coat. A smooth layer of fur, and ears that resembled silver- veined alocasia leaves replaced the scraps of dead skin that had been the dog's previous ears. And a few little grass sprigs sprouted out, making fine whiskers on the thin snout that protruded from the now much sweeter-looking face.

For the scrap of foul material that was the dog's tongue, Zee crafted it anew from a water lily-like leaf, which she guessed would match a real dog's tongue or at least was close as this one was going to get. She loved that she had mastered crafting with just plants, and lastly she showered a few delicate yellow dandelion flowers from the dog's head down its bony spine, making the creature's outside match the beautiful energy that seeped from within it.

'Wow.' Sayde breathed, leaning against the door with her arms crossed. 'I guess that's better.'

Zee held her hand up above the dog's newly adorned head, and tiny seeds sprinkled from her magic, flittering down onto the dog and bursting into tiny jasmine blooms. They filled the air with their sweet scent and crept around her coat to replace the sharp tang of rot that had seeped from it moments ago.

Sayde smirked. 'For someone who doesn't know what they're doing, that's pretty bloody creative,' she praised Zee's work.

'I just matched her outside with what was still clinging to her inside.'

'She?' Sayde asked, refraining from rolling her eyes.

'Yes, she's a she. I think we'll call her Moss. What do you think?'

Sayde actually rolled her eyes now. 'You're not actually keeping that thing, are you?'

'Her name is Moss,' Zemira corrected.

'Oh gods,' Sayde replied. 'Let's get the hell out of here before we both start losing our minds.'

Zee laughed and cuddled Moss one last time before she got up and followed Sayde from the murky room of old relics, the orb secured in her pack and a happy Moss-dog trotting closely by her side, her head bumping up into Zee's hands for more pats.

'Oh darling, you've been alone a long time, haven't you.' Zee's eyes looked down as she comforted her newest companion.

Then she ran straight into an outstretched arm that stopped her in her tracks. The trio were at the edge of the building's third floor in front of a dirty window and about to descend the stairs. The sun was rapidly descending through the thick cloud cover and there, on the streets below, figures *moved*. In fact, hundreds of slow-moving forms now lined the streets. Moss growled, and her dandelions rose along her back in place of where hackles had once been.

'Looks like we're not alone after all.' Sayde swallowed as Zee's stomach dropped, taking in the hordes of walking dead on the streets below them, blocking any way out of the city without a fight.

Snowflake Queen

Zenya, Kymera

Mazda stared out at the sparkling ice-crusted city from her room, which she had spent nearly a lifetime in. The heavy weight on her shoulders made them feel like they could collapse in on her if she even took a second to think about all the things that she feared, the things that were eating away at her piece by piece. Her thumb stung as she twisted the silver ring there, the skin blistered and worn away underneath. The sharp pang of pain tore her away from her worry about Blaze and her coronation for the moment.

Ilga had helped her dress, and had tamed her wild locks into some form of submission. Mazda wore the light-blue gown she had crafted herself long ago for the occasion. The fit was simple but elegant, and small gems that resembled sky-pine blooms glittered from the waist, flowing out in a sheer fabric of white and even paler blue. It looked like an evening sky littered with the first stars of an oncoming night. Mazda truly looked like a ruler of the ice territory, but she just wished Ravaryn were here with her to pass on the title. If it had been under any other circumstances than the world on the verge of war, she would have at least been able to smile for real.

A knock sounded on her door, and Mazda dropped her hands and her stinging thumb, expecting Ilga back. The door opened and there stood Paxton. He had been dressed in a fine soldier's outfit, and Mazda's eye went wide, like cornflowers blooming in spring, as she took in the young man before her.

Paxton's chestnut hair was neatly tied back with a leather band of the same black as his outfit. The snake and wings gold seal of Ravaryn's reign was gone, and instead a silver snowflake tipped with arrows adorned the shoulders. The symbol of Kymera, the one she had chosen to represent her as well, for she herself wanted Kymera to be her top priority. The people here were her number one concern, and she wanted them to know that from the start of her reign.

His smile was huge, and his cheeks coloured as he looked Mazda up and down in her silken blue gown. He entered the room with a glass box in one hand, leaving the door open.

'You scrub up well,' Mazda confided, not even trying to hide the impressed look on her face from him.

He rubbed his free hand over the back of his neck and tilted his head as he said, 'Barrack thought that if I were to be escorting you, I had to look the part. He said if I want, I can join your royal guard, and he's offered to train me himself. If that's, ah – you know, if you wish for me to stay. You look... by the way... I mean, your dress...' His face absolutely blazed as he dropped his hand and stumbled further over the words trying to fall out of his mouth. He stopped himself, then took a second. 'I think blue is my new favourite colour.'

Mazda's freckled cheeks rose high, making her eyes crinkle at the sides as she laughed. Paxton also laughed at the sound, releasing the tension that built up so fiercely when he was around her now. She was like a crisp summer storm in the heat of the wet season back home in Aylenta.

He presented the box he had commandeered from Ilga on his way to Mazda's room. She had said that he was welcome to bring it up to Mazda.

The old chef didn't say much, but the wicked wink she had given him had sparkled through her kind face. 'This – it's for you, from Ilga.'

'Oh Paxton Raker, lucky you're as handsome as you are because you do not have a smooth way with words.' Mazda took the glass box from Paxton's hands, her own petite ones sliding over his before she retrieved it, the wicked grin still plastered on her face from Paxton's earlier attempt at flattery.

Placing it down on the dresser beside her, she opened the delicate silver-rimmed lid, reaching for the crown within. Glass had been blown into twisted ornate swirls, and splashes of gems laced the edges in whites, silvers and deep midnight blue. At the peaks, tiny light blue crystals adorned the small stems, like miniature sky-pine trees in full bloom.

Mazda lifted the crown gently, a feeling of pride and panic all in one swirling within her. She turned to Paxton and presented it to him, his back straightening.

'Will you do me the honour?'

'I ah... I don't think that I should be the one to—'

'Please.' Mazda nearly rolled her eyes. Paxton's change of behaviour since he found out that she was to be queen was flattering, but starting to dig at her. She would have to nip it in the bud before he was set in his ways of treating her like some delicate ornament, which was most definitely not what Mazda had decided she wanted.

Paxton nodded as that all-too-big smile reached his face again, and he carefully took the crown from her. He was a good foot taller than her, especially with her wild locks tamed for the moment in beautiful pinned sweeps behind her, trailing down her back in thick crimson waves. Pax gently placed the crown atop Mazda's head and stood back looking down at her, his smile dropping and his eyes misting over.

'Mazda, you look...' He found his words this time were actually formed with ease. 'Stunning.'

Mazda looked up through her thick lashes as she felt her cheeks flush.

'Are you ready?' Pax asked, his voice deep and his mind entirely elsewhere.

She grabbed at the front of his shirt between the thin plates of finely woven armour and fisted the fabric there, pulling him down towards her. Mazda stopped as his face was just centimetres from hers, and had to tippy-toe to reach up to him. Looking deeply into his russet eyes that swam with want, as though searching for something she needed answers to, she then shut her own sapphire eyes, pulling him into the kiss she had wanted for a long while now.

*

Paxton's hands found her thin waist and slid gently but firmly to encapsulate her. He kissed her like she were the cure to an ailment he had been searching for his entire life. His chest filled with light, and warmth flooded his veins. Her mouth was warm and enticing, soft on his. She pulled away, and he instantly felt the cold. Her breath was uneven, and an alluring smile, one that he had yet to witness from her, made her eyes gleam into his, making him feel he was the luckiest man in the entire city at that moment.

'Now I'm ready.'

Her small hand found its way into his, and Paxton squeezed it tightly as she led him from the room, his head light. He realised that he would let her lead him anywhere in that moment. She'd already made him leap from the rooftops on a wild beast, stab another one that had attacked them in a forgotten land to save her, and now he would stand at her side in a territory that he thought he would never set foot in again. A territory that he had hated to his core. Yet all of it, every last second he had spent with her, had felt comfortable, had felt right. It felt like he had finally found his place in the turbulent world around him, and with Mazda, he thought, he hoped, he prayed to the Mother, that maybe he might even have just found someone who understood what it was like to have to find it all on their own.

Moss Dog

Zee, Sayde and Moss, the newly crafted foliage-clad dog, froze before the grimy window, taking in the mass of gathering undead below them on the streets of the ancient city crumbling around them.

'I think we found them,' Zee said, the nervous waver of her tone not disguised one bit.

Sayde just watched, her eyes slitting to form her animal shift, and her mind calculating. 'They look as though they can barely move! They're staggering all around, even into one another. We'll have to sneak down to the streets then make a run for it. Zee, you'll need to create a path with your flames, and I'll watch your back in case any get close.'

Zee swallowed. 'We still have to find a vial or something that contains a virus in here to add to the orb.'

Sayde swore under her breath. 'You're right. We'll search the levels, but I don't think the undead come in this building that's why the ... "dog" must have been hiding in here. We'll split up, search for anything

that might contain a virus and meet back here when were done. Alright?'
Sayde turned to Zee before heading off.

'Alright.' Zee nodded as she tore her eyes away from the horror show gathering below. 'Come on Moss-dog, let's go.'

Moss stayed at Zee's side like glue, her tail flicking back and forth while they searched the upper three floors. After a long time of searching for anything that might contain some invisible liquid poison, which may have been the virus, she came up with nothing. Diwa had explained clearly what it was, but whatever it was, she couldn't feel anything in this entire building that had the energy signature she was searching for. Sayde met them back at the grimy window and had also come up empty handed. Their time was up. Two poisons would have to do, that is, if they even made it out of the city alive...

*

All seemed too quiet until Sayde, Zee and Moss reached the ground floor. None of the undead were inside the building, which Zee inwardly thanked the gods for. She didn't know why but the thought of long-dead humans that could kill you with one bite was far more terrifying and distressing than any other creature she'd encountered both in the forests of Lamiria and the old Rim world so far. The fact that somehow the ancients had caused this... had done this to themselves made Zee's insides slide around like a snake in thick water, making her nauseas. *Not good. Keep it together, Zee. Now's not the time to feel sick. It's the time to fight.*

She clenched her fists at her sides as they heated with warmth there, stilling her mind before they made a run for the tunnel entrance. *They're not people anymore... they're monsters of their own making.*

Sayde's flat, authoritative tone cut crisply through Zee's thoughts as they watched from the base of the stairwell out to the gathering crowd on the street. 'You've got this, forest queen. I saw what you did in the village to the black dragon, Zee. Just do the same thing now and make a path to get us out of here. I'll have your back the entire time, but you blast them away from the front, and I'll keep them at bay from behind, okay?'

Zee nodded, her face serious, eyebrows knit together in concentration.

Sayde added, 'Dog, you want to come with us? You keep close.'

Moss just twisted her sweet head to the side as Sayde actually addressed it for the first time.

'Moss will be fine, Sayde. She's already dead.'

'Good point.' Sayde smirked. 'You ready?

'Ready as I'll ever be. Let's get the hell out of here.'

'After you, flame queen.'

Zee rolled her eyes, but smirked at the name all the same. This would be fine, these undead moved like they were knee deep in thick molasses and probably wouldn't even get close to the pair. They'd be out of this place before the sun disappeared into the night. Zee took one look at Moss beside her leg, and the dog whined as it eyed the undead humans.

'Come on, Moss.' She set off in a run for the shattered opening that was once the large glass doors to the entrance of the hospital. Zee reached the street with Sayde behind her, but a deep, rumbling growl gently caressed her back and vibrated powerfully through her spine. Zee turned around to take in Sayde in her shifter form: a huge panther-like creature standing high on all fours, feathers on thin strips furrowing out from spots on her spine. Large, glowing eyes narrowed back at her, and Sayde's teeth bared as she growled again, nudging Zee with her enormous purple-black head, her coat rippling as she did.

Zee's initial surprise was overtaken by the screeches that sounded all around them. In a wave of agonising, terrifying noise, the undead had spotted them, the screeches flowing as if they were communicating to one another. Suddenly, the cacophony ceased and the crowd surged towards them, bodies staggering forward in rapid succession. Rotten teeth were bared into vicious snarls and skeletal fingers clawed the air. Zee took off. She sprinted along the edge of the building and away from the oncoming mass of rotten bodies as fast as her legs would carry her, Moss racing beside her. She hugged the edge of the buildings, avoiding the rusted obstacles and leaping over them with grace.

Hands raised before her, she conjured the air around them to disperse their green fire as she blasted her neon-green flames forward as powerfully as she could, sweeping the undead from their path. Sayde snarled and swiped at the bodies that lunged at them from behind. Her huge paws swept the bodies away like flies, crushing them individually, most with just one blow of her powerful feline forearms. The horde before Zee gouged and swiped at her through the flames, but as they came close, they were blasted away before they reached her skin. Within her flames, the undead began to catch alight, the screeching and sound of crackling numbing Zee's mind to all the chaos around her. And still she ran.

Before her, the crowd seemed to thin, so she took a quick second to look back and saw Sayde falling back from her as the fray were now mostly behind them. Zee was too far ahead of Sayde, and there were too many of the corpses, which seemed to be engulfing her like jungle ants to a kill.

Zee's heart thumped in her chest as if to the beat of a raspors wing's. She turned, all around her she spun her flames, wind whipping her hair and concentration pounding in her skull. She was creating a circle around herself.

'Sayde!' she screamed over the noise.

From behind, a monstrous corpse lunged at Sayde's panther form. Its dark, empty eye sockets were pinned on her friend, sharp teeth bared. Most of them were missing, but the gaps made them all the more dangerous if they were to make contact. They would easily tear skin. Zee wasn't going to make it to her friend in time, and everything slowed down around her.

Sayde tried to twist her powerful feline body towards the dead human, but it had leapt and was going straight for her throat mid-air. Zee's heart stopped in her chest, she couldn't suck in any air, and it felt like she was drowning within the circle of flames that protected her. Sayde wasn't going to make it.

In that instant, a flash of elegant green flew through the air, and the elongated body of the streamlined hound connected with the undead form that was about to rip into Sayde's throat. It was knocked away from her as Moss collided with the creature, a violent crunch sounding as its skeletal structure crushed into the others around it. Sayde's feline eyes went wide, and within a moment she swiped the remaining dead from her path. Then she shifted into her lithe-framed woman form that Zee was accustomed to and sprinted into Zee's circle of fire forcefield as they fled the thinning hordes of undead. Tears ran from Zee's eyes as she heard the wails Moss emitted behind them as the dog was overrun with the undead, but Zee didn't, couldn't, look back.

Side by side Sayde and Zee pounded the pavement, their boots in rhythm, both covered in the splatters of vile liquid that had burst from the dead upon attacking their rotting forms. There before them, a patch of decaying and wilted sunflowers marked the entrance to the hidden tunnel, the way out. Zee slid to the earth and dug her hands into it, the ground shifting and the garden marker of dead plants falling to one side.

'In!' she yelled at Sayde, sweat covering her face. She took one last look back at the city and the undead racing towards them and slid down into the tunnel, descending into darkness. Her hands pressed against the earth behind them as they went down into the tunnel, sealing them in, away from the monsters and their city of poison. Zee forced back the pain constricting her throat and burning her eyes at the thought of poor Moss. She had truly been good, whatever she was, and she saved Sayde from a lethal bite, sacrificing herself to the undead.

Zee's ragged breath filled the quiet space around her now, and she conjured a small flame, her hand shaking as she held it out before her, nerves rattling through her body. Sayde reached a hand towards her and clasped her shoulder, helping her up from the dark floor of the tunnel. The two made their way through the almost darkness, where the only sound was catching their breaths. Their hearts pounded in their chests at the horror they'd narrowly just escaped, Moss's howl of pain and fear stilling ringing in Zee's mind.

Arakanai

Kymera

The Kymerian forest was humming with noise. Cicadas sang in the temperate dusk air, and leaves ruffled gently as the ancient rainforest giants creaked in the wind. In their wolf forms, Orion and Aytac watched on, their acute hearing at an advantage. Their gazes were fixed on the centre of the clearing they had created with Ravaryn. This was the trap that lay in wait for an Arakanai to hopefully approach during the night in search of more victims to add to Salvador's army.

Ravaryn could only just make out the two sets of eyes between the thick vegetation, one a brilliant yellow to the right of him and one an emerald green, blending in and barely noticeable just to his left across the clearing. They waited for hours until the song of night morphed and changed with the passing of time as the moon winked in the sky above the leafy canopy. In the centre of the clearing, on a net covered with leaf litter and vines, was a fiddle deer carcass that the pair had hunted and laid in the trap, its life blood seeping from its inert body. This created the scent of a kill that could be smelled by a predator for kilometres away.

He tried not to let his mind wander, but Ravaryn couldn't help the tug of thoughts that led to Zemira. When would she return? Would she even still want him? Would being the new forest queen have changed her? His heart ached to see her again, and his body yearned to touch her. To lose himself in her emerald eyes, even if only for an instant. He couldn't go out in search of her after Gaia had begged for his help, and Diwa had assured him that she was in no danger. Going to her would only cause her to suspect that he thought she was incapable of looking after herself. And she was with Sayde, Aytac's twin shifter, a formidable watcher – as Ravaryn had learned.

Zee was fine, and he knew it. He knew that *he* was the one who needed her, needed to see her, to hold her. He wanted her scent of jasmine and rainforest to intoxicate his senses, to force away any worry in him that she had changed since becoming the forest queen.

He blinked, his eyes growing tired. Maybe this was a bad idea. Maybe the Arakanai wouldn't take this forest path through to Kymera? The trio had made sure they tracked their scents along this trail, and Orion had been adamant they had been here recently. Ravaryn couldn't deny the smells that matched the stronghold and the creatures in his memory. The watchers had worked with him with no objections, just adding their knowledge of tracking and offering to secure the bait. They both probably needed the hunt to burn off some steam and pent-up energy. Ravaryn had certainly felt Orion's burning hate towards him dissipate, if only just a little. He shifted his feet, and a muscle in his leg protested at being stationary for so long. Watchers were well trained in the art of patience, so he stretched the muscle and regained his stance.

The moon was reaching the centre of the sky, so maybe this wouldn't work? Maybe they would have to venture closer to Salvador's stronghold, something Ravaryn definitely didn't want to risk without a force behind him. That place made his stomach clench with rage and disgust. And just a touch of fear.

Salvador was ruthless, an abomination. A simple life wouldn't stand in his way, not even the blood of his own kin. The blood of his blood would mean nothing to him if it stood between him and what he desired. And what he desired was this entire realm at his feet. Whether he had to burn it to the ground or not, Ravaryn knew he would take it either way. All his father craved was power, and to rule.

A faint noise sounded in the distance, along with the crunch of leaves and bark. Ravaryn saw the yellow and green eyes at the far side of the crossing narrow, pupils focusing, and he knew they had heard it with their heightened wolf hearing too. Ravaryn had his wings and his other shifter senses out too. The faint *click, click, click* grew closer, and scattering legs could be heard coming in contact with the soft earth, along with a gentle crackling as they grew nearer, crushing leaves underfoot. They weren't the stealthiest of creatures, but considering how vicious they were and what weapons they wielded on their bodies, he guessed they didn't really have to be. The question was whether they could be successfully contained without their master's command or not. He guessed the three of them were about to find out.

Ravaryn's hand felt for the vial of bundlebay root extract in the pocket of his pant leg that Diwa had given him to sedate the Arakanai. He watched as one of the monstrous things emerged from forest into the clearing, its head twitching from side to side as its multiple eyes darted around to scan the area. That eerie *click, click, click* slid from its open mouth, revealing its hooked rows of teeth. All three watched as it approached the bait in the centre of the trap, thankfully none of its legs catching on the rope net below, hidden with earth and leaf litter.

Come on, come on, you mutated bastard. Take the bait. Ravaryn's eyes watched unblinking, and he felt the roar of success pump into his heart while the Arakanai prodded the carcass with its two front spider legs as it bent its head. Its jagged jaw hinged grotesquely, widening as it took a sickening chunk from the deer's hide, blood spilling from its mouth as it chewed and swallowed.

It was time. Ravaryn was just about to signal Orion and Aytac when the mutant threw its head back and let out a jarring screech that caused the air to vibrate. Orion and Aytac leapt forward in wolf form into the clearing and shifted in seconds as they landed in unison. Ravaryn followed suit, but just as they reached their corners of the net, two more Arakanai broke into the clearing.

The one in the trap raced straight for Ravaryn, reaching him in a flash before Orion and Aytac could even get to their spots. Its multiple eyes narrowed with murderous intent, and it charged towards him. Orion and Aytac were supposed to rush over to pin its legs down as Ravaryn poured the bundlebay into its snapping mouth to knock it out cold, but as the other two creatures approached rapidly towards them, Ravaryn knew he was on his own. The other watchers had their hands full in combat with the jittery soldiers, gold shining from their eyes as Salvador's intent commanded their movements – just as they creatures of the damned had worn the silver sheen of Kyeitha's control and power.

Ravaryn heard the slide of metal being unsheathed as Orion and Aytac wielded their weapons, slicing and dodging the sharp barbed legs and snapping maws of the Arakanai they faced. Ravaryn had no such luxury, he couldn't fatally harm the Arakanai snapping at him, as they needed to capture it relatively unharmed. His foot caught in the net as he dodged another swipe of the creature's razor-sharp front arms, and he tripped backwards. The Arakanai took its chance and stabbed at the earth, one of its blows pinning then tearing through the delicate skin of his wings. Ravaryn grunted out in pain and shifted them away, anger raging in him as the head snapped forth. Foul saliva dripped onto his face as his strong hands forced the teeth away from connecting with him.

Orion slashed like a warrior deep in the dance of the fight, carving the creature up and avoiding its advancing attack with ease, until he heard Ravaryn's sharp grunt of pain. He turned to see the king pinned underneath the Arakanai, which was snapping close to his face. Orion didn't hesitate; he turned back around and dived for the beast before him, rolling as he hit the ground, one of the sharp edges of the Arakanai's legs slicing into him like a sharp trowel through soft earth. He righted himself with teeth clenched against the sharp prick of pain flaring at his side, and forced his knife upwards with all his might straight into the creature's belly. It reared up and screeched violently in a cry of agony, then teetered awkwardly, and before it even hit the ground Orion was on his feet, legs carrying him as fast as they could to Ravaryn. He knew there was a human trapped inside, but this was life or death battle.

Ravaryn had gritted his teeth, as his eyes released the powers he barely ever wielded. Engulfed in utter darkness, smoke poured from his hands and slithered like snakes around the Arakanai's throat. The smoke coiled around its neck, holding it back from his face. He felt strong arms grab his shoulders, but no sharpness or tearing of his flesh followed as Orion's muscled grip tore him from underneath the creature being held at bay by his smoke and shadows.

Orion whipped him around, and in a panicked flash his eyes swept over him for injuries. Ravaryn couldn't hide his look of confusion, and Orion's face turned into a scowl as Ravaryn realised what had been written there: concern. In unison, the pair dodged the scattering feet of the choking Arakanai, Orion pushing Ravaryn out of the way of one of its legs, saving him from being impaled in the ground with the spiked leg. Ravaryn retrieved the bottle of Bundlebay root from his leg pocket and threw it to Orion.

'Orion!' he yelled.

Orion saw the deep blue liquid glint in a strip of moonlight as it flew towards him. He caught it in one hand as Ravaryn leapt into the air and landed on the creature's back. He withdrew the smoky shadows from around its neck that were suffocating it and fed them instead like reins through its mouth. This pulled wide its upper jaw, and at the same time he wove his black smoke around each side of the legs, binding them together and holding the thing back from fleeing.

His black irises met Orion's. 'Now, Orion!' he commanded.

Orion ripped the corked top from the bottle and threw the whole thing straight into the Arakanai's mouth, barely missing the teeth, and connecting with the back of its throat. Ravaryn, without missing a beat, wound his smoky snakes around its mouth, sealing it shut. Orion ducked from its path as the creature crashed to the ground and ran to Aytac's aid as soon as he saw that Ravaryn wasn't in the path of more danger. Just as

Orion reached him, Aytac let out a savage roar and drove his knife deep into the creature's torso that he was fighting. A muffled screech drowned in its throat, and it dropped to the ground in a crumpled heap. Orion watched the pain and emotion spur from his fellow watcher, as he too knew there was a human soul still inside. Orion didn't intervene, as he had been there before, pent-up sadness and utter despair bottling up until finally spilling over.

Ravaryn released his smoke shadows and dropped the Arakanai on its back. The mutant creature was utterly out; it twitched a little in a heap then stilled completely. He came to stand alongside Orion as he watched Aytac punch the ground with his bloodied fists.

'You didn't need to get it to take the entire bottle, you know.' Ravaryn's voice was light and almost mocking.

Orion turned to Ravaryn and looked at him, his sneer melting as he saw the wholly blackened eyes stare back at him. Ravaryn saw the look, and felt the unsaid word slice into him...

Demon.

He forgot that he still wore his shifter gaze. He blinked, and his onyx eyes became sliver-speckled once more. His composure returned as he hid his face behind a cocky grin.

Orion's face once again became stoic, but his words held a somewhat more respectable tone than previously. 'If you had been fighting instead of dancing with that thing, I wouldn't have had to save your sorry arse in the first place.' Orion's thick sliver brow twitched slightly. He bared his teeth, not threateningly, but just a slip of a savage grin showed there, and his emerald eyes shone for just a moment.

Ravaryn felt his core tighten in slight shock as he realised that Orion had just given him a jab, not a direct blow of hate, but an insult laced with acceptance.

'Let's get that thing secured and netted before it wakes.' His face once again wore his usual warrior's expression, unimpressed and severe, but Ravaryn had seen the crack, had seen there could be room for change. 'We'll leave as soon as Aytac's done with his...' he paused, 'as soon as he's done.'

They turned from Aytac and in silence wrapped and bound the captured Arakanai, both assessing up close the horrid transformation of what was once a human.

'Let's pray that your glasshouses, horticulturalists and scientists – whatever you have there – can truly find a cure for this, as I wouldn't even wish this on my worst enemy.' Orion eyed Ravaryn as the words came out.

Ravaryn met Orion's horrified gaze. 'No, neither would I.'

*

Salvador stared out at the desolate grey land surrounding the ancients' once-great building crumbling with age, which was now his stronghold – the place he would begin his rule over this world. Such ingenuity they had once possessed, the humans. They would be perfect to build the cities of the empire he envisioned. Their weak minds and numerous fears made them the perfect vessels to command.

His long taloned feet clamped tightly onto the wide ledge of the tall building as he adjusted his footing while stretching out his enormous black wings. The moon streamed through the clouded sky in short bouts, and shone for a moment on his wings as he stretched, illuminating them like obsidian gems. The moon was growing fuller. His son was running out of time to retrieve Zemira, Thaylon's heir, his true heir who wielded his blood and magic.

Salvador tucked his wings gently back in and focused into the distance as he let his gaze grow glassy. The gold rim around his black irises started to glow as he connected his vision to the groups of Arakanai that had gone scouting to retrieve more humans from the frozen land they called Kymera. He flicked through each of their minds, going from group to group. Visions of both lush and charred forests flicked past in his mind as he searched through his creatures' minds on their way to gather more humans to transform, checking on their progress. Then he entered into one's mind that had found a kill, and was taking chunks from it, gorging itself, not able to resist the temptation.

Salvador growled in anger, feeling the flames build in his throat. *Stupid creature... Move on!* he commanded it. But before it had a chance to comply with his order, it was under attack. Salvador watched as Ravaryn came into view. He pinned Ravaryn's wings down using the Arakanai by controlling its actions, and just as he was about to fight back, the other man his son was with sliced a leg from the Arakanai Salvador was controlling. Salvador turned the creature to retaliate as the warrior gave a fatal blow to its torso. Salvador's mind connection was severed.

A giant plume of fire bust from his maw in fury. He left his spot on the ledge and circled the building's roof as he concentrated on finding the connection again, this time with the other two Arakanai that were grouped with the one that had just been ended. But by the time he found the others again, there was only one that had survived. Its mind was blank and swimming in mist. Alive, but unconscious.

Dreams & Nightmares

Sayde's nose scrunched with the scent of the foul muck that coated her as she crawled from the tunnel Zee had created to give them access to and exit from the undead city. Planting herself on the ground on her arse, knees up for her arms to rest on, she caught her breath as Zee collapsed the last bit of the earth tunnel, now that they were both safely on the right side of the city wall.

The structure of living coral-like fungi rose solidly above them like a reef striving without water in the deadened lands. It groaned high above them with an unnerving pitch, right before shifting in colour. Its dark red façade faded to white, like it were bleached from the sun, directly across from where Zee sat catching her breath. Pieces of it crumbled away in a large patch, and Sayde and Zee jumped up and backed away, planting their stances firmly, ready to fight.

Zee's eyes widened as she thought the worst. *No, no, no.* The undead could not pass through the wall; they could not escape. A rapid panting emitted from the pale patch of crumbling wall, combining with the grind and groan of the towering monolith. The area now seeped with colour and poison, the veins around it pumping a deep blood-red mist outwards. More and more pieces of the wall crumbled away, and a wet green thing protruded from a crevice. A nose... a velvety, mossy nose... poked through, sniffing and puffing.

Moss dog's front paws tore away at the crumbling reef patch of the wall, and finally broke through, tearing towards Zee. She yipped, spinning around in place, a panicky whine coming from within her skinny frame. The wall was now pulsing and seeping liquid to fill the space of invasion, red life pumping back through it, reinforcing the structure. Sprouts that looked like limbs grew rapidly and joined together, sealing the hole Moss had created.

'Moss dog!' Zee's voice was high and sweet as she followed the creature spinning around on the spot. Zee knelt down to inspect her creation. The moss and vines were torn in places but seemed to mingling back together. Moss dog was healing herself, as Zee expended no magic of her own. She let out a surprised laugh. 'Look, Sayde. She's healing herself. It's incredible! It's as if she's now alive with the magic I imbued her with. I'm not doing this.'

Sayde crouched down to inspect the dog's coat in places where it had knitted back together, and a wet lily pad-leaved tongue slid up her cheek. Sayde grunted out in feigned disgust and smiled. 'Thanks for saving me,' she said to the strange creature.

She turned to look at Zee. 'It must be the magic of the forest. You are queen now after all, and you've used your power to mend a life, Zee. You've created something new... very cool.' Sayde ruffled the dog's dandelioned head.

Moss's tail just whipped back and forth, and she stood there vibrating happiness in front of the two women, watching them as if a soldier waiting patiently for her next command.

'Come on, you two. Let's get out of here. We've got what we came for, at least most of it... and I for one could use a warm bath, a cold brew and three days of sleep,' Sayde admitted, standing up and casting a glance at the still-shifting spot on the blood-red wall. Her stomach churned with a strange revulsion at the living, poisonous coral, then she turned, and the three left the city behind to its own fate. Minus one undead soul they now claimed as one of their own. A fizzling feeling of energy crackled in her heart as she studied Moss, and Zee knew deep within her that she could help the undead. She could come back and change the way the radiation had affected them, maybe not heal them completely, but she knew she could do something to make them less dangerous. Zee felt a deep sense of warmth spread through her as she decided that if they were to defeat Salvador, she would return here and do all she could to change the undead for the better.

*

They reached the forest after dark and set up camp. Zee couldn't get their failure to find the third poison out of her mind. An unfamiliar yet ancient scent had kept brushing against her as they'd made their way to the edge of Lamiria. It wasn't Moss, as she now had a fresh jasmine and water lily smell that was uniquely her own. But Zee was too tired to tune in to what the scent was as she coaxed a small fire and beds of vegetation for them to finally rest on. They didn't even bother with preparing a meal, and Sayde had gone quiet on the long hike back. Zee could tell something was stewing in her mind, so she let her be, guessing that they were both exhausted and slightly haunted after actually seeing the city and the undead with their own eyes.

What must it have been like? The Oxygen Wars? How the humans must have suffered in their final days, how much fear and pain they must have endured. Fear. The smell that had followed, it was laced with fear and death. Zee sat up, realisation striking her like lighting in a wild storm. The smell, the virus, was *with* them... *on* them. It was in the pungent, sticky residue of the undead that had dried and crusted on both of the women after battling their way through the horde to escape the city.

'Sayde! We did it—' Zee stopped talking as she heard Sayde's gentle snores from across the flickering camp fire. She retrieved the orb from her pack, Moss at her feet, curled into a tight ball like a caterpillar at her feet. Warmth filled her at the sight. Zee concentrated, and with her powers felt the energy, the tiny capsules of the virus in the dried residue of the undead on her shirt. She grasped onto the unusual energy and willed it from the crusted-over patches. Microscopic molecules of silver floated in the air like dust on the wind towards her outstretched hand as she willed the essence into the orb. It swirled and sparked as the last of the poisons was added to it.

There was a burst within the liquid as the virus mingled with the other poisons, and the colour within turned a metallic grey, like melted mirrors were now moved inside the orb. A shiver ran down Zee's spine despite the humid warm night, and the orb became instantly heavier in her palm. Zee watched it for a few moments longer, feeling the contents within, and it was like the weapon now had a sentience. Like it were alive. Struggling to keep her eyes open, she returned the orb to her pack. Shifting her feet against Moss's back, she curled up into a deep sleep. One where she wandered through the forests and met with a tall ethereal man. One with the darkest eyes of a starry night sky, and dark wings. She found Ravaryn in her dreams... as if it were a reward. A gift for completing to forge the light she would need to protect their world. They kissed and caressed until dawn stole him away again. But happiness swam through her. He was okay, and she would see him, hold him for real very soon. Her heart ached, but she knew it could wait just a little longer.

*

Sayde twisted and turned, her body sweating but her mind deep in dreams. She was inside the Dark Rim again, and grey mud crusted every inch of her skin, under her fingernails, in her hair. Even the creases of her eyes were heavy with the thick clay. She searched the wind-swept cliffs, starved of all colour, that sat high above the glittering black sand of the coves below. The cliffs had been carved by a relentless sea, and the swirling black mass of angry water was coated in a dense layer of hovering mist.

'Noah! Noah!' Sayde was gasping, trying to get more air down into her tight lungs as she ran. A shadow before her in the long-dead grass clawed at the edge of her vision.

'Noah!' her voice was ragged, desperate.

She raced after the shadow, the thick mist before her skewing her vision, her bare feet screaming in pain as they connected with the jagged rocks protruding along the track. The closer she got, the shadow seemed to disappear into vapour then re-materialise further ahead in the mist, and her heart leapt into her throat.

'Noah, please!' Sayde's eyes bulged as she skidded to stop.

A scaly mass towered before her, and her voice disappeared inside of her, her pulse beating like a drum in her ears as she took in the black scales. The monstrous head turned towards her, golden eyes glowing vividly through the mist. Sayde felt her hand suddenly become heavy. She looked down and there within her palm was the weapon Zee had forged, 'the light'. It glowed brightly in the grey mist as Sayde lifted her hand, swung back her arm and took aim. With all her might she threw the orb at the black dragon, smashing into it with the orb, which burst between its shining horns.

The dragon didn't move, just watched her with its glowing eyes as the liquid burst from the orb and started to trickle down its scales. Like a living thing, the shiny liquid ran over the scales, covering the entire dragon and turning its flesh to mist. Sayde watched, her face slack, and she stumbled a step back. *No, no, no! The heart!* She raced forward as the dragon melted from her sight into a puddle of liquid mirror. She started digging through the viscous substance, tears pricking at the edges of her eyes. *The heart.* She needed it.

'*Noah, please.*' A deep chill permeated her skin, and lifting her hands she saw the liquid there, dissolving her. Her bones were stark white in the mist, and her skeletal fingers moved before her. Sayde tried to scramble back away from substance, but it engulfed her body, crawling up and into her mouth, drowning out the scream that wanted to pour from within her trembling core. Then darkness consumed her.

Sayde woke in a cold sweat, her right leg asleep and sparking with pins and needles. She sat up looked around. The fire was now embers, and Zee was still asleep with Moss curled into her chest. She had one arm draped over the dog's body as though it were a pillow she was hugging for comfort. Sayde blinked the sleep away from her eyes and wiped a few stray hairs from her face along with the cool sweat on her brow.

She got up and walked into the forest to relieve herself, the first trickles of morning just starting to seep through the wild canopy above. Birds cooed in early morning calls, and tiny floating bodies of a few spent orcles swept past her. But her mind was reeling and her chest tight from the nightmare. *She couldn't allow Zee to wield the weapon on the black dragon...* realisation bloomed in her like venom and spread painfully through her veins. The heart would be poisoned also, and lost. *Noah.* Sayde ignored the familiar sadness and ache of her broken heart as she returned to the camp. She watched Zee sleep, her eyes fluttering rapidly as if she were reliving her own worst nightmares.

Sayde truly liked the strange woman; she had never had so much ease with anyone else before, had never made a friend so quickly or so easily. Everyone in Lamiria who knew her also knew what Sayde had done... knew why her father ceased to exist... and she saw the glaze of fear in their weak eyes whenever they were near her. Her shifter form was like no other in the realm. She was the only Vallarax shifter she knew, and why she had donned the unique form was a wonder to her. Aytac, her twin and the black wolf, was revered, was looked up to. He had always been loved by all who surrounded him. She, however, had not.

Noah had been the only first true connection that she had made in her life. She would do whatever it took to get him back, to see him, to be with him one last time. She had to see the look that came from within his eyes when he saw her – not one of fear or distrust – but one of wonder and love. Something Sayde hadn't realised she had strived for her entire existence. She had never seen that look before, not in her father's hateful eyes, and not in her mother's for she had passed the day she had brought the twins into this world. And not in her twin's eyes, as his love was something different; it was always laced with worry and sprinkled with a protective layer that infuriated her. Like she was somehow his burden, his responsibility. Like she needed him to always be there to watch her to make sure she didn't do something wrong... to fuck up. *Again.*

No, Noah had been her refuge, the spark that lit up her soul, the stars that shone on a dark night. He was her balance, her *soul flame.* She looked at Zee as she rolled over, black hair in a tangle, Moss stretching her skinny, elegant form out beside her and digging her slender snout into Zee's side. She truly liked the Rim Walker, the new forest queen. She was an absolute mirror opposite to her predecessor, Kyeitha. Sayde's stomach clenched as she thought of all that Kyeitha had taken from her, and the acidic sour tang of fury reached her mouth. She told herself she didn't care, didn't care that she'd made the first real friend since Noah, since maybe ever. Noah was all that mattered... and the dragon's un-poisoned heart... was all that mattered next.

Wings & Phoenix

Lamirian Forest

The trio trekked for the entire day, feet aching, legs weary and reeking of the undead's dried blood on them. The weight of the orb in the pack pulled on Zee's shoulders the entire way, like a formidable evil that lingered in wait. They reached the Temple of Lamiria the following night, Moss chaotically racing around the lake of life's edges as she chased unimpressed millowisps, nipping and snapping at their coloured mist-like tails.

Zee laughed, and surprisingly so did Sayde, the pair feeling lighter as they watched Moss miss time after time, the millowisps now playing back after realising the game. Their tiny little hands threw miniscule sparkling bombs of glittering light at Moss.

'That dog—' Sayde breathed in between gasps of laughter '—is probably the best thing that ever came from the ancient humans!'

Zee's heart burst with love as she watched Moss play. 'I entirely agree with you on that.' They stayed a little while longer, just watching until the millowisps had had enough of Moss's antics and ventured away over the water's surface, far from her reach in the centre of the lake.

'Come with me.' Zee gestured to the edge of the lake where Moss frolicked. 'Let's wash away that trip before anyone else has to be exposed.' Zee wove water through the air towards Sayde.

'What are you doing?' Sayde questioned, eyes wide and pinned on the swirling stream of glowing water coming towards her.

'Experimenting with my new powers, so stay still,' Zee explained as she washed away the trip and spun the dirt and muck from Sayde, leaving her dry and fresh.

'Thanks,' Sayde said as she inspected herself.

Zee repeated the same magic on herself, a proud smirk on her face.

The three entered Tangaroa through the crescent moon-handled door at the back of the temple, then went through the tunnel of rock and into the Valley of Rivers beyond. The falls crashed powerfully into the valley, greeting them as they reached the flattened clifftop above the shimmering city.

Lanterns were lit in small clusters throughout the city below, signalling the inhabitants had returned and now dwelled in the sandstone cottages that lined the riverways weaving through the city. Some walkways had been cleared of trailing vines and overgrown vegetation, and overgrown water plants had been tamed and harvested. The city was not completely revived but it now beat with a life and change. And most importantly, hope. The image was one that made Zee's hands tingle, and her body feel light, like she was a feather ready to be swept away, completely weightless despite the heavy thrum of ancient power emanating from the orb inside her backpack.

She noticed the scent of moonflowers, a cross between jasmine and vanilla that carried on the warm air with a calming effect, and looked over to Sayde whose eyes seemed suddenly distant.

'Do you have somewhere to stay?' Zee questioned, her voice gentle. 'You can come with me to the palace if you like. There are a thousand empty rooms in there. Pick any you like, two if you want.'

Sayde smiled a little at her new friend. 'Thanks, Queenie, but I have a house actually, down there.' Her head motioned to the valley below. 'And no doubt a hovering mother hen of a brother waiting for me to return so he can fluff over me.'

Zee chuckled. 'I don't think I could witness Aytac "fluffing" over anything and not laugh out loud.'

'Oh, it's a sight to behold, alright.' Sayde nudged Zee on the shoulder before she left. 'Goodnight, Moss dog. I'll come see you two tomorrow and check out your one thousand rooms.'

Zee called out to her as she left for the tracks down to the city. 'Thank you, Sayde. Thanks for coming with me, thanks for having my back... and thank you for not making me have to do that trip alone.'

Sayde's heart constricted in her chest, but she shook it off and turned around, a smug smirk in place on her face. 'Anytime you're in need of a Vallarax shifter as a sidekick, you know where to find me.' She winked in the full moon's light and continued down the track to her old home, and most probably brooding twin awaiting her.

A *Vallarax.* Zee mulled the word over in her head. That's what the creature was that Sayde's shifter form took. *Such a powerful form to be able to wield.* 'She's such a badarse,' Zee said aloud to Moss.

Moss just looked up at Zee.

'Don't worry, you're definitely a badarse too, after what you did to save us in the city. You can pick any room you want as well.' Zee patted Moss's head and they started along the mountainside towards the majestic palace that hugged the hill. Suddenly, she felt a deep throb in her arm. She looked down and the blood blooms had opened wide, petals unfurling there. The feelings, the worry, the ache for him she had been repressing since the day he was torn away from her could no longer be held at bay. Her pulse quickened as her heart leapt, and butterflies flickered rapidly in her stomach. *Ravaryn. He's here.* Zee almost sprinted down the last of the track to the flower-adorned pergolas that edged the palace rooms, Moss in tow.

And ran straight into a waiting Diwa.

*

Ravaryn paced the palace room he now stood within. Orion and Aytac were well on their way to Kymera with the Arakanai bound and caged in tow. He had given Orion a letter for Mazda upon them leaving, and Orion had surprisingly accepted it and agreed to deliver it to Kymera's next ruler. As he had left, a gentle yet stern nod was all that he conveyed as a response to Ravaryn.

He knew Zee was on her way back from her mission with Sayde. Diwa had filled them all in upon their return, yet Orion had chosen to deliver the Arakanai safely alongside Aytac instead of reuniting immediately with his daughter. He was growing more and more concerned for Verena's safety, and had to go to her. Only once she was safe inside the valley would he be able to focus on the upcoming conflict. A warm wave then swept through Ravaryn, and stopped him from his pacing. That familiar feeling of her tore him away from his thoughts, just like it always did when she was near.

Ravaryn turned, and there at the entranceway of the candlelit room she stood. 'Zemirah...' his voice was velvety and smooth, and desperate with desire. Within seconds he had made it across the floor and had her against him, wrapped in his arms, his body pressed up against hers and crushing her into his embrace.

Zee breathed in the scent of him, the heady pine and bark calming her with a refreshing clarity after days of travel with Sayde, the pair covered in muck from the city and its rotting inhabitants. Now clean and fresh, her heart and soul were thrumming just to be held in his arms. 'It feels like it's been forever, Wings...' she admitted softly, pulling away to look up at his face, to bask in being back with him finally, her eyes misty. 'What happened? What did Salvador do to you? I want to know; no, I need to know everything.'

He stared at her like his mind was elsewhere, drinking her in like he hadn't laid eyes on her in years.

'Wings. Are you with me?'

'Yes,' he replied after a moment, coming back to reality. 'I am now.'

He smiled that half-hitched handsome grin that always made her stomach do somersaults. Zee tippy-toed up and kissed him, strong and hard, her body pressing against him, like she too needed to have him as close to her as possible. The elation at finally getting her back was making his head light. Ravaryn indulged in the kiss as long as she offered. Warmth spread through him like the sun after a storm. Then he pulled away a little breathless and took in the rest of her.

'Did you manage to gather the poisons? The weapon? Is it—' he stumbled on the words, an expression Zee hadn't seen before lingering in his eyes. 'Is it here?'

Zee dropped her pack and pulled the light from within, its weight now much heavier in her palm. The metallic liquid within was opaque and swirled around, like a serpent lazily sliding through water. Ravaryn's eyes shone as he assessed the object in Zee's palm.

'Incredible.'

Zee stared into the light while she spoke. 'It was strange, to see it all. The city, the creatures that seemed to live without true life inside them, with the ancient ones' creations and objects everywhere. They had created so much, yet it still didn't save them in the end.' She returned the orb to her pack and looked to Ravaryn for the answers he'd promised.

'Come with me. Answers later,' he answered her, as if reading her mind.

Zee replied as if she were remembering the festival in Maya Village when he had been led by her in a similar way to dance in front of the glowing fires. 'Anything for you.'

His onyx eyes sparked, irises blooming wide at her. Her words glowing inside him, his lip curled into his handsome half-smile, and he turned and led her to the far end of the large rooms, through a candlelit corridor and out into gardens lit by the night sky. A few floating glow beetles were going about flower to flower, and a small trail led them to the mountainside behind the palace. From the rockface trickled clear, steamy water into a pool surrounded by gingers and other leafy vegetation.

'Wow, this is gorgeous,' Zee exclaimed.

Ravaryn noted her shoulders slumping as her muscles practically begged for the warm, soothing waters in the spring before her. He gently pulled her further into the secluded space. 'Care for a dip?' his vice was silky, and mischievous.

'What is it with you and secret waterfalls?' Zee face was alight with a beautiful smile, one she seemed to possess just for him.

Ravaryn laughed, the sound melodic and deep, before replying. 'And I'll answer anything you want to know.' He saw Zee's eyes sparkle, and a touch of colour flushed her bronzed cheeks. Answers suddenly seemed not as important now as Ravaryn began to undress her gently, his fingers moving before he even gave them permission. He took the belt from her waist, unbuckling it with sure, steady hands, then unbuttoned her jacket, sliding it off her shoulders and dropping it onto the mossy rocks behind them.

Steam rose around them and no chill could be felt in the air whatsoever, but still Zee's skin turned to gooseflesh. Reactions from her body came from every point his smooth, strong hands came in contact with her body. Her nipples peaked under her cotton singlet as his touch skirted the hem of her shirt there. Before he lost himself in her, he searched her eyes for permission to continue on. Zee's emerald gaze burned up at him with want. Her breaths had quickened, causing Ravaryn's body to respond just from the sound of her. Every fibre of his body was waking up. Coming alive again after being dormant for so long, as his match, his equal, stood before him.

Deep in her core she seemed to radiate with warmth. She had no hesitations, for he was who she wanted, he was the only one she had ever wanted, and she had never felt this way about anyone else – ever. He could tell all this just by the look she was giving him... no words were necessary. She made him feel like the most important person in her world. Like every despicable thing he had ever done in the past didn't matter, and the more she became a part of his life the more she made it all fade away. She was changing him in a way he couldn't even explain. No one could make him burn from within like she did, and both her darkness and her light matched his.

Her hands reached for his black shirt and slid it up and over his head. His skin felt like smooth marble underneath her touch. Where the scars littered his chest and shoulders like veins in the sculpted stone, she ran her fingers lightly over his muscles there, over the spot where his heart lay beneath, and the blooms on her left arm furrowed and opened wide in response. A warm pulse radiated through her hands, warming his skin beneath them. Ravaryn's gaze grew dark, and a deep rumbling groan grew in his throat at her touch, want seeping from him. He leaned down and kissed her before the spring, removing the rest of her clothes as he devoured her soft mouth.

Zee's hands then trailed down over Ravaryn's sculpted chest, past his navel and over the taut plains of his hips that directed her downwards. She undid the belt and slid him free from his own clothing, his hands a tangle in her long hair, his mouth still on hers as his warm, hard length pressed against her. He had longed for this moment for what had seemed half a lifetime, and never did he think he would get to feel this kind of connection again. She pulled away from the kisses they were indulging in, taking a breath, his heart now racing wildly. Bravely taking a look at him, her eyes burned with green light, fire pulsing within her, and Ravaryn didn't miss that her cheeks were heated and flushed with more colour. He was suddenly filled with burning need at the sight of her. She was a goddess, and she had chosen *him.*

Suddenly he needed her, needed her against him, needed to be close to her, every inch of her. He needed to be inside of her, and his body and soul ached for this. Before he could move, she had already started to lead him into the warm water of the spring. He let the waters envelop them. Zee wrapped her hands around his neck, entwined her fingers in his soft, thick curls of black hair and trailed kisses along his jaw, his neck. A deep groan of desire escaped him again, and his composure snapped. His swift, strong hands grabbed her toned legs from beneath her. She complied, wrapping herself around his body, hooking her ankles behind him for purchase. The warm waters caressed them, and Zee tilted her head back to see the stars brightly flickering down in the clear night sky.

Ravaryn saw the reflection in her gaze. A whole world lay within them. *His* whole world finally, safely in his arms. His mouth found the small dip in her throat between her collarbones, and a soft moan escaped her as she utterly lost herself in Ravaryn's touch, as he worshiped every inch of her body. *His* Zemira, his queen, his soul's flame, finally reunited, finally together, and nothing in the world mattered in that moment, none of the pain, the torment, the sadness... it was all so insignificant compared to this moment, this feeling, like a drop of water into an ocean. Two hearts, two souls connected, perfectly balanced. Reunited. Fused as one. Energy and power radiated from them, as black snakes of smoke curled around flickers of cool green flames, combining in pure bliss in the steam of the spring. Two souls danced together, their hearts becoming one under the gentle glow of the stars in the valley.

Part III

The Cut Serpent

The screeches that had rattled from the captured Arakanai upon it awakening inside the cage had finally died down to unsettling clicks. Orion's ears were ringing with the creature's cries from the last few hours. He had badly wanted to knock the thing unconscious again, but they had to save the last of the bundlebay root extract for when they reached the towns in Kymera. It wouldn't be wise to instil any more fear into the humans than they guessed was already present.

Aytac had slid into the warm moscow coat and boots before the icy landscape had even been visible, grumbling about the cold with pure venom in his voice. Orion, of course, agreed, but hadn't needed the protective wear until snow and ice started to crunch underfoot.

The pair dutifully towed the creature forth within the small-wheeled enclosure. Its body was tightly bound, and they could have obtained some battilux or even woverbine to bring the mutant into the old Rim world, but would have had to leave them upon hitting the frozen terrain. They had both decided this would be the easier option. Making good time, they had needed the distraction of the task to keep them from their own minds for just a while until he retrieved Verena from Aylenta.

Aytac pulled a heavy blanket over the creature, making sure to cover its disfigured face and unsettling eyes. They had reached Valomma, where spirals of smoke rose up into the crisp, dry air. Ice shone in crusts over the black-bricked homes, and fitlzeweed crept upwards along the lamp posts then dangled down from the tops, clinging with hairlike vines of leafless growth. But the village was all too quiet: there was no shuffle of the market place, no scents of humseed bread seeping from the town centre. It looked like a ghost town.

'This can't be good,' Aytac said, with foreboding.

'I agree. But we'll find the nearest inn, and get some food and information. I'll go in, as I've had more time with the humans. Trust me, they scare easily. Wait with the creature. I won't be long.'

Aytac nodded, a scowl permanently on his face since reaching the human lands. He tucked his mitted hands in tightly to his broad chest and leaned up against the slick ice-covered wall of the nearest building. Aytac's scowl almost made Orion want to chuckle, but there was an unsettling energy in the air. Something was not right here. He made his way farther into the paved streets of the empty village, until he found the main inn.

Orion's large tattooed hand reached for the door of the inn, the sign indicating that it was called The Cut Serpent. The door creaked on its hinges above him, the sharp noise the only sound to his ears. The door was crusted shut with ice, but an encouraging nudge from Orion's solid shoulder freed it. The fire was only dying embers in the large fireplace in the centre of the inn, and some of the chairs were overturned. Schooners of muddle beer – the local brew made from Kymera's humseed husks – were left half full, and some spilled over the tables.

His eyes were alert as he scanned the empty premise, then a glass smashed behind him, making him turn in that direction. Approaching cautiously, he found a shaking old bartender with a greying beard and wide brown eyes with his hands outstretched. His voice came out like chunks of rocks in an avalanche – rough and strewn.

'Please, I beg you. Don't hurt me...' his voice snapped like taught violin strings.

'I'm not going to hurt you, old man. What happened here? Where is everyone?'

The old man's wide eyes stayed pinned on Orion's until he realised that Orion was not leaning over the counter to attack him. He stood up, cracking noises coming from his joints like twigs snapping. He was short, and from what Orion could see, his belly ballooned out before him, probably weighing him down significantly.

'They're gone... all of them, taken just last night, by these... these *things...*' His eyes widened in fear as he spoke. They were ruddy and ringed with yellow around his brown irises.

'I knew it... I knew the day that mutant girl broke the Rim wall that she would be our doom! The monsters have come, and there's nothing left!'

Orion's face carefully tried to hide the scowl, but this old fool was clearly scared out of his mind, and Orion didn't need him even more afraid or he wouldn't get any answers then.

He smashed a fist down on the wooden counter clenching his teeth, 'Calm down, and tell me what happened here.'

The man's throat bobbed as he rattled a shaky breath in through his nose, nostrils flaring wide and sucking up some of the frazzled grey hairs there with it. 'Monsters came! Last night dozens of spiderlike demons! Underworld things, you know? They pinned the screaming and struggling villagers down. Some tried to fight back... but they took them dead or alive, spun them in golden threads, tight like cocoons, and dragged them away. I only escaped because I hid in the cellar. I just got the balls to come out, then I heard the door creak open, and nearly wet myself again.'

Orion's face was a mask, although he appreciated the old man's candour.

'It was like they were communicating with each other, like some kind of swarm of locusts or something, all clicking and golden eyes. It's the end of the Rim world, I tell you! We're all doomed now without the wall!'

Orion's shoulders slumped and he dropped his head, his forefinger and thumb coming to pinch the bridge of his nose for a moment. 'What's your name?' he asked flatly.

'Everyone round 'ere just calls me Garlic, least they did before they were all taken by giant spiders.'

Orion looked up and slightly raised a brow at the old, wild-looking man, somehow realising the name suited him well. 'Garlic, pour yourself a muddle, and two more for me and my travel companion. I'll be back shortly with him, and if there's any food you can muster it would be greatly appreciated.'

Garlic's brown eyes bulged in their yellow pools then he nodded and pursed his lips within his wispy beard. 'Good idea,' was all he said as he shuffled over and instantly started to pour cold beers.

Garlic had downed three muddles in the short time it had taken to retrieve Aytac, whose lips were blue, and tiny ice crystals had formed on his eyelashes and beard hair, matching his mood perfectly. They left the Arakanai in the stable next to the inn, and ate the modest meal of cheese, bread and jillabee jam with some leftover terrine of undetermined meat, but the pair didn't have time for complaints. If humans were being taken at this rate from Kymera, and most probably the Aylentean towns closest to Lamiria, they were running out of time.

They left for Zenya not long after the respite of the short break, offering to escort Garlic out of the abandoned town with them on to Zenya, but he refused, stating he would rather stay in the safety of his inn. 'They won't come back here, there's nothing left to take! If I go somewhere else, I'll be sure to run in to the horrid things again. Nope! I'll take my chances here. I'd rather die of too much muddle than be a demon's dinner.'

Orion and Aytac respected his wishes, thanked him for the food and brew, and continued on. The vicious cold in Valomma lingered behind them, relenting slightly and giving way to fields of humseeds and grazing moscows as they grew closer to their destination.

Sunflowers

Zemira awoke in a tangle of limbs. A smooth, muscled arm lay under her head, and the smell of sky-pines tickled her nose as Ravaryn breathed gently against her forehead. Her heart glowed from within as she watched his long dark lashes rest against his face, his eyes closed, his face calm in sleep. He was truly stunning, like he were sculpted from a sketchbook of the gods.

Early morning sun spread in through the open pergola windows that looked out over the valley, and there was still a crisp chill to the air hanging on from the clear night. Zee realised for once that she was awake early, and tiredness wasn't weighing her down like it usually did. Her body felt light as though she could float if she mustered the air and willed its energy so. And she couldn't stop a ridiculous smile from spreading across her face.

She carefully withdrew herself from Ravaryn's body so as not to disturb him, and dressed in a flowing robe decorated with small berries, mushrooms and dragonflies. She'd found it in a wardrobe in the regal room. There were lots of garments and clothing neatly hanging, which she guessed had been revived for her since she had opened the doors to Tangaroa as its new forest queen. The whole event still felt like a dream.

The thought still brought a little simmering panic to her stomach, but she swept it away, not wanting to linger on it, not wanting the afterglow of last night to be ruined so quickly by everything she was yet to face. Zee made her way to watch the sunrise over the valley below for the first time in a long time. Golden ribbons were starting to shine as the sun hit the many rivers that wove through the sandstone city. The golden warmth of the sun's rays lit up the landscape and her entire being. As Zee looked out over the valley, the feeling inside of her chest seeped out over the land, and thousands of sunflowers unfurled in the growing morning light. They looked like a wave blooming throughout the valley, spreading light and warmth.

Tears welled in Zee's eyes as she watched her happiness move through the land. She was warmth, light and life all in one. The forest queen's powers coursed through her, like vines creeping out of the ashes of her old self. This is what it was to be a true forest queen – this feeling, this knowing of life and creation. How had Kyeitha become so poisoned? How had she turned this magnificent gift into pain and power? A faint whine echoed from across the grand-sized room, accompanied by a scratch at the heavy door. Zee padded over woven carpets and opened it to let in an excitable Moss, after leaving her in Diwa's care for the night as soon as she had returned to the palace. Moss was all tail wags and pent-up energy upon seeing Zee again.

The dog flew into the room to nuzzle Zee's hand, then leapt through the air and straight onto the bed. Ravaryn shot upwards in bed, awakening just as Moss reached him. His hands glowed with black smoke, and he aimed them straight at the creature.

'No!' Zee's voice ripped from her throat as she rushed to the bed.

Moss bolted backwards, a deep growl rippling over her sharp canines, dandelion hackles unfurling.

'She's a friend,' Zee explained, coming to stand behind Moss, who now stood between the bed and the door of the room as she backed up next to Zee.

Ravaryn blinked rapidly, and his onyx eyes focused on his hands and the magic pooling forth from them. In an instant, he dropped them and the smoke dispersed from the air in a wisp.

'What is ... *she?*' he asked, his voice gravelly from sleep, his brows knitting together as he stared at Moss.

'She's a dog, a moss dog. She saved us in the undead city.' Zee affectionately stroked her luscious green head. Moss's cloudy eyes were still pinpointed on Ravaryn, not quite sure if he were friend or foe.

'It's okay, Mossy, he's a friend.' Zee's voice soothed her as her hands swept her leafy ears back from their alerted position.

'Moss, this is Wings. Wings, this is Moss.'

Ravaryn gave Zee a lopsided smile and swung his legs over the edge of the bed, sheets covering his fine form from the waist down. Zee's eyes took him in, and she felt her cheeks bloom like cheery blossoms once more. He held out a hand towards the strange creature that clearly favoured Zee's presence. Moss rumbled a strange sound and carefully proceeded forth on her long, thin legs, sniffing his hand where he offered it. After a second or two, her whip-like tail swayed from side to side, and she panted instead of baring her teeth. Her bulbous cloudy-sky eyes looked up to Zee as if seeing what her thoughts were on the matter of the man before them. Then she decided all must be alright, and began to wander around the room, sniffing everything else in her path.

'That is one of the strangest creatures I think I've ever met.' Ravaryn scratched his head as Moss sniffed everything in sight.

'You should have seen her before I fixed her.'

'Fixed her?' Ravaryn questioned. He stood up and pulled her into his arms, holding her tightly against him. 'Come here. I have need of some of your "fixing", he joked.

He lay her on the bed and rolled on top of her, lacing kisses down her neck and sliding her robe to the side to reveal a breast. Moss whined. *Loudly.*

Zee laughed. 'I don't think Moss approves.'

A low growl left Ravaryn's throat. 'Well... see her out and shut the door behind her, please. I'm in need of my *queen*.'

Zee's insides tingled with small sparks of lightning as Ravaryn's silky voice caressed her ear. 'I like it when you say please...' Her eyes glowed with a look of want that mirrored his own. She shimmied from underneath him, still smiling. His eyes watched her every movement as she came to the door.

'Moss, come on, go find someone else to pester for the moment.'

Moss trotted over to her, looking back at Ravaryn with a head tilt. Understanding her dismissal, she trotted out the door, leaving Zee and Ravaryn to continue what they'd started.

Poisonous Love

Diwa sat in the ornate cherry-red velvet chair, her legs tucked beneath her with Moss's sleeping head on her lap. She had a dainty cup of tea in her hand and was humming to herself as she took in the valley from the grand sitting room in the centre of the palace. Her shoulders were relaxed, and her free hand swept gentle strokes over Moss's soft head as she smiled gently to herself thinking of Ravaryn and Zemira both returning to the valley safely. For the moment, the short-but-sweet moment, all was calm.

Sunflowers bloomed in the golden valley, and the world beyond the protective walls of the city was forgotten for just a little while. Diwa released a deep breath and sank farther back into the decadent lounge. A set of steps echoed their way towards her on the polished stone floor, along with a rhythmic jingle of metal.

As Sahara approached, she poured herself a cup of tea, her eyes suspiciously taking in Moss as she sat down in the chair adjacent Diwa. 'I see the new forest queen has been playing with her powers.'

Diwa smiled, silver eyes shining back at Sahara, her eyes now crinkling ever so slightly since her transformation back to her younger body, but they still exuded the same warmth. 'Not only that, but she also managed to forge the light.' He eyes glossed over at the mention of the powerful weapon Zee had managed to craft.

'Well, that's good then, so what are you fretting about, you old nanny goat? The sooner that demon is dead, the better for the entire realm.'

'Yes, but what if it doesn't work...?' Diwa's eyes bored into Sahara, searching for answers that she had not yet seen.

'You haven't seen the event yet?' Sahara's brash voice was clipped.

'I have seen images of the battle. I have seen Salvador fall... but I have not yet seen his death.'

Sahara rolled her tongue over her teeth, as though pondering something encouraging to offer. No such luck. 'You're losing your touch, Diwante, getting slack in your old age.'

Diwas eyes opened wide. 'Speak for yourself, you cantankerous little tree viper!'

The two mock-bickered as friends do until a purposeful cough sounded behind them. Both the women turned towards the sound. Eyes wide, Zee looked like she was prey that had been spotted by two large predatory owls. 'Ah... good morning. May I join you?'

'Of course, dear!'

Diwa's mood instantly shifted, and Moss popped her sleepy head upwards. Zee came to sit on the opposite end of the lounge Diwa was on, between the two women. The three now formed a triangle. They had instantly stopped their arguing and eyed Zee with warmth. Sahara just nodded her greeting and poured her a cup of tea.

Clutching it in both hands, she crossed her legs on the lounge and took a small sip. The onyx fingernails on her left hand were in deep contrast to the white and sage patterns on the ornate cup, and the blooms on her arm opened in vibrant bloom as she settled into the chair.

'The valley greets you back, my dear. Have you seen the flowers?' Sahara probed with a curious tone.

Zee's cheeks reddened as she stared into her tea. 'Yes, they're beautiful, and I'm glad to be back. I thank the Mother that they found Ravaryn, and that he's okay. I'm so glad that he's here. Safe.'

Diwa's face eased into a gentle smile. 'Where has he gotten to this morning?'

'He's gone into the city to rally the watchers and anyone willing to train and fight. I'm going to go and help but first there's something I need to ask you about,' Zee confessed. 'It's about Kyeitha.'

Diwa eyed Sahara then brought her gaze back to Zee's.

'Something's been bothering me, and I need to know what truly made her lose her way. She had this power, this gift inside of her. It's incredible. It's like I can feel every living thing and its life force, its joy, even its heart beat if I wished it so. She possessed so much wonder yet she was filled with fear and hate. Why? How could she have become so twisted with this magic inside of her?'

Diwa's silver eyes dulled, and her smile dropped at the mention of Kyeitha.

'Right, well, there is nothing helpful whatsoever that I can add to this topic, and I'd rather not endure having to listen about that particular monster on such a beautiful morning, so I'm off to corral some villagers to man the kitchens around here.' Sahara plopped her empty cup down and shuffled off with her hands gesturing into the air as if sweeping a dirty mist out of her path as she went.

'Fair enough.' Zee shrugged her shoulders as she watched the odd woman walk off.

Moss shifted onto her back, her strange, long legs pointing out in all awkward directions as Diwa spoke. 'When Kyeitha found out what your grandfather... what *Thaylon* truly sought from her, just an heir that he could use to force her to give up the throne to him, she was heartbroken. I tried to console her, and I finally told her what I had done to Salvador, but by then Ravaryn and I had moved far from the valley. He was still a child when she found out that Thaylon had been in alliance with Salvador all along, and that they had in fact come from the same demonic world.

'I was ever suspicious after I saw what Salvador truly was, after the smoke screen and his façade were well and truly gone. But Thaylon was so cunning and kept up his ruse. Kyeitha trusted him with the essence of her core, and he taught her blood magic that she could wield with expertise. She mixed it with her own powers and it was like nothing that I had ever seen before. I tried to warn her, but she would have nothing of it. She thought I was jealous that my own partner had abandoned me and my child. I had my own life to concern myself with and rather than getting on her bad side, I just let it be, because at that time all I had were my suspicions.'

Zee placed her teacup down on the table and her fingers began to fiddle as she continued to listen. Diwa's face grew sadder as her words came out like thorns on a vine.

'There is a reason your father doesn't have the gift of the flames that you do, that he has none of the darkness that you struggle with. Once Kyeitha found out what Thaylon really was, that he was in fact a demon who sought to dethrone her and steal her child, she banished him to live out his days inside of the Rim.'

Zee's eyes widened even more at this, but she said nothing as Diwa continued.

'Using her strengthened powers, Kyeitha cursed Thaylon to a human existence as long as the Rim wall stood. And as her child grew inside of her, she absorbed every bit of his magic from Thaylon's essence into herself. She loved Orion, the child growing inside of her, more than anything in this world – and in her old one. Before Orion was even earth side, she took every drop of magic from his veins that could mar him like his father, but it slowly poisoned her from the inside out. It collided with her true nature and overtook her true powers as the forest queen, until she became what she ultimately did. Thaylon's magic, however, resided in Orion's genes to then carry onto you, but he possesses nothing of what Thaylon truly is. Kyeitha loved her son so much that she let herself be destroyed rather than allow anything to happen to him. But she didn't know that he still carried Thaylon's essence deep in his genes, and that she couldn't fully absorb it from there.'

Diwa looked away from Zee's shocked expression and gently stroked Moss's exposed neck.

'You mean she was actually *good...*?' Zee eyes flared with horror as she realised what, or who, she had really destroyed the day she broke the Rim wall, along with the curse over Diwa and Ravaryn.

'It's not your fault, dear, and you can't deny or feel shame about your destiny. The person you ended that fateful day was *not* the forest queen Gaia had once chosen. There was nothing left of the person Kyeitha had been when we both fell into this world. The magic she absorbed from Thaylon had poisoned her, reaching to her very core. She knew that a Rim Walker child would one day come to end her... I foresaw it... and the prophecy was my entire fault, along with what happened to Ravaryn's babe, and Liara...'

Diwa sucked in a strained breath, her eyes watery. 'But she never thought it would end up being her own blood that would stop her in the end. Don't let guilt consume you, Zemira. You're the only one who could have finished her.'

Diwa's gentle, smooth hands reached over Moss and caressed Zee's cheek, her thumb swirling on the tattooed scar at her temple there. 'You ended her suffering, and saved the realm from her. I'm just sorry that once again you'll have to face a demon to save us, but this time you won't be alone. All of Lamiria will have your back.'

And you'll need us, dear girl. Diwa couldn't help but tremble a little at what lay ahead for all of them, but Zee especially.

*

Thaylon's hands swept over the large iron pot before him, its contents hissing and spitting as drops of blood from his palms dripped into the dense, swirling liquid. The purposeful clip, clip of boots pricked in his ears, pulling his mind away from the magic he was spinning. Salvador was approaching his chambers. By the pace of his gait, he gathered the blood magic for the next lot of humans could wait. His lord needed something. Thaylon sat up from his spot where he leant over the iron pot and wiped his hands clean with a nearby rag, just as Salvador entered the cavernous room above the underground cells that he had turned into his workspace.

The room had all been cleared of the debris from long ago, although dirt and dust coated the floor, but a firepit was blazing on the far wall between two murky glass windows that were fractured but still intact. Metal tables to the far end had rows of jars, each containing the largest of golden orb spiders ready to be infused and transformed once the next group of humans arrived.

Hanging from hooks and cords in a gloomy corner on the farthest wall were assorted human parts, all showcasing carved-out missing chucks. A few errant bugs buzzed around other objects that were rubbed over with ash. The room exuded an off-putting metallic scent mixed with the burning poisoned wood collected from the deadland's remaining skeletal trees.

Salvador ever so slightly flared his nostrils at the smell as he entered, but he gave no other signs whether or not he agreed with Thaylon's methods.

'My lord, what may I do for you? Do you need to replenish your dark magic connection to the Arakanai? There is plenty of flesh prepared and ready now. Not all of the last group of humans the Arakanai dragged back were worthy of being transformed.' Thaylon's dark hooded eyes sparkled as he grinned through the explanation.

'No. I'm fine,' Salvador replied in a short-clipped tone. 'I just witnessed Ravaryn attacking our Arakanai with two other warriors,' he seethed. 'I believe my son has deceived us.'

'Well, did they succeed?' Thaylon answered, unperturbed. He had always known the king was going to be nothing but trouble, but didn't want to anger his lord any further.

'Succeed! They killed two and left the third unconscious, but I think you're missing the point. He's already betrayed us.' Salvador's eyes grew large like spilled ink.

'Not necessarily.' Thaylon clasped his large hands between his knees. 'He could have just been gathering allies to help him search for my heir. Remember the intricacies of allies and alliances, my lord. In Prythorda, your brothers all preceded you for the throne, not because of their status defined by their enormous size over you alone in their dragon forms, but also because they were conniving, traitorous and expertly manipulative in the demon court. Maybe your son has more ruling qualities than you've given him credit for. He made himself a king while banished in the human world, after all. We don't know what kind of characters our heirs possess, having been banished from them for all this time.'

'You've got a point, Thaylon. You were always better at scheming and politics than I,' Salvador replied, his fists unclenching and finding each other behind his straightened spine. He made his way over to the grimy window across Thaylon's work space to glare out at the deadlands surrounding his stronghold. 'If only those brothers of mine could see what I will turn this entire realm into. How they would regret not letting me compete alongside them for the dragon throne.'

'Aye, my lord. Prythorda will be a walk in the forest compared to what horrors you'll create here, I have no doubt. And the new recruits Ravaryn seems to be gathering will all aid in our conquest once he retrieves my granddaughter and brings her to join us, then nothing will stand in our way. It's like I said the day we found ourselves falling into this world through the crack in the realms, "fate has us in her hands".'

Salvador turned around, his eyes narrowing in on Thaylon, who had now come to stand next to him, the mention of Prythorda, their home world, sparking a wicked smile from him. One that bloomed like poison over his handsome face, consuming his features, leaving no trace of the anger remaining.

'You've given me the grandest of ideas, Thaylon. Once we conquer this realm and turn it into a vision the likes of the underworld would be envious of, we will have to invite my dear brothers and the high lords of Prythorda to come and witness what I have created. So they may see what fools they were to deny me my birthright in vying for the crown. We will find a way to tear into the fragile seams of this world and create a doorway between us and our homeland. If it's been done once before, we can do it again. That deity who maintains the balance here will know how to do it. After we take rule over the humans and the forest folk, and I am king, our next venture will be to find her. Find whatever means it will take for her to reopen the tears she once sealed shut.'

Thaylon's face matched Salvador's now. He clapped a hand over his leader's shoulder and nodded once. 'I will dream of the fear on the faces of all of the snivelling zealots in Prythorda once they see what you accomplish here, and take my pick of whose bones to clean my teeth with once we are done with our betrayers.' Thaylon's laugh was a deep rumbling beast as his eyes glittered, imagining the future that was closer now than ever for him and his lord. 'Give Ravaryn the rest of the time you promised him, until the moon's full cycle is up. We'll keep adding to our forces of humans ready to transform with every group the Arakanai drag back. And if he has in fact already betrayed you... well, he's your son after all. I'm sure you will find an appropriate punishment for his decision.'

Ice City

Zenya, Kymera

Never in millennia did Orion think the sight of the ice castle in Zenya city would bring him a feeling other than hatred. But as the shining icy spires glinted in the sunlight breaking through the cloudy sky, he felt relief at finally reaching their destination. Relief to finally be away from the unsettling abomination they had dragged half way across the Rim also eased Orion's tightly strung muscles. The Arakanai had remained covered, and for the most part quiet, other than the occasional few clicks, as it finally realised its predicament.

One of the main guards at the now-open gates to the castle looked at Orion with kind, albeit suspicious, eyes. He explained that he and Aytac were here to urgently speak with the new queen, and had a letter signed from Ravaryn. The proof wasn't needed though, as the guard nodded as if he had been already instructed that they were coming, or somehow knew who Orion was. Barrack was his name, and Orion couldn't help but appreciate his stern but no-nonsense demeanour. He also sensed that the other guards they passed by held a high level of respect for Barrack by the way they stood, their shoulders firm and back, heads held high in his presence.

They left the creature in a secure cell, still bound in the netted ropes to the transport cage, in the icy part of the lower level of the castle. Orion clearly recognised these as dungeons, some still littered with frozen blocks of long-gone prisoners, their preserved shells covered in crusted layers of ice.

An angry scowl slid onto Aytac's face. 'Will the creature even survive down here?' Aytac aired his concern about the thing that had just taken a considerable amount of energy to capture and deliver all the way here. If it just died, it would surely be a massive waste of their time.

'We'll leave it here while we inform Mazda, and then get an escort to the glasshouses. We won't be long, and if it's a creation from blood magic similar to Kyeitha's, it's harder to kill than it looks, trust me.'

Aytac nodded. He knew all too well about the innocent victims Kyeitha had torn apart and rebuilt before his eyes. He could still hear the creatures' cries of agony if he lingered too long on the memories. Too many times she had made him watch her perverse practices, dooming the animals she had made him capture for her.

The pair turned to face Barrack, who just gave them a concerned stare, then led the way out of the lower levels and through the empty yet opulent halls and corridors of the ice palace. But they had to remove their coats upon entering into the warmth of main room, fires blazing in all three fire places.

'Wait here, please. I'll retrieve the queen and have some refreshments brought in for you both. Sit and rest.'

Orion and Aytac eyed each other, clearly uncomfortable with the kind treatment and overly opulent surroundings. Yet they took a seat on the velvety lounge, their dirty clothes probably tracking muck and leaving a trail everywhere. Aytac made himself comfortable, muddy boots finding the coffee table and making Orion smirk his way.

The sound Paxton's boots made as he strode down the hallway stilled as he reached the doorway, drawing the attention of the two watchers to where the young soldier stood. Paxton's eyes widened in recognition, then his face was consumed by his huge smile as he spied Orion. He made his way over to greet him and produced a hand.

'It's good to see you, Wolf.'

Orion's lip twitched in a smile, and he felt pride bloom in his chest at the sight of Pax. He had grown up so much in these last few months, and Orion had barely been able to greet the lad at the palace in the valley as he'd had to furiously rush off to retrieve Ravaryn. Now he wrapped his tall, athletic frame into his huge muscled one, crushing him sufficiently into a rough hug.

'Good to see you again, lad.'

They embraced for a moment then Orion released him and introduced Aytac. Pax shook his hand and Aytac eyed him with a stern nod.

'Hey, have we met before?' Paxton's voice was curious as he tried to place the man, his yellow penetrating gaze too familiar.

'We have, actually.' Aytac smiled in a way that looked more like baring his teeth than an actual smile. 'You and the red-haired lad were visiting the old woman Diwa just as I arrived at her cottage in the woods. The other lad looked like he thought I was going to eat him.'

Realisation made Paxton's brows shoot for his hairline. 'The black wolf,' he said in awe, still holding Aytac's hand, oblivious to Aytac's discomfort.

'That was me.' He withdrew his hand from the excessive shake.

'Nice to meet you, properly. I'm Paxton, but everyone just calls me Pax.'

He came to sit with the men on the lounge to wait for Mazda. The three of them couldn't have looked more out of place in the sparkling finery, with the black sea glittering in angry swells out from the tall glass windows adjacent them.

'What are you two doing here? Did you find *him*... is he–is Zee okay?' Pax questioned, the worry apparent in his eyes.

'Zee's fine. She was completely healed not long after we left when you and Mazda were with her, I was told. Then she and Aytac's sister Sayde left on a task from Diwa to collect rare poisons to fight against the black dragon. When we found Ravaryn, he was uninjured, and he's safely inside the protection of the valley city now. So as long as the insufferable bastard stays where we left him, Zee will be fine.'

Paxton nodded, but Orion didn't miss the sharp sting of hurt sweep over his face for a moment at the mention of the king.

'What about you, lad? I thought you would have stayed in the valley with Zee? And your gear? Are you a soldier now?'

'I wanted to stay with her, but there wasn't anything I could really do there. I feel like I can actually help here... and the Kymerians are not so bad. Barrack has been training with me every morning, and Mazda has asked me to accompany her when she has to speak with the leaders of the other two territories.'

Orion didn't miss the slight flush of red and Paxton's eyes dropping to the floor on mention of the vivacious red-haired queen. He smiled to himself. 'I'm glad you're here.'

Paxton looked up, and his amber eyes misted over.

Orion saw he was biting the inside of his cheek to keep his emotions in check. He knew he was like a father-figure to the boy, and even as Wolf he had had a role in Pax's life – despite him being overprotective of his daughter. He knew the lad felt like he finally had Orion's approval.

Just then Mazda glided into the room like a monarch butterfly, all grace and power, her vibrant red curls a mass of fiery waves, making her look not as domineering as her presence felt. She was in her riding gear and came to sit in the lounge with the three men, but her face seemed drawn, and dark circles were obvious under her dull blue gaze. She was followed in by Barrack. He stood silently, a metre from the lounge, hands crossed in front of him. She was a leader already in her own right. Orion just prayed she would be better than her predecessor.

Orion and Aytac stood and greeted Mazda with a curt nod each. 'Majesty.'

'Please, sit. I don't need any of that. Did you find him? Is he alive?'

Orion's forehead furrowed. 'Yes. Ravaryn is safe in the valley.'

Mazda shoulders visibly relaxed she leaned back into the chair as if it were a soft cloud. 'Has there been any sign of Blaze? The duellerat that saved us from the spider creatures?'

Aytac answered her simply. 'No, Majesty. I'm sorry.'

Mazda's sparkling blue eyes dulled further, like storm clouds dulling the bright blue sky.

Orion produced something from his chest pocket under the strap and handed it to her. 'It's from Ravaryn.'

Mazda's hand reached for the letter. 'Thank you.' She finally looked Orion in the eye, his deep forests of emerald so much like Zemira's. 'I see where Zee gets her eyes from now.'

Orion just searched the young queen's gaze, still unsure of her. She'd been raised by an arrogant monster, so how did she exude so much warmth and kindness?

He spoke. 'We have one of the creatures with us, and we need to deliver it to the glasshouses. Diwa has informed us that there may be a way to reverse the transformation, there may be a cure. There are indeed humans with human souls still inside of them.'

Mazda cringed, and Paxton's face contorted a little on the confirmation.

Orion continued. 'We passed through Valomma on the way here. The town has been raided, and I'm afraid no one is left but the old barkeep. The Arakanai have taken them all to Salvador's stronghold, I'm guessing. We're running out of time. You need to rally the other territories' armies. You need to inform them of the threat. Aylenta I'm sure has already suffered some of the same losses as it borders Lamiria too. We need to get ready for a war, and we will not have much time. I fear if we wait any longer to rally our combined forces, there will be nothing left to fight for.'

Mazda replied, her voice steady as she relayed the information. 'It is already done. I met with both the Aylentean and Thortan leaders the second the rushed coronation was over. There has been no sight of the spider creatures within Aylenta just yet, but I fear that will change as Kymera's villages bordering Lamiria have all now been raided, or evacuated by the guard for the safety of Zenya city. Thorta has only pledged half their forces. They were somewhat unconcerned; I'm assuming that they are the furthest away from the threat and felt that we would deal with it before it reached their borders.'

Mazda held her anger in well, but Orion still caught the furrow of her brow and the tensing of her shoulders.

'But Aylenta has pledged to join with us, and we will gather both forces and head for Lamiria within the week.'

Orion nodded, before adding, 'You should meet just beyond the gates to Lamiria, at a narrow mountainous pass that leads into a vast meadow. I will explain the route before I depart. It will be large enough for both your forces and the warriors from Lamiria to assemble.'

*

After delivering the Arakanai to the steamy glasshouses and securing it in Borztan chains left over from Ravaryn's reign as king, Tye and Hamish's initial shock had worn off and was replaced by ways to cure the creature, setting the human soul free. But what kind of tonics, tinctures and medicinal herbs could force the blood magic from it without harming the human soul inside.

Mazda had insisted that Aytac and Orion stay to recoup before they returned to the valley to gather their own army of shifters, watchers and creatures of Lamiria. Orion couldn't wait any longer, and he left the castle and flew straight towards Aylenta in his large eagle form. Verena couldn't wait any longer. He needed to have her safe in his arms and out of any harm's way.

Mazda sent word to Aylenta as soon as she had finished her discussion with Orion and Aytac, informing them that she would lead the combined armies into Lamiria. She instructed Aylenta that their forces were to meet with Kymera's at the edge of the old Rim wall on the Kymerian border. This was the entrance into the Phoenix Forest, and they would reach the meadow past the gates to Lamiria in a weeks' time. It wasn't long, but it was all they could afford knowing Salvador could burn the world to the ground in a moment if he so much felt the urge.

That night Mazda clutched the letter in her dainty hands, her thumb stained red and the skin raw underneath her silver ring. The perfect scrawled writing of the man who had raised her like a father slid across the worn paper, confirming that Blaze was gone. There was nothing in that moment that could stop the tears from staining the ink, as her heart cracked like it never had before. Not even the loss of a childhood without parents compared to the pain of losing her companion. It ignited a fiery hatred within her that she had never felt before, and she like so many others knew that the black dragon had to die.

He would never have this realm unless every last one of their hearts stopped beating. The leaders had listened to her. She was a ruler now. After all, she had been trained by the King of Kymera who had finally, after 500 years, brought an end to the Rim wall. And he had passed on his methods. Mazda had done whatever it took to convince the other leaders that they must join the war. But her words had all been the truth... there wouldn't be anything left to fight for by the time the black dragon and the Arakanai got to their lands.

The Promise

The valley had been bright and full of hope every single morning that Zee had awoken in Ravaryn's arms. Bliss didn't even come close to the feeling that grew inside of her every time she breathed in his scent. Every time his powerful hands caressed her body, every time their lips met, every time their bodies worshipped each other.

Somewhere deep inside of her soul she felt like she had felt this love before, although she couldn't explain it. It was intoxicating, all consuming, and there was nothing on this earth that would ever compare to his presence within her arms. His darkness soothed her own, and she no longer felt guilt for what she was made of. She felt powerful with him next to her. They had trained every day that week, collecting every willing shifter and warrior in the valley and sending scouts to scour the hidden villages of Lamiria to spread the news.

Creatures and shifters came to the temple day by day, heeding their new queen's orders. Zee had also trained with Diwa, concentrating on conjuring her powers of the forest. At the end of every day, she fell into Ravaryn's arms exhausted, but somehow his mere presence lit her with fire and energy from an unknown source. Just when she thought she was close to utter depletion, he filled her with up again with want, warmth and a powerful, unspoken energy. She knew she loved him deeply with her entire being, and she had for a long while now.

Zee had already learned to control the shadowrens that Kyeitha had used to watch the humans within the old Rim world. Having not completely agreed with their old image and the fear that they instilled upon the humans, she had crafted their feathers into deep purples and vibrant sky blues. Their tail feathers sprouted with jasmine flowers and their eyes, instead of milky white pools, reflected the green forests around them. The shadowrens now represented the new queen, with no reminder of the last ruler's cruel reign now in their appearance.

Each day, a small part of Zee changed. Her hair had started to turn a deep green on the tips of her midnight tresses. The vine scar on her temple had shifted a little, and a fern now peeked out from her hairline and entwined with the black swirls. She didn't mind what was happening to her, as somewhere in her lineage she was already part fae, part human, part demon, so why not be part forest guardian too? She was a woman of four worlds, and she finally felt like she knew where she belonged after a lifetime of being lost.

Ravaryn came to stand behind her and wrapped her in his arms, his chin resting on top of her head as she looked out upon the valley like she had every morning since returning.

'They're so beautiful, aren't they? They're my favourite?' Zee leaned her back against his chest, staring out at the brilliant sunflower blooms decorating the valley before her and running her fingers over his muscled forearms that wrapped powerfully around her.

'There's something I need to tell you,' he began.

'If it's that you're so blessed to have me as I'm the most perfect thing to enter your life... well, ever. It's okay. I know.' Zee's smug face beamed in Ravaryn's embrace.

'I'm serious, Zemirahhh...' he purred in her ear, his deep velvet voice tickling her skin there, sending a warm shiver through her.

'So am I!' She faked shock.

'But, yes, you are indeed the most perfect thing I've ever held in my entire life. Every part of you was made for me, and your soul will always belong to me. In this life and the next, and now that I've found you again, I will never... ever... let you leave me.' Ravaryn's tone changed to something desperate as the words came out.

Zee turned around in his grip to face him in the gentle morning sun, which illuminated the specks of silver in his onyx eyes.

'Wings, what's wrong?' She felt a spark of worry ignite inside of her.

'There's something I have to tell you, but please don't think I'm going mad.'

Zee's brows twitched but she refrained from an eye roll. 'It's okay. Come, sit.' She led him to the bed. 'You can tell me anything. I already think you're mad.' Her smile was wicked.

A deep laugh left him at her words. 'And that's why you're perfect.'

Zee just smiled reassuringly, waiting for Ravaryn to air whatever it was that was worrying him so.

'When I awoke after Salvador had taken me, I was injured so badly that I was dying.'

'I know...' Zee interrupted. 'I could feel it. I could feel your pain as we're connected, you and I, with a blood bond. Forever. What you suffer, I suffer alongside you, and vice versa. We'll never be alone again.'

Ravaryn's eyes glazed over. 'I'm so sorry,' he said.

'You couldn't have known, and we're connected in a way that is so special that I don't mind.'

'While I was near death, a vision appeared. A woman, an ethereal creature. The Mother appeared before me, Zee. The *actual* mother of the earth, Gaia. She healed me... and she told me why we are so drawn to each other, why when you aren't near me I feel like I'm drowning, like there's no point in struggling for the next breath. You're my soul flame, Zemira Creedence, and we've met before... sunflowers were her favourite too.' Ravaryn smiled like he was in pain. 'Liara's favourite. Yes, you are her soul's reincarnation, Zemira, my phoenix risen from the ashes, and nothing in this world will ever take you from me again.'

Zee's eyes grew wide as realisation struck her and she was hit with a long- forgotten memory. She was in a garden tending to her brassicas, and littered between everything there were huge sunflowers smiling all around her. She felt a pull... a flutter of butterfly wings inside of her, and as she looked up, there he stood as handsome and god-like as ever. Ravaryn waited at the edge of the gardens; *Liara's* gardens. She ran to him, his smile wide, and jumped into his arms. He spun her round and round, his young face radiating with joy. By the Mother, she *knew* in her heart that she had once been Liara.

'You're not mad. I've met her too. Gaia. Many times, actually. I knew... the first day I laid eyes on you in the castle, I felt it. I knew I had met you before, that we had a connection... *somehow.*' Zee's eyes grew alert as the second realisation hit her.

'Soul flame,' she whispered.

'My soul flame.' Ravaryn kissed her deeply, cupping her face with his hands and pulling her towards him as close as he could. He breathed her in. The cracks, the giant fissures that had ailed his heart were slowly fusing together, like her essence was healing him from the inside and melting him back together like flame would to shattered glass.

'I will never let you go again. Even if it means I have to promise to follow you from this life to the next.' The words were true, and held power. A promise. And they came from Zee's mouth, her emerald eyes now glowing with the declaration to Ravaryn.

'I promise, Wings. I promise I'll always find you.' She kissed him again in the morning sunlight that spread like sparks from the sunflower blooms below in the valley.

*

Orion had made it to Kali on his journey back from Zenya, and he flew with large white wings into the familiar garden on the cottage on the hill. The patch of flowering chamomile that held Zendara's little soul caught his eye as he landed and shifted back to his human form. Verena opened the door to the cottage as if sensing his return and ran to him. Embracing him around his broad waist in a powerful hug, she wiped her tears into his shirt, holding him tight for a long moment, just breathing him in.

*

Zemira knocked on the door to the sandstone building she had been told Mirabel's family had chosen. When she opened the door, the young girl's glossy blonde hair was dishevelled, and her eyes looked dull against her dark skin.

Zee smiled at her gently. 'Hello, Mirabel. I have a favour to ask of you, and you could say it's a queenly request of the upmost importance.' She moved side to side as she held something awkwardly behind her, trying to contain as it nudged into her.

Mirabel's eyes focused when she realised who stood at her door, and her grief-stricken face lit up a little. 'Hi, Zemira,' was all she could force out.

Then Moss broke free from behind Zee in an exuberant spinning dance, her tail whipping wildly, unable to contain her excitement. Mirabel moved back a tad, but she was quickly waking from her stupor, it seemed.

'What is that?' Mirabel's face dropped in confusion.

'This is Moss, and she needs someone to take care of her while we're gone. She'll be safe here with you, and I trust no one else. Oh, and she's called a dog.'

Moss padded awkwardly on her long, thin legs towards Mirabel, who panicked and raised her hands to stop the creature, but Moss leapt up and ran her thick-leaved tongue over Mirabel's neck and face, knocking her down and peppering her with strange kisses.

'She also needs to be taught some manners too!' Zee added, laughing just as Mirabel erupted in giggles.

This only egged Moss on more, and she whipped around and kissed even more, tickling Mirabel into a state. Mirabel's mother rushed in from the other room to see what the commotion was. As she took in the sight, her eyes watered with the sound of Mirabel's laughter. She looked at Zemira still standing in the doorway and realised what was going on. Pressing her hands together in front of her chest, she mouthed the words to her new queen, 'Thank you,' before dipping her head respectfully.

A Puzzle

Tyson Bramble and Hamish the horticulturist stood side by side a good distance away from the Arakanai bound and enclosed in the compact cage. Their faces scrunched in horror as they looked at the creature now eyeing them with multiple rotating golden eyes. A nerve-shredding *click, click, click* emitted from the abomination.

'So the first thirty-seven medicinal concoctions have failed to produce positive change in form, or behaviour – at least from what we can tell.' Tye's voice was serious as he held the clipboard containing highly organised data from the last week of endless testing on the mutant patient.

He was tired, and his entire body ached from lack of sleep, but he was determined to help whatever poor soul still remained inside of the thing before them. It could be someone's, brother, sister, mother, father, wife or husband. It was someone. And there had to be a way to reverse the blood magic's hold. If there was a cure for snow lung then there was surely a cure for this. They just had to find the right plant extracts, the right balance and then they could help free the people's souls who had already been taken.

'What if we start testing a different category of plants? Stuff we know the ancients used rather than the unknowns from Aylenta?' Hamish offered, his arms tucked in around his barrel chest as he flicked his mop of sandy hair away from his eyes.

Tye stared at the Arakanai, trying to think of a solution to this puzzle. They had been at it all week since the creature had arrived with the Lamirian watchers, and they had not made an inch of progress. He felt like the thing had learned to watch them... like it was listening to each feeble attempt they tried to administer, each failed concoction that didn't result in a cure. He imagined it laughed back at them through its ever-watchful golden gaze.

Hamish came forward to pull the thick hide over the creature's cage. 'I can't think straight while that thing is watching us.'

'We could add some yarrow? And combine that with the kimbledart tonic we already have to see if it brings about any change. Maybe some rudamwort berries as well? It says here they are really good for healing tinctures of skin irritations, so maybe we need to work with healer herbs of the flesh instead of from the inside of the creature? Focus on transforming the exterior back instead of the other way round because we've tried and failed at every internal attempt?' Tye looked up and caught Hamish giving him an assessing look and smiling for some odd reason.

'You never give up, do you?'

'This thing could be someone's family member, Hamish. It looks like it should be just put out of its misery now, but inside, they said that there is still someone in there... imagine being trapped like that? With no way out.'

Visions of a dark cavern swirled terror for an instant throughout Tye's body. He stilled. 'We're their only chance.' His voice grew taught, white knuckles clutching the clipboard of medicinal herbs in his grasp.

Hamish walked over to Tye and pried it from his hands. 'If anything were ever to happen to *me*, please remind everyone that you're the one I want on my side.' He placed the clipboard down on a table full of flowering calendula behind him, and stood closer to Tye than he ever had before. Tye could see the streaks of grey flash through Hamish's bright icy blue eyes.

'I think ...' he breathed so close to Tye's face that he felt his cheeks heat instantly. For a second he was lost in the snowstorm of Hamish's hungry gaze and the tickle of his warm breath against his cheek. '...we need to take a little break.'

Hamish's smile was devilish. 'Come on, I'll make us some wattle seed tea. The Arakanai will still be here waiting for whatever concoction we try next. But you, Bramble...' Hamish reached up as if to brush a hair behind Tye's ear. Tye sucked in a sharp breath, but in the last second Hamish's hand came to clamp on Tye's shoulder. '...need a break.'

He led Tye away from the glasshouse area where the creature was kept and to the open kitchen break area. Vines showered down in curtains to make the space feel as though it were a living room within the houses.

Tye calmed his beating heart at Hamish's closeness. *Don't be ridiculous,* he told himself, *there's no way...* But the distraction was most definitely needed, and as soon as Tye sat down, he felt his stomach ache with hunger, and his head pounded a little from his temples inwards.

Hamish passed him a mug of tea, and his large hands brushed over Tye's briefly, accompanied by a warm smile. He sat down next to him in the break room.

'We're missing something.' Tye hands raked through his wild locks that badly needed a trim. 'I just can't figure out what it is yet...'

*

That night Tye tossed and turned so wildly that he awoke in fright as he fell from his old bunk in the room he shared with his sister Juniper. His head smacked loudly into the rugged floor. Rather than trying to fight to find sleep again, he left the room, along with Juniper's soft snores, and ventured out into the family house's small kitchen to seek the time and maybe a warm cup of tea.

It was still rather early, but his father George Bramble was gone though, having left already for his shift in the bakehouse in the market centre, so it was definitely past midnight. Tye gathered from his absence that it was early morning. His mind instantly started listing herbs and plants that he and Hamish had yet to experiment with. Just as he fiddled for a match in the dark kitchen, a furry body slid around his ankles and startled him. He had just enough time to recognise what it was, and stopped a yell from exiting his mouth as he realised that Edgar was the culprit.

'Eddie, you little ratbag!' he whispered. 'What on earth do you want? Juny's still asleep! Everyone is.'

The sparalinx just turned his fluffy head around, and his wide, dark eyes like that of an owl bored inquisitively into Tye's tired ones. Then he ran up Tye's body to gently encase his neck like a living scarf, shifting from a deep burgundy colour into a gentle lime green, his little feathered ears tickling Tye's ear.

Tye couldn't help but smile with Edgar's soft warmth comforting him. He lit a few candles and finished making himself a cup of strong tea, then sat in his father's chair in front of the embers of the family fireplace. His mind recited the medicinal drafts he would use to try to shift the creature's cursed form back today. What could they have possibly been missing? They had nearly tried every known method and plant extract to reverse the transformation and return the trapped human within, but nothing – *nothing* – had even budged the vile creature's form, not even a little. His head throbbed at his temples as he watched the flames glowing in different patches of the coals in waves of deep red light. *What were they missing?*

Eddie slid from Tye's neck, and he blinked rapidly awake, having almost fallen asleep again on the comfy lounge chair. It was still early but not a ridiculous hour for him to appear back at the glasshouses for work. The clock on the wall above the fireplace said it was past five. He packed a small lunch, rubbed his face over with a damp cloth and raked his fingers through his wild hair. Grabbing his coat and the knitted scarf

Juniper had made him, he wrapped it around double, then left before his mother or sister had a chance to wake.

*

'What if we use more? Like heaps more…? Maybe it's not penetrating through the Arakanai's hard shell?' Tye's voice was becoming desperate.

Hamish just gave him a worried look, noting his dishevelled hair and wild arm movements. 'We've tried that Tye, remember? We left it lathered in thick milkroot and callistem oil salve for an entire night. Nothing. When was the last time you had a good night's sleep?' he asked the question gently.

'What does that have to do with anything!' Tye almost exploded.

Hamish didn't react though, he just stayed put, his calm presence making Tye feel foolish.

'Sorry. I – I just can't believe we haven't figured this out yet, and we're running out of time.'

'I know,' Hamish soothed. 'But it'll come.'

A loud bang behind them knocked a few pots from a shelfing system that swayed as though it had been bumped from beneath. The creature to the far right popped its netted head up, gold eyes wheeling, and it clicked a few curious sounds from its throat.

Tye scowled at the thing then turned to investigate the pots. A blur of bright red hair couldn't be disguised from under the potting bench if it tried.

'What on Mothers' earth do you think you're doing here?' Tye scolded, his voice high.

Juniper's little body, wrapped in brown woollen jumpers, jumped up in fright. She smacked her head again into the metal bench, knocking more potted specimens off the shelf she hid beneath, tumbling soil and plants out everywhere. Juniper crawled out, rubbing her head with a small hand, her eyes crinkling shut at the pain.

'You forgot your lunch that Mum made you – *again*.' She held out a calico bag in her free hand, and her eyes landed on another set of grey blue ones that smiled invitingly at her.

Hamish's face lit up in an impressed smile, and his thick arms crossed over his broad chest.

'Hi, I'm Juniper, but you can call me Juny! Do you work with Tye? Are you his boss?'

'Alright, that's enough. I'm taking you home right now! You shouldn't be here, and I made my own lunch this morning!'

Hamish laughed. 'It's alright,' he said. 'I'm Hamish.' He held out a huge hand to the small firecracker and shook her little hand, totally encasing it in his – and her wrist as well.

A screech sounded from the Arakanai, but the pair barely noticed as they had become so used to the thing by now. Juniper jumped, however, and spun around to see where the noise had come from. Her eyes grew massive, like Edgar's of a night time. Tye panicked and reached out to grab her shoulders and steer her away from the creature.

'No, it's not alright!' he squeezed out, expecting a horrible meltdown and months of nightmares that would all be his fault for letting Juniper see the monster that threatened to become all of them if they lost this fight. He tried to pull her away, to pry her little eyes from its view.

'What *is* that thing?' she said. The sound of excitement, not fear, sparking from her voice was not what Tye had expected in the least.

'It's nothing... let's go. You can't be here.'

Juniper slid out of Tye's grip and slipped over to Hamish, tucking herself half behind him, but eyes still directly on the Arakanai.

'It's horrible! What's wrong with it? Is it sick?' she asked curiously.

Hamish's brows twitched a bit, and impressed by her lack of fear, he offered her an answer. 'Actually, it kind of is. Your big brother and I are finding a medicine to fix it.'

'So this is why you've been working so much?' Juniper's little mind found her own answers, a serious look on her face, as she still couldn't peel her eyes from the Arakanai. 'What kind of medicine have you been giving it? How can you fix it?'

'That's what we're trying to figure out. There's actually a person in there, and they're sick, so we're working on curing it like an illness.'

Tye's blue eyes pinned on Hamish as he stood protectively near his little sister, clearly annoyed that he was pandering to her inquisitive nature.

Hamish just shrugged his way, in an I'm-sorry-but-she-asked kind of way.

'It looks like a spider ate it, then tried to make it a spider, and it didn't really work, because the human bits are all wrong and still kind of there. Maybe you shouldn't be trying to make it better at all. You should be trying to kill the spider parts. Like Edgar kills the spiders at home.'

Juniper scrunched up her face, her dislike of spiders evident, like she was lucky to have a sparalinx like Eddie in her home to scare them all off.

Tyes eye's widened and found Hamish's. The pair looked at each other at the exact same moment.

'Juniper, you're a genius!' he yelled.

The Arakanai screeched simultaneously, and Juniper jumped with a fright.

'I know that!' She clutched at Tye's jumper now. 'Ah... But why?' she added.

'You just are, Juny. Now let's get you home. I'm sorry, but Hamish and I have a lot of work to do.'

An Understanding

Ravaryn watched Orion from the seat of rock he had been waiting upon, and approached him as Orion made his way down to the valley, leading Verena towards the palace. His entire body resisted what he was about to do, but as he called out to catch Orion's attention, the pair both turned. Verena's gaze narrowed, and the look that spread over her face, even from such a distance, would make any grown man cower. She started to march towards him, fists clenched at her sides, back rigid. Orion grabbed her, and the pair exchanged a few words before Verena turned away and huffed off into the palace as Orion came to meet Ravaryn.

'You're back,' Ravaryn stated flatly, hands pocketed in his dark-armoured training wear. 'Did you...? Did Mazda get the letter?' he inquired, ignoring the scene, and the hate, from Verena.

Orion's face, which he had forced into a scowl upon sighting Ravaryn the minute he got back to safety, dissolved as he realised Ravaryn's first words were after the wellbeing of his apprentice queen. He was tired of feeling the consuming anger towards this damaged man. Meeting Mazda and seeing her concern for him had crumbled some of the hate away. He also had Verena safely inside the valley, and her presence near him and the knowledge of her wellbeing eased him further.

'Yes, she did. Mazda is well, and she has rallied the other territories' armies. They will meet us in the meadows just inside the gates. You trained her well.'

Ravaryn was taken aback by the compliment, and he actually stood back a little as if he expected it were a trick, or that a blow would follow. 'She will be one hell of a leader, and she will make a respected queen. She'll do a better job ruling Kymera than I ever did,' Ravaryn admitted.

Orion smirked. 'Not hard to do. But you had your reasons for doing what you did. Not that I agree with all your methods.'

Ravaryn nodded at Orion's olive branch. 'Aytac returned a day ago, and he and his sister Sayde have organised the warriors and shifters in the valley into units. They're very adept, so we might actually have a chance to win this thing. The Lamirian armour has all been coated in a buskstin fern extract that Diwa and Sahara have been working on, as it repels flames and is unable to catch alight. We'll take as much as we can to the meadow for the human armies when we meet them, to paint their armour with also.'

Orion turned to look out at the valley and the groups of warriors that were training. They looked like congregations of ants below them as he spoke. 'Has she seen your true form yet?'

Ravaryn's face drained slightly of its colour, but his composure returned in an instant.

'Because whether you like it or not, we are going to need all the forces we can gather, you included.'

'You know what I am?' Ravaryn's voice was low and flat, as though a fear was being aired.

'You and Diwa left the valley after Kyeitha took over, and you lived in a small village of watchers when you were young. Your father is a dragon shifter from another world, and your shifter form is only half an animal form, as you just materialise wings, not an entire shift. You're like no other shifter I've met. And you possess shadow and smoke magic that I've never seen before. Diwa also has powers that don't hail from this world.

It didn't take much for me to figure it out after I saw the black dragon, and Diwa confirmed that he is your father, but just don't let Zee find out about your true form the same way I did. If she truly cares for you, it won't change the way she feels about you. My daughter has always been accepting of everything that comes into her path, and for reasons unknown, she has found something in you that she deems worthy.'

Ravaryn swallowed hard, his throat constricting like hands were slowly crushing off his air supply. His mind was whirling as he tried to quell the fear that sparked within him, to forcefully contain it from bursting out. His secret that he had kept for an entire lifetime was known... and Orion... he didn't flinch away from Ravaryn as he stared at those fierce, penetrating emerald eyes with his black wells of darkness.

'You hold her life in your hands now, and she holds yours. Treat her well.' Orion turned and walked away, leaving Ravaryn frozen in place by his sincerity: both the admittance of knowing Ravaryn's greatest secret, and the acceptance of his daughter's decision.

*

One day earlier

Aytac made his way over to the group that mimicked Sayde's every move in the training arena, recently relieved of its vegetated covering. Sweat beaded on muscled bodies, the air full of power and focus, the warriors' movements like fluid water – artists wielding their bodies with precision to the tune of the movements.

He watched until the session came to an end and waited for his sister to approach, having no doubt she already sensed that he had returned. She wiped the sweat from her brow and took a long swig from her water sack.

'Good to see you got back in one piece,' she offered, after quenching her thirst and taking a few breaths to calm her heart down after the training session.

'Same goes for you.' He slightly lifted a brow, a tiny smile reaching his face that few had ever been able to conjure. 'Quests with the new queen?

Don't tell me you finally figured out how to make friends while I was gone?' Aytac teased.

'Maybe I was never able to make friends because my haughty, deadpan twin was always hovering around to scare everyone off.' She landed a punch into Aytac's thick arm, not even producing a flinch.

'Ha-ha. I just assumed it was your cheery disposition that kept them all at bay.'

Sayde walked over to sit on a tree stump at the edge of the dirt clearing, and Aytac followed. 'She's different that one,' Sayde explained, referring to Zemira. 'She didn't even flinch when she saw me as a Vallarax. She was, well.... impressed.'

Aytac looked at his sister. She had changed so much since they were young, and she had always been feared after what she had done to rid this world of their violent father. In turn, her rare shifter form brought fear from the other watchers and Lamirians. She should never have had to feel that, not from her own people. She should never have had to be dealt that hand in the first place.

'She is most definitely different. I've known and watched her for some time now, and there's no doubt in my mind that she will restore greatness to this world. There's an acceptance inside of her for all of us, even the most feared and damaged ones, she feels a kinship with. The Mother chose well with her.'

Sayde smiled at the amount of words her usually quiet brother offered, and raised a quizzical brow.

'The day I first saw her, she pulled in an ancient river god from her side of the Rim wall. She wasn't thin compared to other humans I'd seen, and as soon as she laid eyes on the creature and realised she didn't need to take his life for food, she showed mercy. Sent him straight back to his domain without a second thought. Time and time again I have witnessed her put others before herself. I think that we will finally have the queen we deserve.'

*

Sayde felt guilt swirl inside her stomach at the words. She knew Zemira was good; hell, she even would go so far as to say she really liked the strange woman. She saw how even the foulest of creatures captured her heart. No one in their right mind would have even given that death-dog a second thought, but Zee had instantly felt love and kindness towards the grotesque thing. Sayde knew that she was utterly and wholly nothing like Kyeitha had been as queen, and it would make it that much harder when she did what she planned on doing when the time came...

Silver Secret

Valley of Rivers, Tangaroa, Lamiria

'Are you ready?' Ravaryn's voice was gentle.

'Do I look ready?' Zee almost screeched. She paced the floor of the room before him in the ethereal gown that had been woven onto her with the forest's magic the day the throne claimed her. Her dark hair fell in gentle braids down her back, and sparkling gems were woven in and around the midnight lengths that now had vibrant deep-green tips.

'You look—' He walked over and stilled her anxious pacing. 'Absolutely mesmerising. I don't know if I want the entire city's eyes to see you, to see my queen like this. My jealously might drown me.' His smile was disarming and wicked all in one, and he looked down at her with hunger in his eyes, his long lashes seductive as they framed his dark eyes.

'That's easy for you to say. You've had a lifetime of people looking to you to lead. I can't handle all those eyes on me... it's too much. Oh gods, I think I'm going to be sick. I'm sweating, are you sweating?' Zee flapped a hand at her face, taking rapid breaths.

Ravaryn just pulled her to the bed and sat her down next to him, his face passive. 'Never let them see your fear. I never did, and I guessed they assumed I didn't possess any. You'll do fine. I promise. They already love you, so you just have to solidify your confidence in them, and they will fight with passion and loyalty for their home, knowing that you are one hundred per cent on their side.'

Zee's breaths slowed a little. 'Can't I just go slay a demonic dragon instead? Can you just do the speech for me?' she begged.

Ravaryn's laugh bubbled deeply from him, making her stomach settle with his mirth.

'I would if I could. The fact that you'd rather fight a malevolent fire-breathing monster than speak in front of people is worrying.'

'I know.' She squeezed his hands, solidifying in him her trust.

'There's something that I have to do too that I feel is going to make me just as nervous and uncomfortable as you...' Ravaryn confessed, his face ashen.

His eyes dropped from hers to trail along the tattooed vines on her hands. He looked... *scared.*

'Oh gods... What is it? What's wrong?' Zee hated seeing him like this, and her heart instantly ached to soothe him.

'You know that we both contain demon's blood...'

Zee swallowed, not liking the way this conversation was going. 'Yes...' she said.

'Well, yours is present in your ability to control fire. Your emerald flames come from your grandfather, Thaylon, Kyeitha's lover-turned-prisoner and Salvador's returned right hand. My powers are more... distasteful...' Ravaryn tried to explain.

'What are you saying, Wings? I love your wings. They're beautiful, and the fact that you can talk with creatures is amazing, I'm kind of jealous if I'm to be honest. I'd love to know what Moss is thinking.' Zee tried to make light of Ravaryn's sad demeanour.

'That's not what I am referring to. I've learnt to hide my true self, my *true* shifted form. Diwa knew I wouldn't belong, and she wanted there to be no excuse for people to fear me like they do Salvador, so I learned to half shift...'

'Show me,' Zee comforted. 'There's nothing about you that scares me, Ravaryn Black, nothing that you are that I would ever turn away from. Your soul belongs with my soul in any form.'

Ravaryn swallowed and dropped Zee's hands, his gaze intensifying for moment longer. He stood, leaving Zee patiently watching him in all her finery. Moving to the centre of the room, he took one last look at Zee's face and the calm reassurance there, along with her beautiful smile.

Then he shifted. His *full* shift rippled black smoke, and it came to pool at the edges of the room, then slithered like snakes over the floor towards Zee. Ravaryn's eyes grew large, the darkness leeching into the whites of them as they became blackened night skies. His wings material-ised but were so much larger than Zee had ever seen, their span taking up the entire space of the large room. Throwing his head upwards, he shut his eyes, then in a swirl of black smoke, he shifted fully, his roar filling the air, one that Zee felt she had heard before.

Long taloned claws tipped in sharp black nails dug into the woven carpet beneath him. And instead of the black metallic scales of Salvador's form, there stood a sleek, shimmering silver dragon, half his father... but Diwa's light was there, so half his mother shone through the wild and powerful form he now possessed. Diwa's silver specks outweighed the darkness, the balance tipped as their light conquered the night. Ravaryn's eyes were deep black voids, dark horns protruded from his head and thorned barbs rippled over his backbone, following the line of his raised spine. Perfect sharp white teeth like that of the Armilandro lined his jaw slightly ajar maw.

The Armilandro... Zee had heard that roar accompany the Armilandro's in the cave when they'd had to barter for his teeth... *It was Ravaryn.* He had fully shifted back then without Zee seeing. While she had scurried to get away from being pummelled into the stalagmites by the Armilandro's powerful attack, he had shifted to calm the Armilandro and protect her from it.

Ravaryn's silver dragon form roared again, and he moved away from Zee. He opened his mouth and black tendrils of smoke blasted out towards the back of the room. The doorway to the springs caught the brunt of the plumes and disintegrated into black ash. Ravaryn turned around, carefully lifting his long-scaled tail, the tip a ball of silver spikes like polished daggers. He came before her and stood close, facing her with his head hanging down low. A deep rumble came from within him, and he closed his eyes then bowed to his queen, awaiting her reaction to his demon form.

Zee took in the magnificent creature before her, and her eyes followed every plane of his shifted body: the way the silver-plated scales rippled with light in rows at the smallest inflection of movement, and the horned and spiked head that now bowed to her. All her fears of addressing the city dissipated, and she stood on tingling legs before Ravaryn. She trailed a hand over his hanging head. He was twice the size of her, but not as large as Salvador's gargantuan form that she had fought in Maya Village the day he'd burned the forest to ash.

As Zee trailed her onyx fingernails over the silver scales, Ravaryn lifted his head and a purr-like growl came from within him at her touch. His ebony eyes opened and focused straight on her, and she finally spoke, her own eyes wide.

'You're magnificent.' The words hung in the air between them, and Ravaryn didn't move, as if he were now frozen.

Zee just circled him, running her hands over his body as she went, then came around to his opposite side and slid her arms up either side of his vicious-looking dragon face. She placed a soft kiss on his scaled face between his snout and eyes. She stood up right in front of where she had just seen the smoke he possessed being wielded, the black smoke that crumbled objects to ash, and she *kissed* him.

'I don't know why you waited so long to show me this...' Her voice was serious for a moment, 'because this is way cooler than just wings!' And then Zee was Zee again, joking and sweet.

Ravaryn shifted back in an instant before her, and stood right against her within her open arms. He looked down into her forest eyes. 'You are a strange soul, Zemira Creedence, and I'm never letting you go.'

'As are you, Ravaryn. You are *my* strange soul... you are *mine*.'

He kissed her fiercely, savouring the taste of her, his fears gone. He looked liberated at having shifted fully before her, like baring his true self had sparked wildfire inside his veins.

'I'm going to worship you so thoroughly that I will be all you can think of while you address the city. You are wholly, truly... *mine*.' His voice was deep and commanding, the words igniting a feral look in his eyes. 'In this lifetime and the next, and the next.'

Two Armies

Valley of Rivers, Tangaroa, Lamiria

Zemira stood before the entire city, all eyes watching with hopeful sheens towards their new queen. Her heart was drumming within her chest like wings ready to take rapid flight, and a sour taste filled her mouth along with a flood of saliva as her stomach lurched. She felt a tingle in her arm and a pull to her right, and as she looked towards the string of energy calling to her, there stood Ravaryn. Tall and taught, his penetrating dark eyes catching hers as he smiled, his lip pulling upwards to one side, his face saying, 'You've got this. Breathe.'

Did she imagine those words...? Or did Ravaryn's voice somehow just weave through her mind? She turned back to the quiet crowd awaiting her words. The scent of pollen and fresh vegetation wafted up from the blooming valley, and she embraced it into her, the warm earth below her grounding her, steadying her racing pulse.

'People of Lamiria,' she began shakily, her voice not her own. 'Most of you do not know me, but you may know who I am. The Mother has chosen me, and the forest has chosen *me to be your queen*, and this is a decision I promise each and every one of you that I do not take lightly. I will lead to the best of my ability, guard these lands with everything that I have, and put each and every one of you, and every living creature, before my own needs if that is what it takes to make Lamiria great again.

'We have a darkness that has been unleashed upon the land. Salvador the black dragon has shown us his hand and what he is capable of the day he burned Maya Village and the surrounding ancient forests to ash. He plans to rule over this world, to enslave and to punish. To lead with fear and pain, and I will not let that happen.'

A murmur from the crowd rose in the air.

'But he will not destroy us! We have formed an alliance with the humans inside of the old Rim world, and their armies are to meet with our forces. With them, we will take down the Arakanai-formed army that Salvador leads, as I believe he controls them with the likes of magic that Kyeitha wielded to lead her creatures of the damned. I ended her reign...'

Zee's voice no longer shook, and it rose triumphantly as the crowd cheered for her. 'And I will end Salvador and stop the creatures he created. This land belongs to the Mother. To Gaia. And no one and nothing will take it away from her children!'

Zee looked towards Ravaryn, and he nodded, a proud smirk on his handsome face.

'We also have a secret weapon that we will wield in the fight.' She motioned to Ravaryn, and he came forward, his eyes scanning the crowd.

'Many of you may know the son of Diwa who was banished into the Rim world for showing love towards a human. There will never again be such a law, as we are both one and the same now. Ravaryn was wrongfully punished.'

The crowd cheered in agreement, hands fisting the air as Zee continued on. 'And he will be our weapon. His shifter form will match that of Salvador's, so do not fear him. He will show you his true form now so that no one may confuse him with the enemy. He is a Lamirian, he *is* and *always* has been one of us, and he will help us win this war!'

Zee gave the nod, and black smoke started to spiral around Ravaryn's body, starting at his heels. He closed his eyes and shifted in an instant before the crowd. Shocked gasps filled the air and eyes grew wide as they took in the form of the silver dragon before them. The inner ring of the crowd staggered back. Zee stepped forward, sensing the panic, and raised her hand to rest on Ravaryn's scaled jaw before her people.

'Ravaryn Black is a former prisoner of Kyeitha's and a victim of her crimes against her people. He was imprisoned in the old Rim world, along with the humans, who were also her victims. Ravaryn has offered willingly to fight in the battle against our enemy, for his queen and for Lamiria!' Zee's voice was like steel, her words clear, concise and full of pride.

A moment of silence hung between them. The pair didn't move; they just remained standing solid, a reliable force the forest folk could trust. Then a cheer rose from within the middle of the crowd, which grew and spread rapidly. Like a swell in a vibrant sea, a roar of energy sparked a fire from the crowd.

'*For Lamiria!*' the people shouted.

Ravaryn shifted back into his male form, and Zee found his hand. She squeezed it tightly in her own and raised it high in the air. Diwa's proud eyes found hers, shining out from within the crowd, and a silvery tear slid down her cheek that didn't go unnoticed by Zee. She scanned further and there, still and stoic with a gentle smile, stood her father and mother. Together, once again in each other's arms, where they belonged. Orion nodded as his eyes met hers, and his smile reached his bright emerald eyes.

Zee withheld the emotions that coursed through her and kept her composure before the wild energy of the crowd, which flooded her with life. After a moment longer, she and Ravaryn took their leave. Later, Zee instructed the warriors that they were to ready themselves to leave for battle. They needed to say their goodbyes to their families and meet in the meadow to join forces with the human armies at dusk. Now was the time. Salvador could not be left to grow any stronger. Tomorrow their world would be at war. She just hoped and prayed that the weapon she had forged, the *real* secret weapon, 'the light', would truly work...

*

Mist hung over the vast meadows on the outskirts of the temple lands. Dewdrops hung gently from the wild grass, and flower heads sparkled with tiny webs collecting the dew-like jewels in the faint light of dawn. Zemira had met with all leaders from the territories the previous day, after addressing the city, and they were confident with their battle plan. She felt her muscles tighten like taut vines as she stood in the deep heart of the forest and waited for Mazda, Paxton and the entire rallied human forces to arrive through the gates of Lamiria.

Zee had sent a shadowren with a message, and it had shown her that Kymera had joined with Aylenta at the border and the combined armies were ready. The rock guardians were slumbering in their earthly gates. Zee had had Diwa's help to communicate with them and had already given them their orders to lay low until the armies had arrived. They were to follow behind at a far pace until the battle began, and only then coming in to aid their forces. They had limited words for communicating, but Zee had gathered their names, which were fitting for the huge rock warriors: Fungus and Fern. There was no sign of Arakanai anywhere in this part of the realm, no roar or screech from the sky, no fire... nothing of warning in the still meadows. It was peaceful, quiet... and it made Zee's anxiety so much worse. *Where were the territory armies?*

Moments passed and Zee's heart sank. Sharp pangs of disappointment tingled through her. She was so sure the human armies would fight alongside them. Ravaryn stood at her side, his hand finding hers as they both watched the misty gates. Aytac and Sayde appeared at her other side, Sayde gently nudging Zee's shoulder with a pressed-lip smile. Then the mist swirled and the meadow stilled as if holding its breath. A lone figure appeared, a small woman passed through the gates, and the Queen of Kymera stepped forth into the meadow and into Lamiria. Beside her, a young man followed, then an entire force in narrow procession through the mountainous gate pass. They made their way across the field. Mazda spotted Zee and Ravaryn next to her. She tried to hold her composure, but her pace quickened as she sped up. Ravaryn met her half way. Tears pricked at the edges of her bright blue eyes as she squeezed them tightly shut in Ravaryn's arms. Paxton sped up to reach Zee, crushing her in a similar hug. She breathed in the scent of him and felt his heart beat against hers, her body calming with her friend, her dearest ally, her *family* now standing with her. *They had arrived, they had come.* It was time to meet Salvador before he met them with any more destruction and death.

*

After organising the regiments of Lamirian warriors and mixing them with groups of human soldiers to optimise their chances of survival, Zee again met with every one of them to explain the risks, the plan and how they could best work together. They would need to have each other's backs to throw the balance of this fight. The Lamirians helped to coat their new allies' armour with the buckstin fern coating, to protect against the flames of the black dragon. The scattered attack of Arakanai would have no chance if the groups stayed together and fought as one. They planned to immobilise the creatures if possible without killing them, downing them by attacking the legs and taking them out from underneath. To try and save the human souls inside the morphed monsters. The day was long, and Zee slept heavily that night, wrapped in strong arms and dark wings. The next morning dawned on the meadow all too soon, and the tension in the air was as thick as raspor's honey when the armies broke camp and set out early to reach the deadlands that was home to Salvador's stronghold.

The orb weighed heavily on Zee's shoulder in the sling wrapped around her side, tight against her armoured attire. A cold vibration niggled where it rested against her, and it hummed as they reached the edge of the forest that met the deadlands. Black-plated armour adorned her entire body, and her hair had been tightly woven into fine braids against her head, which swept down her back. Dark kohl lined her eyes, and she looked every part the warrior beside her dragon king. Ravaryn stayed close, and he and Zee led the first large group of the army, followed by Aytac and Sayde with the second, and Mazda and Pax in the third, which held more human soldiers than the first two.

Zee didn't know how she had managed to win the argument with her father, but she had – *just*. She had begged him to stay with Mazda and Paxton's regiment, as there would be nothing she could do to protect them while they were in battle. Her sole focus was stopping Salvador, and she knew deep down that she couldn't bear for her father to be there if anything went wrong, if she or Ravaryn didn't make it. She wouldn't be able to think straight if Orion stayed by her side. If he had to witness something happening to her. He had reluctantly agreed to lead with Mazda and Paxton, but only after crushing Zee into a fierce hug that went on for minutes longer than it should have. Her father had held her in front of the campfire that night for the longest of moments, holding her head to his chest in his large tattooed hand, as if he was saying a goodbye just in case.

Zee felt emotion try to trickle into her, but she stopped it before it could take hold. She must be focused. Diwa would remain behind to protect the valley and make sure that if they failed, no harm would come to any of the people inside. Her power alone would be enough to protect this last stronghold if something went wrong. One thing that none of them had to worry about was Diwa and Verena being in harm's way. Even though Diwa was more powerful now than she had ever been, her magic having returned to her from the breaking of the Dark Rim, she was still the precious old woman in their minds. She was the bond, a single precious tie, which was the only thing that connected all three of them in a positive way. They all held Diwa dearly in their hearts as a mother, a grandmother and a dear friend.

Thank the Mother she had agreed to stay behind to protect the venerable folk and the entire valley if they should fail. Even if they didn't make it, at least Diwa and her mother would be safe. The thought brought a tiny shred of calm to Zee's zinging blood, then Zee looked to her left and over to the man who led the way for the armies through the forest. Ravaryn's demeanour was stoic. He had always emanated darkness, a threat of power, but today he was terrifying in his presence beside her. He was in his armour from Lamiria this time. Not Kymera. He exuded ancient power but appeared youthful all at once.

They reached the edge of the forest where the lush green foliage had not been assaulted by flames. Golden strands of strong silk coated every tree trunk, exposed branches and leaves, forming a tunnel of spiders' webs into the opening at the edge of the deadlands. An eerie chill in the air sent a shiver up Zee's spine, along with the snapping of threads as their boots crunched over the numerous strands of the golden webs.

Golden orb spiders scuttled and scattered through the trail as their webs stirred, but no Arakanai were in sight. Not yet. Small lumps were cocooned in the golden death traps and hung limply from the webs as grotesque little frog fingers reached out towards Zee.

The armies pushed their way forward through the unsettling mass of golden webs, and Zee spotted more and more victims trapped in them. Hollow eyes of finches and other larger birds stared vacantly, their heads popping from the cocoons that had been their end. Zee shivered, imagining them instead as her friends, as her family that she had worked so hard to find, being caught and held for fodder by the Arakanai. She brushed off the feeling and continued on through the landscape of sticky webbed cages, until stepping out into a windy grey emptiness.

Zee never thought this wasteland would ever be a reprieve to reach, until now. The web tunnel was suffocating to say the least, so maybe she should have changed tactics and let Fern and Fungus lead the way. They would have smashed a path through there with such ease. She took in the vast grey tundra of poisoned land and steeled her mind: Salvador could not be allowed the chance to rule. He would decimate the earth, and smother it with his creations, burning all beauty and life to the ground. It would become a land of fire and ash that would never recover. Gaia wouldn't survive it, Zee knew. No. They had to win today, or die trying, because a world like this wouldn't be worth living for.

Zee took the lead out past Ravaryn, leading the forces behind her onto the desolate, arid grey soil. Quiet murmurs filled the stagnant air, then a rumble vibrated the ground beneath her. Pebbles shook on the cracked plates of dried-up poisoned mud, rattling them like puzzle pieces on the crusted surface. She quickly knelt down on one knee and placed a hand to the ground, momentarily shutting her eyes. And there beneath the earth, she saw it...

'Get ready!' she screamed. 'Weapons at hand!'

As she screamed, a mud muncher, the monstrous larkaden, burst through the dirt. Clumps of rock and debris showered the front procession of soldiers, and dust blanketed the air all around them. The horrific head with its huge gaping mouth was open now, full of rows of needle-like teeth that lined its insides, and down into its dark throat.

And it lunged straight for Lamiria's new forest queen.

Phoenix in the Storm

The Deadlands

Zee's hands ignited in brilliant green plumes of fire. She thrust them forward, and the blast of emerald fire collided with the larkaden's oncoming attack, a brilliant light illuminating the dusty air all around them. The mud muncher reared back with a shrill, ear-piercing screech before it could mount its attack. The ground shook with the force of its body landing as it was thrown backwards from Zee's blast.

Soldiers crowded around their queen, readying to strike. Zee saw the flashes of sliver blades all around and for a moment she felt a pang of fear, sharp and strong. But it wasn't her own. The larkaden retreated from the blow, and although it had no face as such, Zee's could *feel* its energy. It was angry, but also afraid.

'*Stop!*' Zee commanded her soldiers, holding steady. She was poised and ready, but not approaching to engage. The soldiers were confused by her command.

Turning to Ravaryn she said, 'Can you communicate with it? Tell it to leave us be, that it doesn't have to attack, for surely it will die.'

Ravaryn's face was clearly conflicted, but given her soft heart for even for the most vicious of creatures, he nodded. 'I'll try, but if I fail, be ready.'

As the larkaden inched up farther, poising to strike again, Ravaryn shifted in an instant and roared defiantly back at the creature. His silver scales flickered with his movements, and his wings spread wide to shield the soldiers and Zee.

More animalistic sounds were exchanged, with the larkaden swaying slightly as it screeched. The earth rumbled again, and it its body rose higher from its hole, then it turned to its right and ploughed into the hard earth there, its mouth carving a way back into the darkness below, and away from the confrontation.

Zee whooshed out a breath. *He did it... it worked! What an incredible gift!*

Ravaryn shifted back, surrounded by wisps of dark smoke tendrils, and looked at Zee with a head shake and a cocky smile.

'What?' she pushed. 'What did it say?'

'It said it would rather live. I can't believe it actually spoke. I didn't know they were intelligent, and I can't say I've ever spoken with one before.'

'There's a first for everything.' Zee's eyebrow rose. 'I knew we didn't have to fight it as I could feel its hesitance. So thank you.'

The human soldiers spoke animatedly around them in awe of seeing the larkaden, while everyone was in awe that Ravaryn had actually convinced the thing to let them pass without conflict.

'It also said that spiders have spread over its lands like a plague and even fill the underground tunnels...'

Zee felt her face drop. *They were using the underground tunnels? But why?* 'Let's get going. How far do we have now till we reach it?' Zee questioned.

'Not too far. We'll be there soon enough.' Ravaryn's face darkened.

Zee nodded and chewed into the inside of her cheek as they marched on, making their way across the vast, misty grey land.

When they reached the crumbling ancients' concrete stronghold, there was not a living thing in sight. No Arakanai... and no black dragon. The army halted as the wind sped up, scattering gritty dust all around.

'Where are they...?' Zee's voice was almost a whisper to Ravaryn.

He stood close and stared out at the empty building. 'I don't know. We should wait as it could be a trap.'

Ravaryn's voice was low, but Zee sensed the tension. He wasn't sure either. They waited a few moments, the soldiers all tense and at the ready. Suddenly, a man appeared from the shadows of the crumbling building, his towering bulk moving slowly towards them, sinister hooded eyes pinned directly on Zee.

Ravaryn bristled and an angry growl emanated from his throat that wasn't remotely human. Zee felt a spark of panic zip through her, but instantly hardened herself. *You're the forest queen, the destroyer of the Rim walls. You ended the previous queen, so don't be fearful for no reason. You're a force to be reckoned with. No one is like you, and no one can do what you can do.*

Zee wasn't sure if the words were even her own as they swirled with black smoke through her mind, encouraging her. But they helped. She felt calmer, and her energy sparked within her at the ready as the man approached.

Thaylon's eyes narrowed as he stood metres from his descendant, his granddaughter and heir by blood, an eerie smile curling his lip on a face that made Zee's skin crawl.

'A queen already. How fitting.' His voice was like oil, deep and all too smooth for his bedraggled appearance. He turned to Ravaryn. 'I see you brought back a real leader with you, little dragon.'

Black smoked weaved around Ravaryn's ankles as he stood just in front of Zemira, a deep growl the likes of which Zee had never heard rumbling in his throat again.

Thaylon stalked closer, his eyes not leaving Zee's for a second. 'My heir.'

He produced a smile that would make even the most battle-hardened warrior's stomach turn. Thaylon looked pure evil and more than a little unhinged. Zee felt a curl of disgust and shame coat her insides. *I came from that...?* She moved forward bravely and spoke with the voice she had summoned when she had addressed the city.

'I am under no circumstance here to join you, nor do I agree nor want any part of what you plan for this realm. Kyeitha was right to banish you. You will submit to me and reverse the effects of your blood magic on the humans you abducted and made into Arakanai. Or you will have this entire army end you.'

A rumbling laugh left Thaylon as he watched Zemira, his smile still present, but it didn't reach his eyes. They shone brightly with something else. 'We'll see about that.'

His palms moved to face outwards as the words slid from his sneer. Bright crimson flames transformed into balls of blood fire, flaring brightly. Thaylon then lifted a hand and blasted crimson plumes of burning heat towards them. Zee instantly raised her own cool flames of bright green and weaved a circular ring, blocking his attack from connecting with her, or Ravaryn and her soldiers.

Loud screeches and clicks, as if a plague of cicadas had instantly appeared, surrounded her and the soldiers behind her. The Arakanai started to rise from the crusted grey earth, their sharp-barbed spider's legs emerging from the ground beneath and all around them. Then more and more stampeded towards them from behind the concrete stronghold. It was an ambush, and chaos ensued all around them.

Thaylon blasted more vicious flames towards Zee, singeing the ends of her braids as she hurled a powerful blast back, green and red flames colliding. Ravaryn shifted and instantly came to her aid, taking out the legs beneath every Arakanai that came into his path. His black smoke blasted forth and caught Thaylon in his surprised face. Thaylon deflected just in time, but the smoke caught the side of his skull. Flesh disintegrated into ash there, and a roar of rage tore from him. He bared his teeth in a wild half-grimace, half his face eaten away to the bone, and black liquid streaked down from where his eye had been.

'You'll pay for that, you fucking wyrm!' Thaylon moved his hands wildly around each other, his movements so fast as if the blow only fuelled his fire more. He transformed red fire into blades, his remaining eye now glowing a terrifying brilliant red, like the sun blaring through a smoke-laden sky. Then he blasted the fire blades straight at Ravaryn's dragon form.

Zee's heart leapt into her throat, and she almost cried out in fear as she watched the blades hit their mark. Then she *felt* a sharp hot-white pain blast into her own side. Ravaryn leapt from the ground and took flight, shifting into his dragon form, but the blades caught him just as he took off, piercing his flesh and wings. He dropped to the ground and rolled into the chaos of soldiers and Arakanai fighting behind him. Zemira cried out with the pain of the blow that had also wounded her.

Thaylon's eyes flew to her and back to Ravaryn, sighting the glow of bright blood on the dragon's abdomen and Zee holding her side, crouched over in pain. His face glowed with sick amusement. 'Well, well, well. A blood bond. This day just keeps getting better and better.'

Ravaryn shifted to re-gather himself, his eyes entirely black with rage. Thaylon clapped powerful hands together and spoke a loud, clear command in a strange language. Every Arakanai in the close vicinity turned, glowing eyes shifting from golden globes to red, and they headed straight towards Ravaryn.

Zee screamed in fury as she watched him being attacked by so many of the Arakanai at once. He defended with precision and grace but they were still getting in blows to his unguarded side. She realised what Thaylon had just done, and what it meant. Stopping Salvador would break the hold he also had over the Arakanai, just like it had done when she'd stopped Kyeitha and her hold over her creatures. The transition of power of the few he aimed at Ravaryn proved that Thaylon didn't control the army entirely, Salvador did.

Zee rushed forward, her hands outstretched and blasting flames towards Thaylon without reprieve. Black talons erupted from her fingers, alight with flames of brilliant green. An Arakanai stumbled into her path and was instantly consumed by her fire. It screeched as it scattered away, crying out in agony and taking the flames with it. Zee's eyes were no longer her own. They glowed with flames. All over her body, flames ignited, making her blasts more and more powerful.

Thaylon grimaced, his teeth crushing together, his own large hands before him matching her attack. 'You're soul flames!' he roared. 'It couldn't be more perfect, the power we will wield! Do you know what this means!?' he spoke through her fire as if they were old friends, but he was wavering at being pushed back.

Over the noise and commotion, a roar shook the crumbling building behind Thaylon, and brilliant orange-white light lit up the sky, stark against the dull grey. Salvador in his black dragon form perched on the edge of the middle-floor window opening then dived into the air towards the battle, dark wings spread wide.

Thaylon smiled viciously as he withheld Zee's attack. 'You won't win!' he yelled like a preacher. 'You have no idea what you're up against. Join us! Rule with us! We are family, we are blood! That fire in your veins is mine, mixed with the dragon blood from the bond of Salvador's heir. We are the same, you and I. You could rule this entire planet with the power you possess, Zemira!'

Zee gritted her jaw so tight she thought it might break. Her hands were wavering, her eyes were stinging and the pain in her side pounded. She couldn't keep this up. She leapt away from Thaylon's ever-consistent blast of powerful fire, tucking and rolling on the hard earth and out of his line of attack. Sweat poured all over her as she panted in deep, dusty breaths, and the orb smacked into her hip bone as she landed hard. Her nose filled with the metallic scents all around her, mixed with faeces, the smell now thick in the air as the battle raged. Soldiers' bodies lay still, strewn on the ground in pieces. Chunks of them were missing on the ground around her, and the innards of both humans and Arakanai were littered in wet clumps of sticky wet blood. It pooled around the fallen Arakanai bodies that lay eerily still. This was hell, and all because of this man, this blood demon before her, who'd created the creatures just to suffer.

'NEVER! I am *nothing* like you!' she thundered, her body filling with the desperate and chaotic energy all around her.

Zemira then burst into a giant ball of light, her flames flowing like water licking at the air. Feathering out from her body were wings of brilliant fluid green flames. They unfurled from her back like freshly hatched but-terfly wings uncoiling for the first time. She rose high above the mayhem, and Thaylon's face for the first time cracked into shards of shock.

His one bloodshot eye watched her ascend, his mouth slightly open. She rose above him, her eyes never leaving his, like a phoenix in a storm of death all around her. And then she dove for him, black smoke in her wake as she collided with her ancestor. *Ravaryn's* black smoke followed her attack, her soul flame's powers becoming a part of her own as she pummelled the blood demon into the grey earth. She punched her fiery hand into his chest, melting the flesh as she went, and Thaylon's wide eye never left hers, his face a stunned mask. He watched her as she melted her way through him to reach his heart within.

'I am the queen of the forest, and I will protect it! I will protect them all from monsters like you,' she rasped, venom lacing her tone.

They were the last words Thaylon heard slip from Zee's mouth before the life left his remaining eye. Zee watched the red dull, and the life leave him.

'I am *nothing* like you,' she spat, convincing herself the words were true as an orange cloud of light lit up in Thaylon's dead gaze, reflecting the sky above them back at Zee through his empty eye.

Salvador's fire was blasting from the grey clouds right towards where she crouched over Thaylon's now-still body, his heart melting into a pool of black in the palm of her hand.

A Dragon's Heart

Zemira sprinted over to aid Ravaryn, who had one of his wings hanging at an awkward angle as he tore away at the Arakanai limbs that came near him. His face was a swirling mass of rage as he sliced through the Arakanai bodies still attacking him in the centre of a circle of carcasses. These humans unfortunately could not be saved in this life-and-death battle.

'Are you badly injured?' Zee yelled as she took in his contorted face and blackened eyes, her voice tight.

He disabled the last of his attackers, and his eyes met with hers like two magnets, instantly receding into their usual onyx and silver starry-night skies. Her face dropped as she saw the rips in his wings up close. Thaylon's blades of fire had torn into his delicate skin there, leaving some of it in tatters.

'I'm fine,' he grunted. 'But we have to find Aytac and Sayde.'

Zee nodded, and they set off blazing a trail back towards where the second half of their army was battling more Arakanai. They just kept appearing, coming from every direction, not affected at all by the screeching wails of their injured.

Orange wildfire licked the air behind them. Zee turned back and produced a shimmering shield just as Salvador blasted the ground with liquid heat, melting everything in its path. Ravaryn held onto her to balance himself, just a little, trying to shake off the blow to his delicate wings and making Zee realise that he was definitely *not* okay. She knew he was wounded in the same spot on her side where she felt the blasting pain, but she didn't have his wings... his injuries were a little worse.

Zee pulled him down on the ground, the shield around them still holding for the moment, even though her energy was becoming depleted.

'What are you doing?' Ravaryn was thrown off guard, not by the actual battle but by Zee mounting him and forcefully holding him down.

'You're hurt,' Zee stated as if he were daft.

'Yes, but I don't think right now is the best time for you to be consoling me about it.' He smirked devilishly.

'Oh, grow up.' Zee couldn't hide the smile from her face as she pressed her palms into the ripped tatters of Ravaryn's wings. She pressed them down hard, amidst the chaos all around them.

He groaned loudly. 'My love, your foreplay has truly escalated.'

Zee blushed. 'Shhh, you big baby.' She removed her hands.

And where they had been in contact with the torn skin lay perfect handprints of green mossy life holding the damaged structures together. The thin patch of greenery stifled the blood that had been oozing from the wings, holding them temporarily together.

Ravaryn turned his head to see her very temporary mend, and raised his eyebrows in approval.

'Let's go,' she urged. 'Aytac and Sayde can't be far, and we have to reach them before Salvador finds us.'

But as if her words had summoned his very presence, wind blasted them. Zee's shield was now gone, and the black dragon's large body shook the earth as his weight pounded into it before them.

Zee pulled Ravaryn upwards, her hand firmly grasped within his. 'This is it,' she said, sounding more confident than she felt.

He nodded, his eyes telling her soul just what she needed to hear. *I'm here, I'm with you. We can do this together.*

Salvador's roar blasted the hair back from Ravaryn's face, and Zee squinted her eyes against it. His scaled lips snarled in disgust, showing his sharp teeth through the sneer as his eyes narrowed on the pair.

'JOIN ME OR DIE.'

His booming voice vibrated the very veins in Zee's body. Such dark energy emitted from him, and she saw a flash of a land riddled with fire, ash and stone, with a reddened sun. The vision flickered before her eyes – a promise of what was to come. She stared into his gold-rimmed pools of black, and the Arakanai around them stopped in battle and came to gather around their lord, his huge form towering over them all, like ants below a god.

From behind the fighting emerged Aytac and Sayde. Sayde shifted from her feral Vallarax form, and they both ran to join Zee and Ravaryn. They were panting and blood-spattered but were an utterly determined and powerful pair. Zee felt the orb emit a chilly presence into her as her hand came to protectively rest against it. Her other hand found Ravaryn's, thinking it would maybe be the last time she got the chance to have hers held within his.

'WHAT... WILL... IT... BE...?' Salvador's demonic voice rumbled.

Zee's face lit with pure fire, her face a determined scowl. 'Go back to hell. Go back to where you came from!'

She ignited, flames bursting powerfully, and her new wings shot her upwards before him, distracting Salvador from the others around her. She then blasted him with all of her might, her energy fully concentrated into her flames as she directed them straight at his face.

He roared in anger and blasted back with his own fire. Ravaryn shifted fully, his wings still damaged, but he didn't need them for this part of the plan. He came around to Salvador's flank, Sayde joining in as she shifted from human back into her Vallarax form. She rounded around the dragon's other flank. Each took a wing and shredded the thick membranous skin there. They tore away fiercely as Zee took the brunt of his fire.

Salvador spun in fury as he felt the attack. His large head whipped around to throw them from his flanks, and Zee's flames scolded his neck and shoulder as he turned, causing him to roar with more rage. Aytac ran forward as Salvador was distracted by Ravaryn and Sayde. He threw himself on his side feet first, sliding under the black dragon's chest to his soft underbelly, his sword held firmly in his powerful grasp. While sliding, he thrust it upwards in a forceful slash, and with the tip of his sharp blade he created an opening, the wound just penetrating the armoured scales in a gash on his softer chest plates.

One of the black dragon's feet lifted and slammed down on Aytac. His foot was penetrated by Aytac's blade, but also forced the watcher into the ground with a bone- crushing impact. Zee's hands dropped from the air, as did she, while Salvador was distracted by the others. She ran for the dragon's underbelly, finally withdrawing the orb, 'the light'. The weapon that she had forged from the ancients' poisoned things was firmly in her palm, the lethal silver swirling within.

She saw Aytac crushed under the dragon's foot, terror coating her skin, but she didn't stop. If he was dead, she wouldn't let it be in vain. She raced forward as Salvador blasted away at Ravaryn's side. Wild gusts of angry orange flames lit the air around him, but he countered with his black smoke, charring some scales on Salvador's face. Zee slid underneath the dragon and thrust the orb upwards, straight into the slice of flesh Aytac had created.

She tasted victory. But just as she felt that they were going to win and that the realm would be free of this darkness, Sayde leapt between the open wound and Zee, knocking the orb straight from her hand before she could deeply imbed it into the dragon's body there and poison him from the inside.

Sayde shifted into her human form as Salvador staggered away from Zee, defending himself against Ravaryn's attack. Zee was left reeling in the dirt. Her heart was cracking at the realisation of what had just happened. There was a groan from Aytac's crumpled body beside her. Then Ravaryn was thrown by a powerful blow to the ground, and her own body doubled over in excruciating pain as he crumpled into the dirt metres away.

Ravaryn shifted back into human form, the impact knocking him far from the others into the chaos of fighting Arakanai and soldiers. Sayde sprinted forward and heaved her sword upwards, deep into the slice Aytac had made, causing Salvador to rear back in pain. But Sayde had shifted from human to Vallarax and was digging into him with her Vallarax claws – as though she was trying to crawl *inside* of the dragon's chest.

What on earth was she doing!

Just then, a shimmer of silver flicked her attention to her left, away from Sayde and Salvador.

Diwa raced towards the orb that had been thrown afar, lying on the ground in all the debris as soldiers and Arakanai danced around her in battle. It still shone like a beacon, and Diwa grabbed onto it, her nimble hands holding it tightly. Salvador's giant body reared upwards then landed back down with a thud as Sayde attacked his open-wounded chest. He narrowed hateful eyes as he instantly spotted Diwa.

Diwa stood still in front of him, her head held high, her silver eyes glaring into his. There was no fear, only pure determination on her face. His scowl deepened, his hatred so pure in that moment that not even the shifter burrowing inside his chest deterred him from his revenge. He blasted a roar of undaunted rage towards her, and Diwa closed her eyes and stood as still as a mountain against a hurricane. She didn't move a muscle as Salvador's mouth stretched open wide and he snapped her up whole, devouring her entire body. Her entire being was *gone* in one split second.

The Light

Zee's heart shattered within her chest. *NO! It's not real! I'm not really here, and she's not here. She stayed behind, she promised! DIWA! She shouldn't be here!* Zee's mind was frantic within her skull, trying to process what had just transpired before her. Salvador looked around him, and his eyes pinned on her. Zee swore a sinister smile adorned his charred face, and he stomped forward – the parasite at his chest entirely forgotten as he approached his final enemy. He discarded Sayde, flicking her out like an errand tick from his body. The otherworldly look in his eyes shook Zee to the core.

This is it. This is the end, there's nothing left. The weapon is gone, Diwa is gone...

Her energy sapped away from her. She was now totally depleted. Even if there were the slightest trickle of power left to wield, she couldn't wield it. She had been beaten, and there was nothing left to muster... there was nothing left.

Diwa is gone.

She's gone...

Salvador reached her where she lay between the bodies and discarded weapons of her soldiers, his eyes gleaming with victory. He towered over her, shadowing her with his body.

His deep dragon's voice boomed down on her. 'You could have been the one to rule alongside me. But now you will die just like she did.' He opened his maw just like she'd witnessed moments ago.

She should shut her eyes, scrunch them tight as her soul was taken from this world, but she didn't. With her last bit of strength, Zee's eyes ignited with the forest's green fire within her, and she stared into Salvador's gold-rimmed dark wells of hell.

'Never,' she croaked.

Salvador snarled, exposing his gleaming teeth. But just as he lunged to end his prey, he froze, his pupils growing wide. The black grew wider, consuming some of the gold that rimmed them, then transforming into a mirror-like sheen. Zee watched, unable to move, as she was reflected perfectly within them now, her bottom lip hanging limp, tears running down her dirty cheeks as silver liquid started to spiral from within his open maw. It was circling up from his dark throat and spiralling outwards from within him.

It moved over his flesh, coating it with a thick metallic-mirrored liquid. He roared and staggered back from her, his front claws tearing at his own throat as he thrashed, his tail smashing into his own side. Then his bulging eyes locked on Zee, and he fell forward, his body rumbling the earth as he fell. The liquid consumed his entire face, sliding over each individual scale.

Zee scooted back from where his sharp-toothed maw landed just inches from her feet, dust blasting over her, and she heard a desperate cry.

'NO!' Sayde shot forward from where she had dragged Aytac's limp body away from the fight. She ran towards the fallen dragon and slid on her knees before the gash on its chest, ripping into the flesh and diving in deep.

Zee watched in horror as again Sayde gouged into the dragon's body, her tongue coated in a sour tang as nausea threatened. What on Mother's earth was she doing? Had she gone mad?

Sayde reappeared from within his chest cavity, coated in his black blood, just as the metallic liquid crusted over the flesh and turned it to hardened silver. She held Salvador's dragon heart in between both hands. Tears of relief flooded Sayde's blood-splattered face, and she laughed manically as she held the heart up in the air before her like it were some holy relic.

'Noah,' she praised the heart. 'I will see you again.'

But just as she went to devour the heart, it bled out with a silver sheen that spread over it like a crawling disease, just as it had done over the entire dragon's body. Then it slipped through her fingers as it turned into shimmering dust.

'NO!' Sayde screamed, eyes frantic. Then she wept as she dropped to the ground, trying to sweep the fragments together.

As loud as lightning rolling over the hills, a crunching and cracking of the dragon's hardened stone-like corpse sounded around them over the ongoing battle. From within his thorned backbone, a sprout emerged. It forced its way forth, rapidly shooting upwards towards the clouds. Roots snaked down, and branches thrust upwards and outwards as a massive fig-like tree encased the metallic stone body of the fallen demon. The fig tree was twice as large as the entombed dragon, its roots encasing it like a cage. The tree's leaves were fresh and shining with a rich green, twinkling as they sprouted. Then small blooms furled open into little jellyfish-like wisps of cottony white flowers, which gently floated out from the tree in the air.

Zee observed all this as though she were watching from someone else's perspective, a calm numbness washing over her pain. The little blooms landed all over the fighting field and spread wide. Each and every Arakanai they came in contact with instantly became still, eyes glazing over with a silver sheen before falling stiff and still to the ground, as though they had been rendered into a deep sleep.

Sayde was beside herself and weeping on the ground in pure agony. Her mourning poured out from within her in wracking waves. Zee willed her numb limbs to move and crawled over to where Sayde wept.

'It's over, Sayde. Whatever were you doing, whatever... Sayde?' Zee pulled her friend's hands away from her face and forcefully gathered her close in an awkward embrace. 'Sayde, shhh. It's okay, whatever it is. It's over now.' She tried to soothe her friend's pain, having no idea what had happened, just that she was suffering.

'It's not okay!' she screamed at Zee. 'He's gone! That fucking monster killed him, and the only way I would ever see him again is if I died eating his foul fucking heart!'

Zee was at an utter loss, not having a clue what Sayde was ranting about. Maybe she had taken a blow to the head in the battle?

'I'm sorry,' she rambled. 'I'm so sorry, Zee. I didn't mean for anyone to get hurt... I just–I just needed the heart.'

Zee's chest constricted in pain as she saw Diwa in her mind's eye being devoured again, almost not believing it had really happened. 'It's okay,' she soothed again, as tears trickled down her face.

The women wept together, unable to move. Zee just held onto Sayde and stared at the stone dragon before her, the fig's branches moving in the wind. Then after moments, like time had slowed to a snail's pace, Zee spotted a familiar bright aura making its way through the slaughter. Gaia reached them, and knelt down in the blood-crusted ground.

'You did it.' Her eyes shone like they contained lakes of anguish within them.

Sayde lifted her head from Zee's embrace as if she couldn't help but be drawn to the Mother's presence. 'Who are you?' She sniffed, then wiped a hand over nose where she smeared black dragon's blood, making her look even more unhinged.

'Sayde, my child.' Gaia smiled, her lips straining like it caused her discomfort in the environment surrounding her. 'Do you want to see him again, my dear? Do you want to be with your soul flame again?'

Sayde's pupils grew wide, her brows crushing together in her forehead. 'Yes,' she breathed. 'Please, I'll do anything.'

Zee watched as Gaia nodded at Sayde with a strange expression on her face, her hands reaching for the distraught shifter. Gaia pulled her up and led her away through the bodies that now lay still in the battlefield, past the soldiers who staggered around trying to find their comrades or make sense of their enemy just dropping in mid-fight. As the two disappeared from sight, Zee's aching body crawled the best it could towards where her heart told her Ravaryn's body lay.

She found him, the blood crusting on his brow now soaking through his dark curls. She lay awkwardly against him, panting with the exhaustion it took her to find him. But he was breathing, and Zee could feel the gentle rise and fall of his chest against her head. She wept into him. After a long while, a rattled cough came from him, and he opened his eyes.

'Wings.' She kissed him, relief flooding her system. 'We did it,' she reassured him.

'How?' he coughed out. 'I saw… I saw Sayde. She betrayed us and took away our only chance at infecting him with the orb.'

'She did,' Zee confirmed as her eyes dropped to his chest, her hands holding fists of fabric and armour, not wanting to let him go ever again. 'But someone else managed to use it against him…'

Tears fell from Zee's face as she spoke, and she couldn't hold back the agony any longer.

'What?' Ravaryn tried to sit up. 'Zemira. Look at me. What happened.' He tilted her face so her eyes would meet his.

'She's gone, and I'm so sorry, Ravaryn. She destroyed Salvador with the orb, but now she's gone… Di–Diwa's gone.'

Zee thought she could see nothing more painful than the murder of her dearest friend in front of her very eyes, but she knew in that moment that she could… as she watched Ravaryn's heart fracture into a million pieces before her.

In Another Life

Sayde was shaking as Gaia took her into the forest. The ethereal being had promised her what she wished for most in this entire world, to see her soul flame again. When they reached the lake of life, Sayde could barely hold herself up; her legs were like liquid and exhaustion rattled her very bones.

'Do you understand that you forfeit this life for another? That you will not appear as you do now, and that this version of you will end forever?' Gaia's eyes were large on her delicately framed head, her smooth antlers adorning her like a crown, furry ears flickering ever so slightly.

'Y-Yes,' Sayde stuttered, fear coating her tongue, but more than that... *hope.* Hope that she might once again be happy, belong. That her heart would stop beating with the pain she could no longer live with. 'As long as I'm with Noah, I don't care. I don't care how, or in what way. I just—' Her tears flowed freely now. 'I just *need* him, more than I need to breathe, more than I need the sun, more than I need to live this life without him.'

Gaia's own eyes shimmered and welled, like deep oceans. 'I'm so sorry you suffered so, my child.' She reached out a delicate, elongated hand.

Without a second of hesitation, Sayde took it and followed her into the waters of the lake of life.

*

Tye's hand shook with anticipation. Fear? Doubt? Really, it was a mixture of all three. *Please, please let this work...* This had to work. They were all out of ideas. Well, that was obvious as this wasn't even their idea, it was Juniper's. Trust the mind of a curious, creative child to come up with a solution that trained and experienced adults wouldn't even have thought of.

Poison instead of medicine... it was a risk for sure, but they had expended every other option.

'You ready?' Hamish's calm tone enquired as he held the net over the Arakanai's unusually still form.

Tye took a quick breath in. 'Let's just pray to the Mother that this works.' He scooped up the vibrant yellow paste from the mortar it was in and smeared it over the extended and pinned-down leg of the creature. He smeared it on thickly in a smooth patch, and it looked like he was a beautician from one of the large cities preparing to wax the thing's leg. The hilarious notion made his upper lip twitch, and he almost wanted to laugh. At first, nothing happened. Tye and Hamish just watched the patch of poison they had carefully concocted do, well, nothing.

Tye's shoulders slumped, and his ocean eyes lost their anticipated sparkle. It was a failure. He moved away to place the mortar and paste back behind him.

'Come on, let's get this thing back to its holding pen.' Tye's defeated voice was a monotone.

'Wait, something's happening.' Hamish's eyes were wide as they met with Tye's, and his whole face scrunched in pure disgust.

As Tye came closer, completely confused, he smelled it too – a foul, acrid scent that hit his nostrils like a wasp's sting. Hamish couldn't help himself from gagging, and Tye covered his nose as he came forward to inspect the salve. It was bubbling and disintegrating the hard outer shell-like membrane of the Arakanai's spidery legs.

The Arakanai started screeching and bucking violently in its restraints, awoken from its calm under the protective hide. Hamish was either thrown off, or could no longer handle the repulsive fumes. Tye scrambled back and watched as the leg sticking out from the hide disintegrated into dust before his very eyes. More guttural screeching sounds and thrashing carried on, and Tye realised that Hamish was puking on his hands and knees.

He ran to his aid, dragging him a safer distance away and brushing his sandy hair back from his face as he retched. Suddenly, the lump under the hide went quiet and still. Tye offered a clean towel for Hamish to cover his mouth and nose with, and the pair sat at a safe distance as they stared at the unmoving mass.

'You think we killed it?' Hamish asked, disappointed.

'Only one way to find out,' Tye replied, knowing that it couldn't be a good sign.

He approached the unmoving, albeit much smaller, mass that lay underneath the hide. He tensed and prepared for a melted pile of vile mess, and the possible murder of a creature he'd been responsible for.

Tye pulled the cover away from the Arakanai, and his eyes burst wide as he took in the human woman curled in a foetal position. She lay shaking in a pile of powdery yellow dust, her hands clasped firmly around her head. Hamish leapt up and came to stand beside Tye, his yell of triumph piercing the air and making Tye jump with the sudden realisation of accomplishment. They had done it; they had reversed the blood magic's effects...

Hamish pulled Tye towards him into a passionate hug, squeezing the oxygen from his lungs in the process, as he crushed him to his chest. 'If I hadn't just barfed, I would kiss you! Tye, you're a genius!'

Tye's cheeks burst into red blooms at Hamish's words. He smiled back at him, his deep breaths replacing the oxygen that was forced out of him from Hamish's embrace.

Hamish held him at arm's length and said, 'Oh, fuck it!'

He planted a hot kiss right on Tye's blushing cheek, and Tye didn't care that he had just emptied his stomach contents moments ago, or that they had just accomplished the impossible: saving countless human lives with their discovery. He couldn't wipe the stupid smile from his face, even though the room still reeked of rotten meat and disintegrated flesh.

All his mind could do was let him enjoy the flutter of wings invading his stomach as it sang to him, 'He likes you back...'

*

Weeks had passed since the battle, and most if not nearly all the Arakanai that could be saved had been transformed back to human by Tyson's miracle salve. The old Rim territories were beyond grateful, and he and Hamish had been honoured with their own festival in Zenya. So too had been Queen Mazda and Paxton, and the leaders of the armies that had survived.

There had been significant losses, but somehow the restored Arakanai humans eased that pain just a little. Orion, Paxton and Mazda had found Zee and Ravaryn passed out in each other's arms in the battlefield, after Salvador had been poisoned and the remaining Arakanai had all fallen into slumber. Orion had stayed back to lead the human armies behind the Lamirian soldiers. After the battle had died down and all the now-dormant Arakanai had been captured and immobilised, he had shifted into Wolf and followed the scent of his daughter. Verena, Orion and Pax all took turns watching over Zee back in the Tangaroa palace. Paxton didn't leave Zee's side until she was fully recovered, and he could barely even trust her wellbeing with another person then either. She and Ravaryn had both healed slowly inside the valley's palace.

Ravaryn graciously allowed Paxton's presence and said not a word as he hovered over Zee, spending countless hours beside her. He instead gave them the space they needed, expertly avoiding Verena in the process, and spent most of his time with Mazda, or alone. He still hadn't accepted that his own mother was truly gone, and the feeling was like a giant hole inside of him as he never saw how it came to be. He had asked Zee just once how it had happened, and he figured that Diwa had always known that it was to be her fate. She must have seen her future and what she must do.

He just prayed that it hadn't been for too long that she had known, and she hadn't had that burden weighing on her for more than it had to. But deep down, he knew his mother, and he knew she must have known for a very long time what her fate was to be. He just wished he had had a chance to tell her how amazing she truly was, how much he idolised her, how much he loved her. He knew she had known he did, but still it didn't feel like it had truly been enough. And he guessed it never would.

*

One month later

In Tangaroa, at the base of the falls paved with smooth river stones, Sahara's gravelly voice echoed. 'Zemira Creedence, Queen of the Forest, Guardian of Aylenta and the human lands, and Ravaryn Black, son of Diwa, protector of the queen and both the Lamirian and human races, come forward and address your city as their newly wed queen and king and rejoice!'

The valley echoed the yells and cries of the people's praise, and showered them as they entered the crowd. Petals all shades of the rainbow littered down upon them as Zee's new-improved shadowrens flew overhead, dispersing the decorative rain of petals. Musicians performed joyful music and wine began to flow as the celebrations got underway.

Aytac's face was still sombre, but he managed a proud nod as the new couple passed him on the way to their first dance. No one had seen Sayde for weeks, but Zee had assured him that she had seen her being taken away by the Mother. After Aytac had heard about what Sayde had done… that she had sabotaged their attempt to poison Salvador, he held no hope that she would return. He knew the sister he had once known was long gone, but it didn't make his heart ache any less.

Zee and Ravaryn twirled in each other's arms. They wore elegantly crafted outfits that the people had chosen. Zee's deep emerald-green gown flowered out around her like a bud in full bloom. All eyes watched them as they had their first dance as queen and *king* of the forest.

'This doesn't mean you ever get to tell me what to do.' Zee's voice was teasing as under her thick lashes, her eyes sparkled into Ravaryn's.

'No, your majesty. Never.' His cocky smile was wicked with delight.

'I only married you so that I could protect you...' Zee jested, rolling her eyes at him as he guided her through the smooth dance steps, his large hand firm and warm against the small of her back.

Ravaryn's dark eyes glittered as he laughed. 'Protect me?'

'Yes.' Zee looked to the far left of the crowd where Orion stood with a proud smile on his usual stoic face. But a beautiful Verena wrapped in his arms pinned Ravaryn with a threatening look that said, '*If you step a millimetre in the wrong direction, your head is mine.*'

Ravaryn caught her glare for a second, and he cleared his throat. 'I am forever in your debt, your majesty,' he said sarcastically.

'I love you, Wings, in this life and the next.' Zee's voice was filled with passion, and Ravaryn's looked grew hungry and protective.

'In this life and the next, Zemirahhh.' He kissed her deeply before the entire realm. His wife, his queen, his soul flame – in this life and the next.

A cry that sounded like a woverbine crossed with some kind of bird called out in the sky above the clearing. Everyone looked up as another call cried out. Two large sets of elegant-feathered winged creatures were descending from the far edge of the valley. They soared through the air together as though they were in a joyful dance all of their own. As they got closer, Zee recognised that they were creatures she had once seen in a book – but never in real life.

They had four hooved feet and wild, shimmery manes that flowed down behind their pointed ears and along their necks. They had long swishing tails of the same shimmery long hair.

'Are they...? Are they Pegasi?' Ravaryn's face beamed with a surprised smile.

The pair of shimmery white and grey creatures landed delicately and came before Zee and Ravaryn. One of them made a ruffling noise, and the other a whinny. Both tucked their magnificent wings in behind them and bowed on bent front knees before the queen and king.

'Oh, you are not going to believe this,' Ravaryn said.

'What? What is it?' Zee pressed. 'What did they say?'

Ravaryn withheld the information for a second longer knowing how it would irk his wife to wait a second longer than she had to.

'Tell me!' She laughed and stomped on his toe with her heel.

'Ow, Zee. Sayde—' Ravaryn paused, waiting for his words to sink in. 'Sayde would like to introduce you to her soul flame, Noah. Noah, this is Zemira. Zee - Noah.'

Zee's eyes misted, and she brought her hand to her heart. In that moment, she recognised the darker grey Pegasus that stood up from her kneel as Sayde. She stepped forward and clasped her hands tightly around Sayde's muscled and beautifully smooth neck.

'How...?' Zee breathed.

Sayde made a noise, and Ravaryn answered for her. 'Gaia,' he said simply.

Sayde tucked her large Pegasus head around Zee's and breathed in her scent.

'Go get Aytac! Now!'

She let go of Sayde's neck and turned to Noah in complete awe. 'Oh, Sayde this is a miracle,' she said as she stroked Noah's face, his sweet eyes gentle and warm. 'We can all fly together now!' Zee said excitedly. 'Wings! I told you to get Aytac!'

'No need.' Ravaryn's smile was smug and full of joy.

Beside him stood a stony-eyed Aytac. He was frozen to the spot, just staring at the beautiful animal before him. He knew... he already knew. He felt his twin, his comrade, his closest friend for his entire life, in his veins. He felt her presence and already knew it was his sister.

Sayde whinnied, and Ravaryn translated. 'She said she's so sorry, and if there's any chance that you'll forgive her for what she did, and for leaving you behind, she will try her entire lifetime to earn your forgiveness.'

Aytac's stony face cracked. A deep cough was all he produced as his eyes glazed over and he stepped towards his sister, his yellow eyes flaring wide as they met with Sayde's new ones. Yet somehow they were the same… the same huge mahogany irises suited the Pegasus body like it was her true form all along.

'About time you showed up.' Aytac came forward and crushed her neck into his arms, realising that he no longer needed to worry. He realised that for the first time in her life she was free, and she had found where she belonged, *who* she belonged with, and he no longer had to worry about her finding the happiness she deserved.

Epilogue

Zee made her way slowly through the winding track that led out to the vast grey tundra of the deadlands. They were no longer so desolate though, as the winding path that she had taken numerous times since the battle had begun to sprout with moss and small green tendrils of growth. Little vermillion mushrooms littered around here and there, trying desperately to grow in the harsh environment.

The forest queen had brought life back to the damaged soil here, and she threw out seeds from her pockets, nestling them into the hard earth with her magic as she went. Zee was also working on a plan to save the undead from their wretched fate in the Undead City. But for now, she approached the fig tree that sprouted from the stone dragon monument. Moss dog was zooming around and kicking up grey dust before her in happy abandon. Zee reached the looming body of crusted mirror-like stone that was now dulling with weather as it aged. The fig tree's roots were still encasing it like a cage, as if it were holding the black dragon's bones down, keeping the world safe from him forever.

She climbed up and perched herself on the flattened area atop the dragon's back, to sit before the trunk of the giant fig. Its branches were rhythmically swaying, although hardly a breeze tickled over the deadlands that day. It was quiet, and even the energy around Zee was barely noticeable. There was hardly a pinch of life except for the giant tree. It always made it easy to think when she was here, as it was so quiet. Devoid of most life, but still peaceful at the same time.

Zee sat cross-legged and shut her eyes. She cleared her mind for a moment as Moss sniffed and skulked around the tree's thick roots. A sharp squeal of fright pierced Zee's concentration, making her jump, as Moss came flying towards her in panic. She opened her eyes at the interruption and pinned them on Moss dog. Just as Moss reached the safety of Zee, a thin, dangling tendril root hanging from the fig's canopy whipped at Moss's rear end, making a snap as it made contact. This caused another high-pitched yip from Moss.

Zee's eyes widened, and she couldn't help but stifle a laugh. *But what on Mother's earth was that?* Zee stood, her eyes searching the tree and taking in the twisted trunk and the hanging leaves that curtained her, searching for any movement there. Had she imagined it? Moss cowered against Zee's legs, her cloudy eyes large with worry just as a root of the fig tree shot upwards like a snake and flicked at her again.

Moss howled and took off, racing away from the tree. Zee unfurled her wings in an instant, and they gently but quickly flew her out into the air away from the spot near the strange happenstance. Her illuminated green wings held her in place as she hovered mid-air and watched the tree with curiosity. Then the smooth patches of coloured bark *moved*.

Thick knots of the tree's trunk were shifting before her eyes, branches swaying like a dance, and the roots rose up a foot then gently resumed their original spots as the huge tree contorted and shifted, like it were stretching awake. A cracking and creaking of wood sounded in the still air as she watched the tree morph before her stunned eyes.

A face started to swirl in the centre of the tree trunk, and two crinkled ancient eyes formed, along with a small slightly buttoned nose. A huge smile crunched wide, its sides upturned in a vibrant smile. A warm, crescent-moon grin. Zee's wings swept her forward towards the flat spot in front of the trunk, and her eyes misted over with emotion as her heart burst with sparks of warmth. It was as if the tree beckoned her to it like it had cast a spell.

The tree trunk's familiar face looked down at her, and its eyes seemed to tear up as well. 'Hello, dear Zemira...' it said.

The voice was ancient but familiar, and it was the voice Zee had longed for every second since it had disappeared from her world. Tears fell from her now and ran freely down her face, and Zee laughed and cried with pure joy.

'Hello, Diwa,' she managed, her voice constricted, thick with both disbelief and longing. 'I've missed you...'

Acknowledgements

A massive, MASSIVE thankyou to my editor and publisher Juliette Lachemeier, managing editor of The Erudite Pen. There is no way this book, or the series, would have become what it is without you. Thank you so much for all your commitment and hard work to make this story, and the two before it, what they are now. Writing a third and final book in this series was so much trickier than I ever expected. I hope all the hard work, creativity and yes tears that went into creating this epic finale for Zee and Ravaryn has made it a worthy finale for everyone.

Judith San Nicolas, thank you for the beautiful cover that completes the series perfectly. I love everything about it! And my arch nemesis, the golden orb spider, looks just as perfect and menacing as it did from my dreams when I was growing up!

Thank you, Kaitlynd and Davo, for once again being my beta readers, cheering me on and supporting my stories even when they are in their first draft stages, and are still painful to read! You two are seriously lined with gold. Rubes and Andy for always backing me and convincing me when I need to hear it that I can do this. You are a pair of legends. A big thank you to George for all your 'there there's' when I whine. I love you lots and lots.

Thank you, Summer, for rolling your eyes at me and bringing me back to reality when I think I am cool because I write books. Mum, thank you for reading and for the hordes of golden orb spiders in the garden we all grew up with.

Katie for your hilarious shenanigans and opinions, and all the childhood gems that pop up for brilliant inspiration. Brenden and Edie for always being there supporting me and my books. Annie for being the most inspiring woman, and the spark that created Diwa – you fight demons in real life and I've never met anyone braver.

But most importantly a ginormous thank you to all my readers! This book literally would not exist without you. Thank you, thank you, thank you!!!! You have given this little author the encouragement to continue creating, and without you, *The Girl Who Forged the Light* wouldn't exist.

xxx

ABOUT THE AUTHOR

Fantasy Weaver | Wordsmith | Dream Architect

Immerse yourself in worlds of magic and mystery with Publishers Weekly rising-star author Renee Hayes. As a true dream architect, Renee crafts captivating tales that transport readers to realms where the extraordinary becomes reality.

With a boundless imagination and a heart that beats for fantasy, Renee weaves enchanting stories that resonate with both young and new adults. From daring heroines to mythical creatures, her characters come alive on the pages, inviting you to journey alongside them.

Whether it's uncovering hidden secrets, battling ancient forces or embracing the power within, Renee's narratives explore the depths of courage and the wonders of the unknown. Her spellbinding prose and vivid worlds will sweep you off your feet and into a world of endless possibility.

Enjoyed the book? You can follow Renee Hayes at:

Facebook: www.facebook.com/profile.php?id=100086763157926
(Renee Hayes Author)

Instagram: https:/instagram.com/reneehayesauthor

TikTok: Renee Hayes Author

Email: rennnay@outlook.com

If you liked the book, please leave a review on Amazon, Goodreads or
with the author directly. Reviews are invaluable in supporting an
author's hard work and are greatly appreciated.

9 780645 587142